DAUGHTER OF SECRETS AND SORCERY

HR MOORE

Titles by HR Moore:

The Relic Trilogy:
Queen of Empire
Temple of Sand
Court of Crystal

In the Gleaming Light

The Ancient Souls Series:
Nation of the Sun
Nation of the Sword
Nation of the Stars

The Shadow and Ash Duology:
Kingdoms of Shadow and Ash
Dragons of Asred

Stories set in the Shadow and Ash world:
House of Storms and Secrets
Of Medris and Mutiny

The Cruel Goddess Series:
Bride of Stars and Sacrifice
Daughter of Secrets and Sorcery
Book 3 – coming soon

http://www.hrmoore.com

CONTENTS

MAP

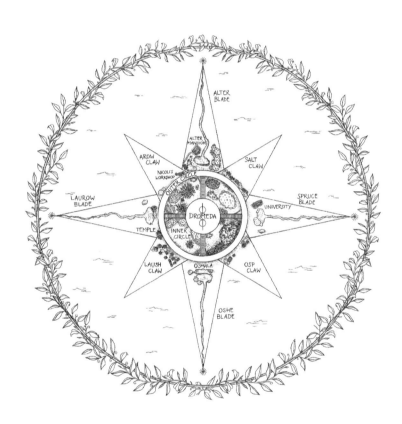

RULE TWO

The second rule of Atlas:
Time is not a constant.

Chapter One
Maria
Two Days After Dromeda Started Spinning

Maria gritted her teeth as two maids fussed with her hair, plaiting it in elaborate fashion so it fell artfully down her back. It wasn't so much the hair that had her ready to burst a blood vessel—although that certainly didn't help—but the dress that hung on the wardrobe door, if a few flimsy scraps of fabric could reasonably be called a dress.

It reminded her of a child's attempts at clothes-making and would do little more than cover her most intimate places. It was so far past immodest as to be laughable, not that she was in a laughing mood, seeing as she was expected to wear the abomination to dinner.

The maids stood back, beaming as they admired their handiwork and looking as though they expected praise for dolling her up to Cane's exacting standards. But it wouldn't do to make enemies among the servants, so Maria plastered a smile on her face and gave them the praise they so obviously desired.

Which only served to heighten their excitement as they helped her into the monstrosity.

Had Maria not seen Sophie—the first daughter of Laurow—dressed in similarly risqué fashion in recent times, she would have questioned the maids' sanity. But Maria didn't know if the people of Oshe—the land in which she currently resided—regularly dressed in this way, also, or if Cane intended to humiliate her as well as hold her hostage.

At least it hid her nipples, she supposed, grasping for anything positive as the fabric slid into place.

'Now this,' said a maid.

Maria raised her arms once more, allowing them to pull a second layer over the first, this one sheer, embroidered here and there with delicate cobwebs and buttercups.

The second layer hugged her flesh, and although it did little to hide her near-nakedness, it made her feel a little better, a small defense against the ogling eyes of the men she'd no doubt encounter at dinner.

She wasn't allowed shoes, and the maids attached bracelets to her wrists and ankles so she jangled as she moved. They threaded gold earrings encrusted with brightly colored gems through her earlobes that hung almost to her shoulders, then adorned the other holes in her ears with vibrant studs to match.

As a final touch, they put rings on each of her hands that joined in swirling patterns across the tops of her fingers, then rouged her lips, heavily kohled her eyes, and ushered her from the room, closing the door behind her so she stood alone in the silent gloom of the corridor.

Maria felt suddenly small in the flickering light of the wall sconces, and when her eyes finally adjusted, she found two guards outside Cane's bedroom watching her, waiting for her next move. Maria almost cowered, but then her grandmother's stern face flashed before her eyes. *Stop it*, the imagined woman silently snapped. *You will not give them the satisfaction of your embarrassment. You are the first daughter of Alter. You will not let them win.*

Maria steeled herself, drawing back her shoulders and lifting her head as she padded along the corridor, trying to ignore her jewelry's ridiculous tinkling. She was reminded of the feral hunting cats of her homeland, where farmers tied bells around the animals' necks to give their livestock fair warning.

The thought warmed her, for if she was the dangerous beast, Cane was the hapless chicken, but then the idea turned so hot it burned because the truth was Cane was a cat so feral the farmers would have drowned him long ago.

She'd only been in Oshe a few short hours, but already it felt like a lifetime since she'd seen Elex. She hoped he was okay, that Cane hadn't sprung some other trap or killed him ... If she'd learned anything from her time with Oshe's first family, it was that Osheites were a barbaric people, so unlike those from the land of her birth.

She pushed the unhelpful thought aside. She was where she was, and wishing and longing would do nothing at all, aside perhaps from summoning the imagined voice of her grandmother.

A guard stepped into her path as she approached Cane's door. 'Wait here,' he said, his voice clipped, his eyes, thankfully, looking somewhere over her left shoulder. 'Lord Cane will escort you to dinner.'

The guard whirled and strode away, the second falling in behind him, leaving Maria alone with only the unease in the air as company.

The door to her brother-in-law's bedroom was ajar, and as the guards' footsteps faded, the sounds of soft moans floated through the gap. Maria froze, unsure what to do. Should she continue to the banqueting hall, retreat to her own bedroom, or stand dumbly as she'd been instructed? Any of those could result in punishment. Perhaps that was Cane's plan, she realized.

'Harder,' said a man's voice, a choked version of Cane's whiny tenor. Maria clamped her hands over her ears, dearly wanting to rip them off.

'Like this?' said a woman, one that sounded a lot like Erica, Maria's hands doing nothing to diminish their voices.

'Fuck ... yes ... more.' Cane grunted out the words, and Maria closed her eyes, trying to ignore the sounds, telling herself to think of something else ... anything else. *Ponies. Sunsets. Triffling. Her still room. A list of deadly poisons that she would dearly love to feed Cane ...*

Erica's moans joined Cane's grunts, ricocheting higher and higher, until, thank the Goddess, they were over, and Maria sagged in relief. She drew her hands down her arms in vigorous strokes, as though she could somehow brush off the noises stubbornly refusing to leave her mind, but she quickly dropped them at the sound of shoes clicking on stone, and then the door swung inwards.

'Ah, Maria,' said Cane, as though surprised to find her there. A sadistic smile lingered on his lips as he stepped out into the corridor, a flushed Erica on his arm. Behind them, trailing by two paces, was Opal, Erica's near double in looks, but not in demeanor, her cheeks red, her head tilted towards the ground, shoulders hunched as though trying to make herself small.

What the fuck? Maria's eyes were stuck on Opal, her brain trying to decipher what had happened, what Cane and Erica had done to her, if she was okay ...

'Come along,' Cane snapped, holding out his free arm for Maria, his hand still wrapped in cloth from the night when he'd tried to steal Maria from Elex, but instead had ended up plunging his own hand into a vat of boiling oil. His face still bore a few red marks also, and the sight of them bolstered her.

Maria could think of few things she'd like to do less than to touch Cane, but making a fuss would do nothing but give him what he wanted, so she took his arm, keeping her grip as light as she reasonably could, an uncomfortable prickling sensation creeping across her skin.

Try as she might, Maria couldn't help her mind from conjuring thoughts of what Cane had subjected Opal to in that room. Opal, who had seemed so strong, self-assured, ballsey even when Maria had first laid eyes on her only a few hours before. Now she was a shadow of her former self. Unlike Erica, who, on Cane's other side, practically glowed. Maria would have liked to give the woman a piece of her mind.

But even if she'd decided to throw caution to the wind, there was no time. They were nearing the light at the end of the tunnel, and that finally forced her to consider other things. Like being ogled by a gaggle of old men in her skimpy getup, and who knew what other terrors Cane might have planned for the evening.

But as they stepped through the double doors that led to the modestly sized banqueting hall, her mind cleared of thoughts entirely and her breath froze in her lungs.

Elex.

Standing in the doorway on the far side of the room.

She flinched as her body tried to run to him, but self-preservation rooted her in place, pain swelling in her chest at the internal conflict. She longed to take his hands, press herself into the warmth of his chest, to feel his arms around her. Her heart thudded against her ribs like a blacksmith hammering a sword. Slow and persistent and with so much force it was a wonder her bones didn't fracture.

Her breaths became short, shocked puffs as she fought to wipe all expression from her face, while he looked as he always did, relaxed, confident, handsome, and dressed head to toe in black. Although his hair was a little messier than usual, and his features, although set in a fearsome mask of calm, had a gaunt tinge that saddened her. She wondered where he'd been since they'd parted.

'Ahhh, brother,' said Cane, pinning Maria to his side with a little too much force. What did he think Elex was going to do in a hall half-filled with Cane's guards? Even if every part of Maria wished he would try to grab her and flee, she knew there was no hope of it.

Elex inclined his head, the tension about his eyes the only sign of anything amiss, aside from the overwhelming darkness rolling off him in waves.

Cane pulled Maria away before she was done examining her husband, so she let her eyes roam across the space, determined to look anywhere but at her captor.

Through the fog of shock and pain, she managed to note that the room was cozy, and under pleasanter circumstances, Maria would have felt quite at home between the two large fireplaces, amid the banner-covered walls and low-hanging lighting fixtures crammed with candles.

The long wooden table seated twenty or so, and aside from the spaces reserved for Cane, Elex, and the three women, every chair was filled with aging men of all shapes and sizes.

Cane steered Maria to the seat to his left, the cold flagstones under her bare, jangling feet making her feel vulnerable and childlike, but she did her best to square her shoulders and ignore the weight of stares as she slid into the gap Cane created by pulling out her chair.

The supposedly chivalrous move was yet another reminder of how she was at his mercy, and she lowered her eyes to the table as she sat, taking deep, centering breaths. But that drove the cloying smell of his sickly-sweet cologne deeper into her lungs, the scent lingering even after he'd stepped away to seat Opal on his right. Maria turned her head, seeking fresher air, but could find none. She wished she could bury her face in Elex's neck and breathe him in, but he was out of reach, all the way across the other side of the wide expanse of wood.

He was so close, but too far away to even touch his foot under the cover of the tabletop. Part of her wanted to slither off her chair and crawl to him, desperate for contact, for reassurance, but of course that was a ridiculous notion, and anyway, Cane was already leaning towards Maria, demanding her attention as Erica rounded the table with sultry steps to sit beside Elex.

'We have been treating you well, haven't we, my dear?' he said, his face too close, his breath acrid.

'Perfectly fine, yes,' said Maria, hating to give him the words he sought, yet also glad they were true.

'Good girl,' he said, slapping his hand down on her thigh and squeezing.

Maria grabbed his hand and yanked it off, throwing it away. 'So far, at least,' she added through gritted teeth.

Elex's sharp eyes followed her movements, his shoulders tensing, lips pursing the tiniest fraction, the movement so small she doubted anyone else would have noticed. But it was enough to ground her because in that tiny movement, she saw her own rage and hurt and desire for vengeance reflected back at her. They were a team, she and Elex, and Cane was their enemy. She took strength from that, knowing that they would make him pay.

'And Opal?' said a man to Opal's right—one of the two men who'd been at the bridge when Maria and Elex arrived in Oshala, his small frame and receding hairline at odds with the power in his tone.

'*Father!*' Opal chastised, looking as though she wanted to melt into the cushion below her backside.

'Has your new husband been treating you well?' the man pressed, unperturbed.

'Yes, of course,' she said quickly, her eyes turned down towards her hands.

'Hmmm,' said the man, lifting his goblet, not seeming in the least bit convinced. 'I hope that is true.'

Cane gave a small cough, diverting the table's attention away from Opal and her father, then leaned back, swirling the wine in his goblet, a vindictive smile on his lips as his eyes fixed on Elex. 'Are you enjoying your return to Oshala, brother?'

Elex picked up his own goblet and eased back in his seat, returning Cane's stare as he let silence stretch for a beat longer than was comfortable. 'So much has changed in my short absence, and yet nothing at all.'

The brothers' eyes held, and Cane's sudden stillness hummed with a promise of violence that made Maria deeply nervous, but still Elex didn't retreat.

The whole room watched on, so silent the crackling fire became deafening, Maria's pulse thudding in her ears as dread threatened to eat her whole. What would Cane do in the face of such a challenge?

But eventually, Cane bellowed, 'Food!' snapping the tension. The room collectively exhaled as the servants hurried to deposit individual plates in front of each person at the table. It was different to the custom of Alter, where they all helped themselves from central platters, and that, more than anything, made Maria feel vulnerable, a reminder that she was a stranger here, that she didn't know these people or their ways.

The food itself was also different. Plain fare—meat and potatoes and some kind of gravy—which smelled pleasant enough, the familiar scents of garlic and rosemary hitting her nose, although it was a stodgier meal than was her preference.

'I think I will keep your cook,' said Cane, through a large mouthful, narrowing his eyes at Elex. 'Her food is excellent, is it not?'

Elex didn't even look up from his plate, slowly cutting a slice of succulent meat.

'And your librarian. She has a fine ... aptitude for her work.' Cane paused meaningfully, but Elex remained silent. Cane threw down his cutlery, which clattered against his metal plate, then picked up his goblet. 'And perhaps even your masseuse.'

Elex stubbornly refused to engage, while the rest of Cane's guests kept their heads down, eating politely and quietly, staying out of the fray, although their eyes scurried around like timid mice anytime they thought it safe.

'Maybe I should take your head from you, also,' snapped Cane, putting down his goblet hard enough that red wine splashed over the rim, the liquid pooling in the small divots at its base.

Elex met his brother's cantankerous gaze, but still he said no words, nor did his features betray any hint of feeling.

Cane clenched and unclenched his fists as he sat rigidly in his seat. 'Answer me!' he screeched.

Elex paused another moment, then tilted his head. 'What is it you would like me to say?'

Cane slammed his fists down on the table. 'You will regret this insolence,' he hissed. 'You will—'

Erica pushed back her chair, its feet scraping noisily across the flags, rising with a feline smile on her full, pouting lips, her golden hair freshly tousled.

Cane's attention moved from Elex to Erica, and he blinked, then sat back, nodding to Erica and beckoning her with his hand. She moved with not a second's hesitation, sashaying her way to him.

Maria wished she could see Opal's face. Was she happy to leave Erica to deal with their husband, or green with envy that she wasn't the object of his attention? Her father certainly didn't seem happy, and Maria wished she knew the dynamic between the men. Who held the power? How finely balanced was their agreement? What would happen if Opal's father withdrew his support?

'I will take my leave,' said a deep, male voice to Maria's left, pulling her back from her thoughts. It was the other man who'd been at the bridge, she realized, this one tall and stocky, his face flushing a ruddy shade of red as he angrily slid back his chair.

'Goodnight, Father,' Erica said calmly, pausing in the tiny gap between Maria and Cane's places.

'Goodnight,' he growled, not looking at his daughter as he marched for the door.

Erica slid onto Cane's lap, wrapping an arm around Cane's shoulders, her back to Opal, while Cane casually laid his injured hand on Erica's thigh, the other on her hip.

Maria averted her gaze, glancing at Elex, who was finishing his food as though this were normal, which, she supposed, it might be. Elex had warned her things were different here. He was different, too: aloof, detached, and seemingly uncaring.

A cold weight settled on Maria's thighs, startling her, and she looked down to find Erica's bare feet in her lap. Erica rocked them back and forth, both her and Cane studying Maria closely, watching like fascinated terriers playing with an unfamiliar insect.

Maria pushed back her chair and rose to her feet, surprising herself more than them, if their unphased expressions were anything to go by. Erica giggled cruelly as her feet dropped to the flagstones, and the sound summoned a handful of vicious bees to Maria's eyes, their furious stings inciting tears.

It wasn't the giggle itself that upset her so much as her powerlessness, the injustice of having to put up with being treated this way, of having no escape and no ability to fight back. 'If you'll excuse me,' she managed, thanking the Goddess that her voice didn't shake. She didn't want to leave Elex so soon, but it was either that or capitulate, and she refused to retake her seat like some puppet.

Cane caught Maria's wrist as she turned, the movement awkward seeing as he had to move his good hand across his body, pushing Erica out of the way. Maria swallowed hard, her heartrate spiking. It took every ounce of self-control she had not to yank her hand free and to hide the revulsion in her eyes as she looked down at him. He swiped his thumb back and forth across her pulse. 'Goodnight,' he crooned, then released her with a lingering slide.

Maria's shoulders drew inward and her insides spasmed as though she might be sick, her brain unable to focus on anything but getting away.

She walked on numb, frozen feet towards the corridor that would take her back to her room, imagining a world where she could have balled her hand into a fist and punched Cane in the face, rage replacing the sick feeling in her stomach, consuming her, so it was a surprise when a hand grabbed her arm and spun her. Her chest slammed against a solid torso, which forced her backwards until her back hit a cold stone wall, and she screwed her eyes shut, worried it was a guard who had pinned her at Cane's command, that he was preparing to humiliate her further.

But the scent of oak moss and cedar had her eyes flying open, relief chasing away her debilitating terror, the feeling soaking through her veins, turning her tense body loose. 'Elex,' she breathed, finding they were in an alcove partially hidden from the room by heavy drapes. She pressed her face to his chest and inhaled him deep into her lungs.

He wrapped his arm around her head but twisted away, Maria panicking that their time was up already. 'Come closer and I will gut you,' he said calmly, threatening someone behind them. His lethal tone must have worked because when she opened her eyes, she found his face hovering just above hers.

'Are you okay?' he asked, his voice a concerned whisper.

She nodded, losing herself in the intensity of his deep brown eyes. Euphoria crashed through her when she realized it was the Elex she knew looking back at her, soft and strong and gentle. 'Are you?'

His answer was a kiss, and she pulled at him until he pressed himself more firmly against her, needing to feel him everywhere, not letting up until almost his full weight pushed her against the stone.

'Where have you been?' she said as he cast a wary look over his shoulder, checking on the guards.

He returned his gaze to her, stroking her cheek with his thumb. 'With friends.'

'What happened? How did Cane take your quarter?'

He shook his head a little, then looked behind again. 'I'm still piecing it together, but it sounds like one of the kitchen boys betrayed me. He's dead now, and not by the hands of my people.'

'Cane?'

Elex nodded, the skin between his eyebrows puckering.

'I'm so sorry, Elex.' Maria kissed the v of flesh visible at the top of Elex's shirt, and he exhaled sharply, so she did it again.

He gently angled her head upwards and kissed her lips. It was all Maria could do not to moan, something about the situation heightening every caress, but she knew the loss of him would be worse the longer she let it last, so too soon she pulled away, burying her face in his neck and fighting the choking, cloying desolation threatening to close her throat, to cut off her air.

He stroked her hair with soothing slides, then leaned back and looked down at her, raking his eyes up and down. 'Cane made you wear that?'

She nodded, biting her lip.

He stroked her neck. 'No one should see you dressed that way but me.' He leaned closer, growling, 'You look good enough to eat.'

Maria's stomach clenched. 'Elex ...'

He nuzzled her neck. 'My brother is a dead man,' he murmured between kisses. 'Whatever he does or makes you do, remember that.'

She gave a breathy exhale as he squeezed her through the flimsy fabric.

'You're stronger than all of them,' he continued. 'More resourceful. More determined. Together—you and me—we'll beat him, no matter what he does. No matter what it takes.'

She wasn't sure if she believed him, but she was grateful for his confidence and strength, for the distraction and hope.

'We're a team, my little hell cat,' he said, pulling back and looking down into her eyes.

She bobbed her head, unable to form words. Their time was coming to an end, and the sheer despair of that had robbed her of her voice.

'I'll be back tomorrow night.'

She nodded and slid her hand into his thick dark hair as he pressed one final kiss to her lips. 'Stay safe,' she whispered, then tore herself away, Elex shielding her from the room as she stumbled on unsteady legs along the corridor. He was still watching when she reached her door, and her heart nearly imploded as she pushed inside.

Elex spent an infuriating half hour losing the tails his brother had put on him, weaving between the jumble of buildings—the unkempt and sparkling standing side by side—careful to avoid pickpocketing fingers and the streets loyal to his enemies. Only when he was sure he was alone did he return to the small tavern in an unassuming residential quarter where he'd found his friends drowning their sorrows earlier that day.

He slipped inside, glad to throw back the hood of his cloak as he shoved the door closed behind him, the taproom blissfully empty, save for three men sat around a low table by the fire.

Elex raked his eyes over his oldest friends, Tallin, Sol—Tallin's cousin—and Elex's bastard half-brother, Zeik. Tallin and Sol could have been twins, although two years separated them in age, both tall, with brown eyes and shoulder-length hair dyed an unlikely platinum blond. Zeik was short and skinny, a messy mop of dark, wavy hair sitting low on his forehead, wire-rimmed glasses covering his shrewd green eyes. He bore a passing resemblance to Elex, but no more.

The tavern, a homely yet warn place, belonged to a distant relation of Tallin and Sol. It had been closed for years on account of the owner marrying a wealthy merchant and no longer needing to toil for a living, so he hadn't hesitated to hand over the keys when he'd heard what Cane had done.

'How did it go?' asked Tallin, striding to the bar and pouring Elex a tankard of beer from a half-full jug.

Elex moved to stand by the fire. 'As expected: he hasn't hurt her, but he'll do what he can to humiliate her and try for a rise out of me.' He closed his eyes and faced the wall, images of Maria dressed in nothing but scraps of cloth flashing across his mind. He leaned forward, bracing his hands on the mantel.

'We'll get her out, brother,' said Tallin, clapping Elex on the back. He handed over the beer with an assured smile, then dropped into a chair, sprawling back in a relaxed, self-confident fashion.

'And we finally have a lead,' said Zeik.

Elex snapped his head towards his brother.

'A guard swears he saw a woman with dark ringlets—he suspects a prostitute—leaving the compound just before the attack,' Zeik continued. 'The guard was on his way to the gatehouse to check all was well when everything went to shit. He got out but was scared to come forward because he knew we'd been betrayed, that we barely got out alive. He didn't know who to trust.'

Elex looked down at his beer. 'Who was the woman?'

'We're working on it,' said Tallin, playing with a loose thread in the embroidered arm of his chair.

'Looks like it ...' Elex bit back. He could still smell Maria's eucalyptus scent, could still feel her on his lips, his fingers twitching as though still on her hip. It had taken everything in him not to throw a knife at his brother, a knife that would have hit his heart, but Cane had been clever in marrying both Erica and Opal. In one fell swoop he'd bound both of their father's most powerful allies to his side.

'Cane's kept a number of your servants,' said Zeik, ignoring Elex's harsh remark.

Elex nodded, turning back to face the fire. 'Including our cook, librarian, and masseuse.'

'Fool,' laughed Tallin.

Elex gripped the mantel harder. 'But the men he's allied himself with are not, and nor is Erica. They'll be watching and will slowly replace our people with their own.'

'Then we should strike soon,' said Sol, his chair creaking as he leaned forward. He was a man of few words, except for when it came to spilling blood.

Elex shook his head, then turned to face his friends. 'If we harm Erica or Opal, their fathers will strike back before we have time to consolidate our position, and I won't risk Maria. As long as they have her, we must tread lightly.'

'She's truly worth that? Risking everything?' said Tallin, no small hint of incredulity in his tone.

Elex stilled, his eyes boring into his oldest friend. 'She's my wife.'

Tallin blew a derisive breath through his nose. 'She's a woman you've known but a score of days.'

Elex stepped towards his friend, his features fierce. 'You would question my judgement?'

Tallin barked a laugh. 'You wouldn't question mine if our roles were reversed? If I acted like some love-sick—'

Elex closed the distance between them with lightning speed, shoving Tallin so hard he tripped over the low table, sending the tankards flying.

'Your short trip to Alter appears to have addled your mind, my dear *Black Prince*,' Tallin said with a mocking grin as he righted himself. 'Anyone with half a brain would question your sanity.'

'Tallin, leave him be,' said Zeik, mopping up the spilled beer.

'Or we'll have to bring up your love for his wayward sister,' Sol added, rounding on his cousin with a sly smile, 'wherever she's run off to.'

'Fuck you,' Tallin and Elex said together.

Sol chuckled, leaning back in his chair. 'We must be swift in our rescue. The longer we leave it, the stronger Cane becomes.'

'And the more likely Elex is to do something stupid,' added Tallin.

Elex scowled and threw himself into a chair, gripping the arms as though they were Cane's throat.

'But how?' asked Zeik. 'How do we get Maria out without risking her?'

Sol opened his palms as though the solution was obvious. 'The only weakness is the front gate, so our only option is to walk her right out from under their noses.' He paused meaningfully. 'And then we kill them.'

Elex blew an angry exhale through his teeth. 'But first we must find out how Cane took what is ours. Someone betrayed us, and we can't let that happen again.'

CHAPTER TWO
AVA

Ava landed hard on her feet, stumbled a few steps, and smacked straight into a brick wall. Although, it didn't hurt as much as it should have, the wall somehow softer than customary.

With the Atlas Stone still grasped tightly in one hand, she pushed herself off the sandy-colored stone and looked up. Familiarity hit her like a sledgehammer. Not that she was surprised Kush had sent her here, to her childhood home.

The house was set back from the road and protected all around by a high wall, the big, square-fronted building covered in the same dainty, sweet-smelling white rose she remembered from her youth.

Nostalgia gripped her, as did trepidation and a little fear. Part of her wanted to rush inside, to see what she could find, but she held back, cautioned by the part of her that was worried about what she might learn. What if her parents were the evil monsters B had made them out to be, power hungry, aloof, and inhumane?

But she didn't know how long she'd have before Kush would arrive—perhaps with his father in tow, ready to haul her off to enslavement—and she wanted to uncover the truth for herself, especially if it was bad. She shoved the idea aside and told herself to stop gawking, then approached the pillared porch that shielded the front entrance and wondered if she would even be able to get inside.

Perhaps she'd have to throw a brick through a window or maybe one of the items in the package B had given her on her eighteenth birthday would allow her entry, although she doubted a twisted piece of wood or a vicious scalpel could be used as a key.

She climbed the wide, creamy steps with her heart in her throat, the swell of it blocking her airway, allowing no breath to pass. She looked left and right, her eyes snagging on the well-kempt bay pompoms on either side of the door, and her forehead pinched.

Was someone here, looking after the place? Her insides rushed inwards at the thought. She couldn't remember a housekeeper or maid, but Ava couldn't remember her parents ever doing domestic chores, either, and from her vague, hazy memories of them, they hadn't seemed the type to sully themselves with such things. Perhaps they'd paid someone to look after the place. Perhaps that person had never stopped ...

Hope and excitement fluttered in her chest as she stepped up to the wooden front door. If there was someone inside, maybe they could tell her the truth about the past. Maybe they would help her figure out who to trust. But even with that additional enticement, it took a moment and several long breaths for her to work up the courage to place her hand on the ridged brass doorknob, then another moment before she twisted it, mostly expecting the door not to give an inch. But as she held her breath, the house seemed to let out a sigh, and the door swung open on silent hinges, a warm yellow light from a lamp on a polished console table welcoming her inside.

'Fuck,' she whispered, pausing on the threshold because surely a light meant she wasn't alone, and the thought suddenly occurred to her that whoever was inside might not be friendly. She froze for a beat, considering her options, but it wasn't like she had anywhere else to go, and it was unlikely that someone who had kept the house in such an excellent state of repair would want to hurt her, wasn't it? Without letting herself dwell on the potential dangers, she stepped cautiously inside, her eyes scanning left and right, then following the line of the stairs as they speared upward, straining to hear any sound.

The place was silent, so she closed the door with a gentle click, and leaned back against the wood, attempting to suck reassurance from its steadfast grains. She surveyed a scene that hadn't changed since her youth, memories coming thick and fast, so potent they threatened to choke her.

The same hat stand stood to the left of the door, her mother's wide-brimmed straw hanging there, exactly where it always had. Opposite the entrance, between the doors to the boot room and kitchen, hung a grand, abstract painting in hues of blue and green that had always looked to Ava like trees spawning trees, the first thing any visitor saw when they entered. Her eyes lingered for a moment because she'd forgotten the painting entirely, but then the scent of a florist's shop filled her nose, green and fresh and sweet, pulling her attention back to the console table, where, beneath an antique mirror and beside the lamp, stood a vase of blousy blooms that looked as fresh as though they'd been picked from the cutting garden that morning.

A thud of foolish hope struck her heart. What if it wasn't a housekeeper or someone employed by her parents that tended to the house, but her parents themselves? What if they were still alive? What if their deaths had been an elaborate ruse, nothing but make-believe to get the other Gods off their backs ...

'Hello?' she asked the silence, then a little louder, 'Hello?'

Ava moved without thinking, rampaging through the house, moving from the grand drawing room to the dark study to the impressive library to the homely kitchen, not stopping until she reached the lofty solarium with its inviting blue swimming pool. But, aside from everything being perfectly clean, tidy, and well-aired, she found not a single sign of life. No dirty dishes, no fresh food in the cupboards, no discarded items of clothing hanging haphazardly over the back of a chair.

'Urgh!'

She raced past the pantry and utility room with its door to the garden, then climbed the back stairs, taking them two at a time in her haste. But she stilled on the first-floor landing, a chill running down her spine, the wide corridor empty and foreboding. She couldn't face it yet, the place where her parents had died, so instead she headed farther up, the steps narrowing as they turned back on themselves and reached towards the attic.

In most houses of that size, the rooms in the eaves would have belonged to the servants, but her parents had turned them into work spaces, filled with whirling, spinning contraptions, books, parchment, lengths of wood and metal, and bottles filled with every herb and mineral imaginable.

She had never been allowed up there as a child, aside from on the rare occasions when she'd been tasked with delivering a message or ingredient, but it all looked different now. The picture of dainty fireflies and silvery spiders' webs looked more like a map of connected worlds. The etching of a tree cut through the middle from canopy to roots—a fairy tree with libraries and shops split over different levels—was no longer a far-fetched fantasy, but the study of a specific tree ... The tree she'd recently escaped.

And the endless books and journals and letters that were scattered around on every surface were no longer boring tomes she would one day be expected to read. Now they were treasure troves she couldn't wait to inhale. Although, her reading was so rusty, it would probably be more a series of laborious, frustrating sniffs. Even so, a thrill of excitement raced through her as she reached for the nearest book: *Notes on Portal Discomfragmentation.*

She put it down—probably too advanced a place to start. But where should she start? As she surveyed the room farthest from the stairs, which contained a workbench, blackboard, and walls lined with books, she became overwhelmed by the same artifacts that had, only moments before, seemed so full of possibility.

She was no sorcerer. She'd never been trained in anything. She could barely even read. Perhaps basic texts aimed at children were where she should start. At least she might have some hope of deciphering those ... if she could find any.

Or perhaps she should start by searching for journals and letters, anything that might help her determine who to trust, and to tell her the truth about her parents. But what if the truth wasn't something she wanted to hear?

She slumped against the bench, suddenly exhausted. Perhaps she should nap before beginning her search, although that would mean exploring the bedrooms. If anyone else was in the house, that was the only place she hadn't yet looked, but surely they would have heard her by now and made themselves known.

Ava pushed upright, not letting herself think too hard about the possibility that her parents' remains could still lie in their bedroom only a flight of stairs below. Whoever had been keeping the place clean and in fresh flowers would likely have dealt with that, too, Ava reasoned, as she forced herself back towards the stairs.

She steeled herself as she descended the thin, creaking steps, visions of twisted, blood splattered bodies bringing bile to her throat and giving her pause as she reached the landing. She wasn't sure she had the energy for this.

Coward. It was her mother's voice in the back of her mind, taunting her. Although her mother had been kind most of the time, she could be cruel, with exacting expectations and erratic moods. Neurotic and changeable, excitable and brilliant, her mother had shone brighter than the sun, but her light had also burnt with searing heat.

Ava swallowed hard, then crept towards the closest of six large doors off the wide, light-filled corridor, the rug atop the floorboards absorbing her footsteps so the only sound was her short, anxious breaths as she approached.

She stopped breathing entirely as she placed her hand on the door's white paneled wood and pushed. It swung inward with the barest of groans, apprehension squatting on Ava's chest like a toad, but as her eyes scanned the room, she found no bodies or gore, only a carefully made bed covered by the same floral bedspread she remembered.

This room, too, was dust and cobweb free, well-aired, and sweet-smelling, with a bunch of vibrant orange dahlias on the dressing table by the window. The chaise longue brought back flashes of her glamorous mother relaxing in a silky red patterned robe with a book in her hand. The bed was where Ava had run at night when scared, sometimes allowed to climb in, other times turned away. Behind the curtains was where she'd hidden when her parents had visitors, her ear to the floorboards, straining to hear their words in the study below but almost always failing.

And then her mind's eye showed her Novak—the man in black—as he hurried her from this house that fated evening, his face white and haunted.

'Where are we going?' she'd asked, her six-year-old voice high-pitched and panicky in her memory. 'Where's Mama and Papa?'

'They're dead, child,' he'd said with no ceremony, no pre-amble, no compassion.

Her first instinct had been to laugh, as though he was playing some morbid game, but something about his quiet voice and fearful features had stolen the impulse. 'No! You're a liar!'

'Killed in their bed,' he'd said gruffly, as he yanked her through the front door and out into the dawning night. 'You're not safe here.' He'd turned and stared down at her just before they'd passed through the open gates. 'Forget this life,' he'd commanded, 'and everyone in it.'

Ava shivered as the memory receded. It seemed to take with it almost all her energy, but she forced herself into action, searching the room for anything useful, starting with the nightstands on either side of the enormous bed. Only one notebook showed any promise. As she leafed through the pages, she found it crammed full of diagrams and complex equations, but she quickly threw it aside with a frustrated sigh. She could decipher none of it.

She poked her head into the other bedrooms, all clean and tidy, but seemingly unused. She saved her own room for last, tears welling in her eyes as she stood on the threshold, a wave of homesickness crashing through her. Her things were still there just as she'd left them, the room a time capsule of her former life.

A puzzle sat half-finished on the floor, a book lay open on the unmade bed, her tortoiseshell hairbrush still contained a nest of the lighter-colored hair of her youth. She sat heavily on her childhood bed, vaguely wondering why this room was the only one that hadn't been straightened. She closed the book—*An Introduction to Portalry*—picked up her long-lost toy otter, kicked off her tattered shoes, and lay down, cradling the lavender-stuffed toy to her chest as the past settled over her like a blanket.

The washed-out purple bed linen, earth-pink dappled walls, and beige drape curtains embossed with little muted dots of color were so familiar. As she stared, it was easy to imagine she'd never been away, that her parents were alive, that she was still a six-year-old girl living a childhood filled with learning and love and delicious food and so much possibility.

As her limbs went limp and all her energy drained away, she thought she must have imagined the slight shaking sensation, then the small thud that invaded the silence, for it had been a long, traumatic day, and there was no one in her room but her. Her and her memories. Memories that flooded her mind as she embraced the enticing comfort of sleep.

CHAPTER THREE
HALE
TWO DAYS BEFORE DROMEDA STARTED SPINNING

HALE TRIED TO IGNORE the slight uptick in his heartrate as Maria and Elex left the library, leaving him alone with Sophie, the woman who believed he was owed to her. But he had no intention of marrying anyone, and certainly not some jumped up little liar from Laurow who'd manipulated his brother, John, into believing she cared for him. She'd dropped all pretense of that as soon as Hale had returned. The blasted minx.

And now she would try to seduce him, no doubt. But he was ready, and skimpy outfits and batted eyelashes would get her nowhere. Unlike his brother, Hale was wise to the world, and he'd known his fair share of women like this one.

'You're an ass,' said Sophie, leaning back on the couch and looking at the ceiling.

Hale flinched, then realized he must have misunderstood. 'Excuse me?' he said tersely, scowling hard. Not that she could see him. She was still busy admiring the cornicing, which was rather well done, he had to admit.

Her loose auburn hair slid over her shoulders as she leaned forward, her full lips splitting into an elegant smile as she fixed him with a lighthearted look. 'You heard.'

He gritted his teeth. 'I don't understand your meaning.'

Sophie barked a laugh. 'You don't know what it means when someone calls you an ass?' She threw herself backwards as though exasperated. 'And they say you're the clever one …'

Hale pushed to his feet. He would retire to his bedroom, he'd more than fulfilled his duty of hospitality. But he faltered because try as he might to overcome it, his curiosity got the better of him. He'd expected her to simper and flatter, not to insult him, and he didn't like the feeling that he'd missed something.

Hale poured himself a large whiskey, then returned to his seat, making himself comfortable, gearing up for a verbal joust, which was fine by him ... Probably just what he needed, in fact. He had plenty of steam to blow off after the way his uncle had treated him at dinner. 'And what is it they say about you, exactly?' Not his strongest opening gambit.

Sophie sat forward slowly, a coy smile tugging at her lips as she appraised him, and Hale got the distinct impression that she was delighted about something, although he had no clue what it could be. 'No one says much about me at all. I'm far too insignificant.'

He wanted to ask her what that meant but refused to give her the satisfaction. Was she insignificant? He'd certainly tried to brush her aside as though she were, but she could be both insignificant to him and significant to someone else, to her own family, for example. Did they treat her badly? Was that what her words implied? Or merely that they overlooked her, as was so often the way with women. Or perhaps she merely wanted to tip Hale off guard, to make him feel sorry for her. Well, he wouldn't be so easily pushed off course. He took a sparing sip of his sweet, smooth drink, rolling it around his mouth as he met her gaze, most of the liquid evaporating before he swallowed. 'Are you going to tell me?'

A small crease formed on her brow. 'Tell you what?'

'Why you consider me an ass,' he said, tilting his head. 'Do keep up.'

'Oh, right, you're still stuck on that.' She batted her eyelashes in what seemed to be a strange parody of her former self.

'Well?' he pressed.

'No.'

He scowled. 'Why not?'

'Because I'm certain you already know.'

Her words rendered him speechless, his mouth falling open for a moment before he remembered to clamp it shut. Who was this triffling woman?

The silence stretched to discomfort, and Sophie exhaled loudly, then spun in her seat, resting against the arm of the couch and stretching her legs along its length, facing away, her back to him. *What in the name of the blessed Goddess?* This was no ordinary seduction ...

Hale took another mouthful of whiskey, at a complete and total loss.

Sophie turned her head briefly and glanced up at him, her neck at an awkward angle. 'What was it like?'

He frowned in confusion. 'What was—'

'The edge of the world.' Her voice had a soft, dreamy quality, like maybe her interest was genuine. It made him want to tell her, especially as no one else seemed to care much about the epic adventure from which he had only just returned, and on which he'd almost died many times over.

'It was incredible,' he said quietly.

She stilled but didn't look at him.

'Quiet. Beautiful. Powerful. Awe inspiring.'

'Did you go right to the edge?' Her voice was breathy and her fingers gripped the couch cushion, Hale's eyes glued to the movement.

'Yes.'

'Did you touch it?' She turned her head, her expression hungry.

He paused as he remembered the way the edge of their world had sucked at him, trying to pull him in. 'It almost killed me.'

'You nearly fell over?' Her words came out in a rush, and if her interest was feigned, her acting skills were enviable.

'No.' He shook his head, then told her the whole story, answering her never-ending stream of interruptions as he went, surprised by the depth of her questions and her acute attention to detail.

'But why did you come back when you did?' she asked, when they'd exhausted every part of how he and his crew had sailed the circumference of their world.

He shrugged. 'We were all ready for a stint on dry land.'

'It was a coincidence, then, that you arrived back at the exact moment you did, in the middle of the weddings?'

Ah. Now things were falling into place. She thought he'd come back for her. He sucked in a long, tortured breath. 'If only I'd been twenty minutes later ...' Sophie would have married John, and he would be free of all this bother.

She turned away, the movement sharp, and a barbed silence settled.

'Why did you do it?' he asked, surprised to find he'd said the words out loud.

'Do what?' she snapped, but the tension holding her whole body rigid told him she knew precisely his meaning.

'You pretended to have feelings for John. You allowed yourself to be *hand-tied*. You—'

'I did what I had to do to make the whole thing tolerable, and the *hand-tie* shows just what kind of a man your brother is. It was an imitation of Elex's actions to save your sister. In their case, a romantic last resort. In ours?' She scoffed. 'What was I supposed to do, Hale? Publicly refuse to hand-tie the man I had already agreed to marry? But fret not, future husband, it's very much broken. Now,' she said in a more reasonable tone, swiveling her head to look at him once more, 'you said you sailed anticlockwise, and that you passed the Hellen Islands before Scallia, but that's impossible because you would have met them the other way around.'

He scoffed. 'Don't be absurd.'

'Oh,' she said, spinning her legs to the floor and launching to her shoeless feet, 'I assure you, I am being anything but.'

She practically danced to the section of the library reserved for maps and pulled a large, rolled piece of parchment from a tall basket. 'Help me,' she ordered, unfurling the map across a nearby desk. Hale reluctantly obliged, sliding two round weights onto one end as Sophie did the same at the other.

As one, they pounced on the section of map above Laurow Blade, moving together so their arms brushed as they leaned forward and traced their fingers across the string of islands.

'Parta, Meonope, Caranil ... Ha!' cried Sophie, her voice full of triumph. 'Scallia, then Hellen.'

Hale pushed her fingers out of the way and studied the words more closely, choosing to ignore the pleasant warmth of her skin. 'Hmm,' he said, reading the words over and over. 'It would appear you are correct.'

She huffed a triumphant laugh, then straightened, and Hale did too, not wanting to give his enemy a clear shot at his back. Unfortunately, that put them close. Sophie moved to step away, but Hale's hand came up without thinking, holding her arm to prevent her from running. A flash of uncertainty crossed her features before he hastily released her, but she didn't attempt to move again.

Hale's forehead pinched as he tried to focus, her honeysuckle scent fogging his mind. 'Where did you study? I thought the women of Laurow—'

She *tisked*. 'We are not allowed to attend the university, but that doesn't mean we can't study in the moments when we're not used as pawns, when everyone's forgotten we're alive.'

She said the pointed words sweetly, but they landed like a slap across his face, mostly because his sisters hadn't been allowed the luxury of formal study, either. One day he would change that archaic rule.

He appraised her with fresh eyes, feeling as though he were back on his boat, listing wildly after an unexpected wave. This was not at all the woman he'd anticipated, or the woman he'd met earlier in the day.

They stood there, seconds ticking by, nothing but the sounds of their breathing punctuating the tight silence. He tilted forward, wanting a closer look at the flecks of gold in the soft grey orbs of her eyes, then travelling lower to the plump pink bow of her lips, which were pressed together just a little too tightly, betraying apprehension, perhaps, or annoyance?

'Who the fuck are you?' he breathed, her lips so close he could feel the light puffs of her breath on his skin.

She exhaled through her nose, emitting a noise that sounded almost like a snort. 'I'm your future wife, Hale.' She pulled back, breaking the spell, then spun, pocketing a triffle from the table by the sofas as she headed for the door. 'Goodnight, darling,' she said, the word *darling* tripping off her tongue as easily as if they'd been married for years, and then she left without so much as a backward glance.

Hale blew out a heavy breath and leaned against the desk, needing something solid to hold onto. He didn't believe in the small magic of triffles, not really, but as he headed for his own sleeping quarters, he snatched one up, filled with the uneasy knowledge that he'd grossly underestimated his adversary and would need all the help he could get.

CHAPTER FOUR
AVA

AVA TRIED TO IGNORE the irritating shaking. She was so very tired, *needed* to sleep, would deal with whatever it was later. But the shaking didn't stop, so eventually it won, her mind crawling reluctantly back to wakefulness. And then panic gripped her insides because although she could open her eyes and move her head a little, she could do nothing else.

Her breathing sped, her heart rate rocketed, and a terrible realization dawned because she'd felt this way once before, back at the Atlas Tree. *Stone sickness.* Only this time she was alone, no one to find her Herivale—the antidote—or to administer it.

She would have cried if she was able, her mind desperately searching for an escape, a way to get help. But Kush was the only one who knew she was there. He'd said he would come for her, but who knew how long that would take, and unless he arrived soon, she would die alone in her childhood bed.

Or perhaps that was Kush's plan all along ... He was the one who'd urged her to use the Atlas Stone, after all, and she still had no idea who she could trust. Maybe no one.

She cast her eyes wildly around, and as she took in the well-dusted, cobweb free space, a small fire of hope kindled in her belly because whoever had been looking after the house might come back. They might help her. They might—Her first thought was stopped in its tracks by a second. *Herivale.* Her heart plummeted. Even if anyone found her, what good would it do? The antidote was almost impossible to find, its distribution tightly controlled by Var, and no doubt outlandishly expensive.

It would be worse still if someone found her and could do nothing.

She closed her eyes, thinking about how short her life had been, about all the things she might have done, the places she might have visited if only she hadn't taken Kush's advice. If only she'd stopped to think before using the Atlas Stone again. *Fucking magic.*

She tried to will her mind back to sleep, at least then she wouldn't have the torture of her own chastising thoughts, but her mind would not comply, too preoccupied with her foolishness. An hour ticked by, maybe two, perhaps more—Ava had no way of telling the time aside from the movement of the sun across her window—and she wondered how long she would have to lie there and what it was like to die from thirst, her mouth already dry.

She was so deep in thoughts of her body shriveling from the inside out that she almost missed it when the shaking came again, light like the buzzing of a bee. She dismissed it as a symptom of stone sickness, wondering if it would get progressively worse the closer to death she came, and then a voice filled her mind, a voice that brought feelings of joy and dread in equal measure.

'Ava!' Kush shouted, and she could hear his voice both inside her head and through her window, albeit a muted, distorted version. *What the fuck? More magic?* She waited for him to burst into the house, to rush up the stairs and rescue her. If she could have wept from happiness, she would have because she wasn't going to die after all, Kush the one person in all the many worlds who could get the Herivale she needed. Maybe he already had some with him. Maybe he'd planned it all along.

But seconds ticked by, and he didn't burst into the house or rush up the stairs, and Ava wondered if she was hallucinating, if the shaking and his voice were more tricks of the sickness.

'Ava!' the voice screamed. It was so real, so like Kush, and then the sound of a rattling metal gate filled her ears, and she remembered the magical wards that had kept everyone out for over a decade.

Fuck. The news the wards still worked would have been a relief in any other circumstance, but as it was, they were about to cause her death.

'Ava! Let me in!'

She tried to say something, silently pleading with her body to let her speak, but it was no use, her voice locked inside an iron box, and she was too weak to lift the lid.

The shaking came again, this time more violent, almost as though it was angry. Was the bed cross with her? The house? The stone sickness?

'Let me in!'

I can't.

More shaking.

What is your problem? She silently screamed. *I can't speak!*

The shaking became so violent, it was almost painful, and she inhaled sharply. It was then she remembered she could still breathe on demand, and if she could do that, perhaps she could ... do what, exactly?

The gates shook, and Ava imagined Kush's back slamming against them in frustration, the sound so clear it was as though she was standing right next to them. How was that possible? Was it some part of the wards? Some layer of the spells that had made the place a fortress? Would that fortress even answer to her?

But the magic had let her in easily enough, the front door had opened to her touch ... If she could only communicate with it, perhaps she could convince it to let Kush pass, too.

But how? She couldn't speak!

She exhaled as forcefully as the stone sickness would allow, but it made only the barest of sounds, and if she could have growled in frustration, she would have.

The slamming sound of a weight against the gates came again, and it was as though their emotions were tied, hers and Kush's, each of them seeking an outlet for their hopeless aggravation.

She tried to make her breath carry sound, tried again and again until it made her breathless, and seeing as her chest was restricted as though someone had wrapped a belt around her ribs, it made her lightheaded and panicky, unable to get enough air. She worried she would pass out and Kush would leave, which only served to scare her more.

The gates rattled furiously, as though Kush was trying to break them down, but his physical force wasn't enough, could never be enough in the face of such powerful magic.

'Ava! Let me in!' Kush bellowed, and strangely, his upset calmed her, helped her come to terms with the idea of her impending death. At least he might miss her, even if no one else would.

Seconds ticked by, turning to minutes, and she imagined that she and Kush sat side by side outside the gates, her head resting on his shoulder, sucking in his strength and warmth.

She'd been an outsider since the night her parents had died, belonging to nothing and no one. But with Kush, she'd felt as though she might belong to him one day, and maybe ... maybe he could belong to her, too.

'I have to go, Ava,' he said, his voice quiet, defeated. 'I understand why you don't want to see me, but I'll come back tomorrow if I can. I just want to know that you're okay, that you're ...'

No! Kush! She could be dead by tomorrow. If he said more words, she didn't hear them, terror ripping through her. She dug deep within herself, dredging up every last ounce of force she could find, refusing to accept this fate, refusing to lose Kush to his father, knowing even if he wanted to come back tomorrow, Var might send him away for a month, two, or on a mission that got Kush killed!

No. No. No. No. No! Kush! Don't leave! KUSH!

A sound came from her throat, surprising her. It was supposed to be the word, 'Kush,' although it was really more of a croaky click than anything. But somehow the magic understood her intention, and the whole house seemed to zip tight as a squealing sound filled Ava's ears.

Was that ... the gates? Were the gates open?

Then the sound of rushing footsteps, the front door clattering open, her name many times as Kush moved around downstairs. She closed her eyes, emotion welling in her chest, causing it to somehow squeeze even tighter. Kush was here. Inside. He could help her, stay with her. Var couldn't get them while they were behind the wards, and that added to her colossal relief.

As she listened to Kush rampaging through the house, she realized how much she hated being alone. It hadn't occurred to her before, but she did hate it. She wanted to be part of something bigger than herself, like she had when she'd lived with her parents, and again in the Cleve—even if she'd despised most of her life there.

'Ava!' Kush breathed, dropping to his knees beside the bed. '*Shit.*' He pulled a vial of Herivale from his coat and ran the tonic across her lower lip, then cradled her face in his hand. 'I'm so sorry, I had no idea it would be this bad already.'

The sweet flavor coated her tongue, and as before, the medicine worked in an instant, her body coming back to her as though it had never been out of reach.

'Hey,' she said, her voice cracking.

'Thank Atlas.'

'Thank you,' she whispered, as he rested his forehead on her arm.

'I would have come sooner, but Mother saw me in the temple.' He lifted his head to look her in the eye. 'She insisted I use the healing pools, and I couldn't think of a way to say no without making her suspicious. I told her I'd come to apologize after the visit on her birthday ended so badly.'

Ava studied him, glad to see he looked much better than he had the day before. His arm was no longer in a sling, he was moving more freely, his face had the same luster as the very first time she'd seen him, and there was not a trace of Mezz in his beautiful blue eyes.

He also seemed bigger, if such a thing was possible, his shoulders even broader, his arms more muscled. Or maybe that was because her childhood bedroom wasn't meant for someone like him, his presence so potent it took up most of the space.

'I'm just glad you came,' she said, sliding her fingers into his hair.

'I always will. I can't lose you, Ava. You're all I have.'

She scowled at that. 'Aside from your father—who's a God—and your mother, and no doubt all the other powerful people you grew up with.'

He kissed her, cutting off her words. She wanted to push him off, to take him to task for his insensitive, privileged whining and demand answers to her many questions, but more of her wanted to do the opposite, wanted to pull him into bed beside her and keep him there forever.

He pulled back, breathless, his eyes full of tenderness as he pushed a strand of hair behind her ear. 'But you're the only thing that's real, Ava. The only thing that's true.'

Chapter Five

Sophie

Two Days Before Dromeda Started Spinning

Sophie pushed into the suite of rooms she and her mother had been allocated for their stay. Not as large as the wing set aside for the Oshe contingent, but still nothing to be sniffed at. Although her mother had done precisely that, and often, since their arrival.

Sophie swung the door closed, and a flash of movement followed, too quick for her to react, a hand swiping across her face with a sickening *thwack*. Her head flew to the side and she gasped, then she ducked and whirled, pulling her hands up to protect her face in case of a follow-up.

But she needn't have worried on that score because when her eyes located the attacker, she found the tall woman with a dark bob who had birthed her, her hands on her hips, a deep scowl on her forehead.

'What the fuck do you think you're playing at?' Linella hissed, stepping menacingly into Sophie's space.

Sophie averted her eyes. *One, two, three, four, five, six, seven* … She counted quickly in her head, distracting herself from the desire to lash out, to retaliate. She'd done it once and it hadn't ended well.

'Well?' demanded Linella, a spec of spittle flying from her mother's mouth, landing on Sophie's cheek.

Sophie concentrated on blocking out the stinging pain from her mother's slap. She knew from experience it would ease quickly——and with it her desire for revenge——although she'd have to cover the marks with make-up for many days to come.

'I'm doing exactly what you wanted me to do,' she breathed, trying to keep her voice light.

'You walked away!'

'Tonight?' In the library? Had her mother been spying on her?

'You had him in the palm of your hand, and you *walked away*.'

'I *have* him in the palm of my hand precisely *because* I walked away,' Sophie spat, refusing to back down. This was her mission, and she would complete it as she saw fit. 'He's not the same as John. John was easy, Hale is ... not.'

Hale was taller, broader, darker, more worldly. Hale induced a tugging feeling in her chest that John never could. A raw attraction, nothing more, but the feeling made her role more complicated.

'Seduce him. Marry him. Bed him. Get with child. Kill him——not necessarily in that order. It is simple.'

'Simple,' Sophie agreed, allowing the barest hint of sarcasm to creep into her tone, although not so much as to provoke another attack.

'Figure it out.'

'I am, Mother.'

'This is our chance,' said Linella, as though Sophie hadn't heard those words a hundred times before. 'Our chance to take control of Alter Blade. It should have been ours for generations.'

Because some ancestor had bested some past leader of Alter at cards.

'You think you know all, but you do not,' Linella sneered. 'There are forces at play that you do not understand.'

The words stopped Sophie in her tracks, and she studied her mother carefully. 'What forces?' It was unlike the older woman to be cryptic. Cruel, yes, but she rarely withheld information that could aid Sophie in her tasks.

Linella let out a harsh breath that turned into a growl. 'I am not supposed to tell you, but I worry if I do not, you will make the wrong decision.'

Every fiber of Sophie's body stilled. 'Tell me what?' she breathed.

Linella folded her hands over her chest and clutched her upper arms. She tapped her thumbs on the sleeves of her silk gown, the rapid staccato setting Sophie's nerves alight. And then she stepped close. 'Laurow is in league with the Claws,' Linella said so quietly, Sophie had to strain to hear the words.

'What?' The blood drained from Sophie's brain as she struggled to make out her mother's meaning. Her family hated the people of the Claws. Like many in the water-rich Blades, they looked down on the Claws, felt superior, willfully disregarded all the Claws had done to keep Celestl turning. 'How?'

'We've been helping them acquire food for years, and allowing them to store it on our land—for a fee, of course. But with everything that's going on with Nicoli and the Claws, well ... it leaves us in a precarious position. If Nicoli should tell the other Blades ...'

'They would imprison us,' whispered Sophie, her voice tiny, scared of lurking Alter servants or that the walls might have ears. 'And execute us after that.'

'Yes. But if we can take Alter, we'll have the might of Alter and Laurow together. We'd be evenly matched against the other two Blades, and no one wants another war.'

'Fuck,' said Sophie, part of her wishing her mother hadn't told her. 'We're traitors to the Blades?'

'Don't be naïve,' Linella hissed. 'The other Blades would have done the same in our shoes. It's a lucrative deal, and why shouldn't we sell food to those with the coin to buy it? Especially when the Claws have worked so hard to ensure our survival. It was an investment in our future. And anyway, Danit's hiding something, I'm sure of it. So pull your finger out and do to Hale what you so easily did to John. Buy me the time I need to unearth his secrets.'

Sophie reeled, feeling as though she'd taken a blow to the head, that she might topple at any moment. Before, it had been easy to convince herself that her actions were righteous, that she was rectifying an—albeit dubious—wrong. Settling a gambling debt. But now?

'Sophie,' said her mother, snapping her fingers in front of Sophie's face.

Sophie closed her eyes for a beat, exhaling heavily. 'I'm trying, Mother. Believe me, I'm—'

Linella grabbed Sophie's chin between her thumb and forefinger, squeezing to the point of pain. Sophie knew better than to reveal her discomfort or try to pull away, counting once more in her head to give her something to focus on other than her anger. 'Well, if you value your life, child, try harder.'

Chapter Six

Ava

Ava let Kush hug her until her strength had fully returned, inhaling the scent of him, allowing herself to feel relieved that he looked so much better than he had only a few hours before. But it was remarkable how quickly the Herivale worked, and when she was entirely back to normal, she pushed him off, scowling hard, her doubt and anger returning with her vitality. 'You lied to me, Kush,' she quietly accused.

He tried to hold onto her. 'No, I ...'

'Yes!' She shoved him away.

'Ava ...'

'You're a demi-God, and your father killed my parents. Wants to kill me! And you knew! You *helped* him. You kept my past from me. You knew who I was, and you never told me any of it!'

He paused for a beat, visibly collecting himself, pulling his shoulders straight. 'I hid you. I kept you away from him, and Father didn't kill anybody.'

She laughed cruelly. 'We both know that's a lie.'

Kush closed his eyes, shaking his head in frustrated little jabs.

'You left me in the tavern on my birthday,' Ava continued. She desperately wanted for things to be okay between them, for him to explain, to understand why he'd acted as he did, but it also felt good to finally have it out with him after days of hurt and confusion. 'You *ran*.'

'I'm sorry.' He tried to take her hand, but she pulled it away. He brushed back his dishevelled hair, grabbing hold for a moment. 'I thought it would be better for you if B didn't see me. I planned to return, but then Father arrived, and—'

'You fell into line like the good little soldier you are.'

'Ava ... No! I led him away, didn't want him to find you.' His tone contained a note of warning, but she refused to heed it.

'Why are you even here, Kush? Spying on me for Daddy?'

'I'm here for you.'

'Liar.'

His brows pinched. 'Don't say that.'

'Or what? What are you going to do, my lord *demi-God*. Kill me?'

'Ava!' His features betrayed his shock, how he was appalled and hurt, and she almost felt guilty, but then his face hardened into the predatory mask he used with the rest of the world, and a hot bolt of awareness shot through her. 'You're a demi-God, too, remember.' His eyes were molten, his voice commanding, and her mouth went so dry she couldn't speak, not that she could think of any words. He rocked forward, crowding her, and this time it didn't even cross her mind to push him away. 'I'm here for you, Ava. Because I love you. Because you're all that matters to me.'

He pulled back, and she only just stopped the protest that rose to her lips, unable to bear the loss of him, the idea that he might leave like a knife in her guts. She sorely wanted to believe him, but he had lied to her, had blindly done his father's bidding, and what if he was only there on Var's orders?

'I don't want to fight with you,' he said quietly, then stood and turned away.

Ava loosed the lungful of air she'd been holding, watching his shoulders move up and down with his breaths, his hands balled into fists. 'How do I know I can trust you, Kush?' Her words were little more than a whisper, and she was terrified of his answer, but she needed to know, both because her life might depend on it, but also because he was the one person she desperately wanted to have on her side.

He turned slowly and gave her a sad look. 'You don't.'

Their eyes held, and Ava stared into his for a long moment, searching for any waver or sign of deceit, using the trick she'd often relied on during her life in the tavern. But unlike most of those she'd interrogated in the Cleve, Kush didn't shy away. He stood open and vulnerable, staring straight back, letting her see right down into his soul. 'Do you plan to stay?'

He nodded, their eyes still fused.

'Why?'

'I told you why.'

'What about Var?'

He shrugged. 'He'll be angry, but he can't get to us here.'

Us. Her heart pulsed at the word. She had a million more questions, but he was here and planning to stay. They had time, and she didn't want to risk driving him back to his father. She pressed her lips together and nodded, then climbed out of bed, accepting his offered hand, but as her foot hit the floor, she cried out and clutched at him because she'd trodden on something cold and cylindrical that rolled out from under her, upsetting her balance. 'What the ...!'

'What is it?' Kush asked in alarm, looking down as soon as she was steady on her feet. He bent and picked up a large glass vial, holding it up to the light. 'Wow, it's—'

'Herivale,' Ava finished for him. 'But ...' Had that been there when she'd entered the bedroom? Surely she would have seen it. And then she remembered the thud when she'd drifted off to sleep, the one she'd been too tired to investigate. 'Fuck.'

'You didn't see it?' Kush asked tenderly.

'No. It wasn't there when I came in. It ...' She trailed off because she wasn't sure where it had come from. 'I think someone must be looking after the house. They must have put it here.' But she would have heard footsteps, wouldn't she? 'They must have used magic.'

Kush fixed her with an almost pitying look. 'No one can get in, Ava. The Gods tried every trick they could think of to get in here, and when that didn't work, they had the house watched. No one ever came or went.'

Ava held up her hands, gesturing to the room around them. 'Then how is it so clean?'

He shrugged. 'Magic?'

The shaking. Had that been magic? Thick, cloying self-loathing sank into the pit of her stomach and sat there like a stone. If only she'd paid more attention. If only she'd used her head instead of sinking into the melancholy of the past, instead of pining like a lost child for her dead parents, she could have saved herself. She wouldn't have needed Kush at all. She wondered if she would have let him through the gates so easily if she hadn't been dying.

Kush frowned. 'What is it?'

She waved him off. 'Nothing.'

'Ava ...'

'We have to focus. Var wants to get in here because he thinks the house is hiding the location of his soul, correct?'

Kush froze, then nodded reluctantly. 'His and the other Gods'.'

'Then let's find out if he's right, and what other secrets my parents were hiding.'

He hesitated for a moment, watching her closely, seeming conflicted, but then he stepped back and held out his arm, gesturing for her to lead the way.

They explored the house from top to bottom, searching for anything that might help them locate the parts of the Gods' souls her parents had hidden. But aside from a few scribbled notes they didn't understand, they found little that seemed promising among the piles of academic tomes, maps, and letters.

By the time they'd finished their first sweep of the place, their stomachs rumbled and their fingers hurt, but the kitchen was bare, nothing but condiments and spices filling the cupboards. 'Maybe there's food in the garden,' said Ava, leading Kush through the utility room and out of the back door, but Ava came up short as she cast her eyes over the jungle that had once been her mother's pride and joy.

Pristine raised beds and beautifully edged paths were now hidden under weeds the same height as Ava that encroached on either side as they passed. Fennel fronds and hollyhocks brushed her arms, and they had to push their way through an overgrown buddleia to get to the vegetable garden at the back of the walled space.

'My mother would not be pleased,' said Ava, and her chest clenched once more with homesickness as memories she'd long forgotten rose to the surface of her brain.

'Was she ... violent?' Kush asked haltingly.

'No. Well, she had ups and downs, I suppose. I can't remember all of it, but I don't think anything like ... like what your father does to you.'

She slipped her hand into his and squeezed, choosing to ignore her doubts about his loyalty at that moment.

He gave a heavy exhale. 'I'm used to it. It barely even hurts anymore.'

Ava wasn't sure she believed him, but then again, what did she know about family? 'What happened after I stole the stone?' she asked as they approached an old, gnarled apple tree that, thank goodness, was groaning under the weight of its red and green speckled fruit.

They stopped beside a low-hanging branch, and Kush looked away, his fingers pulsing gently against hers. She wondered if he realized he was doing that, and if he would answer …

Memories rushed across Ava's mind, of Kush's mother groveling on her knees, Var ignoring the woman, his plush green cape fluttering in the breeze, and Kush lying battered on the ground. The visions sickened her even more now than when she'd witnessed them in the flesh.

'Nothing good,' Kush said eventually. 'My parents went inside and left me in the dirt. Father told me if I got up, I'd regret it, and Mother cared only about saving herself, worried Father would blame her for what I'd done, for standing up to him and for … for losing the stone.'

She squeezed his hand, regret sucking at her insides. 'I'm sorry.'

He turned and pulled her so she was standing in front of him, looking down at her with an earnest expression so fixed it could have been carved from stone. 'I was glad you took it. Glad you escaped.'

She turned her head away as the memories kept playing. 'I almost didn't escape.'

He exhaled a long breath. 'I know. When Father came out of the house, he was buoyant, smug, convinced he'd outsmarted you. He said you'd sent yourself into his custody.'

She met his regretful gaze. 'His goons almost got me. Novak sold me out.'

Kush's eyes flew wide. 'Novak? The new Master of the House?'

'According to Billy, selling me out is how he got the role. Novak was the one who took me to the tavern the night my parents died. He forced B to take me in, and before B kicked me out, she gave me a parcel Novak had left for my eighteenth birthday. It had the coordinates I used to escape inside.'

Kush shook his head. 'And Father had enforcers waiting at those coordinates?'

She nodded. 'Billy rescued me. Turns out Novak was playing both sides, although I don't know why.'

'Then he's playing a dangerous game. If Father finds out … He was furious, he …'

'He took it out on you? Your injuries … That was him?'

Kush dropped her hand and moved to the other side of the tree, surveying the apples as though looking for the perfect one. 'The Mezz helped me through.'

She remembered the silvery blue sheen in his eyes, even if she didn't know what Mezz was or did. She plucked an apple for herself and took a bite, chewing silently for a moment, savoring the sweet juice that ran down her throat as she considered all the ways she'd like to hurt Var.

'What is that?' asked Kush, invading her daydream.

'What?' She moved to join him.

'Down there.'

'Oh.' Near the garden's back wall, a steep, grassy slope angled down to a circular door in the earth beneath a large alter tree.

'What's down there?'

'It's like a bedroom, I think. I went in once and my parents freaked out. There's nothing inside, but my parents would go in occasionally. They'd be in there for hours, and they always seemed a little strange when they came out.'

Kush smiled broadly, then raced down the slope.

'Kush! What are you doing?'

'If this is what I think it is …' He pulled the door open without hesitation, stuck his head inside, then reappeared, his smile so wide Ava couldn't help but return it. 'It is!'

'What?'

'An echo chamber.'

'A …'

'Come look.'

Her feet moved before she'd told them to, her chest scrunching tight with anticipation and excitement. 'What is it? Wait! Take your shoes off!'

Ava hadn't bothered to put on her uncomfortable, hole-riddled moccasins when she'd got out of bed, so she stepped straight inside while Kush pulled off his supple leather boots. Dry leaves crunched underfoot as she stepped across the threshold, the dim space exactly as she remembered, walls made of roots, the occasional little white flower appearing on them, accompanied by a low murmuring noise she couldn't decode.

Kush closed the door behind them, and a soft bluish light filled the darkness. A tinge of unease made Ava still because she hadn't got much farther than this in her youth, and she half expected the door to fly open and a furious parent to pull her out.

Kush stooped as he surveyed the contents of the thin shelf packed with small glass vials attached to the back of the door. He read the labels, then carefully selected one that seemed to be filled with coarse flakes of something dark, holding it up for her to see.

'What is that?' asked Ava, half excited, half terrified.

He gave her a coy smile. '*Lost.*'

'Come again?'

'We're going to get lost in the Atlas Web.'

'We're going to ... Kush, I don't understand. What does that mean? What is this place for?'

'Excellent questions,' he said as he pulled off his long coat and socks, then dumped them unceremoniously on the leaf-covered ground. He had only a shirt and breeches underneath, and the shirt came off next. Her eyes traced the perfect triangle of his torso, lean but muscular, and she quickly turned away, rubbing her forearms as an outlet for her awkwardness.

'Ava,' he said, and she jumped a little, whirling guiltily towards him as he grabbed a piece of fabric from a cubby by the door. He stepped towards her. 'Did you hear me?'

'Uh ... Sorry ... I'm ... Um ...'

'You'll be more comfortable if you take off your dress. It can get pretty intense inside these things.'

'Kush, I can't. I ...'

'Here,' he said, handing her the fabric—a thin cotton nightdress.

She took it and clutched the soft garment to her chest. 'What do you mean, *intense*?'

He grinned, and she'd never seen him look so carefree, the boyishness of it warming her heart after everything he'd been through. 'You'll see.'

She puffed out an exhale, then reluctantly nodded her agreement, her eyes flicking briefly back to his torso as she said, 'Turn around.'

He did as she asked, and Ava shrugged out of her dress. She realized, as it fell to the ground, that she could get new clothes now, perhaps by trading something belonging to her parents. Or maybe her mother's dresses would fit her and she could burn the ugly monstrosity B had forced her to wear for so long. She tossed her dress atop the pile of Kush's clothes, then slipped the nightgown over her head. 'Okay,' she said, and he turned back towards her.

'Don't look so nervous!' he said with a hearty laugh. 'There's nothing to worry about. Echo chambers show us small fragments of lives in other worlds. Like an echo, they're not precise, and only the loudest or most potent make it through the web of roots and magic.' He held up the vial and shook it. 'This helps clarify the voices and direct our journey.'

Ava's stomach clenched tight with unease. 'But why are we doing this?' They had endless books to read, and they had to find food, and Var could be hammering on the gates at that very moment. Not to mention, her parents had yanked her out of this very chamber when she was young, had told her never to go back inside, that it was dangerous.

An endearing, childlike smile graced Kush's lips. 'We're doing this for fun.'

'For ... fun?'

He stepped closer, so she had to tip her head up to meet his eyes. 'When did you last do something just because you wanted to?' he asked in a low, soft voice.

'Well ...' She racked her brain, but his proximity was scrambling her thoughts. She took a deep breath, buying some time, but that just made it worse, his subtle, spicy scent filling her lungs. She probably smelled terrible. When was the last time she'd washed? Did washing count as something fun?

'See,' he said, 'never. And it's been too long for me, too. I've only been inside an echo chamber once, when I was a child, but it was exciting and hilarious and,'—he shrugged—'fun.' He leaned his lips down to her ear. 'I want to have fun with you, Ava.'

Oh, Gods ... She rested her forehead on his chest to escape his searching eyes, but it was no help. His skin was smooth and firm and warm, and she wanted to kiss him right where his ribs joined in the center of his chest. She tried to remember that he'd lied to her, that she should be at least a little angry with him.

He wrapped his arms around her and tugged gently on her hair, bringing her eyes back to his. 'Please?' he said, his smile gone, replaced by a look of doubt that made her chest lurch with alarm. Her hands came up between them and rested on his ribs. She savored the feel of him for a moment, then said, 'What do I have to do?'

He gave a quiet, delighted smile and tipped a line of flakes from the vial onto the back of his hand. He licked half into his mouth, then reached his hand expectantly towards her. She almost recoiled. 'Um ...'

'It's nothing to worry about, Ava. It just clarifies the voices, and perhaps lowers inhibitions. Some of them do that.'

She hesitated for a moment more, briefly wondering if this was some terrible trap, but she was also intrigued to see how the chamber worked, wanted to understand every part of her parents' lives and anything that might give her an insight into them, so she took his hand in both of hers and licked.

The flakes were bitter and fizzed a little on her tongue, but they soon dissolved, and then the incoherent murmuring in the air around them morphed into words ... Far too many words for her to understand.

Kush slid his hand into Ava's and led her to the middle of the domed space, to where a circle of fragrant white flowers carpeted the ground beneath the arching tree roots above.

'Lie down,' said Kush. 'It'll make it easier to concentrate, to navigate the voices, to pull them apart and hear the threads. It starts fast, but it'll settle in a moment. And the flakes might make you feel ... strange. They all have different effects. I don't know what *Lost* will do to us.'

She did as he said, lying on the soft mattress, and when her eyes turned to the ceiling, she gasped at the trail of little white flowers springing to life along a root. They disappeared just as quickly, only to be replaced by new ones.

'Kush,' she breathed in wonder, turning her head to face him, finding him close, his eyes watching her.

'Give in to it,' he whispered. 'Follow where it leads.'

Ava closed her eyes, trying to let go of everything but the voices, seeking a single thread. A haze descended across her mind as though she'd walked into a cloud, making the voices blend together once more, and then out of the fog came a single soprano voice, as clear as though the woman was inside the chamber with them. 'We will never let them through again,' the woman said bitterly, and Ava opened her eyes to find only one tiny white flower on the roots above.

'They'll kill us,' said a man's voice, his tone grave.

'Better dead than a slave.'

'Better dead than *their* slave,' said a third faint voice, drifting away, back into the indistinguishable chatter.

'What was that?' said Ava, turning her head towards Kush, then rolling onto her side. 'Who was that?'

Kush shrugged, a slight frown on his brow. 'Someone in another world.' He entwined their fingers. 'You're the most beautiful person I've ever known,' he said, resting his forehead against hers. 'From the moment I saw you, I could barely look away.'

'Kush ...' She bit her lip, trying desperately to keep her head, to remind herself he'd lied to her, that he was probably lying now seeing she was no great beauty. But it was hard to ignore the rushing in her chest, made harder still by the heating echo chamber, the soothing chatter, and the scent of him in her nose.

'Did you know who I was then?' she asked almost shyly. 'The first time you saw me in Mrs. Kelly's shop?'

He smiled a small, secret smile, and her chest pulled tight. 'No.'

'When did you know?'

'The day Father made me kill Malik.'

'Oh.' Her forehead puckered. 'I don't understand.'

He lifted his fingers to her brow and smoothed the lines with his thumb. 'When we were leaving the Clouds to come to the tavern, he told me to search for a girl named Ilyavra, especially in Santala. He said you'd be about fourteen, and he showed me a portrait of your parents, thinking you might look like them.'

Her heart gave a painful tug. 'Do I?'

His thumb moved to her cheek, caressing her cheekbone. 'You have something of them about you, mostly your mother. Enough to confirm it was you he was looking for.'

Ava felt strangely lightheaded, almost giddy. 'But you didn't tell him.'

'I … no.' He turned his eyes to the ceiling. 'I wanted to get to know you first. I already knew I couldn't trust Father, and I couldn't bear the thought of handing you over without knowing *why*, especially not after I'd met you.' He tilted his face back towards her. 'I wanted more of you from the first moment I saw you. I'd never felt that way about anyone else.'

She tried not to let his pretty words sway her, a near-impossible task given how they had scrambled her brain. 'That's why you followed me to the stream?'

'It was the only place you were ever alone.'

'But you still didn't tell Var.'

'I never would have.' He pushed a strand of hair off her face.

'Why? Why are you telling me this?'

'Because I'm in love with you.' He pressed his lips against hers and her eyes fluttered closed. 'Obsessed, really. I can't get you out of my head. I want you to trust me, and for that you need to know how I feel. I *want* you to know how I feel.'

'Kush,' she breathed, opening her mouth to him, 'I—'

A booming male voice stabbed through the chatter. 'We should close the portal.'

'We need the trade!'

'Fuck the trade and fuck the taxes. They're killing us. They're stealing from us!'

'Laurant, don't be so stupid. They're Gods! What are we in the face of their might? They take what is rightfully theirs. They protect us, keep the portal safe, provide a market for our goods! You'd be so quick to sentence us to death?'

Laurant's frustrated roar faded into the background as a large flower shriveled and died on the chamber's roof.

Kush rolled onto his back and puffed out a long breath. 'The Federation is under so much strain.'

'The Federation?'

He tilted his head towards her. 'Worlds that swear fealty to the Gods in return for protection and open trade.'

'The people don't like it?'

'It's not that simple ...' He thought for a moment. 'You grew up in the Cleve, right here in Santala, in a federated world.'

She pulled back in surprise. 'Santala?'

He nodded. 'The temple, my father's patronage, the protected portal: all hallmarks, and yet plenty of ordinary people don't know the significance of any of it. Don't know about the Atlas Tree and the portals and the opportunities the Federation presents. Like anything, it works for some but not others, and there's always been tension.'

'Between the people and their rulers?'

'Yes, and between the worlds and the Gods. Some federated worlds do better than others. That leads to mistrust, and the worlds sometimes fight among themselves. Then there are the unfederated worlds ... Some of those go as far as to accuse the Gods of hoarding all the magic for themselves.'

Ava's eyes flew wide. 'Do they?'

Kush's face scrunched. 'No! Of course not.'

Silence settled for a beat as Ava processed what he'd told her. 'What did that man mean about taxes? He was angry ...'

Kush shrugged. 'The Gods keep hiking taxes, but they don't have any choice.'

Ava raised a skeptical eyebrow.

The hint of a scowl marred Kush's forehead. 'Running the Federation has a cost, not to mention, the Gods are expanding, which will benefit all federated worlds eventually. But someone has to pay for it.'

'And if the federated worlds don't want that?'

'The Gods don't answer to the Federation. They do what is right for the system in the long term, and if there is a cost for that now, it must be paid.'

'But what about the people we heard? What can they do? Can they leave?'

Kush turned his gaze to the ceiling. 'The Federation must be protected, no matter the personal cost.'

'So those people don't matter?'

He pursed his lips.

'Nobody matters?' she pressed. '*We* don't matter?'

'My life matters little.'

'Well it matters to me,' she said hotly.

Silence pulled the air tight, then Kush exhaled a long breath and rolled towards her, pressing his forehead gently to hers. 'And yours matters to me, but in the grand scheme of the Atlas Web, we matter not at all.'

'No,' she whispered, trying to convince herself as much as him. 'We do matter.' She pulled back, looking him in the eye. 'My parents mattered. Your father, unfortunately, matters. Our actions have consequences, and I don't want mine to hurt people.'

'And yet, what do you think happened to the people who helped you in the Atlas Tree?' he said defensively, his eyes instantly flashing with regret.

'What?' breathed Ava. She'd assumed B and Billy were fine, that they'd escaped, that Var's guards had only cared about capturing her. 'What happened to them?' She held her breath as she waited for his reply.

'I'm sorry, Ava, I didn't mean to—'

'What happened, Kush?'

He looked up at the ceiling. 'The man escaped, but B was captured.'

Ava wasn't sure how she felt about that. She couldn't trust either of them, but they'd also kept her alive when the stone sickness had hit, and B had taken her in when her parents had died, even if she'd had no choice and had treated Ava like scum for years ...

'Billy comes from a magical family,' Kush added. 'They were once respected, although they've fallen from favor since your parents' death. He has a navigator and used it to escape.' The same way Billy had saved Ava from Var's men when she'd first landed in the tree.

Ava probably shouldn't care after the years of B forcing her to live in a cellar, but for some reason, she felt both guilt and concern. 'What will they do with her? Will they hurt her?'

'They might,' he said slowly. 'It really depends on her.'

'Can we get her out? She knows things that could help me understand who I am, who my parents were, their magic.'

'Things that would help Father, too ...'

'Shit.'

Another flower bloomed, this one on a root to the side of the chamber, and a child's voice filled the air. *'Just jump in,'* it hissed.

'We can't! We're not allowed!' squealed a second child.

'Oh, come on! Don't be a baby. They'll never know.'

'They *always* know.'

A shout sounded, followed by a splash, then a laugh, then, 'Gods! Get out!'

'What? Why? Stephen, come back! Help me out! We're not supposed to ... Oh ... I ... I'm so sorry, Lord Bombardier, I—'

'What do you think you are doing, Boy?' The male voice was deep and terrifying. 'These pools are for healing *important* people, not for you.'

'I'm sorry. I—'

The boy's screams echoed all around them. 'Make it stop,' Ava whispered, pressing her face against Kush's chest.

Kush wrapped his arms around her as the flower died, and Ava realized there were tears in her eyes. 'Men like him give the Gods a bad name,' Kush ground out, his hold on her fierce.

Ava pushed herself away. 'You know him?'

'He's my godfather,' he said bitterly.

'Oh, Kush ...'

'A vicious, twisted man. He was always hateful, but then his son ran away, took his family's Atlas Stone, and he's been searching for it ever since. It consumes him, no longer being like your family and mine.'

'Your family and ... what do you mean?'

Kush interlaced their fingers. 'We have Atlas Stones. He does not.'

'My family has an Atlas Stone?'

'Your family had all three at one time.'

'Where is it? Who has it?'

'No one knows, although Father's convinced it's somewhere in your house. One of the many reasons he wants to get inside this place.'

'And because he wants back the missing piece of his soul,' said Ava.

Kush lifted a shoulder. 'Just like B and Billy want theirs.'

But Billy and B hadn't wanted her to come here. They'd wanted her to slink off into the shadows never to be seen again. 'Wait ... what did you say? B and Billy are ...'

Kush nodded. 'Long-lives, yes. You didn't know?'

She shook her head, her mind reeling. That changed everything ... maybe. Did it? She had to think. Why didn't B and Billy want their souls back when all the other Gods did? Kush gave a heavy exhale, then rolled towards her, cupping her face. 'You can't trust any of them, Ava.'

But can I trust you? She didn't ask in reply.

CHAPTER SEVEN
MARIA
THREE DAYS AFTER DROMEDA STARTED SPINNING

MARIA HOVERED AT THE open door of Cane's bedroom, no part of her wanting to enter. She cast her eyes across the room and her stomach dropped because something about the unusual curve of the desk, the abstract tapestries on the walls, and the plush-yet-practical rug made her realize whose room this really was. Certainly it didn't fit the flashy painted peacock.

'Ah, Maria,' said Cane, with a sadistic curve of his lips. 'Come in.'

Maria took a tentative step into the room and found Erica and Opal standing side by side by the bed. She stifled a gasp as she took in their identical blood-red dresses, if the slivers of fabric warranted the name; the monstrosities were devoid even of a sheer overlayer like the one she'd worn the night before. But her gasp wasn't because Cane had dressed them up as twin dolls, but because Maria's own dress was an exact match for theirs.

'Be a good girl and stand beside Opal,' said Cane, drinking in her reaction.

She did as she was told because what option did she have? And as she took her place in the lineup, Cane sat on the edge of the bed.

'Erica, my dear,' said Cane. Erica stepped forward with the efficiency of a well-drilled soldier, not stopping until she stood between his thighs. His hands slid up her legs until they rested on her waist, and then he gripped her with his good hand and pulled her to her knees before him.

Rushing sounded in Maria's ears as horror filled her. He couldn't mean to …

Cane stroked Erica's hair as she unbuttoned his breeches.

No.

Maria glanced at Opal, whose features were vacant, as if it wasn't the first time this had happened. She stared straight ahead, a glassy sheen shielding her eyes.

'Eyes on me,' Cane grunted, and Maria turned back to face him, not bothering to try and hide her shock.

'Over there,' Cane snapped at Opal, pointing to the end of the bed as Erica began moving her hand up and down. 'We wouldn't want you to miss the details of your lesson.'

Opal moved without question, standing at the foot of the bed where she could see Cane and Erica side on.

'No,' Maria breathed. He couldn't do this. Treating his wife this way was abhorrent—even if it was his right by law—but to do it to Maria ... 'You promised not to harm me.'

'And I plan to keep my word,' said Cane. 'Now move or I'll call a guard to make you.'

Erica dipped her head, and Cane closed his eyes, cupping Erica's nape. Her head began bobbing up and down, and Maria eyed the door, wondering how far she'd make it if she ran.

Not far enough, she knew, and she didn't doubt that Cane would have a guard haul her back. Her skin crawled and tears pricked the backs of her eyes.

'*Now,*' insisted Cane, his tone husky. 'I won't ask nicely again.'

Maria reluctantly obeyed, moving to stand beside Opal. She closed her eyes, trying to steady her roiling stomach.

'Watch,' Cane commanded, locking his eyes with Maria's as she lifted her eyelids. She refused to let him see her cry, so she squared her shoulders and blocked the scene out as best she could, copying Opal, making herself dead inside and letting her eyes glass over, aware of the spectacle, but not focusing on it.

Erica continued to move up and down, using both her mouth and her hands, and Cane grunted and groaned, alternating between looking down at Erica, and checking he still had the attention of his audience.

'Fuck, yes, Erica,' he gasped, taking hold of her head. '*Fuck.*' Erica's pace increased, and Cane pushed and pulled her up and down with no care for her comfort.

It continued like that for what seemed like endless seconds, and Maria wished she could block out the sounds, just like she wished she could block out the sick feeling in her stomach. But it was too much of a shock, too disgusting, too violating, and not only for her, but for Opal and Erica also. Thank the Goddess she hadn't been forced to marry this man. It was the only thought that gave her any comfort.

Cane made a series of strangled noises, and then Erica pulled back, looking up at her husband as though he was the reason she breathed—the same way she'd looked at Cane's father, Maria recalled.

Cane leaned forward and captured Erica's mouth in a bruising kiss. She met him move for move, then pushed upwards, climbing onto his lap so she straddled him, making gasping, mewling noises as he squeezed her breast.

A cough sounded from the doorway, and they all turned their eyes to see a guard standing there, all except Opal, who seemed lost in some kind of trance. How many times had she been forced to endure such sights?

'Sorry to interrupt, sir,' said the guard, seeming not at all embarrassed by the scene, 'but you asked to be informed when your brother arrived.'

Maria's chest lurched painfully. Elex was here. So close, and yet he might as well have been a thousand miles away. Even if she made it past the first guard, there would be at least two more outside.

'Very well,' said Cane, still massaging Erica's breast. 'We will continue after dinner.'

'As you wish, husband,' Erica said coquettishly, climbing off him and straightening her dress.

Cane grabbed Erica's jaw as he stood, pulling her roughly towards him. He held onto her for several long moments as though looking for a slip in her adoration, but Erica didn't slip, she doubled down, melting into his touch and tipping her head back, letting her lips fall open. He ran a callous thumb across her bottom lip, then shoved her away.

'Well, girls?' Cane asked as he came to stand before Maria and Opal.

Neither of them said anything.

'Oh, come now, Opal may be dumb as a fucking post, but you've never been shy about running your mouth,' he said to Maria, leaning in, far too close.

Maria cast a quick glance at Opal, wondering if she was okay. She was so vacant Maria wondered if she needed a healer. Maria turned her gaze back to Cane. 'Well, what?'

Cane moved with lightning speed, grabbing Maria's hair and pulling her head back, his lips close to her ear. 'You are lucky, are you not, to receive such excellent tutelage?'

Maria froze, incapable of anything—movement, thought, words—but then some inner strength seeped outwards from her stomach, and she smiled sweetly, imagining the satisfaction she would gain from ripping off his balls. 'Of course, brother. You are most kind.'

CHAPTER EIGHT
AVA

AVA WOKE WITH A start, then looked around in confused panic as she tried to remember where she was. Roots, dim light, a strange weight on her ribcage. *The echo chamber. Right.* She dropped her head back to the ground as the panic dissipated, while Kush rolled away and stretched out beside her.

'How did you sleep?' he asked, his cheek flat against the mattress of flowers as he turned to look at her.

'Fine, I think. You?'

'Great,' he breathed. 'Best sleep in a long time.'

Ava's cheeks warmed. 'Really?'

He smiled, then rolled towards her like he planned to kiss her, but Ava pulled away.

'What's wrong?' he asked, looking a little hurt.

She took a long breath, lifting a hand to her forehead and rubbing her fingers back and forth, trying to erase the nagging worry. 'What is this?' she eventually asked, the words coming out before she'd fully thought them through.

His smile morphed into confusion. 'What's what?'

'This!' she exclaimed, throwing her hand in the air, then added in a small voice, 'Us.' She could still feel his kisses on her lips from last night, the delicate skin bruised and tingling. But the looming threat of his father dominated her thoughts, and whether Kush was on her side or his.

'I don't know,' he said softly.

'Are you lying to me, Kush?'

He flinched. 'Why ... What do you mean?'

'You've lied to me from the moment we met.'

He paused, looking from one of her eyes to the other as his brain chewed over her words. 'What would you have had me do, Ava? I didn't know you then.'

'Well, you know me now.'

'And I'm here!'

She rolled away, folding her arms. 'So it's just a happy coincidence that your wishes and Var's align?'

Silence settled for several long beats, and as it stretched, Ava's jaw started working worriedly back and forth.

'You want me to go?' he asked gravely.

'No,' she breathed, sitting, wrapping her arms around her bent legs, the idea of being alone filling her with horror. She needed help navigating this new world, and he was her only friend. 'But ...'

He sat too, the muscles of his bare chest contorting as he leaned towards her. 'You can trust me, Ava. I know it's a lot to ask after everything that's happened, but I'm here. I want to be here. I want to be with you. I ... I meant it when I said I loved you.' He looked at the place where the wall turned into floor, something about him vulnerable as he waited for her, giving her space.

She dearly wanted to believe him, to believe he was on her side, that he wouldn't abandon her when his father called, that they wouldn't keep going around in the same circle forever.

She supposed she just had to decide one way or another. Trust should be earned, but they didn't have time for that, and being suspicious would do nothing but waste their time together and drive him away. He said he loved her, and she'd looked deep into his eyes and found no trace of anything sinister, yet still a small, vexing doubt lingered, like maybe there was something he was hiding. Perhaps that was merely her lifetime of hard-learned suspicion at play ... Either way, if she wasn't going to ask him to leave, she couldn't second guess him at every turn.

'I'm sorry, Kush. Trust isn't easy for me, not after everything that's happened. But I'm glad you're here, and I want to be with you, too.'

He met her eyes, a tentative smile on his lips as he reached for her hand, and she gave it willingly, the tension in the air melting away. 'It will take time. I know that.' He kissed her fingers. 'But eventually you'll see that you're all that matters to me.' He leaned close and ghosted a kiss across her lips. 'Are you hungry? Shall we find something to eat?'

Her stomach rumbled in answer, her mouth parched, so they dressed and emerged to find a misty, dewy morning, the grass heavy with beads of moisture, the air thick.

They pulled a few apples from the tree, then skirted around the house, looking for anything edible growing in one of the many raised beds. The pickings were slim, and aside from a few leaves that looked like spinach, there was nothing else to go with the fruit.

'We can use the Atlas Stone to get food,' said Kush. 'You need to make a few trips anyway, to cure your stone sickness.'

'Travel to other worlds?' The idea hadn't occurred to Ava until that moment. 'Where will we visit?'

'I'll take you to my favorite first,' he said, as they rounded the corner of the house, heading for the front door.

She grabbed his arm and squeezed, unable to contain her excitement. 'What's it like?'

His features morphed into a devious look. 'You'll just have to wait and see.'

Ava grinned as she swiped him on the arm. 'You're so mean.'

He chuckled. 'We can go now if you want. I'm starving.'

'Wait,' said Ava, her eyes snagging on something on the ground just outside the iron gates, 'what's that?'

Kush spun, his shoulders suddenly tense, his smile vanishing. He narrowed his eyes. 'It looks like ...'

'Food.'

They shared a confused look, then moved cautiously towards the gates, scanning as much of the far side as they could see around the perimeter walls.

It was still early in the morning, no one in the street beyond, but Kush kept looking while Ava read the note, which had been written in a slanted, irregular scrawl.

Saw activity. Thought you might need food. I've reopened your old account. Welcome back. You were missed. This one's on the house. Grace.

'Who's Grace?' said Kush, glancing down at the box, which contained fruit, vegetables, bread, milk, cheese, yoghurt, and a pile of enticing packages wrapped in brown paper.

Ava shrugged. 'Maybe she owns a nearby shop?'

'Hmm,' said Kush, just as his stomach gave an audible rumble.

'We could grab it quickly,' said Ava. 'There's no one here.'

Kush scanned the street again, craning his neck to check as far as he could on each side. 'You open the gate, and I'll grab the box.'

Ava nodded. She was starving, and the freshly baked bread smelled wonderful.

'Ready?' said Kush. 'Go!'

Ava slid the bolt free and swung the gate inward a fraction. Kush rushed out, grabbed the box, then hurried back inside, but before he'd cleared the opening, a force rammed into him from behind, sending him sprawling to the ground, the groceries flying everywhere.

A slight man jumped over Kush and sprinted towards the house, Ava slamming the gate shut, then whirling to get a proper look at him. By the time she'd turned around, Kush was already giving chase, rapidly closing the distance, pumping his arms and legs.

Ava watched, her heart in her mouth, as Kush launched himself at the short, ginger-haired intruder just shy of the steps to the front door. *Was that ... Billy?* She went after them, hampered by her lack of shoes, and by the time she reached them, Kush had already spun Billy over and pinned him to the ground.

'What are you doing here?' Kush hissed.

Billy protected his face with his hands. 'I had nowhere else to go!' he squealed. 'Var wants to kill me for helping Ava.' He parted his fingers so he could peek up at Kush. 'You know what a belligerent old grouch he is, and Ava owes me! The least she can do is provide me with a place to hide. And she has this,'—he waved his hands in the direction of the house, then paused as though he'd seen a ghost—'monstrosity, just sitting here.'

'She owes you nothing, you little snake.'

'Well, she's obviously not being choosy about her house guests if she let *you* in.'

Kush lifted Billy a little by his shirt, then smashed him against the ground, winding him so he lay gasping for breath. Kush turned his head, looking expectantly at Ava, as though waiting for her to throw the intruder out.

'I can help you,' Billy spluttered, twisting a little so he could look her in the eye. 'I knew your parents. I know this house. I know Var, who has minions in every world, including this one, spying on you.' He flicked his gaze to Kush, then back to Ava. 'Ask him. He knows all about spying for Daddy.'

Kush scowled as he shoved Billy flat against the grass. 'My father doesn't know I'm here.'

'Ha!' laughed Billy. 'Lies.' Kush pressed a hand to Billy's neck, so his next words came out as a constricted wheeze. 'Or naivety. Either way, you can't trust him.'

'But she can trust you?' Kush asked cynically.

'I'm not the one working for Var.'

Kush shoved away from Billy as though physically restraining himself, rolling to his feet and looking down with furious eyes. 'What do you know of work? You do nothing but get drunk and undermine the Gods.'

'I *am* a mother fucking God!' spat Billy, climbing to his feet and dusting himself off. 'I'm here for a safe place to stay, and in return, can offer help to Ava. You're only here because Var wants access.'

'I am not!' Kush snarled. 'I told him I couldn't get in.'

'Well, you're in now,' countered Billy, turning his eyes to Ava, his expression deeply chastising.

Ava scowled. 'Why do you even care, Billy? You tried to stop me from coming here!'

'Why?' demanded Kush, rounding on Billy, the word dripping with suspicion.

Billy gave a little shoulder shrug. 'It's usually best to leave the past in the past and all that. But it was more of a B thing than a me thing. You don't survive as long as I have by refusing to be pragmatic in the face of a curveball. You're here now, and it's as good a place as any for me to hide—the best, really—so ... what's a guy to do?'

Kush scoffed. 'You expect us to believe that's the only reason you're here?'

'Look, you little runt, this whole thing started because *her* parents refused to return *our* souls. B and I didn't want to be tied to another world. We wanted back the parts of ourselves we'd lost. We envied Novak his freedom. His aging. His—' He stopped himself abruptly, his eyes flicking back to Ava. 'Well … everything.'

Ava's insides crumpled. She so wanted to believe her parents had been good and kind, that there was some perfectly reasonable explanation for their behavior, but the more she heard, the less likely that became. 'Why didn't you tell me my parents hid your souls too?' She supposed she probably should have worked it out, given Billy's youthful appearance, but B was the kind of woman who was ageless. She could have been thirty or fifty.

Billy slid his glasses down a little and pinched the bridge of his nose as though the conversation was giving him a headache. 'Do you have anything to drink?'

'No,' said Kush.

Billy gave a long sigh, then rubbed his eyes with the heels of his hands. 'B and I were their guinea pigs. The first. We're tied somewhere different to the other Gods. When we asked to have our souls back, after they'd proven it worked, your parents said it was too difficult, that they'd never tried it, that it was too dangerous, that they didn't have the time … Endless excuses. But really it was about power. And they hated B for what she did.'

'What did she do?' asked Ava.

Billy gave Ava a long, regretful look, then crossed his arms over his chest. 'It's a long story.'

Kush cocked his head to one side. 'One that ended with you killing Ava's parents.'

'I did not!'

'Not what I heard.'

Billy took a step towards Kush, waving his hands around. 'They were out of control, power hungry, selfish … I didn't kill them, but I also didn't prevent it. And honestly, if you'd have been there, you would have done the same,' he said with a flounce.

The blood drained from Ava's face, and a heavy silence settled over them. 'Who?' she said quietly. 'Who killed them?'

'Ava ...' said Billy. 'It's ... a long story.'

A clatter sounded from the street, invading the tense moment, shaking them all out of it.

'We should go inside,' said Ava.

Kush stood still for a moment, then nodded reluctantly. He stalked to the gate, retrieving the food while Ava and Billy headed for the front door.

'You can't trust him,' Billy said in an urgent whisper. 'However good he is, however good he wants to be, he's been brainwashed by his father. Never forget that. The Federation is bad. Evil. Var is evil, and he's been working on Kush for his entire life.'

'Just like my parents were evil?' she asked. That was what B had called them shortly before she'd thrown Ava out of the tavern. 'Out of control? Power hungry?' She hurled Billy's own words back at him like a challenge. 'I am not my parents, and Kush is not his. He's his own person.'

Billy abruptly stilled, almost as if he'd hit a physical barrier. He appraised her for a long moment. 'There's just so much you don't understand.'

She gritted her teeth, irritated by his condescension. 'Perhaps because no one has ever told me anything real!'

Billy cast a wary glance over his shoulder at Kush's approaching form, then angled his head as he returned his gaze to Ava. 'If I knew I could trust you ...'

Ava rolled her eyes. 'Don't be dramatic. Here's the deal: if you help me, you can stay, if you don't, I'll kick you out, just like B did to me. And Kush isn't going anywhere.'

'Oh, for fuck's *sake!*' Billy huffed, flicking his fingers into the air on either side of his head, then stomping up the steps in front of her. 'You're just like your mother.'

Chapter Nine
Maria
Three Days After Dromeda Started Spinning

MARIA PASSED DINNER IN a trance, the world hazy, so she barely even felt it when Erica's feet landed in her lap. Not that anyone noticed Maria's lack of presence. At least, no one except Elex, whose eyes rarely left her face.

Maria dearly wished she could get to Elex, to feel his reassuring touch, but a guard had escorted her to dinner, and now he hovered not far behind her chair, presumably on account of the stunt Elex had pulled the night before.

How long would it be before she could touch him again?

Erica giggled at something Cane said, and Maria appraised them out of the corner of her eye. Was Erica truly besotted with Cane or was it all just a ruse to survive? Erica was convincing, but she'd been equally convincing with Barron, too. 'You're so much cleverer than your father,' Erica whispered, her lips pressed to his ear yet loud enough for Maria to hear; they'd both had more than a few drinks.

'And I look after you better, don't I?' Cane murmured.

'So much better,' she confirmed, and Maria nearly vomited into her food.

'We're alike, you and I,' said Cane, stroking Erica's face. 'I understand you like he never could. We were meant to be together.'

'Mmmm,' she agreed, nuzzling her face against his neck, then she straightened, pulling back her shoulders, her lips in a slight pout. 'Then why is Opal in our bed, my love?' Maria almost choked on her mouthful of chicken.

'Because I need her,' said Cane, his tone light, his fingers playing with Erica's hair.

'You don't need anyone.'

Cane huffed a laugh. 'You know that is not true.'

'Do you love her?'

'I love you.'

'That's not what I asked, husband,' Erica whispered, her tone sharp.

He slid his hand to the base of her neck, and Erica stiffened. 'She doesn't have a mind like yours.'

Erica lifted her hand to Cane's face, tracing the line of his lips. 'But she's younger ... Is that it? You like her because her flesh is more supple than mine?'

He caught her hand in his, halting her movements. 'She has a rich, powerful father who commands many men.'

Erica leaned her face closer to Cane's. 'Her father is not in our bed.'

Cane chuckled as he took her face in his hand, sliding his thumb along her cheekbone. 'Jealousy suits you, my dear. It is surprisingly enticing.'

She closed her eyes and rested her forehead against his. 'Is my rich and powerful father all you want from me, too?'

He dug his hand into her hair, holding her to him, then said almost gently, 'You and Opal are not the same to me, Erica. You have fire in your belly, she does not. Fret not, my love, you are my first wife in every sense, your position above hers, your talents many and varied, far superior to anything she can boast. She is a pretty trinket, while you are a dazzling gem.'

She slid her hand down his chest. 'Then send her away tonight. Let me have you to myself.'

He exhaled heavily. 'But I like it when she watches.'

Erica shoved his arm. 'Just like your father ...'

She made to get up, but Cane yanked her back into his lap. 'My father was a great man,' he growled, 'a noble leader, a—'

'You think I don't know that?' she hissed. 'But he never put my needs before his own, and neither do you.' She slumped back against him, seemingly defeated. 'You promised it would be different between us.'

Cane stayed silent for a moment, his bandaged hand stroking Erica's bare thigh as his eyes completed a sweep of the room. Maria turned her head towards the man on her left, only daring to turn back when Cane started speaking again. 'Am I not a man of my word?' he whispered, grabbing

Erica's chin and forcing her eyes back to his. 'Have I not shown you that already?'

If Erica was intimidated, she kept it from her features, and Maria had to respect her for that. 'It is not keeping your word, husband, if you would have done the same regardless. It is only keeping your word when you put my needs first, above your own.'

He released her and reached for his goblet. 'Such a needy little creature.'

'You would prefer me meek and mild?'

'Ha!' he exhaled darkly. 'You know the answer to that.' He took a swig of his wine. 'It will be just the two of us tonight, then, if that is what my favorite wife requires.'

Erica's face lit up as though she was a cat who'd found her way into an unattended dairy, her smile feline, eyes hooded. She kissed him tenderly. 'Thank you, my love. I can't tell you what this means to me.'

He pushed a strand of hair behind her ear, then cupped her nape. 'It pleases me that you are pleased, my dear, but sacrifice goes both ways. Remember that. Now, hop off, I must speak to a man about a water pump.'

Maria excused herself at the earliest possible opportunity, but the few snatched moments with Elex she dreamed of were nothing but that—a dream—her guard never more than a pace away.

It went on like that for nights on end, guards keeping her and Elex apart. She wondered how long it would take for him to get her out, if he'd discovered who had betrayed him, if there was any hope at all of taking back what was his. But she couldn't ask. All she could do was observe him longingly from a distance and pray to the Goddess that she wouldn't be trapped under Cane's roof much longer.

After a few days of Erica's feet in Maria's lap, Cane became bored of the joke and shunted Maria a little father up the table to make way for more important visitors. It was a blessing in a way, but also left her more exposed to the roving eyes of the other guests, and meant she couldn't hear Cane's conversations—not that he'd said much of interest to date. She tried to glean what she could from her table mates, but no one took her seriously, women seeming to occupy a lowly place in Oshala, no doubt made worse by the skimpy scraps of fabric in which she was endlessly draped.

Elex's attention was never far away, although he also seemed to use the nightly dinners as an opportunity for conversation with those Cane wanted to keep close. She wondered if Elex had wooed any of them to his side or learned anything useful. If only she could get to him to ask.

After another week, Cane sent Maria to sit on the far side of the table, two chairs along from Elex, a rotund man between them. It was a new form of torture, and Cane watched them with interest as though daring them to make a move, but neither of them tried, the likelihood of success too low.

It was unbearable, night after night being so close yet so far, two guards behind her, and a human barrier to her side. Mostly the barriers seemed oblivious to their part in Cane's game, the one tonight particularly clueless, monologuing animatedly about his endless achievements while quaffing large quantities of wine.

He leaned closer and closer to Maria as the burgundy stains around his lips grew, a palpable tension in the air as Elex monitored the man. A servant with a flagon of wine leaned between Maria and her table mate, loading his goblet for the umpteenth time. The servant finished, and the man made a grab for the silver stem, but he misjudged the movement and knocked the vessel toward himself, the contents of the newly-filled cup spilling all over the table and running into his lap.

The man jumped up, throwing himself and his chair backwards to avoid the spill, cursing the servant, blaming the poor woman for his drunken clumsiness.

'Move!' barked Maria's guard, the panicked word alerting Maria to the opportunity in front of her. The blustering man, his chair, and the servant he was busy admonishing were blocking the guards from getting to the table, meaning nothing but open space lay between Maria and her husband.

They moved almost as one, Maria throwing herself across the gap as Elex pushed back his chair. He caught her and spun her behind him, his left arm holding her in place as he faced down the guards who'd yanked the drunk man and his chair out of the way. 'One step closer and you'll understand how I earned my nickname,' he growled, his tone ferocious enough to halt their approach.

Maria pressed her forehead to Elex's spine as the room froze around them, the chatter evaporating until a pin drop would have been deafening. She could easily imagine the hungry eyes of Cane's guests, the guards' fearful glances between themselves, no idea what to do and terrified of the consequences of failing in their duty.

And then Elex turned, putting himself and Maria chest to chest and sliding one arm around her waist, his other hand delving into her hair. For a moment, they just stared into each other's eyes, their breath mingling as they spoke without words. And then he kissed her, chaste yet deep, so when he pulled back, her lips tingled and her head spun.

She dearly wanted to fold herself against him, to hide in his arms, but Maria was a court creature as much as any at the table, and she knew their every move would be weighed and measured. So as Elex guided her down onto his lap with a firm grip, she kept her spine straight. She sat tall, her crossed legs hanging down between his as he leaned nonchalantly against his chair, his hand scorching against her bare hip.

The room held its breath, the guests' eyes flitting nervously between Maria, Elex, and Cane, who now resembled a statue, his features carved in furious lines, eyes narrowed, mouth thin.

Maria angled her head towards her husband's, keeping her regal posture as she murmured, 'Will he force us apart?'

Elex turned his head so their noses almost brushed, his eyes dipping to her lips as he breathed, 'It will make him look weak if he does, and he won't want to cause more of a scene.' Elex's lips pulled into a harsh smile, and before her eyes he became the ruthless, terrifying Black Prince of his reputation. A mask for the benefit of those around them, and a warning to his brother. 'Cane holds these dinners because he needs support, and to demonstrate his power over me, but if we refuse to heed him ...'

'He risks looking powerless,' Maria finished. He squeezed her waist in agreement, and she clenched her thighs against the sensation his touch sent to her core. She leaned her lips towards his ear. 'What about getting me out?' She could hardly bear to hear the answer, but she had to ask ... was desperate to be back by his side and not trapped with his brother.

Elex inhaled deeply as he returned his gaze to the room, sliding his thumb back and forth across her bare hip bone. She straightened, not trusting herself as her body melted under his touch, so preoccupied by the rough graze of his thumb against her skin that she almost missed it when he said, 'We're working on it but we don't have anything concrete yet.'

Maria looked down at her hands, telling herself not to be disappointed.

'You see,' Cane announced, his voice projecting around the room, 'even my brother, the aloof *Black Prince*, has finally succumbed to a woman's wiles. But when you see them together,' he continued, pulling Opal onto his lap, grabbing her neck to hold her in place, 'one can't help but wonder which of them wears the crown ...'

Opal whimpered, and her father abruptly stood, his chair screaming as it scraped across the flagstones. Cane cast a quick glance at the man, then continued as though nothing had happened. 'It seems my brother has gone soft, and all it took was marrying him off. I, on the other hand, know that a firm grip is the best grip when it comes to my wives. I'm sure the gentlemen present will agree.'

Opal's father huffed, flung his napkin on the table, then stormed from the room, but a movement at the edge of Maria's vision caught her attention, and she turned just in time to catch a split-second break in Erica's adoring mask. The look was gone in a heartbeat, and it was hard to interpret, but it had almost seemed like hatred. Maria wondered who the emotion was for. Did she wish it was her on Cane's lap? Was she angry about the way Cane had spoken about his wives? Or was it something to do with the way Opal's father had left the meal?

Opal seemed to have slipped into the same trance-like state Maria had witnessed in Cane's bedroom, her body swaying obediently to meet Cane's demands, but her mind elsewhere.

'Do you think Erica loves him?' Maria whispered, moving her mouth as little as possible.

Elex exhaled a gentle laugh that sent a shiver down Maria's spine. 'Erica loves nothing but herself and power.'

'She acts as though she's jealous of Opal.'

'Doesn't look like she has much to worry about.'

Maria scowled. 'He humiliates all of us, Erica included.'

Elex's thumb stopped moving. 'You mean the clothes?' he asked darkly. 'The stuff at dinner each night?'

Maria refused to sag under the weight of Cane's abuse, but she struggled to find the words to tell Elex what Cane regularly made her witness, managing only, 'He makes me watch.'

Elex went still, like a snake about to strike a lethal blow. 'I'm sorry, Maria.' He squeezed her hip. 'I hope you know we'll make him pay for everything he's done.'

'I'll willingly stick a dagger in his back,' she breathed, surprised to find she wasn't joking. She turned her face towards him, languorously bringing her hand to his cheek and leaning close to obscure their lips. 'I can do it while he sleeps.'

Elex gripped her waist a little too hard, making tiny shaking movements with his head. 'Maria ...'

She moved her cheek so it pressed against the hint of stubble on his. 'I could do it, Elex. We'd be rid of him ...'

He gently pushed her back, waiting for her to look him in the eye before murmuring, 'You'd never make it out alive.'

If she hadn't been acting for their audience, she might have argued. Instead, she sat poker straight as he kissed her cheekbone. 'I hate it too, my little hell cat, but we'll find a way to free you soon, I promise.'

Maria nodded, filling her lungs with the smell of him, trying to block out all else. Some part of her brain considered trying to keep him with her, to beg him to stay the night even though she knew it wasn't possible, that it made no sense. 'Why does he let you go?' she asked instead, the question often on her mind.

Elex slid his hand back to her hip, cupping it gently. 'Cane has people following me. He's greedy—wants to capture my friends and anyone helping me—and he knows I'm not going to disappear or move against him while he has you hostage. With me roaming free, it makes him look strong and carries little risk.'

The servants cleared the final plates and glasses from the table, and the guests began to make their excuses, meaning Maria's precious time with Elex was almost over. He took hold of her chin with his thumb and forefinger, gently tugging her eyes to his, reassuring her with his gaze. He kissed her, sending heat skittering across her skin, and her body softened as she pressed herself to him everywhere she could. He drew back too soon, helping her to her feet as he stood, then escorting her to the corridor that led to her bedroom, all of it happening too quickly, making her want to dig in her heels like a stubborn mule.

A guard followed nervously, another moving to block the alcove Elex had backed Maria into last time, all eyes tracking their every step. Elex stopped on the cusp of the corridor, the dark tunnel out of the bright candlelit hall reminding Maria of the tunnels beneath an amphitheater, which was fitting, seeing as she felt like the entertainment.

Elex pulled her in front of him and looked down one final time. 'Stay strong, my little hell cat,' he murmured, then after the barest ghost of a kiss against her lips, he was gone.

Chapter Ten

Sophie

THE DAY DROMEDA STARTED SPINNING

THE WHOLE OF SOPHIE'S world narrowed to the men and women lying dead before her. Her mind struggled to make sense of it, her body feeling distant, and time seemed to slow, even noises sounding strange.

Dromeda was spinning once more, Nicoli had killed Danit, Elex had killed his father, and it had all happened in the space of a hundred frantic heartbeats. Now Maria stood between John's raised bow and the man who'd killed Danit, and Hale, who stood to John's side, was deadly calm.

Sophie's eyes found her own mother, only a pace away, holding her horse and watching the spectacle with panicked features and ghostly white skin. For a terrible moment, Sophie considered doing what Elex had done—killing her in cold blood. It would be easy enough to slit her throat from behind. Would that free Sophie from her life of servitude or would it just make everything a hundred times worse?

Linella looked back, almost as though she'd sensed Sophie's thoughts, and Sophie snapped out of it, shocked she'd even considered the dangerous notion. Her mother was a conniving, devious sort, but that didn't warrant death. Linella was loyal to her family, always acting in their best interests, and that was what Sophie should be doing, too.

Sophie turned her attention to Hale's broad back, to the man who seemed to take a perverse pride in publicly rejecting her. Just that morning, he'd done it again in front of their whole travelling party, telling John in a loud voice that Sophie only wanted Hale for his title, that John was welcome to her. The comments had smarted because Sophie had thought she'd made progress two nights ago in the library, and last night at dinner he'd sat beside her when he could have sat elsewhere. The stories of his adventures circumnavigating the world had stirred something inside her, a feeling she'd almost never felt before. Respect. The kind that was earned, not demanded.

She'd never felt even an ounce of that for John because he didn't deserve it. He kept his head down, did as he was told, and bickered with his sister like a child. But Hale ... Hale was different. He did what he wanted, but perhaps that was clouding her judgement, making her wishful and naïve just like her mother had said.

Hale had freed the man who'd just killed his uncle, a thought that sent a cold sensation trickling down her spine. Had Nicoli and Hale worked together? After all, few stood to gain more through Danit's death than Hale. Not that it would make her think less of him. But did he have it in him? She wasn't sure ...

If Hale was working with Nicoli, what would he do next? Now Dromeda spun, the Claws had lost their control over the water—their power. Would Hale use their misfortune to his advantage? She sensed not, but did that make him honorable or a fool? Her family certainly wouldn't hesitate to brand him foolish.

Sophie's eyes flicked back to her mother, who, like always, was calculating. Sophie could practically see the cogs turning in her mother's mind, reassessing their position, determining the best strategic route for Laurow Blade. But Sophie already knew where her mother would land. It was even more important now that Sophie marry Hale. He would be the new leader of Alter Blade, equal to Sophie's own father in rank, whereas John would never rise higher than second son, increasingly irrelevant as time ticked by.

'You'll be leaving now, I assume,' said Hale, snapping Sophie's focus back into the moment. Maria had talked Nicoli down, and the drama seemed to have come to a close for the moment.

Linella's lip curled, which didn't bode well for Sophie, although, thankfully, her wrath was currently aimed squarely at Hale. 'Your people signed a pact, and that pact is not complete until *you* marry my daughter.'

Some of the tightness in Sophie's chest eased. *Yes. Good.* They couldn't leave yet. She was glad to know she and her mother were aligned on that much at least.

'The pact promises her the first son,' said Hale, not so much as glancing in Sophie's direction, 'which is now my brother.'

'That depends on your definition of the title,' countered Linella, 'and in any case, he was not first son at the time of the agreement.'

'Of little consequence.' Hale batted Linella's words away with a swipe of his hand.

Linella pulled herself up a little straighter. 'It is of great consequence to me.'

He was so cold. So hateful. Had he felt nothing last night? Had it really all been an act? John turned hopeful eyes on Sophie. 'No,' she snapped without thinking. She would not marry some wet fish like him. 'No. Hale is the man I was supposed to marry. I will wed him or no one at all.'

Hale rolled his eyes. Actually fucking rolled his eyes. 'Sophie, it's nothing personal. You need to be reasonable.'

'No,' Sophie said again, crossing her arms, refusing to let his barb wound her. '*You* need to honor the pact.' She lifted her chin defiantly. 'Or face the consequences.'

Hale threw up his hands in exasperation. 'Look around! The pact is dead, and good riddance. Alter will no longer treat the people of the Claws as lesser, and if the other Blades disagree, the pact is irrelevant to me.'

Sophie watched his features for a beat, searching for any chink in his armor, some softness, but finding none. He began to turn away. 'Then we should broker a new arrangement as part of our marriage contract,' she said quietly. 'One that includes the Claws.'

Her words brought him up short, his brow pinching hard. 'You will marry John,' he said slowly, as though she was an idiot. 'It is a perfectly reasonable solution. You get the first son you were promised, and we are assured of your alliance in helping bring peace to Celestl. But do not look to me for a husband because I do not take liars to my bed.'

The words punched a hole in Sophie's stomach, her muscles clenching against the pain. 'Or maybe the Goddess has returned because she wants us to be together. Maybe it is her will.'

Hale looked at her for a beat, cocking an incredulous eyebrow, although Sophie wasn't sure if it was her sentiment or the razor-sharp edge to her tone that had caused his reaction. He dismissed her regardless, in a way that made Sophie want to stamp her foot.

'We will return home and regroup,' Hale snapped, then started barking orders at everyone around them.

Sophie clenched her fists but forced herself to relax as a presence moved up beside her. She turned her head, surprised to find Hale's sister, Maria, standing close, leaning in conspiratorially.

'I believe you have the measure of my brother,' she said, a mischievous light dancing in her eyes.

Sophie inclined her head, unable to quash her half-smile as Maria moved away, and when she looked up, her eyes collided with Hale's, making her breath catch in her throat. Their gazes held a beat too long, and every muscle in Sophie's torso pulled tight, his lingering appraisal giving her hope and confirming what she already knew, that she would accept no one less, that she would not rest until he wanted her, too.

Chapter Eleven
Maria
Two Weeks After Dromeda Started Spinning

After Maria and Elex's stunt at dinner, Cane doubled down on the pre-dinner sexual displays, much to Opal's obvious torment. Maria endured the same treatment night after night, dressed in skimpy clothes and forced to watch alongside Opal as Erica pleasured Cane in increasingly inventive ways. Maria learned to make herself dead inside, just as Opal appeared to have, switching off her mind so she was only vaguely aware of the acts taking place before her.

Until Cane forced Opal to join them. Then the sick feeling returned in full force, and Maria finally lost the battle against her tears. She didn't wail or sob, but wet streaks tracked silently down her face, dripping off her cheeks, and her eyes must have been red and puffy when they entered the banqueting hall because Elex's jaw ticked, and he ate not a bite of dinner.

Cane had moved Maria back to his side at the dinner table, eliminating any hope of Maria making it to Elex, so she excused herself as soon as she could each night, breathing a sigh of relief as soon as she'd reached the safety of her room and had ripped off her stupid, demeaning clothes.

But that night, when Maria excused herself, vaguely wondering if her eyes still told the world of her distress, she made it back to her modestly sized room and immediately heard a rap on her window. She froze, wondering if she'd imagined it, but then it came again, and she raced to the glass, her heart in her throat, barely daring to hope. It couldn't be Elex, could it? He'd been at the banqueting table only moments ago, but maybe this was her escape. Perhaps Elex was creating a diversion while someone else got her out.

But the window was made of three long panes of glass, far too narrow for Maria to climb through. She pressed her face to the left-hand pane, shielding her eyes with her hands to block out the light from her bedroom. 'Elex!' she breathed, as his face came into view on the other side.

Maria quickly swung the pane open, and Elex took her hand, kissing it, then reaching through the window to cradle her face. 'What happened?' he demanded. 'Why were you crying?'

She shook her head, swallowing hard, hardly believing he was really there. 'More of the same,' she breathed, then pulled Elex's lips to hers, refusing to waste a single moment of their precious time together. It was awkward, the space narrow, but the press of his lips against hers refilled her soul in a way nothing else ever could, his kisses assured and firm but also deep and gentle.

Elex pulled back, casting a furtive glance behind him. 'I don't know how long we have. I knocked out my escorts, but someone will find them soon enough, and it won't take much for them to work out where I am.'

Maria drew him back to her and rubbed her face against his, savoring every touch, losing herself in the unexpected moment of respite.

'What happened, Maria?' he asked again.

She shook her head, her skin still pressed to his, then tried to find his lips once more, but he denied her.

'Tell me, sweetheart. Please.'

'You first,' she whispered, kissing his cheek then leaving her lips pressed against his skin, wishing she could fall asleep against him, that he didn't have to go, that they had more than stolen moments with barriers in their way.

He huffed a light breath against her skin. 'We think a prostitute—tall with ringleted dark hair—distracted the gate guards. It's our only lead, but we can't find hide or hair of her, so I've sent messengers to Nicoli. If we can take back the water, that will give us the edge we need to retake the quarter, and then we can weed out any traitors from the inside.

'Erica and Opal's fathers have thrown their weight behind Cane, but most of the other power players in Oshala are letting the dust settle before committing to any new alliances. That means they won't side with us, but they're keeping Cane at arm's length, too, stalling him, so at least that buys us a bit of time, and shows they're not fully committed to Cane as their leader.'

Maria nodded as she pulled back just enough to look into Elex's warm, brown eyes, and he squeezed his hand into the space between them, cupping her neck as though knowing she needed his touch as much as she needed the breath in her lungs. 'There's no other way?' She hated that it always came down to water, that if Nicoli could help them, it would mean threatening the wellbeing of everyone in Oshala.

Elex shook his head. 'Not unless we raise an army and bring bloodshed to the streets. And even if we could call enough troops to our side, success is less likely that way.'

Maria gripped Elex's wrist as she pressed her forehead to his. Hadn't the pact been supposed to end the war that plagued their lands? But Cane couldn't care less about his people. The conversations Maria had overheard at dinner showed he thought only about lining his own pockets, building influence, gaining the respect of the wealthy men of Oshe, and placating Erica. The wellbeing of his people wasn't high on his list of concerns.

'Can I do anything to help?' Maria asked, lifting her head and looking hopefully up at him. Her days were filled with nothing but boredom.

He shook his head. 'The messengers have already gone. Now please, tell me what happened.'

He stroked his thumb along her jaw, then across her lips, and she turned her gaze down to the ground as she told him what Cane had done to Opal earlier that night, leaving out how the abuse had become worse after Maria had sat on Elex's lap at dinner. Maria didn't let herself consider what Cane might do after tonight—assuming the guards were brave enough to tell him—but whatever the price, it would be worth it for these snatched moments with her husband.

'I'm so sorry,' Elex said eventually, tugging her forward so he could press his lips to her temple. 'My brother is a dead man many times over.'

'Hopefully soon,' she whispered.

'We're doing everything we can.' He held her against him for long moments, stroking her neck with his thumb. 'I have to go,' he breathed, his voice strained.

He covered her lips with his, and she imagined that they were back in Alter, in her bedroom with all the time in the world, no threat of discovery by Cane's brutal guards, no dinner guests watching their every move, nothing but the two of them. They kissed as though it might be the last kiss they would ever share, as though the world might end the second they pulled apart.

'I love you, Elex,' Maria breathed into his mouth, the words out before she could stop them. He faltered. They'd never said those words, hadn't had the time to build up to it, but the feeling in Maria's chest was unrelenting, pulling so hard it caused physical pain every time they parted. She opened her eyes. 'You don't have to—'

'I love you,' he said, his eyes boring into hers, his hand cupping her jaw. 'More than I would have ever thought possible.'

Her lips parted in a small smile, and he covered it with a final tender kiss.

'I love you, my little hell cat, and I promise we'll get you out soon.'

Chapter Twelve
Ava

The first thing Billy did when he entered the house was to make a beeline for the drawing room, an expansive space with large windows, formal furniture, and an extensive selection of elaborate glass bottles filled with brightly colored liquors. The room brought back snippets of Ava's childhood, of glitzy drinks parties where she'd snuck downstairs to get a peek at the guests.

Billy threw open the drinks cabinet doors and rubbed his hands in glee as he surveyed the contents. 'Vintage *Foggy*!' he cried. 'Oh, *Atlas*! *Hazard to Oneself!* That one's been discontinued!' He looked at Ava as though she should understand his utter delight. 'This might be the only bottle left in existence!' He snatched it up like a child in a sweetshop, then reluctantly put it back. 'Probably not the best place to start.'

'No,' said Ava, as Kush headed to the kitchen with the food, shaking his head darkly. 'The best place to start is by telling me about my parents.'

'Yes, yes,' Billy said dismissively. 'But to do that, dear Ilyavra, I need to be intoxicated.'

Billy sifted through the seventy or so bottles in haphazard fashion, pulling a few out with excited squeals and shoving others to the back with sounds of horror.

Ava watched, deciding she would get what she wanted more quickly if she let him continue, but dropped onto an upholstered sofa, sensing it wouldn't be a short wait. The springs were still surprisingly firm.

Kush joined them, and Ava gratefully accepted the ham and cheese sandwich and glass of water he offered. He sat beside her, also watching Billy's erratic behavior, although he seemed to find it offensive, whereas Ava only thought it exasperating.

'He hasn't spotted the *Mind-Boggle* yet,' Kush said in a low voice.

'WHAT did you say?' said Billy, scanning frantically. 'Where?'

'The *Sozzle*,' said Kush. 'It's right there.'

'You little wretch,' huffed Billy, with a disbelieving shake of his head, then he poured himself a large measure of something blue.

'What is that?' asked Ava, as Billy threw himself down onto the second sofa, somehow not spilling a drop. He sprawled, his feet up on the cushions, head leaning against the arm.

'*Fortification*,' said Billy, before taking a long sip.

'Oh, right,' said Ava, not really any the wiser. She took a bite of her sandwich, and her tastebuds fired in all directions, her mouth filling with saliva. When had she last eaten anything substantial? And this was good. *Really* good. 'Thank you,' she said to Kush. 'It's delicious.'

Kush smiled, his eyes lingering on hers, and Billy lifted his head, surveying them speculatively. 'Was this Var's plan all along? For you to seduce Ava?'

'Billy!' Ava half-shouted, but a part of her wanted to hear Kush's answer because the thought had crossed her mind more than once.

Kush shook his head slowly. 'No,' he said bitterly. 'I'm here because I care about her, unlike you.'

Billy sat and leaned forward. 'I want back what's mine,' he hissed. 'That's why I'm here. Unlike you, I have a solid motive and no allegiances elsewhere.'

'So you'll use her until you get what you want, and then what?'

Billy downed his drink, then went to pour another, setting his hands on the cabinet, facing away from Ava and Kush. 'Her parents took something from me when they split my soul. It was the same for all of us, including them. We became ... altered. Maybe if we can get those parts of ourselves back, we can ...'

'What?' Ava pressed.

Billy ducked his head. 'The Federation's broken. Everything to do with the Atlas Web is broken.'

'The Federation is a force for good,' Kush said hotly. 'I know my father isn't a good man, and the Federation's not perfect, but nothing ever could be. It works. It brings trade and prosperity. I've seen it with my own eyes.'

Billy laughed cruelly as he turned around. 'You've seen what your father wants you to see. You're a tool he's shaping for his own ends, nothing more.'

'Billy, stop it,' said Ava. 'Can you please both just stop it.' Billy downed his second drink, then poured another and stalked back to his seat. 'You said you'd tell me about my parents. About the past. Can we just focus on that? Start there?'

Billy pulled his legs up and folded them so he sat cross-legged on the sofa. He wriggled himself backwards, then cleared his throat. 'What do you want to know?'

'Everything, obviously.'

Billy inhaled deeply, held it, then released in a loud whoosh. 'It was all such a long time ago.'

It seemed strange, that this erratic man had known her parents, had been their friend. She had so many questions about that, too, but she didn't interrupt him because he seemed to be collecting his memories, deciding where to start.

'Your father's great great great great,' he waved his arm, 'etcetera, grand-parents were the ones who discovered Atlas. The tree, the magical instruments, the portals. They gobbled up that power, but let a few others in. Friends who had magic, the early explorers from other worlds ... but not many. Fifty families or thereabouts. They set up shop at the top of the tree, and when new people came along, they made them live below, forced them to accept the rules they'd created, the hierarchy.

'They bumbled along like that for, oh, a long time, but over the generations, your father's family—the Blackwoods—lost their sparkle and certainly their magic. The others forced them to trade away two of the Atlas Stones, which meant sharing their power, and by the time your father came along, his family's prospects were grim. The Blackwoods were falling to their knees, whereas the Vars were on the ascension, and they were ambitious.'

Ava flicked a look at Kush, but his features were unreadable.

'The Vars would have taken over,' said Billy, 'had your maternal great-grandmother, Celia Sprucelion, not come along at just the right moment to save them. Now, Celia was an absolute firecracker,' said Billy, throwing his head back and lifting his arms. 'The little rodent ferreted her way into the Clouds as a teacher of magical things, and, due to her considerable abilities, as part of the deal, negotiated that her granddaughter—your mother, Ava—would attend her lessons, too.'

Ava could hardly breathe. Billy's words had woven an enchantment around her, holding her captive. Billy paused as he refreshed his drink, and Ava pressed her hands together to prevent herself from barking at him to continue.

'Now, your mother, Ava—'

'What was her name?' Ava asked quietly. The pain of her admission, that she couldn't remember, was like an iron fist squeezing her heart, her insides flooding with shame.

Billy paused, his mouth open. 'Oh. Ava ...' His eyes softened, but Ava didn't want his pity.

'Just tell me,' she snapped.

'Pollyana,' he breathed. 'Polly, for short, and she was ... mesmerizing. Captivating. The moment your father'—Billy eyed Ava speculatively—'Rupert, saw her, he was a goner. It was comical, actually.' Billy threw his feet over the arm of the sofa, lying with his head flat on the cushions and looking up at the ceiling. 'We were in some magical lesson or other, and in she walked. I've never seen a polite scrum quite like it as the young men of the Clouds fell over themselves to offer her their seats. But she just smiled this little knowing smile and walked all the way to the back, as had been agreed. She sat next to Novak, who was at the back because his family was the lowest of the low—they didn't start off in the Clouds ... Scraped their way in somehow ... Can't remember how.

'Anyway, Rupert and Var and the handful of others at the front—there weren't many, an exclusive group, you understand—spent the next few weeks casting furtive glances over their shoulders. But the only one who ever got to talk with her was Novak because our teacher—her grandmother—would scurry her away at the end of lessons.

'But one day, Rupert put an end to that. He blocked her path as she headed for the exit and invited her on a walk around the perimeter. She could hardly say no, of course. No one denied your father's family—not openly, at least—so off they went, him parading her around, announcing to the world she was his. The rest of them were spitting, let me tell you, and she and Rupert were inseparable from that day forth. Rupert even sat at the back of the class with her. A few thought it romantic, the rest of us thought him a fool.'

Billy sighed. 'Ahhh, those were the days, all so perfectly simple, young love the only weight on our shoulders.' He looked dreamily up at the ceiling, his eyelids half closing a few times, and then they closed completely, the crystal tumbler rolling from his hand, its pink contents spilling on the plush cream carpet.

'Billy!' Ava cried, casting aside her plate and rushing to him, kneeling and shaking him hard, relieved when his chest lifted with a massive inhale, but he didn't open his eyes.

Kush moved to the drinks cabinet, then held up a bottle. '*Sweet Dreams are Made of This*. He'll be out for a while.'

'Urgh,' Ava growled, slumping to the floor. 'He's such a rat.' She shifted to the side, remembering the spill, but when she looked down, the stain was gone. 'What the ...' She sent Kush a questioning frown. 'Where did it go?'

CHAPTER THIRTEEN
HALE
THE DAY DROMEDA STARTED SPINNING

HALE POURED OVER THE documents scattered on Danit's old desk, trying to focus, to learn, to understand his late uncle's business dealings, but his eyes kept creeping back to the agreement he, Elex, and Maria had discovered earlier in the night. The one where Alter Blade had agreed to secretly hide stolen water for the Claws.

He could do little about it until the morning, but sleep was proving elusive, and the only other thing his mind wanted to focus on was Sophie, which was unacceptable, so he would persevere with the ledger in his hands, which was about ... He had no idea. He snapped it closed and threw it down with a huff, then sagged back in his chair.

*Auburn hair, big grey eyes, pouty lips—Don't think about Sophie. Think about ... what to do about the Claws. No. Think about Nicoli. My old fr—*But everything that had happened by the lake came back and hit him like a cold slap across the cheek. Hale had thought he and Nicoli were friends. Hale had helped him countless times over the course of their lives, and yet Nicoli had kept his plans a secret.

The reasonable part of Hale understood why. It was for the safety of all the people of the Claws, but still ...

The squeak of a creaking floorboard sounded outside his study, and Hale grabbed the lantern, jumped to his feet, and was halfway to the door before he'd had a conscious thought. *A distraction. Perfect.* Who was sneaking around at this time? Had John returned? The wet blanket had disappeared after Sophie had rejected him by the lake and hadn't been seen since. Hale's spirits lifted; ribbing his younger brother was exactly the kind of diversion he needed.

Hale stuck his head out into the corridor, but there was no one there, so he stepped fully out and pulled the door closed behind him. A mystery——even better, so long as it turned out to be a small one; he had too much on his plate for anything big.

The main staircase in front of him was devoid of life, so he turned left and headed around the bend. Was John heading for Sophie's room? This was perfect. Hale could admonish him for good measure. Hale hurried farther up the dark corridor, closer to the wing where they'd housed their guests, but still, he found no sign of life. He slowed, frowning a little, not wanting to risk getting caught snooping outside Sophie's room, then stopped, pursing his lips as he considered his options. Maybe the noise had just been the house moving in the night ...

He waited for a few moments, listening and watching, straining every sense, hoping if there was someone there, they would break cover. Nothing. *How irritating*. He huffed loudly, then dimmed his lamp and walked backwards along the corridor, retracing his steps as though giving up, hoping to lure out his prey. Still nothing. Ordinarily, he would have given up, but with only problems waiting in his newly inherited office, he rounded the corner, dimmed his lamp entirely, and then tiptoed back to peek around the edge.

He almost chuckled at his own ridiculousness, feeling like a child playing hide and seek, wondering what the servants would think if one of them found him. He gave it another few moments, holding his breath, wondering if he should use the triffle in his pocket—not that he really believed in their magic—when the tiniest flash of movement caught his eye, a shadow crossing a moonbeam through a window.

He dashed forward, hurtling along the corridor while opening up his lamp, hissing, 'Stop!' as loudly as he dared. The fleeing form careened towards a set of servants' stairs on the right, but they couldn't get the door open in time, and when Hale stepped closer, he found a woman in a long, white nightdress crouching with her back against the wall, her face hidden. What was a servant doing here at this hour? Hale grabbed the woman's arm, hauling her into the light, ready to read her the riot act.

'Hale, don't,' snapped the woman, in a way no servant would ever dare, and in a voice Hale recognized. Several things came together simultaneously in Hale's mind. First, it was Sophie, second, his hand was pressed directly against the soft skin of her upper arm, third, they were alone in a dark corridor in the middle of the night, and fourth, this might be a trap.

Hale dropped his hand as though her skin burned and took a half step back. To his surprise, she didn't come after him, didn't even look at him, her face still resolutely turned away. Was she ... hiding? Her arms were folded over her chest, her shoulders hunched forward, devoid of any of her usual pep or vigor. In fact, she looked like she wanted to disappear into the shadows. *What the fuck?*

Hale stepped back into her space, but still she refused to look at him, turning even farther away and giving her head a little shake.

'Sophie?' he said gruffly, his voice quiet.

'If you'll excuse me,' she said, trying to escape.

Was that a wobble in her voice? Hale caught her arm, and she instantly stilled, something that sounded an awful lot like a sob coming from her lips.

'Sophie?' he said again, ducking his head to try and see her face. She wouldn't let him, so he gently took hold of her jaw. She shoved him off, but he needed to see, had to know what was wrong with her.

He tried again, and she winced. He immediately released her, surprised when she continued turning her face towards him, apparently resigned to her fate. He clenched his teeth as he took in the red, swollen mess of her face, then the emotions raging in her eyes: embarrassment, hurt, anger, pride.

Fury filled Hale's chest, raw and sharp. 'Sophie,' he said, consumed with the need to hunt down and drive a dagger into the heart of whoever had left her in this state. Just like he would for any guest, really, or his sisters. 'Who did this to you?'

Tears trickled from her eyes as she lightly shook her head, biting the insides of her lips as though trying to pull herself together.

Hale set down the lamp and tugged her forward into his arms. She didn't fight him, a sob wracking her body as she brought her hands to his chest and grabbed his shirt, then turned her head and pressed her cheek against him.

It was awkward, with Sophie's arms between them, Hale careful not to put pressure on her face, but it was also ... nice. When had he last hugged a woman like this? Certainly not since before he'd left for the edge of the world, and now he was hugging her, he found he wanted to do more besides. His men always talked of visiting the red districts when returning to land, but Hale had never found much solace in the women of the docks. With Sophie, though ... Oh, Goddess, he wasn't in his right mind, that was the only explanation. Perhaps he *should* find a lady of the night.

But before Hale could persuade himself to release her warm, soft form, Sophie pushed away, her tears dried up and a no-nonsense expression on her features. 'I need something cool for my face,' she said, as though they were only just meeting in the corridor, 'or the marks will be obvious for all to see tomorrow. It'll work better if I get something cold onto it quickly.'

This had happened before, then. 'One of your guards did this?' he said, but he didn't need the scoff Sophie sent his way to know he was off the mark. 'Your mother ...'

'Are you going to help me or stand around gawking like some half-wit?'

Hale cleared his throat, then picked up his lamp and led the way to the kitchen, where he opened one of the wooden ice boxes in the cold pantry, found a good-sized chunk of ice, and wrapped it in a scrap of cloth.

When he returned to the main expanse of the kitchen, Sophie was perched on the edge of the long wooden table, already holding a metal goblet to her face, her eyes closed. He hesitated for a second, watching as she turned the goblet. She winced as she pressed the other side to her skin, then exhaled as though finding some relief.

He crossed the distance to her in a few long strides, and she opened her eyes, warily tracking his progress. She lowered the goblet and held out her free hand for the ice, but he stepped closer, cupping her face and pressing the damp fabric to the worst of the redness.

She hissed, her eyes squeezing shut as she adjusted to the shock, her breaths sharp puffs of air through her nose, her jaw locked tight.

'Is the pain bad?' he asked, moving the ice a little.

She flinched, then opened her eyes, lifting her hand to cover his. 'I've endured worse,' she said, trying to prize his hand away and take the icepack from him. He stroked the line of her jaw, then traced the column of her neck, and she froze, looking up into his eyes with an unreadable expression, her fingers gripping his atop the ice.

He hadn't paused to consider whether his instinct to touch her was wise, he'd just acted, wanting to see what she would do, wanting to prolong their contact. And it seemed to have worked, seeing as she was no longer trying to get away.

She averted her gaze, her lips falling open as he kept stroking, her eyes falling closed. He didn't think he believed in magic, but some spell wound around him as he watched the rise and fall of her chest, felt the pulsing heartbeat in her throat, heard the catch of her breath. And then he realized that she was watching him, too. 'Hale, what are you doing?' she whispered.

He looked from one of her eyes to the other, both of his hands on her face, and if this was a trap, he'd fallen for it hook, line, and sinker. He cleared his throat. 'Does this happen a lot?'

She appraised him for a long moment, and then she pushed him away and grabbed the icepack, pressing it hard against her cheek. 'Are you working with Nicoli?' she asked in a level, no-nonsense tone, taking him completely off guard.

Hale's chest lurched. Did she mean about the water or because Hale had freed him? He had to start using his head. What was he thinking? This woman was a liar, her sole mission to make him hers, and he was sleep deprived ... Not at his best. He stepped back and ran a hand through his hair.

'Oh, don't look so shocked,' she snapped. 'I'm not sure anything could surprise me at this point.'

'I'm not working with Nicoli.'

She laughed. '*Please*. Yesterday you freed him, and today he killed your uncle, making you the leader of Alter Blade. Bit of a coincidence, don't you think?'

She tilted her head as though she had him on the ropes, and a swell of irritation rose through his chest. 'You're delusional.'

'Ha! You're guilty,' she said triumphantly, leaning forward. 'I can see it in your eyes.'

'I'm ...' He clamped his lips shut; he didn't answer to her.

'How would your siblings react if they knew you'd all but killed the man who raised them, and worse, that you were too chicken to do it yourself?'

He clenched his jaw. 'You're wrong.'

'Sure about that?'

'I'll escort you back to your room.'

She didn't move. 'Running away? Who would have thought, the great Hale Alter ...' Her tone was playful yet somehow also menacing.

'You walk a dangerous line, Sophie,' he snapped, then made for the exit without bothering to check if she was behind him. One minute she was all demure and vulnerable and the next she was like a wounded dog, snarling in warning as he got too close.

The thought hit him like a sledgehammer as he reached the top of the stairs, and he stopped short. *A wounded dog.* He'd got too close ... She was deflecting. 'Sophie,' he said, starting to turn, but she grabbed him and yanked him into the shadow of an enormous bird sculpture with surprising strength.

'What—' Hale began, but Sophie clamped a hand over his mouth, then extinguished his lamp.

'Shush,' she breathed. 'Listen.'

Hale went rigid, trying to listen, but the hand over his mouth was warm and feminine, her thinly veiled body pressed to his, and his heart was beating fast, pulsing in his ears, making it very hard to discern anything beyond her closeness.

He opened his mouth, intending to speak, but she pressed harder, her middle finger sliding between his parted lips. He froze, horrified. Appalled. Wondering why she hadn't immediately withdrawn the offending digit. But then his tongue accidentally brushed the crease of her skin, and he felt her go rigid.

Huh. Perhaps this wasn't so bad after all, if he could make her as uncomfortable as she was making him. He clamped his lips together, trapping her flesh between them, and she exhaled a shocked gasp that puffed against his nape. He bit her, his jaw moving without conscious instruction, and she fisted a hand in his shirt, pinching his waist.

He released her skin slowly, letting it slide between his teeth. Still, she didn't remove her hand. Instead, she pressed her forehead into the groove between his shoulder blades, so he could feel her hot, humid breaths against his spine. He bit down again.

'Hale,' she breathed, her voice strained, the sound lighting a fire within him. He sucked, pulling her flesh into his mouth, and she made a noise halfway between a hum and a moan, then dragged her nails down his back from shoulder to waist.

At some point between the biting and sucking, he'd forgotten all about trying to make her squirm, had started to enjoy himself, had developed strong urges to do other things with this mystery of a woman.

Which was a terrible idea. But he was the kind of man who embraced terrible ideas. Who saw them as adventures, like going to the edge of the world. It had almost got him killed, but it had been worth every second in the end.

Was Sophie that kind of adventure? Or was she the kind that drank a man dry and left him a husk of his former self ...

He tugged her hand away from his mouth, then turned, keeping her close as he assessed her in the blueish light of the moon, her free hand on his waist, her eyes looking up at him, too shadowed to read. He should unhand her, send her back to her bedroom—back to her homeland—but he didn't want to. He wanted to see what she would do if he pressed her against the wall, if he slid his mouth over hers ... Would it rile her, would she enjoy it, or would she slice him with a cutting remark the moment their lips parted?

She was a firecracker, and certainly more intelligent than anyone gave her credit for—more knowledgeable about Celestl than most Hale had trained with at the university—but she was also an enigma, someone who pretended to love his brother one minute, then cast him aside the next. Was this the real Sophie before him or was it simply a different face to the lie she'd put on for his brother? A seduction designed specifically with Hale in mind.

Did he care? He would give no version of her what she wanted. Although it might be fun to beat her at her own game for a while ... and to taste her full lips. His eyes dipped to the parted pink cushions, studying them for a moment, and then he bowed his head. For a heartbeat, she swayed towards him, but then, to his surprise, she pulled back, shaking her head.

'The noise, Hale. We should investigate.'

He growled in annoyance because she was right, but she was also so Goddess-damned distracting. Ever since he'd first laid eyes on her on the bridge, looking regal despite her disheveled state, he'd wanted to know more about her. What did she really want? Hale's hand in marriage, of course, but it seemed like more than the simple desire for an advantageous match ... And why had Linella attacked her? What had Sophie done to deserve the punishment?

Hale was a fool. He should put her from his mind and send her back to John because even if she was the most interesting person in their world, Hale would rather cut off his right hand than fraternize with a woman who had been with his younger brother. Although, maybe he could fraternize a little ... If he never planned to give himself to her, what could it hurt?

His eyes flicked back to her lips, but then he sighed and pulled away. It was a problem he would have to ponder tomorrow because if someone was sneaking around late at night near his unlocked study, he really should take Sophie's advice and at least make sure there was nothing incriminating on his desk——

'Shit.' He pushed past Sophie and ran. He flung open the study door, startling Linella, who was hunched over his desk, but her look of shock almost immediately morphed into triumph because she had in her hand the agreement between Alter Blade and the Claws. The one that spelled out how Alter helped the Claws steal water from the Blades and allowed them to store it on Alter land.

Sophie appeared in the doorway behind him. 'Mother?'

Linella's eyes flicked from Hale to Sophie and back again, and her smile broadened further, if such a thing was possible.

'This was your plan?' said Hale, rounding on Sophie, who was glaring at her mother with bright hatred in her eyes.

Sophie slowly turned to look at Hale, and her forehead furrowed, as though taking a moment to make sense of his words. 'No!' she breathed. 'Hale—'

If she said anything further, Hale didn't hear because he launched himself forward, his priority getting the agreement out of Linella's thieving fingers.

'Like mother, like daughter,' hissed Hale. 'Liars and schemers both.'

Linella chuckled as he snatched the parchment from her hand. 'That's a bit rich coming from you.'

Chapter Fourteen
Maria
THREE WEEKS AFTER DROMEDA STARTED SPINNING

THE DAYS WERE TEDIOUS and stale, and since Elex had told Maria he loved her, the ceaseless itching for him had taken on an edge of fire. A fire that not even the tepid bath in which she sat could douse.

Her bedroom had no bathing chamber attached, but Cane had at least been kind enough to set aside the one across from her room for her exclusive use. It was a functional room, filled with nothing but an ugly metal tub that butted up against the wall's tongue and groove cladding, a wooden shelf protruding from the wall just above the lip. The thing drained through a hole at the base, but servants carried heated water from the kitchens to fill it, which cooled all too quickly.

The room was almost empty, with no window and few adornments, but Maria found she liked the simplicity. She had spent many hours wallowing there since her arrival, wondering whose bathroom this had been when the quarter had been controlled by Elex.

She selected a vial of bath oil from the shelf and uncorked it, the smell of eucalyptus and lavender wafting up her nose, eliciting a pang of longing for her old life in Alter. In her homeland, her days had been full of distilling oils like these, then trading them for treasures and secrets both in Alter Blade and Arow Claw. She'd been so busy, she'd often been late for meals or appointments with the seamstress, and she missed it dearly. Sitting still had never been her forte, and yet here, it was all she could do.

She poured a little oil into her palm and ran it over her skin, first down her arms, then her legs, but as she reached for the vial again, she paused, an idea taking root in her mind. Perhaps sitting still wasn't all she could do …

She stoppered the vial, which was still three quarters full, and cast an eye over the other five on the shelf. She sniffed them, paying attention for the first time to the fact that they were all high-quality and therefore expensive. From what she'd seen, Oshala was not a place filled with abundant wealth, and Cane certainly didn't treat his servants well. That meant the oils were not only desirable, but most likely valuable, too, so maybe she could use them here just as she had in Alter.

But where to start? Who could she trust? Certainly not the two women assigned to dress her and fix her hair every night. She would find someone, carefully, and she would ask Elex, too, if she could ever get close enough.

But Elex wasn't at dinner that night or any night for a while, and Cane took great pleasure in telling her it was further punishment for their bad behavior. Had the guards told Cane of Elex's trip to her bedroom or was Cane just bored and taking his frustration out on them? Maria had never wanted to stab anyone more. Had never come closer ...

Maria distracted herself by concentrating on her new enterprise, but another full week passed, and Maria was beginning to give up hope that she'd ever find the first rung on her new black market ladder. She was fractious and preoccupied when she headed into Cane's room that night before dinner, so she didn't notice Opal's maid until she barreled headlong into her, upsetting the tray in her hands.

The tray went careening to the floor with an almighty clatter, dishes smashing, Cane scowling and cursing. Erica soon placated him, climbing onto his lap, and the guards who'd rushed in returned to the corridor, while Maria crouched to help the maid gather up the spill.

Maria collected bits of crockery, cutlery, ruined cakes, and bruised fruit, making quick work of it alongside the other woman, until she spotted a small, sharp fruit knife, and her hand lingered. The maid cast her eyes downwards and rocked forward on her toes, reaching for an apple. 'They're watching,' the woman whispered, her face still angled towards the floor. 'It's a test.'

It took every shred of Maria's self-control not to react, to hide her surprise. She picked up the knife and placed it on the metal tray with a light clink, then retrieved the vial of oil she'd worn strapped to her inner thigh for nights on end—the only place she could think to hide it in the ludicrous outfits Cane made her wear. Maria placed it carefully in the remnants of a teacup, then covered it with a napkin. 'Thank you,' she breathed.

The woman gave no acknowledgement, just cleared her throat, then bustled the tray from the room.

The interaction with the maid left Maria energized in a way she hadn't been since arriving in Oshe, and the feeling made her hungry for more. So instead of waiting for another chance encounter—which might have taken weeks—the following morning, she went in search of the same maid.

Maria slipped out of her room just as the sun was rising, taking her guard by surprise as she pulled open her bedroom door. 'I'm going for a walk,' she announced, not giving the anxious-looking man a chance to order her back inside or to call for backup. 'I've been cooped up long enough and need to stretch my legs.'

'But, ma'am, I ...' the guard spluttered.

Maria stared him down. 'I am a *guest* here, am I not? And seeing as this quarter is a fortress, there's little risk of me making an escape.'

The guard stared blankly at Maria's face for a moment, then said, 'Ma'am,' in a deferential tone, snapping his feet together before falling in a step behind her as she set off at a brisk pace down the corridor. She silently chastised herself for not thinking of doing this sooner. It was so unlike her to wallow, and she'd wasted valuable time when she could have been collecting information to help Elex or aid her own escape. Many inside the quarter would be sympathetic to their cause, she just had to find them, and hope the vials of oil stuffed in her pockets would be payment enough to elicit their help.

Maria headed through the banqueting hall and out into the courtyard, the main gate before her. It was closed, the gate guards sending nervous looks her way, but she ignored them. She turned in a slow circle, taking in every detail of the walls, the gatehouse, the guards, and the paths that headed off in all directions.

The stone building of Cane's residence stood off to the right, and past that on either side stood a great many other buildings laid out in a haphazard jumble. A few were made of stone, although entirely devoid of carvings, scrollwork, or any other adornment, but most were built from wattle and daub. They looked as though they were piled atop one another and overlapping in places, the curved roofs—which she'd come to recognize as standard in this land—seeming to sit across multiple structures so it wasn't clear where one building ended and another began.

They were mostly well-maintained, unlike what she'd seen across the rest of Oshala, many boasting flower boxes outside the windows, and with planters dotted here and there.

Once she'd memorized the courtyard, Maria headed off at a brisk pace along the path beside the left-hand wall. She walked its entire length, past buildings of all shapes and sizes and a large, grassy, open area that seemed to be a park. Nothing struck her as particularly noteworthy until she came to the end, where the sight was so breathtaking it made her gasp, the path falling away into an open void.

The whole back edge of the quarter was little more than a cliff top, no barrier between the livable space and the perilous fall.

Maria inched carefully forward, hugging the wall to get close enough to peer over the edge. She reeled as she took in the huge distance to the enormous lake below—the source of Oshe Blade's power.

Her eyes traced the edge of the lake until she came to the place on the right-hand side where great channels had been carved into the ground, and what looked like an entire village had been flattened. Her stomach dropped because it was undoubtedly the result of Nicoli's stunt. She prayed to the Goddess that no one had died ... unlike in Alter.

'Ya' shouldn't stand s'close to the edge,' said an old, gnarled man pushing a cart filled with woven goods—rush mats and baskets and hats. 'The fall might suck ya' right over ... assuming someone don't push ya' first.'

Maria stepped hastily back. The sunrise fall had been and gone, but the ground was still a little wet, and she had no friends in this place. Even those loyal to Elex didn't know her—perhaps even blamed her for Cane's takeover—and those loyal to Cane certainly had no reason to keep her alive.

The man trundled off down a street slightly bigger than the others, and Maria followed him, wondering where he was taking his wares. They passed several small shops and a tavern before the street opened into a small market square with a circular font of gurgling water in the middle. Maria's eyes went wide.

This must be why so many of Elex's servants had chosen to stay when Cane had taken over. A plentiful supply of water was not something any in Celestl would give up lightly, and the people appeared to be helping themselves without restriction.

'Impressive, heh?' said the man with the cart, parking up a few paces away.

'Yes,' Maria agreed, moving towards him. 'You can just take it?'

'No more than a half-bucket a time,' he said, then his mouth pulled into a gruesome smile. 'If any takes more, they lose a hand. I've lived here my whole life an' works just fine. An' stops people killing themsels trying ta' get it from the fall.'

'Oh,' said Maria, feeling green at the mere thought.

'My wife's from the village below—I saw ya' lookin'—a right mess ... many died. That's when his lordship Cane attacked, when most fightin' men had gone down ta' help.'

'Careful, old man,' said the guard, who Maria had all but forgotten was behind her.

'I mean nothin' by it,' the man replied gruffly, raising his hands. 'Makes little difference ta' me who's in charge, so long as I can make a livin'.'

'I'm sure,' growled the guard.

'G'day ma'am,' said the stallholder, nodding then turning bruskly away.

'You didn't have to be like that,' Maria said to her guard, then clamped her mouth shut and started moving before he could reply. From what she'd seen, Cane did little to keep his men in line, and although this one seemed placid enough, he could easily have a nasty side.

Maria explored the market, which was just warming up for the day, stopping to speak to stallholders, asking them about their lives with genuine interest, keen to hear every detail. Most were hesitant and reserved with her guard's heavy presence at her side, but Maria got some sense of their lives, and those tiny nuggets were worth a great deal. It meant she knew which of them she would approach first when she found a way to shake her tail.

Maria was careful not to outstay her welcome and headed back to Cane's residence in time for lunch. She usually ate in her bedroom, but decided to join Erica and Opal in the smaller eating room off the main banqueting hall. It was light and welcoming with windows on three sides and sage green walls. It felt more intimate than any of the other rooms she'd been in, something she pondered as she helped herself to steak and wilted vegetables from the platters waiting on the sideboard, the silence staunch, and she could feel Erica and Opal's eyes boring into her back.

Erica and Opal were already seated at the oval table in the middle of the room, and Maria took the seat opposite Opal, who looked at Maria, then at Erica, then back, while Erica cocked her head in question. The silence stretched tighter with every passing second, but Maria took a mouthful of spinach covered in steak juice before addressing them.

'I was bored,' said Maria, the delicious flavors exploding against her hungry tongue. 'And the food's always cold by the time the servants bring it to my room.'

'Hmm,' said Erica, picking up her water glass and swilling the liquid around before taking a sip.

Maria ignored them, quietly eating her food, and they eventually returned to theirs and then to their conversation, which was the real reason for Maria's appearance.

They spoke of mundane topics mostly, dresses and menus and flowers. They occasionally referred to Cane, but only ever in reverent tones that made Maria want to roll her eyes.

'Did you have a good morning?' Maria asked during a lull in their conversation, fed up of their frippery.

They sent her matching quizzical looks. 'We only just rose,' said Opal. 'Cane keeps us up so late ...'

Erica set her cutlery down with a *clink*. 'And we women must do what we can to rebuild our strength. Sleep is so important.'

'Of course,' said Maria, thanking the Goddess one more time that she was not married to Cane.

'You didn't find the same with your husband?' asked Opal, her tone superior and lightly mocking.

Maria flushed. 'I've spent so little time with my husband ...'

'A pity,' said Erica, wiping her mouth with a pristine white napkin, 'for that one has stamina to rival any.'

Maria's tongue tied. 'Uh ...'

Erica tittered. 'I always forget that not every woman was lucky enough to have the upbringing I did.'

Maria's brow creased. 'Upbringing?'

'Oh,' said Opal, leaning in as though the conversation had become fascinating. 'Erica had—'

The door cracked and two maids entered. Opal sat back in her seat, looking irritated by the interruption. 'What is it, Mina?' she asked sharply.

'My ladies,' the maids said in unison, bobbing matching curtseys.

'Your baths have been drawn,' said Mina, stepping forward, and Maria's heart leapt when she realized it was the woman she'd knocked into in Cane's bedroom.

Erica gave a little huff, then tossed her napkin onto the table and got gracefully to her feet. 'I suppose we wouldn't want them to get cold. Thank you, Mina.'

Opal followed meekly along, but the maids lingered. 'Shall we give you the usual amount of time?' said Mina, speaking to Erica's feet.

'Mmm hmm,' Erica replied, already at the door.

The two women left, and awkwardness settled over the room, the maids clearly hoping Maria would leave them to the leftovers before they were required again. And seeing as Maria was in the business of making friends, she was only too happy to oblige.

The two maids began to clear the table, and Maria waited for the second woman to turn her back, then held up a vial of oil so Mina could see it. Mina nodded minutely, and Maria slid the vial into her napkin as she rose.

'Thank you both,' Maria said warmly, but she didn't quite pull the door all the way closed behind her when she left the room, and she hovered in the deeply recessed doorway, her ear against the door jamb.

'Ridiculous,' said Mina, her high voice pitched low.

'What is?' said the other.

'Erica. The way she talks about her upbringing like it's something to brag about.'

'It was a *high-end* brothel she lived in, mind,' said the second maid, her sarcasm palpable.

'Oh, well, there you go then. Surely the childhood every woman wishes they'd lived. Education via prostitute.'

'Courtesan, excuse me,' the second woman joked through a mouthful of food.

'Makes all the difference, I'm sure,' Mina retorted. 'Her father pretends he's squeaky clean, but I dread to think what that poor girl must have witnessed ... What she would have been forced to *do*.'

'Not much poor about her now, that's for sure. And she's not a girl any longer neither.'

Footsteps approached, and Maria's guard jumped up from the chair he shouldn't have been sitting in a few feet away. Maria hurried out into view, trying not to make a sound, trying to put herself as far from the door as she could in case whoever was approaching decided to speak with her. But the man paid her little mind, too busy scowling at her guard before striding away.

Over the next few days, Maria repeated the same pattern again and again. First a circuit of the market, lunch with Erica and Opal, and then a bath, where she was careful not to use too much oil.

She heard little of use, but she scouted for nooks where she could discretely hide vials of oil, and picked up small tidbits of information, like which maids and which guards were sneaking around together, and whose toes she'd be stepping on if she struck up a full-blown black market trading enterprise.

Maria's guard trailed her everywhere she went, so she had to be creative when building trust with the maids and stall holders, taking every available opportunity for a quiet word or a covert smile. She carefully reshared the gossip she heard, although only when confident about how the information would be received, and soon her acquaintances became less guarded with their stories in return.

This filled her gossip reserves but provided little that would be useful to Elex or that might aid her escape, everyone preoccupied by whether the Goddess had returned and what that meant for Celestl. She needed to ditch her guard as no one would truly open up with him looking over her shoulder, but he was proving remarkably committed to his post.

Erica and Opal rarely said anything that caught Maria's attention, although they invited her to massages, tea in the library, manicures, music recitals, and various other entertainments. They saw Maria as their plaything, poking her with mean jibes and trying to get a rise out of her, which Maria mostly let roll off her like water off a duck's back, but days later, Maria's tolerance was running thin.

She'd learned almost nothing, had had the opportunity to trade only a handful of vials, and was beginning to wonder if Elex would ever show up at dinner again. She itched to see him, even just from a distance to make sure he was okay, seeing as Cane was resolute in mentioning him not at all.

'Well, it's not like Maria's husband is keeping *her* up at night,' Erica snickered as they sat in a beautifully mosaiced hot pool one afternoon. Erica watched Maria with feline curiosity, her fingers playing casually across the top of the water, and Maria narrowed her eyes, pouting a little as Opal moved the conversation on to the menu for Cane's birthday dinner.

Erica's attention shifted to Opal, but Maria had no desire to discuss how to make her captor happy, and she desperately needed an outlet for her angst. 'Don't you ever get bored?' Maria asked, her tone too sharp.

Erica and Opal stilled, Erica's eyes flicking up like a hawk honing in on a mouse. Making enemies of these women wasn't wise, but Maria's opening gambit had felt so good, and a mental scuffle was just the thing she needed. In her past life, Maria and Nicoli would debate topics for hours, neither pulling their punches, and she missed it dearly, her mind needing exercise more than her muscles.

A smile tugged at Erica's lips as she met Opal's gaze, Opal deferring in her usual grating way. Their eyes held for a long moment, and then Erica pushed Opal's wet hair back over her shoulder. 'Are we bored, Opal?'

'No,' Opal replied, twisting her head towards Maria. 'We have plenty to do.'

'But you're clever,' snapped Maria, 'both of you.'

'That is not desirable in a woman,' Opal said with a little shrug, 'but what ability we have, we offer up in service to our husband.'

Erica took a long sip of the wine she'd been swigging since lunch. Cane had business elsewhere that evening, so there would be no formal dinner, the night their own, and it seemed Erica planned to take full advantage.

'Well,' said Erica, drawing a slow circle on Opal's shoulder, 'much as my fellow wife is correct, I will admit I sometimes miss being indispensable.'

'To Barron?' asked Maria.

Erica tittered. 'Goddess, no.' She looked at the ceiling. 'To my father. But then Barron came into my father's establishment one evening, set his eyes on me, and refused any other woman from that moment forth.' She stretched her arms along the pool's edge, arrogance dripping from the set of her shoulders and tilt of her head. 'My father bargained hard, Barron and I married, and he kept me in a manner any woman would kill for.'

Maria held her challenge of a gaze for a long moment, then said dryly, 'A true fairy tale.'

'Twice over,' agreed Erica. 'Because now I have Cane.' She turned back to Opal. 'And we are the luckiest women in the world.' Maria didn't believe Erica's words. No one could truly believe they were *lucky* to be married to Cane. Even if Erica wanted to be Cane's top dog, she was too clever to be so mindlessly devoted.

'The luckiest,' Opal echoed, her words so earnest and her demeanor so placid that Maria almost did believe her. But then the women smiled at one another as though sharing some great joke, which, try as she might, Maria could not work out, and that made Maria's mood even blacker than before.

Chapter Fifteen
Ava

Kush took Ava's hand as they meandered down a charming cobbled street that was clean and bright and filled with flowers. Well-dressed children dashed about, squealing with glee as their parents ushered them towards the schoolhouse a little farther along, the bell ringing, summoning them inside for the day.

'I understand why you like it here,' said Ava, turning her head so she could see him around the hood of her cloak.

He smiled an enigmatic smile, then kissed the back of her hand. 'It gets better,' he said, tugging her along at a brisker pace.

She squeezed his fingers, relishing the feeling of being together in public, walking down a street like a normal couple, trusting him enough to simply follow and see where he led. Not that they were a couple ... not really ... were they? She blushed at the thought as they turned off the street into a small, manicured park. Kush seemed to sense her discomfort because he pulled her to a stop under a dazzling rose arch in full bloom, the scent of the big, blowsy blooms bold and sweet.

He kept hold of her hand as he drew close and looked intently into her eyes. 'Whatever Billy says about me,' he said, 'it's not true. I'm not here because of my father. I'm here because of you. Because I love you. Because you're all I can think about ...'

He lifted his spare hand to Ava's neck, and she looked nervously up at him, biting the edge of her lip. 'Are we ...' She looked away, then pressed her forehead to his chest, his hand sliding around to the back of her head.

'What, Ava? What is it?' He gently forced her to look at him, and the distress on his features made her heart hurt.

'I mean, are we ... a couple, do you think?' Her cheeks burned and she tried to look away, but he held firm, his whole face softening, the lines on his forehead smoothing out in relief.

He pressed his forehead to hers. 'Yes,' he breathed, swiping his thumb across the sensitive skin of her neck. 'I want that.'

'Me too,' she said in a rush, and then he pressed a gentle kiss to her lips, and for a moment, that was all there was in the world, in any world, just her and Kush, their bodies joined, some energy pulsing back and forth between them that Ava didn't have the words to name.

Kush cupped her nape when they parted, then pulled back and retrieved a pocket watch from his coat, checking it with one hand while he continued to hold her hand with the other, stroking his thumb over her skin. 'We probably don't have too long before Billy wakes, although time moves more slowly here than in Santala.'

'It does?' she asked, as Kush started walking again.

'Just a little. Not like whatever world the Gods' souls are tied to. There it moves very slowly indeed. Slow enough that they're practically immortal.'

They reached the far side of the park, the path spitting them out into a bustling market, and Ava's eyes couldn't take in all the delights fast enough. Brightly colored squares of something dusted with sugar, nuts with a sweet cinnamon coating, chickens cooking on rotisseries, small paintings of animals doing improbable things ... They bought a straw basket with soft leather handles, and then filled it with every treat they could find, Kush handing over coins embossed with an image of the Atlas Tree to pay for it all.

It was the most fun Ava had had in as long as she could remember—perhaps ever—the feeling of being allowed to do as she pleased and Kush telling her to select whatever she wanted a foreign delight. How many times had she watched the well-to-do of Santala go about their business, wishing she had even a fraction of their means. And here she was now, all the means she could ever need, chewing on a stick of dried meat even though her belly was far from empty. How lucky she was.

'Why do they accept coins from the Atlas Tree?' Ava asked as they exited the market on a wide open street heading towards the outskirts of town, their purchases slung over Kush's shoulder.

He shrugged. 'Every federated world does. Sharing a currency makes it easy to trade.'

Ava had never had money of her own, but she'd never seen an Atlas coin in the tavern. 'They use it in Santala, too?'

'Most worlds use both Atlas currency and their own coins. Santala doesn't export much, so not much Federation money makes it in.'

'Oh.'

'This world exports a lot. Precious metals and clothes and food,' he said as they approached a modest temple with pillars carved from creamy white marble. He led her up the steep marble steps, stopping under the stone pergola at the top. 'This is my favorite world,' he said, his gaze fixed on the vista on the far side that had come into view. Another flight of marble steps led down to a small lake filled with crystal blue water encircled by gently sloping moorland hills painted in purple heather.

'Oh, wow,' she said, taking a few steps towards it.

He smiled, clearly pleased by her reaction. 'The lake's healing. The water comes up from deep underground, passing through pockets of magic that infuse the water with the ability to restore. It's the biggest natural healing pool we've found.'

'Oh, master!' said a beautiful woman in long robes the same color as the water, rushing up the steps from the lake. She bowed low, her silky black hair falling around her face. 'It is an honor to see you. It has been so long!'

Kush beamed at the woman. 'It is good to see you, too.'

The woman flushed as she straightened, and jealousy grabbed Ava's chest in a fierce hand. 'Should I prepare swimming robes for you and your guest?' The woman's eyes flicked to Ava, her warm smile seeming genuine, and Ava attempted to push the jealousy aside. She failed.

Kush looked at Ava, but she'd gone mute, unable to speak on account of having just realized the woman had called Kush *master*. Was Kush the master of this temple? 'Yes, please,' said Kush, and the woman bowed again, then hurried away. People here *bowed* to Kush ...

'Ava?' Kush said gently, putting his hand on her arm. 'Is this ... okay?'

'They think you're their God?' she blurted. 'They worship you?'

A guarded, questioning look rolled down across Kush's features, and he dropped his hand. 'I'm a demi-God, Ava.' His words were edged with defensiveness, and he leaned backwards, increasing the space between them. 'Father gifted me this world on my eighteenth birthday. Every God presides over at least one federated world. It's how we see to their needs and make sure their interests are represented at the Council of Federated Worlds.'

'They *worship* you,' she repeated, this time so quietly, she wasn't sure if he even heard her words.

'It's a small world with a tiny population,' he countered. 'It's a token, nothing like what the full Gods have. And as a demi-God, you're entitled to one, too.'

She swallowed hard. 'Did my parents ... Did they have worlds?'

He faltered, thinking for a moment. 'I would think so, but I don't know. We can ask Billy. Or there are records ...'

She gave a shaky nod, and he softened, pulling her to him, hugging her to his chest and stroking her back in soothing circles. 'Let's swim,' he said into her hair. 'You've been through so much, and I promise it will make you feel better.'

Chapter Sixteen
Sophie
THE DAY AFTER DROMEDA STARTED SPINNING

Sophie descended the stairs earlier than usual the following morning, worried because there had been no sign of her mother in their rooms. Hale had had murder in his eyes only a few hours before, when he'd discovered Linella in his office, and Sophie feared the worst.

Had he locked Linella up after he'd kicked Sophie out, or sent her home, or done something so terrible, Sophie refused to acknowledge the possibility. Hale wouldn't, would he? Perhaps he would ... What did she really know of the man, after all? He'd shown her kindness, had helped her ice her face, but what had her mother discovered on Hale's desk? Was it to do with Danit's death? Had Hale lied about his involvement?

The arrogant, irritating fool! Sophie had been the one to make Hale investigate the noise, and yet he'd accused her of working with her mother, of distracting him while Linella snuck around. He should be thanking Sophie, not accusing her.

Sophie stalked silently into breakfast, crackling with the energy of a rolling storm. She found Hale alone at the table, eating a simple meal of porridge and fresh berries, and she took the seat beside him, helping herself to a bowl while clinking everything just a little too hard. 'Where is my mother?' she asked, picking up her spoon.

'Good morning to you, too,' said Hale, not looking up from the document he was reading.

'Did you lock her up?'

His forehead puckered the tiniest fraction. 'No.'

'Did you kill her?'

Hale's eyes finally met hers, his features incredulous. 'No.'

'Then where is she?'

'She's gone back to Laurow.' Hale returned to his document.

'She's ... why?'

He inhaled as though her comment had irritated him. 'She agreed to keep her mouth shut about what she read in my office, and I agreed to let her go on the proviso she would never return without an express invitation.'

'That's it?' said Sophie, her mind reeling. 'And she just ... went?' Sophie couldn't see her mother giving up so easily if she had a trump card. She would have pushed for ...

'No, that is not *it*.'

'You agreed to marry me,' Sophie breathed, hardly able to believe it, her chest rising with joy as something like disappointment clenched in her guts. If she had to marry any of the men she'd met, she would choose him, but this wasn't how she'd hoped it would happen.

'Don't get too excited, it won't be for a while,' he replied, his tone bitter.

'Oh, get down off your high horse, you arrogant ass,' she snapped, unable to help herself. Her nerves were frayed, and he was so insufferable, especially after what they'd nearly done last night—what he'd instigated.

'Excuse me?' he said, lifting his gaze to hers once more, his eyes as hot as molten rock.

'You heard me,' she hissed, leaning into his space, refusing to be intimidated by his fierce features. 'You are swift to call me names as though you are some pillar of morality, but whatever was in that document proves you are not. So you can accuse me of being a liar for making the best of my forced betrothal to your limp fish of a brother all you want, but what exactly do *your* actions make *you*?'

Hale flexed his jaw as though she'd punched him. 'What was in that document has nothing to do with me,' he growled, his voice low and dangerous. 'Did you stop to think that perhaps I am making the best of my situation, too?'

Sophie pulled back a little and cocked her head. No, she hadn't considered that. She studied his eyes, wondering if she should believe him. She wanted to, but was it wise? 'Well,' she said, in a mock petulant manner she hoped would defuse him, '*you* started it.'

Hale gave a small nod and shifted back in his seat. 'How is your face this morning?'

'Much improved, thank you for asking.' She'd covered the remaining redness with a thick layer of make-up.

'You look,' he said, then paused for a moment as though carefully considering his words, 'like you always do.'

Their eyes held for a long moment, and then the sound of chatter pierced their bubble. Hale cleared his throat and turned away.

Sophie barely noticed as Elex and Maria joined them at the table, too preoccupied by the knowledge that she would be Hale's wife after all, if he didn't find a way to weasel out of it. A small, stupid part of her had hoped he would come around to wanting her, that they would build something like Maria and Elex had so quickly constructed between them. Their trust in each other seemed real, even after what Elex had done to his own father, and Sophie longed to ask how they'd done it.

Unfortunately, Sophie would get no chance to steal a quiet word with her future sister-in-law because before long, Maria and Elex were rising from the table, ready to embark on their journey to Elex's homeland. Without thinking, Sophie put her hands together and nodded her head. 'May the Goddess protect you on your journey.'

Maria's face fell, and she faltered for a moment. Sophie wondered if she'd said the wrong thing. In her homeland, it was a customary farewell, and now Dromeda was spinning again, it was more important than ever to stay on the Goddess's good side.

Maria had gone a little pale and was gripping the back of a chair. 'You think she's returned?'

Sophie shook her head in confusion. 'How could she not have?'

Maria's forehead furrowed. 'Then you think the Toll Bells will chime?'

Oh. Maria was worried about that? 'No! Toll Day is past. The next tolls are not due for ninety-nine years.'

Maria didn't look convinced, but she nodded, then wished Sophie the best before following her husband outside. Hale and Sophie trailed them, watching from the top of the steps as they mounted their horses and left the courtyard with little fanfare.

When they were gone, Sophie's eyes rose above the walls to where Dromeda spun in the distance, and a shiver ran down her spine. She had felt so confident only minutes earlier that the Toll Bells would not ring for decades, but now she watched the spinning behemoth, she didn't feel so sure. Her eyes flicked back to the house, to the bell tower that protruded from the top of the mansion, looming ominously above them.

What if the Goddess changed the rules? Could she? And if she did, who would Alter Blade send as their sacrifice now Maria had gone? Would they send Sophie? Would that even satisfy the Goddess? Or would Sophie's father call her home to Laurow to do her duty for her own people?

Hale was watching when she finally tore her eyes away, and her face flushed with embarrassment, convinced he would think her a fool. 'Whatever happens will happen,' he said gently. 'We have no power to change it either way.'

But there *was* something she could do. 'I want to leave an offering at the gate.'

Hale raised his eyebrows. 'You believe it will make a difference?'

She gave him a long look, then shrugged. 'It can't hurt to try.'

Chapter Seventeen
Elex
Five Weeks After Dromeda Started Spinning

'Bad news,' said Zeik, slamming the door behind him as he entered the tap room. The other three pushed up from the floor where they'd been holding stress positions.

'You contracted the pox again?' asked Sol, wiping sweat from his eyes.

'You remembered it was you who invited the prostitute into our quarter the night Cane seized control?' suggested Tallin, heading for the water jug.

'Just spit it out,' snapped Elex, breathing heavily, their joviality grating.

Zeik scowled in a way that told Elex to stop being a grump, which only made Elex more irritated, but he bit his tongue as his half-brother punished him by grabbing a tankard and filling it with beer before sharing his news. 'An informant confirmed the current location of Erica's father's brothel. He asked for a full line up to pick a new … um … *companion*, but swears they showed him no one who fitted the description of the woman in our quarter the night we were attacked.'

Tallin leaned casually on the bar. 'Was this informant, in fact, you, Zeik? Have you been in a brothel all day?'

Zeik made a crude gesture at Tallin with his fingers. 'He asked specifically for someone tall with dark, ringleted hair, and they swore they had no one to match.'

Sol scoffed. 'Did he ask—'

'Yes,' Zeik said in a long-suffering tone, 'he asked if anyone fitting that description had recently left their employment. He was told *no*.'

'So they're either lying,' said Sol, 'or Erica's father isn't our man.'

Elex threw up his hands. 'Or the woman has started wearing her hair differently or she wore a wig that night or she works elsewhere but Erica's father is still involved.'

'Exactly,' said Zeik. 'Completely inconclusive. As I said, bad news.'

It was fucking hopeless.

Zeik took a seat by the fire, crossing his legs as he lounged, a self-satisfied smile on his lips.

'There's more?' asked Tallin.

'There's more,' Zeik confirmed. 'Elex didn't give me this job for nothing.'

Elex rested his hands on the mantel above the fire. 'Elex is beginning to regret his appointments.'

'Ha!' laughed Zeik. 'Very funny.'

'Just get on with it.'

Zeik huffed dramatically. 'Even if it wasn't Erica's father, we know it was someone in *our* father's inner circle who led the coup.'

'We do?' said Sol.

Zeik raised his shoulders and tilted his head. 'I came with good news, too.'

'Which is?' Elex snapped.

Zeik leaned forward in his seat. 'Father's troops were among the attackers.'

A beat of silence stretched as they all processed the news. 'But they struck when we were helping the village by the lake,' countered Tallin. 'It was opportunistic.'

'But well organized,' countered Zeik.

'Your father probably issued a standing order to attack whenever the opportunity arose,' said Sol, deflating, leaning against the bar for support.

'Then it could only have been Erica's father or Opal's,' said Elex.

'Exactly,' agreed Zeik. 'Father didn't trust anyone else.'

'Then we trail them both and hope they lead us to the woman we need,' suggested Sol.

'Fuck the woman,' said Elex. 'We know enough, and I'm not waiting any longer to get Maria out. The longer she's in there, the bolder Cane will become.'

'But we still don't know who we can trust,' said Tallin.

'We never will for sure,' said Elex. 'We know now it wasn't our own people who turned against us, and that's all that matters. It's enough.'

'If you get Maria out, Cane will ransack the city to find you,' said Zeik.

'It's risky,' said Sol.

'Tell only those we know are loyal,' said Elex, ignoring their objections. 'Be ready on Cane's birthday. My wife has been there long enough, and it's the perfect time.'

'Lots of people, I suppose,' Tallin said slowly.

'Lots of distractions,' added Sol.

'Oh, fine,' said Zeik, folding his arms over his chest. 'I suppose we can't live like this forever.'

Tallin flexed his fingers. 'And we haven't had a good fight in far too long.'

Chapter Eighteen
Maria
Five Weeks After Dromeda Started Spinning

Maria's chest fell as she walked into dinner because once again, Elex was nowhere to be seen. She hardly ate, pushing bits of carrot around her plate until the servants took it away, and Cane barely cast an eye in her direction when she left for bed. This was exactly what he wanted—to break her spirit—and even though she knew that, she couldn't shake the lead weight pulling her down.

But as she rounded the table, heading for the corridor to her bedroom, Elex appeared in the entrance from the courtyard. She froze mid-step, but he didn't hesitate, striding towards her with single-minded focus. Maria moved to meet him, with no guards to stop her seeing as Elex wasn't supposed to be there.

'Brother,' said Cane, launching to his feet while his eyes flitted to the nearest guards. 'What a nice surprise.'

'I missed you,' Elex said to Cane as he laced his fingers with Maria's. 'I'm so glad to find you in such good health.'

'Your masseuse really is a marvel,' said Cane, not missing a beat, 'and the water here is so healing.' But Elex ignored him. He tugged Maria into the nearest alcove and gently pushed her back against the wall.

'He's been keeping me away,' said Elex.

'Then how did you get in?' Maria's heart pulsed. If he'd snuck in, maybe they could both sneak out.

'I still have friends here.'

'Who? I'm gathering information, but it's slow. If I had someone I could rely on to help ...'

Elex shook his head again. 'Trust no one.' He cupped her face and pressed his lips urgently to hers. 'Be ready on Cane's birthday. You've been here long enough.' He whirled away, the interaction so brief Maria wondered if she'd dreamed the whole thing. But then she saw the quiet fury on Cane's features, and she knew it was real. She hurried to her bedroom and leaned back against the door.

It felt as though she'd been punched in the chest. But beside the gaping crater Elex had left was a tiny spark of hope because Cane's birthday was only a few days away.

Chapter Nineteen
Ava

Kush had been wrong, the swim didn't help. It had been nice enough when she was in the water, but as they arrived back at the house, Ava's overriding feeling was that she was drained and needed a nap. Was that how healing pools were supposed to work?

'Ooh,' said Billy, after a long, star-shaped stretch. 'I'm hungry! To the kitchen, I think.'

Ava liked the sound of that so headed after him, or at least, tried to, but the next thing she knew, she was flat on her face on the floor, shaking.

'Shit,' said Kush, by her side in a heartbeat, pulling the stopper from his vial of Herivale.

It soothed her symptoms almost as soon as it brushed her lips, but when she looked up, she found Billy standing over them, hands on his hips. 'Why's her hair wet?' he asked, his eyes narrowed.

'We went for a swim,' said Ava. 'Help me up.'

Kush took her hand, but Billy didn't drop it. 'Where?' he demanded.

'In Xonia,' said Kush.

'In the healing water?' Billy asked incredulously.

'It was lovely,' said Ava, feeling the need to defend Kush against Billy's disdainful glare.

'It was *lovely*?' Billy asked with a flounce. 'Almost dying was *lovely*, was it?'

'What are you saying,' said Kush, scowling hard as he slid an arm around Ava's waist.

Billy stuck his head forward, looking like an angry bird. 'The magic of healing waters can be fatal to those with stone sickness, you absolute moron.'

'They ... can?' said Ava, feeling suddenly sick.

Billy folded his arms tightly across his chest. 'The Atlas Stones confuse us to start, so our bodies don't know where in the worlds we are. Stone sickness is us adjusting to that shift, learning to deal with it. The pools interfere with the natural process.' He rounded on Kush. 'And she could have died. At the very least, it will take her longer for her to become immune to the stone's effects. What *do* they teach in school these days?'

Billy spun and stomped to the kitchen, where he began pulling out all the available food. 'Yes, good,' he muttered, arranging the meats and cheeses and vegetables in a line on the countertop. 'I can work with this.'

The kitchen's worn wooden cupboards gave the space a cozy feel, as did the big, scarred square table behind the island and the painted window with twelve small panes that overlooked the garden. Hanging from the ceiling were a series of little cages, each with a pile of four or five stones inside, and Ava gasped as Billy muttered words she couldn't hear, and they illuminated.

'Ha!' said Billy. 'Your parents had some good ideas, I'll give them that much.' He selected a series of jars from a dresser behind the table—dried herbs and spices, fruits and nuts—then planted himself behind a wooden board and began to chop.

Ava and Kush slid onto the wooden bar stools on the other side of the granite-topped island, and Billy poured them all a generous measure of *Pleasantly Pickled*. Ava took a large gulp and found it lived up to its name—cool and tingly and a little bit tart. She felt herself relax after just one swallow.

Billy eyed her warily, his knife suspended in midair. 'Pace yourself, my dear. You don't strike me as a practiced drinker.'

Ava took another long sip, and Billy rolled his eyes, muttering, 'Don't blame me when it all goes south.'

'Don't be dramatic,' Ava shot back. 'I grew up in a tavern, remember?'

Billy leaned over the counter, placing his pointer finger tip-down on the chopping board. 'This stuff is not the same as that watery beer and paint-stripper you're used to. This stuff has the Atlas seal on the bottle, and that means it was brewed according to the recipes perfected by *my* family, infused with a little magic, and not to be trifled with.'

Ava stared him down for a moment, her features carefully blank, then she took another sip. 'So, tell me, how did my parents go from falling in love to dead?'

Billy's eyes sharpened, and the atmosphere turned heavy. 'I never said they were in love. Your father, certainly, but your mother, well, the jury's still out on that one.'

Ava didn't know what to say to that, so she waited for him to continue, while Kush put his hand on her leg under the lip of the island. She put her hand on top, something about the casual intimacy so distracting, she almost didn't notice when Billy started talking.

'Well, anyway,'—Billy waved the knife around—'they spent *all* their time together, your parents, and given Rupert was still at the top of the social tree, the rest of us had no choice but to accept Polly, despite her lowly birth. And she was fine, I suppose, if a little uncouth.' He huffed out a breath and put his hand on his hip. 'But she and Novak always had a special relationship. Perhaps something to do with them both being outsiders, I don't know ...'

Billy started chopping again, his knife skills impressive enough to put every chef Ava had seen work at the Cleve Arms to shame. 'Then this one day, Var and Novak were making fun of Novak's poor relations in Santala, and Polly overheard. She said she wanted to meet them, so Novak agreed, desperate to impress her, and as soon as Rupert discovered your mother's wish, well, off we all went at her command. Novak soon realized he'd made a mistake, that reminding everyone of his grubby roots wasn't wise after how hard his family had worked to claw their way into the inner circle, so he tried to distance himself from B's lot by being even more vile about them.'

He looked up, brandishing the knife. 'The beginning of the end.' His expression turned sinister for a beat before he went back to chopping onions. 'But of course, we weren't to know that at the time.'

Kush refilled their glasses, and Ava smiled appreciatively, glad of the gentle fuzz settling over her mind.

'So, we turned up at B's tavern—'

'Wait,' Ava blurted. 'The Cleve?'

Billy waved an impatient hand. 'Well yes, of course.' He inhaled sharply. 'As I said, beginning of the end.'

Ava gave an almost imperceptible nod as the axis of her world shifted, then took another sip of her drink. Her parents had visited the tavern before she was born. Which table had they sat at?

'Var came too—wanted to see what all the fuss was about—and seeing as he'd recently been made Ambassador of Santala, we didn't have much choice but to let him tag along. He invited a few others, and we sat in that tap room like we were Gods—before we were Gods, that is. The others were foul to B and her parents, laughing, joking, calling them scum. Var even called B over at one point and made her join us just to poke fun.'

'While you did, what?' Kush said accusingly. 'You make it sound like you were nothing but a bystander.'

Billy started chopping again, this time more slowly. 'I was ... different back then, before ...' He put down the knife, huffed a long exhale, and rested his hands on the counter. 'Turns out when a part of your soul is removed from your body, it alters you. I wasn't always like this. Var wasn't quite so selfish, Rupert wasn't quite so aloof, B wasn't quite so heartless, and Polly wasn't quite so intense. It affected us all differently.'

'What about you?' said Ava. 'What weren't you quite so?'

Billy raised an eyebrow. 'I wasn't anything. I was bland. Barely even there.'

'And you want to be like that again?' said Kush, folding his arms across his chest.

Billy closed his eyes as though imagining it. 'In a heartbeat,' he said with a hopeful smile.

'Why?' asked Ava. Billy was vibrant and full. Magnetic. A little erratic, yes, and wildly eccentric, but interesting. He was *someone*. She dreamed of being even half as much of someone as he was.

Billy tipped his head. 'Because the person I used to be is who I really am.' A pregnant pause pressed down on the room. 'Anyway,' he said, snapping out of it and downing his drink, 'we are where we are.'

He slid the onions into a skillet and clattered it onto the hot stove, then turned his attention to the carrots. 'So,' he said, as though the conversation hadn't taken a deep turn, 'there we all were, in the Cleve Arms, and your mother liked it not at all how we treated B. Polly was an outsider herself, still didn't really fit, and she made a show of befriending B, asking her questions about her life, her dreams, her opinions. She near ignored the rest of us.'

Kush leaned forward. 'How did Rupert take that?'

'Oh, he was fine,' said Billy. 'So laid back he was horizontal, that one, although Novak wasn't happy.'

'Why?' asked Ava.

'Because from that day forth, your mother took B under her wing. Invited her for lunches and on shopping trips and to parties. They were thick as thieves, and Polly made Novak tag along, too. I don't know if he was jealous of the time Polly and B spent together, the connection they had, or hated the constant reminder of his family's humble roots, but he frequently told the rest of us that he didn't think it was right, their friendship. And *my sweet Atlas*, we should have listened, but it seemed harmless enough at the time.

'Eventually, B took over the tavern and couldn't get away as much, so your parents moved to Santala—they were married by then—built this house, and spent most of their time here. Your mother had become the most revered of physics, and your father still doted on her, devoid of meaningful skill as he was.

'But with great power comes great potential to fuck everything up,'—Billy stirred the frying onions, then waved the wooden spoon in the air—'and just because you *can* do something, doesn't mean you *should*.'

'You mean turning people into Gods?' said Kush.

'Yes.' Billy jabbed the spoon in Kush's direction. 'Exactly. Now you're getting it.' He turned back to the stove. 'And if doing whatever thing involves using your friends as guinea pigs, then definitely steer clear.'

Ava accepted her third drink refill and tipped her head against Kush's shoulder. It was so strange to think of the past in these terms, not at all what she'd imagined.

'So, long story short, your parents gave me and B eternal life—or something close to it—then did it to themselves when they found it worked. But word got out, some of the other Cloud-dwellers weren't happy, and they made your parents do it to them, too. Your parents added the soul-napping kicker to keep control, things got ugly, and here we all are in a colossal fucking mess.'

'But not everyone in the Clouds became Gods,' said Kush.

'Not everyone wanted to, and all the oldies thought it was a hoax. Most of them had handed over control to their kids by then—had all but checked out. They lived a luxurious life in the Clouds and let the rest of us deal with the tree and the portals and the other worlds and our family responsibilities. They were content hosting parties and playing cards and lying about in echo chambers. By the time they realized the eternal life thing was true, it was too late—Polly and Rupert were dead—and no one else knew how to do it. But now most of the oldies have popped their clogs, too, so ...'

Ava giggled, finding something about the flippant way he said the last bit coupled with his eccentric shoulder shrug hilariously funny.

'Ummmmm, o-kay.' said Billy. He drizzled oil over a tray of sliced carrots, shoved it in the oven along with some whole potatoes, then began tearing up a lettuce.

'Sorry,' said Ava. 'I just ... I think it's the *Pleasantly Pickled.*'

Billy raised his eyebrows. 'Thought you could handle it, having grown up in a tavern and all.'

Ava barked a laugh. 'B tracked every last drop, even the beer. If I'd even thought about sampling the goods ...' She drew a finger across her throat and widened her eyes.

Billy narrowed his gaze, a triumphant gleam in his eyes. 'But you said ...'

Ava shrugged, feeling suddenly frivolous. 'I lied because you were being annoying.' She kicked off the sturdy shoes she'd fished out of the hall cupboard before going to Xonia, the feeling liberating because she wasn't used to the freedom of being able to wander around barefoot on plush carpet and smooth tile. In the tavern, she'd have ended up with a nail through her toe.

'Urgh, I *really* need to get new clothes,' she said, pulling at the fabric of the tattered monstrosity B had given her. 'In fact, I'm going to burn it.' Suddenly the dress itched, irritating her skin. She had to get it off.

'Um, Ava,' said Kush, as she scratched at her laces, 'what are you doing?' She still had the presence of mind to notice his words were a tiny bit slurred, and that made her beam at him.

She put her hands on his shoulders. 'You're drunk too!' she said, then pecked him on the lips.

'No,' he said, shaking his head, then re-filling both of their glasses as though that was somehow proof of his sobriety.

'Yes!' she insisted, returning her attention to her laces.

'Come with me,' said Billy, setting down his knife, pulling the onions off the heat, and racing out of the kitchen.

'Where's he going?' said Ava, jumping down from her stool and rushing after him towards the stairs.

Kush passed her just before the first step, laughing like a kid. 'Hey!' she shouted, trying to keep up, but he was too fast, her malnourished thighs no match for his impressively muscled ones, although her view of him was so good, she immediately forgot all about the race. Still, she was breathing hard when she joined Kush on the threshold to her parents' room, and she paused there while Kush moved inside, some part of her not wanting to invade what she'd begun to think of as a shrine.

'You're almost the same size as your mother, you know,' called Billy, disappearing into the walk-in closet. 'You're scrawny, but with a few solid meals, you'll fill out, and she had big bazookas, just like you, and surprisingly big feet ... Her clothes should fit you just fine, and her shoes, give or take.'

Billy reappeared with an outrageous, full-length yellow dress, nothing like the mustard of B's horror show, but bright like the sun and covered with zigzag patterns that seemed to be all the colors of the rainbow. 'Here,' he said. 'This one might actually be comfortable, too.'

'Oh, wow,' said Ava, the dress drawing her into the room as though she were a moth lured towards a very yellow flame. She'd never seen anything like it, even in the upmarket areas of Santala, and she wanted to know what the silky, slinky fabric would feel like against her skin.

She took it from Billy and rubbed it against her face. It was cool and soft and smelled vaguely of flowers.

'Change,' Billy snapped impatiently, and although she scowled at him, she did what he said, making the two men turn their backs as she pulled off her old dress and dropped it to the floor.

She slipped the new one over her head and sighed as it slid across her skin, telling the others they could turn back around as she tied the belt at her waist.

She was met with a stunned silence that made her wonder if she looked ridiculous, and then Billy clapped his hands. 'Yep! I was right. Just like your mother. It's disgusting ... I mean, who can pull off yellow?' He handed her a pair of soft fabric slippers, which were like pillows under her feet, so comfortable she almost cried.

'Now,' said Billy. 'Food.'

Billy was gone in a flash, but Kush snagged Ava's hand before she could follow him. 'You're beautiful,' he said, her heart fluttering at his closeness, then racing as he stepped closer still, Ava having to tip her head back to meet his dark, smoldering gaze. 'Mesmerizing.'

Her lips parted and her chest pulled tight, and then he captured her mouth with his and a breathy moan escaped her.

It seemed to snap some leash within him, and he pressed more forcefully against her, sliding his thigh between her legs, a rich, guttural sound coming from somewhere deep in his chest.

'Kush,' she breathed, as he moved his lips to her neck. She dug her hands into his thick hair and pressed herself against him, the fabric of the dress sliding sensually across her skin.

'Get down here, now!' said Billy's voice from downstairs, somehow loud in their ears. They jumped guiltily apart. 'When someone slaves over a hot stove for you, the least you can do is turn up when the food's ready.'

Ava giggled as Kush looked almost bashfully down at his feet, then he entwined their fingers and pulled her towards the stairs. Billy acting like an overbearing father was comforting in a strange way, the three of them like a dysfunctional family, and the thought had tears pooling in her eyes. Kush paused as they reached the entrance to the kitchen, looked down at Ava for a beat, then wrapped his arm around her shoulder and dropped a kiss on her temple.

'Voila!' Billy said with a flourish, somehow having laid the table, lit candles, produced three plates of seared beef, potatoes, carrots with yogurt, and salad, and selected a bottle of something new to drink in the short time they'd been alone upstairs. The bottle made a deep popping sound when he flipped the lid.

'Found this hidden behind the cool box,' said Billy, pouring them each a glass. 'Drink creation is my thing—my family's—and it would seem your dastardly parents even thought they could do that better than the experts, the swine.' Billy took a sip of the lightly colored, gently sparkling mixture, then screwed up his face. 'Fine, it's good, but it could be a touch tarter, don't you think?'

Ava sipped the drink, and the bubbles spread out across her tongue, popping and filling her mouth with crisp citric notes. 'Tastes pretty good to me.'

'Well, you would say that,' said Billy, sinking daintily onto a seat, taking the place at the head of the table.

Ava and Kush sat on either side of Billy, and Ava took a moment to pinch herself. How was this her life now? Only a couple of days ago she'd been a tavern girl, serving others and grateful for scraps. Now look at her, clad in silk, eating steak, and sitting at a table with a God and a demi-God … and the demi-God loved her.

'Wow,' said Ava, around her first bite. 'Billy, this tastes incredible!'

Billy saluted her with his glass, a gesture that said both, *I will take your praise and am pleased with it*, and, *naturally, because I'm a genius*. Ava giggled, high on life and alcohol and the thrill of varied company. She imagined her parents at this table with their friends, eating and drinking and laughing.

'Were they happy?' asked Ava. 'My parents?'

Billy looked down at his plate, loading his fork. 'In their own way, I suppose.'

'Then why did they do it? Why split their souls from their bodies? Why risk it, especially after they saw how it changed you and B?'

Billy shrugged as he swallowed, then picked up his glass. 'Because they could. Because they were power hungry and ambitious and didn't want us to have something they didn't. Because your mother especially was driven by an insatiable need to push the boundaries of knowledge and experience, and she didn't care if she had to bend the rules to do it. Her grandmother bent the rules to get them into the Clouds, and Polly was no different. Cut from the very same cloth, and desperate to have something that set her apart from the others.'

Kush's features turned black, his eyes hooking like claws into Billy. 'But how did the others find out?' he asked, as though he already knew the answer.

Billy froze, giving Kush a pursed look. 'B told them,' he said eventually. 'She had a crush on Rupert—always had—but Rupert only had eyes for Polly, no matter how long B hung around. B hated how Polly treated Rupert, and how Polly treated Novak, too.'

'What do you mean?' said Ava, a rushing sounding in her ears, her voice shrill. 'How did my mother treat them?' Ava so wanted to think of her parents as kind, friendly people, but here was yet more evidence to indicate her mother was a villain, not a hero. And now it sounded like they didn't even treat each other well.

'Oh, she was careless with them,' said Billy, swirling the liquid in his glass, then throwing himself back in his chair, his arms aloft. 'She was divine even before we became Gods, and, well, Novak loved her. She broke his heart more than once, and B—who, as your mother's very best friend, had a ringside seat to every twist and turn—couldn't stand it.'

'So she told everyone about the soul-splitting?' said Ava, her voice small.

'Yep,' said Billy, popping the p. 'It was a *mess*. B nearly got herself killed, Novak gave up his position in the Clouds to save her, the others demanded they be made Gods, too—or they swore to devote their lives to taking down your parents—Novak hated B for betraying Polly, Polly made B's life a living hell—even though B hunkered down in the tavern and didn't dare show her face to anyone—while Var and the others ended up as Gods.' Billy threw up his hands. 'As I said, a *mess*.'

'You forgot about the part where Polly and Rupert took the others' souls hostage,' said Kush.

'Well, yes, but they only found out about that later, when Var tried to kill Rupert and Polly ... That was a whole other thing.'

'Oh,' said Ava, glad, in a perverse way, to be reminded that her parents weren't the only ones with dubious morals.

'Pudding,' said Billy, getting noisily to his feet.

He bustled about, then set before them a fresh fruit salad and some kind of cream liquor. '*Light and Stormy*,' Billy announced, pouring a liberal quantity over his fruit.

Ava practically inhaled her own bowl, then sat back, her stomach set to burst. 'That was truly divine,' she said, groaning a little in discomfort. 'I suppose I'll have to find a job now, if I want to keep myself in such luxuries.'

Billy gave her an incredulous look, then turned his head to Kush, who'd paused with his spoon midway to his mouth. Billy's eyes flicked back to Ava. 'You're serious, aren't you?' he said accusingly, before rounding on Kush. 'You haven't told her, you monstrous toad.'

Kush set his spoon back in his bowl. 'When I got here, I was more concerned with saving her life than picking over the details of her fortune.'

Ava's stomach squeezed so hard she thought it might eject the food. 'My ... what?'

Billy rolled his eyes. 'I mean, obviously, as well as this place, which is, frankly, priceless, everything your parents owned is now yours. Gold, books, *magical objects* ...' He looked at her expectantly, as though she should understand some deeper meaning from his words. 'Assuming *he* hasn't already found it and squirreled it away,' Billy said, tipping his head at Kush.

Ava frowned. 'Found what?'

Kush took a deep inhale, as though this wasn't how he'd wanted to have this conversation. 'He's talking about your family's Atlas Stone.'

She pushed her bowl aside. 'But—'

'And you're a demi-God, don't forget,' Billy continued, as though that was a small detail, practically frivolous. 'More than that, you're a Blackwood. You could claim an entire world if you wanted, perhaps even two or three.'

Ava pushed back her chair and folded forward, something about that last part screwing a vice around her lungs. She was a demi-God. She had a fortune. She could *claim multiple worlds*. She'd been delighted with a dress and a roof and shoes that didn't half cripple her. It was too much, it was ... She couldn't get enough air, and the edges of her vision went black and grainy as she tried to force her lungs to function, but it was just ... It was ...

And then Billy put his hand on hers, and suddenly she was fine. Detached, but perfectly fine. Everything would be fine. Until it somehow wasn't, and everything went black.

Chapter Twenty

Sophie

Six Weeks After Dromeda Started Spinning

Hale had ridden with Sophie to leave an offering for the Goddess. They'd walked right up to Alter Gate, Hale carrying the basket of flowers and sweet things, refusing to hand it over until they were mere meters from the circular gate. Sophie had placed it atop the large pile of offerings then backed away, but it had made her feel more hopeless, not less.

'The flowers are gone,' Sophie had said to Hale, looking up at the bare roots above them. 'They were so pretty for Maria's wedding.'

Hale had done little more than grunt, cold, businesslike, and aloof. She'd hoped to prompt a discussion about their own nuptials, but instead, he'd spun on his heel and strode back along the bridge.

That had been weeks ago. Since then, she'd had only herself for company, Hale apparently avoiding her at all costs. She'd even stopped taking meals in the dining room because she'd grown so tired of eating alone, unable to stand the pitying looks from the maids and guards. She'd retreated to the library, spending most of her time alone there instead.

Sophie poured over maps of Alter Blade for the third day in a row, determined to commit to memory every detail of her new land. If she was truly to wed Hale, she would become the First Lady of Alter, and she was determined to do a good job, even if her mission was to ultimately rob them of their leader.

She pushed away from the desk, the thought making her want to gag. It had seemed like a game when her mother had first briefed her back in Laurow. Marry the first son, get with child, kill the first son, live happily ever after. The idea had been acceptable when it had been John on the receiving end, but the thought of injuring Hale, of killing him ... It made her chest ache just thinking about it.

Which left her where exactly? She could be a traitor to Laurow or a traitor to her unrequited feelings. She could run away, she supposed, but where would she go? She had no family anywhere but Laurow, no friends, and no means of supporting herself. Not to mention, she didn't like the idea of leaving Hale. She'd thought they'd been getting somewhere, that something had been growing between them, or at least that he didn't loathe her quite so much as before. And then her mother had forced his hand, he'd agreed to marry her, and he'd promptly disappeared. Is this what her marriage would be like? A life alone? Assuming Hale didn't delay so much that they never even got as far as marriage ...

Sophie put away the maps with a sigh and moved farther into the library, running her hand over the ancient tomes, looking for something good to read. Perhaps a forbidden romance, or a fairy tale that spoke of different lands, or a fable about how the Goddess had created Celestl from nothing but thin air. But she couldn't find any such books. She couldn't find any novels at all.

What a strange land this was. But then, despite Danit's many flaws, the people of Alter seemed happy and prosperous, even if there was nothing salacious to read. Everyone she'd come across had enough, the soldiers brawled only occasionally, and the first family seemed assured of their safe- ty—they often moved around without accompanying guards and didn't even have food tasters. It was not the same in Laurow, where the first family had learned to sleep with one eye open. What did that say about the way her parents ruled?

Her parents, who cared only for themselves, and who would assume control of Alter if Sophie killed Hale. That hadn't bothered her before, but now the idea of her parents leading this land seemed unfair to its people, even if it was a staid and frigid sort of place with a leader hiding something so bad he'd agreed to marry against his will rather than risk its reveal ... *Urgh, what a mess.*

Sophie leaned against the wooden end panel of a stack, closing her eyes as she let her mind noodle on all her many problems, hoping a solution would simply pop into her mind. A cracking noise came from the entrance, followed by the whoosh of a swinging door, then more than one set of footsteps. Sophie froze.

'Anyone here?' called Hale's rich tenor, and Sophie froze as someone walked the entire width of the place and back again. 'It's empty.'

More footsteps walked back and forth, and then a second man said in a low voice that Sophie had to strain to hear, 'Then get on with it and tell me what you need to say.'

'You first.'

Sophie heard a huff. 'I plan to inspect the Inner Circle again tomorrow,' the second man said quickly, his voice slightly louder than before.

'I'll come with you,' replied Hale's assured tone. 'I'm keen to see Dromeda up close myself.'

'It's dangerous. Several have already ventured too near and have paid the price, and, of course, the Inner Circle could fill with water at any time.'

'Touched as I am that you're concerned for my safety, Nicoli, you won't change my mind.'

Sophie sucked in a breath. *Nicoli?* The man who had killed Hale's uncle and waged war on the Blades ... Did this mean he and Hale *had* plotted Danit's death together?

'Well, I can hardly stop you, Hale. If you have no better way to spend your time than watching me work, then by all means, come and hold my bag.'

'Perhaps I'll find something you've overlooked.'

'Unlikely.'

'Ha!' Hale's laughter betrayed his absolute confidence in his own abilities. 'This is not my first adventure, old friend.'

'Any news from your sister?'

The conversation came to an abrupt halt, and a heavy silence descended for a beat. Hale sucked in a long breath. 'A messenger arrived this morning, but I'm afraid it's not good news. Cane has taken Maria prisoner, and he has control of Oshe's water.'

'How the ...'

'I don't know, especially because it seems as though Elex is wandering free. He's requested you go to Oshala and help him take back control.'

Nicoli scoffed.

'Oh, save it. We both know you'll go. Even if Cane didn't have my sister, the challenge is too good to pass up. Just think of the glory ...'

'I'll help them,' Nicoli snapped, 'but they'll have to wait. There are things I must do here first.'

'Hmm,' said Hale, the sound strained. 'Like check on your water stores?'

Something thick and acrid filled the air, and Sophie wished she could see their faces. *What water stores?* The Claws didn't have any, that was the whole reason for their near poverty.

'Did Danit tell you?' Nicoli asked so quietly Sophie almost missed it.

'No. Maria found the contract.'

'She knows?'

'And Elex.'

This time the silence was deafening.

'And it gets worse, I'm afraid,' said Hale, 'because although I'm willing to uphold the agreement, and I trust Elex and Maria to take the secret to their graves, Linella broke into my office and found the contract.'

'What the fuck? You left it somewhere it could be discovered?'

'I left my office for hardly any time at all, but—'

'*Fuck.*' Footsteps sounded, followed by a growl of frustration. 'Will it be a problem?'

'For whom?' Hale said dryly. 'I've agreed to marry the daughter, so they'll keep their mouths shut at least until that's done, but I doubt we can rely on them forever.'

'They're snakes.'

'Oh, don't worry, I know.'

Sophie's face flushed with shame and anger. She didn't agree with all of her family's choices, but they were still her family, the only one she had and all she'd ever known.

'Sophie really did a number on John,' said Hale.

'He's doing well … Enjoying his freedom. He's recovering.'

'I'm glad to hear that. Thank you for looking after him. He's an insufferable toad, but …'

'He had a lucky escape.' Nicoli chuckled. 'I'm not sure you'll be able to boast the same when all is said and done.'

Hale sighed. 'I'm resigned to my fate, to my *duty*.'

Nicoli snickered. 'Pray to the Goddess, old friend, because only the Toll Bells can save you now …'

'You think they'll ring?' Hale asked almost hopefully.

'Ha! No. But you can wish.'

Sophie clenched her teeth. How dare they talk about her that way. *Laughing* at the idea of her life being sacrificed to the Goddess.

'I have to go,' Nicoli continued. 'I'll see you at the Inner Circle tomorrow, immediately after the Sunrise Fall.'

'I'll be there.'

Footsteps followed, and then the sounds of the door opening and closing. Sophie waited for a handful of long moments to make sure they were really gone, then she let out a furious shriek and stomped towards the exit, blood rushing in her ears, guts twisting, tears stinging her eyes.

But when she emerged from the stacks, she found Hale leaning back against the door, arms folded across his chest, watching her with an amused expression on his face.

Fuck.

'Like mother like daughter once again,' he said, pushing off the door.

Sophie scowled hard. 'Says the man conspiring with the traitor who killed his uncle.'

Hale cocked an eyebrow in a way that made Sophie's lip curl.

'And you're working with the Claws,' she continued. 'You're helping them steal your peoples' water!'

'What if I am?'

Sophie shook her head in disbelief. 'You're a traitor to the Blades!' And then she remembered what her mother had told her, that Laurow was selling food to the Claws. Was this the same? Did every Blade have their own deal with Nicoli?

He stepped closer. 'And what will you do about it? Risk our betrothal?'

She froze, hating the feeling of powerlessness that made tears threaten in earnest.

He shook his head conceitedly. '*Exactly.*'

Sophie made for the door but paused as she passed him, something about being in motion making her remember that she also knew how to land body blows. She turned her head towards him. 'You act as though you're somehow superior, but you constantly blunder. You interrupted my wedding to John, you left that contract on your desk for my mother to find, and today, you didn't properly check the library to see if anyone was here. But your head is so far up your own arse—oof.'

Hale shoved her back against the door, then crowded her, his eyes ablaze, and Sophie had to bite her lip to keep it from wobbling, the feeling of powerlessness flooding back. She moved her hands to his chest and tried to push him away, but he wouldn't budge—yet another reminder of how she was at his mercy. 'Move, Hale. We are not married yet.'

He chuckled, and she saw red, hammering her fists on his chest so hard she managed to force him back a pace. But then he caught her hands and held them to his chest, stopping her assault with a mirthful gleam in his eyes.

'I might be a joke to you,' she hissed, 'and you might hate my family, but I *will* have your respect, Hale Alter.'

He tilted his head. 'Or what?'

Her eyes flew wide with fury. 'Or *I* will refuse to marry *you*. Now fucking let me go!' Sophie yanked her hands free and stared him down for a few frantic heartbeats, then she threw open the library door and left.

CHAPTER TWENTY-ONE
AVA

KUSH'S VOICE PULLED AVA back to wakefulness even though her mind resisted it. She took stock as she lay there, eyes closed, and was relieved to find her body seemed to be in good working order—if a little sluggish feeling.

'What did you do to her?' accused Kush, drawing Ava's attention back to the voices. She kept her eyes shut, interested to hear what they would say, given she was quite comfortable, lying on something soft and velvety.

'Nothing much,' said Billy. 'Just calmed her, but between the Atlas Stone travel and the little healing pool trick you pulled it had a more profound effect than expected. A tad too much juice, that's all. I'm out of practice. She'll be fine.'

'You knocked her out!'

'Just a little rest. Good for the soul.'

'Why are you even here, Billy? What do you want from her?'

'I think we both know the real question is what *you* want from her, or more accurately, what Var wants, because if I know him—and I do—he wants *everything*.'

'I love her,' Kush hissed.

Billy scoffed. 'You're young. You don't know what love is. It will surely pass, and when it does, where does that leave Ava? At the mercy of Var, that's where.'

Ava's eyes flew wide, but before she could turn her attention to the bickering men, her vision snagged on the art on the ceiling: an illustration of a tree with clouds at the top and roots shooting out into a series of circles at the bottom, each with a different symbol inside. Words were scrawled underneath that she and Kush hadn't been able to decipher when they'd searched this room—the library—the day before.

'Ava!' said Kush, crouching at her side. Still, she looked at the ceiling, something about it not letting her go.

'The first map of the Atlas Tree,' said Billy, following her gaze upwards. 'That's an heirloom. It depicts the connections to other worlds before Gods and unnatural portals. Your parents moved it here and built it into the ceiling.'

'How ... decadent,' said Ava, trying to work out how such a thing could be moved. It was so big, and presumably fragile.

Kush took her hand. 'How are you feeling?'

'Fine,' she lied, because Billy's words were playing on a loop in her mind. *It will surely pass.* It couldn't pass, could it? He loved her and she ... It—

'Ava?' Kush said gently.

'The map shows the Federation?' said Ava, shoving her fears deep down inside and letting Kush help her sit.

'No,' said Billy, 'that came later. It shows the worlds that were already attached to the tree when your ancestor discovered it, that the tree had already linked to of its own volition. The *natural* portals.' Billy threw an accusing look at Kush as he spoke.

'Hey, don't blame me. It was you and your friends who fucked everything up,' Kush snapped.

'You don't know what you're talking about, and you're only here for one thing.'

'What?' breathed Ava.

'The Atlas Stone,' Billy said darkly.

'That's not true,' snapped Kush. He stood, towering over Billy. 'And Ava still has mine.'

Ava nodded. 'He hasn't even asked for it back.'

Billy folded his arms over his chest and narrowed his eyes. 'But you looked for the Blackwood stone, didn't you.'

Kush's features scrunched in distaste. 'No.'

'You searched the house though, right?' Billy asked Ava, craning his head so he could see her around Kush's large frame.

She shrugged. 'Yes.'

'Every nook and cranny?'

'I don't know … Everywhere we could find.' Her head began to pound. 'Why?'

'Because that's what Var really wants. Aside from his soul back, and to be grand master of the whole fucking web, he desperately wants your parents' stone.'

'Why?' said Ava, at the same time as Kush said, 'No, he doesn't. He doesn't want any of that.'

Billy rolled his eyes. 'Tell yourself whatever you need to, dearie.'

'He doesn't! He wants what's best for the Federation, for the whole web.'

Billy blew out a skeptical breath, then moved back and perched on the varnished top of the oversized wooden desk. 'You're a goner, truly. Drunk the Mezz juice. Hook, line, and sinker.' He stamped his foot on the wooden floor, the move surprising enough and the noise deafening enough to make Ava jump. 'Ah ha!' He dropped to a crouch and pulled up a section of floorboard, extracting a pocket watch from the void below and setting it on the desk. 'Didn't find this one, did you?'

Kush and Ava shared a bemused look. 'How did you know that was there?' asked Ava.

'Rookies,' said Billy, shaking his head, and then off he took, flying from the room with a cackling laugh.

'Billy!' But he was gone, rushing up the stairs, Ava and Kush left with little choice but to follow, although Ava had to move more slowly, her legs like those of a baby horse finding its feet for the first time.

They caught up to Billy in Ava's parents' room, where he was frantically slapping a section of wall beside the bed.

'Come on,' he said. 'Come on, my lovely little … Oh, you … Ouch!' He yanked his hand away, shaking it as though trying to rid himself of a crab holding on by its claw.

'What was that?' said Ava, her head starting to pound.

'Oh, just the house getting cross with me,' he said as though that was a perfectly customary thing to say.

'Does everyone in the Clouds have houses like this one?' Ava asked slowly.

'Ha! Heavens no.'

It had been the house, then. All of it. The shaking, the disappearing stain from Billy's spilt drink, the gates opening to let Kush in, and the fact the place was spotless, even though it had been empty for years. The house ...

'This is the only one like it,' said Billy. 'Obviously. Your parents were such showoffs—no offense—but the house also gives off a small trace of magic every time it acts, which means we can find *all* its secrets. There's something in there the house doesn't want me to see.' He tipped his head towards the section of wall he'd been slapping. 'One for you to peek at later.' He waggled his eyebrows, and then off he went again, but Ava had to put her hand on the wall to steady herself, her head throbbing.

'Ava?' said Kush, grabbing her arm.

She pushed him away. 'Follow him. I need to lie down for a while. I'm a little ... I think the alcohol ... I'm not used to ...' Kush hesitated. 'Go! Before he finds something useful and hides it from us.'

He nodded, her words stoking urgency in him. 'I'll be back as soon as I can.'

Ava leaned fully against the wall, closing her eyes and taking deep breaths as she listened to them rampaging around the house, moving through every upstairs room, and then racing downstairs to her parents' study. By that time, Ava had gathered enough strength to edge towards her own room, although sheer exhaustion gripped her limbs, pulling them down.

She didn't know if it was the alcohol, stone sickness, whatever Billy had done to her, or a combination of all three, but she was weary to her bones, the thought of reaching her bed—of sleep—the only thing she cared about. *Her* bed. *Her* house. How strange that was.

She made it to her room, where a dusky pink nightdress waited on her bed, presumably courtesy of the house, too. 'Thank you,' she whispered, and was sure she felt an answering vibration in her toes. Or maybe that was just the exhaustion ...

Ava didn't bother with the nightgown. She just crawled under the covers and went out like a light.

Chapter Twenty-Two

Maria

Six Weeks After Dromeda Started Spinning

'No, Mina,' said Opal, her tone more forceful than Maria had come to expect, so Maria paused at the entrance to the sitting room Cane had set aside for Opal and Erica's use. 'Erica insisted on white.'

'But, ma'am,' said Mina, cowering a little, holding a skimpy black dress in her hand, 'your husband—'

'I will not repeat myself for a third time!' snapped Opal. 'Erica has a surprise planned, and I will not ruin it.'

Mina bowed her head, eyes on her feet. 'Yes, ma'am. Of course.'

'But only Erica and me. Put Maria in whatever Cane wants.'

'Ma'am.'

Maria stepped through the open door. 'Morning,' she chirped brightly.

'Urgh.' Opal waved an irritated hand as she barreled out of the room.

Maria cast her eyes around to make sure she and Mina were alone. 'Everything okay?' she asked the short, plump maid, who stood in a corner collecting herself, her head still bowed. Maria had never seen Opal behave that way. 'What happened?'

'Morning, ma'am,' Mina murmured, then she bobbed a curtsey and made for the exit.

Maria caught the maid's arm as she passed and slipped a vial of oil into her hand. 'Do you know a tall woman with dark ringlets who visited the quarter the night of the attack?' she whispered.

Mina wrenched her arm free but pocketed the oil. She met Maria's gaze with a terrified, wide-eyed look. 'I have much to do. I must be getting to the seamstress in the market, seeing as Erica and Opal require different dresses for the party.'

Maria worried she'd pushed Mina too far as she watched her leave. But ... the seamstress in the market ... It was oddly specific, and if Erica and Opal had their own plan for their dresses, wouldn't they have made arrangements already? Maria spun on her heel and headed after the maid. Perhaps Mina meant Maria should meet her there or perhaps she didn't, but Maria had little to lose either way. And she was due a trip to the market as she hadn't been in a few days.

Maria's guard hurried after her along the perimeter wall. It killed Maria to take such an indirect route, to waste valuable time, but it would arouse suspicion if she deviated. She stepped out, however, her pace brisk, hoping against hope that Mina would still be there when she arrived.

When she finally reached the market square, Maria forced herself to browse casually, flitting from one stand to another as though she had no specific target in mind, but after a few minutes, a woman she'd only spoken to once greeted her warmly.

'S'pose you've come to see the beautiful baby boy?' said the short, skinny woman with limp blond hair whose name Maria didn't know.

Maria froze, her mind whirring.

The woman linked arms with Maria, and Maria went willingly as the woman tugged her towards one of the buildings at the edge of the square. 'Still in the birthing room behind the seamstress. Hasn't gone home yet. I was just there. I'll show you the way.'

'Wonderful!' said Maria, clasping her hands, mainly at the mention of the seamstress, but she made it only two paces before her guard stepped into her path.

'No,' he said, with a vehement shake of his head. 'Men are not permitted in the birthing rooms.'

'Fathers are,' the woman countered.

'*I* am not permitted in the birthing rooms,' he clarified.

'So?' said Maria. 'You can wait outside.'

'Where you go, I go.'

Maria smiled warmly. 'You'll be a few paces away the whole time, and a newborn baby is hardly a threat to my safety! What are you worried about?'

'And there's only one way in,' the woman added, leaning towards the guard, 'in case you think she might make a run for it. Mind, she'd have to find a place to hide inside the quarter, seeing as the gate's locked and guarded, and I shan't think many'd be stupid enough to hide her.'

The guard hesitated, so Maria pressed their advantage. 'I'll be five minutes,' she said, coaxing her features into the most placid, reassuring arrangement she could manage. Then she sidestepped and let the woman guide her towards the building, beaming at her guard as she passed him, trying to seem overjoyed by the idea of meeting a new baby.

Maria held her breath as they neared the building, convinced the guard would come to his senses and stop her. She could almost feel his hand closing around her arm. But the hold never came, and then she was inside, casting her eyes around a small, dingy room that smelled of chamomile with an open fire, a single bed, and three women crouched in a circle on the flagstone floor.

Maria's escort left, heading deeper into the building, and Maria looked over the women, feeling a pang of apprehension as she identified Mina. Had Maria misjudged her? Was she in danger? Was Mina loyal to Cane after all? But the second woman was nursing a tiny baby, her hair sweaty, features puffy, blood-soaked rags at her feet.

'Congratulations,' Maria said slowly, taking a careful step forward, a genuine smile on her lips. 'What's his name?'

The women remained silent, and Maria wavered. 'May I?' she asked, pointing to the unoccupied space beside Mina, wanting to bring herself down to their eye level.

'Please,' said the third woman, who had greying hair and wizened features. 'Mina tells us you have questions.'

A shot of fear fired through Maria's blood, knowing her guard would be listening. 'Such a beautiful baby,' she said loudly.

'Ha! He won't hear a thing, dear,' said the older woman. 'This place was built to contain the sounds of birth.'

Oh. Maria nodded, then looked hesitantly at Mina, wondering how much she could say ... Who these women were.

'She wants to know about the attack,' said Mina. 'About the woman who was here that night, the one with dark ringleted hair.'

'Does she?' said the older woman, her hazel eyes pinning Maria in place, assessing her.

Maria swallowed, then gave a small incline of her head. 'And anything else that might help Elex piece together what happened. He said the quarter was attacked when most of the men were helping the village by the lake, and he hopes if he finds the woman, he can find whoever masterminded the whole thing. To understand it.'

The baby finished nursing, and the mother shifted the child in her arms, holding him upright on her chest, rubbing his back.

'And please, take these,' said Maria, handing over all the oils she had. 'I'm sure you need them more than I do.' She put them on the floor in the space between them, then waited, not wanting to risk saying anything that might convince them to stay quiet.

'The *prostitute* you speak of,' said the older woman, practically spitting out the words, 'is my daughter.'

Maria tensed and eyed the exit. Maybe this was a trap after all.

'And the kitchen boy who got her into the quarter was my son,' said the woman with the baby. 'Dead now for his troubles.'

Silence fell for a beat. 'I'm so sorry for your loss.'

'He thought they'd pay him handsomely, that he could help provide with the new baby coming. But to them, he was nothing ... A loose end they tied up.'

'Did they ...' said Maria, looking at the older woman. 'Did they do the same to your daughter?'

The woman waved her hand. 'Oh no, she's right as rain. She's Kiran's mistress, holed up tight in his tender care.'

'Kiran was behind the attack? Erica's father?'

The older woman spread her hands wide. 'That's all I know, but if you find my daughter, feel free to give her a good hard slap from me. She betrayed us, all of us. Elex was a good leader, and now look at the pompous, self-important shit we have lording it over the whole of Oshe. And Kiran and Paul, strutting around like they own the place. Making demands. Undercutting our trade. And my *daughter*,'—she stuck herself in the chest with her index finger, repeating the movement over and over—'my ungrateful hag of a daughter seduced and drugged the gate guards, then let the motherfuckers in.'

The air rushed from the room, so when the midwife finished, it was hard to breathe. Maria's forehead crinkled, her mouth falling open, her heart going out to these women. 'I'm so sorry.'

'Elex must take the quarter back,' said Mina, leaning forward, her words vehement. 'Cane and Erica and Opal ... they have no place here. Them and their selfish ways.'

'And their fathers,' added the older woman.

Maria nodded. 'He will,' she promised, 'but he doesn't know who he can trust.' Despite their disappointed expressions, Maria refused to give them false hope. 'He'll never give up. He cares about all of you, but he'll only get one shot.'

'Then tell him we'll be ready when he strikes,' said Mina. 'Us and the whole quarter, ready and willing to rise.'

Maria swallowed the lump in her throat. 'I'll tell him, and I'll tell him the other things you told me, too. Thank you for trusting me, for sharing your stories.' Maria couldn't find the right words to convey how grateful she was, how she understood what they were risking by talking to her, and that she didn't take their faith in her or Elex for granted. Maria had never doubted the kind of leader her husband was—despite his reputation for brutality—but still, the loyalty of these women was such stark evidence that her chest pulled tight and pride had gooseflesh rushing across her scalp, rippling her hair.

'You should go,' said Mina. 'Your guard ...'

Mina was right, so Maria got quickly to her feet, but she turned back when she was almost at the door. 'Really, thank you.'

'Where is she!' shrieked Cane, his robe flying open as he jumped to his feet.

Maria stood in her usual pre-dinner position at the foot of Cane's bed, while Opal, wearing nothing but a silk slip, rushed to her enraged husband's side, sliding her hands over his shoulders and looking placatingly into his eyes.

'She has a surprise for you,' Opal cooed. 'A special birthday surprise. You'll like it, I promise.'

'I need her, and she has defied me.'

'She's doing it for you ... because she loves you,' said Opal, sliding one hand down to his cock. 'As do I, my love.'

Cane growled his dissatisfaction, but sucked in a sharp breath as she took him in her hand. Maria snapped her eyes up and adopted her usual mid-distance stare, thinking of anything but what was taking place before her.

'You,' grunted Cane. Maria jumped a little, realizing his eyes were on her. 'Get over here.'

'I ...'

'Now,' he said, drawing out the word.

Maria's heart thundered, and bile rose from her stomach, stinging the back of her throat. 'You promised not to hurt me.'

'I may do as I please. Especially on my birthday.'

'But—'

'Now, or I will call a guard to force you.'

Maria moved on heavy feet, taking as long as she dared, while Cane pushed Opal down onto her knees. 'Just as Erica taught you,' he said, then put his hands on Maria's hips and pulled her so close, her bare thighs pressed against Opal's pulsing back.

Cane closed his eyes with a grunt, and Maria swayed backwards a little, trying to break contact with Opal, but Cane's eyes opened into slits and locked with hers as he held her tighter. He shook his head, then grunted again as Opal did something Maria—thankfully—couldn't see.

Cane held Maria's gaze, and never before had she felt such visceral, primal anger. She wanted to tear his throat out with her teeth ... Would have done it if she thought she had any chance of escape. But tonight, perhaps she did have a chance. Elex had told her to be ready on Cane's birthday, and the lavish party Cane had planned might provide an opportunity for them to slip away.

Opal moved faster, and Cane tilted his head, his mouth open, forehead creased as he dug his fingers into the flesh of Maria's backside. Maria held her body rigid, worried her jaw might fracture from the force of her gritted teeth, but then Cane made a series of unintelligible noises, and Opal's movements lost their urgency while Cane made small, erratic movements with his hips.

Cane exhaled a self-satisfied breath and finally stopped staring into Maria's eyes, looking down at his wife. 'You're not a patch on Erica,' he said cruelly, stepping back and pulling his robe shut. 'Now get dressed.'

Opal rose to her feet and scurried from the room, and Maria couldn't help but feel sorry for her. Opal was as much a victim of Cane's cruelty as anyone, and Maria refused to believe she'd asked for this life.

'You, wait there,' said Cane, spinning away and calling for a servant to help him into his clothes.

Maria's chest heaved, needing huge amounts of air to feed her frantic heart. She wanted to collapse to the floor and sob, to spew the contents of her stomach, to curl into a ball and shut out the world, her anger chased away by despair. How much longer before someone put a sword in Cane's guts and left him to bleed?

'Where is she?' Cane demanded of the servant who'd helped him into a white military uniform trimmed with gold and the light blue of Oshe. Maria's outfit was a series of interwoven strands of gold, blue, and white fabric to match, and she wanted to rip it from her skin.

'I'll get her right away,' said the man, bowing his head, then rushing to the adjacent room while Cane admired himself in the mirror. But the servant returned moments later, ashen faced. 'She's ... she's gone, my lord.'

'What the fuck do you mean?' Cane said in a quiet, menacing tone.

'I'm so sorry, my lord. I'll look again,' he said quickly. 'Perhaps I ... Perhaps—'

'Guards!' roared Cane, shoving the servant aside.

'Sir?' said the first guard through the door, his features earnest as he scanned for threats.

'Where is my wife?'

The guard hesitated. 'Which one, sir?'

Cane's face turned an alarming shade of puce. 'Which ...' He looked down at the floor as though unable to believe the guard's stupidity. 'Which one? The one who was here mere moments ago but who has now vanished from right under your noses.'

The guard stood up tall and snapped his heels together. 'I'll—'

'Oh, go away,' Cane spat. 'My wives deserve no fanfare after their behavior tonight, and I have no patience to wait. Come, Maria. I will punish them later.'

Maria reluctantly took his offered arm, keeping her touch as light as she was able, and held her breath for the entire walk to the banqueting hall so as not to infect her lungs with his sickly scent. Cane's dark mood sucked everything good and lively from the music-filled corridor, turning it heavy with the possibility of malice. An angry Cane was an unpredictable Cane, and that didn't bode well for Maria or the night ahead.

The banqueting hall turned deathly silent the moment they stepped through the open doors, the decorations jarring, the walls draped with white and gold banners filled with Cane's feathery insignia, the table pushed up against the far wall to make space for dancing. Guards filled every nook and alcove, and the sight lit a tiny flame of hope in Maria's chest. Did that mean Cane had invited Elex? She hadn't seen him for so many days she'd lost count.

Kiran and Paul—Erica and Opal's fathers, and Cane's closest allies——approached first, each of them bowing their heads as they halted before Cane. 'Happy birthday,' they said in turn, then handed Cane gifts in matching leather boxes.

Cane gave them a curt nod, then instructed two servants to take the presents to a nearby table that was already groaning under the weight of a mountain of gifts.

'To a prosperous year,' said Kiran, saluting Cane with his tall, thin glass. The man's formal doublet was a little too tight around his throat, and between that and the hair combed over his bald spot, Maria decided that he was ungracefully holding onto his long dead youth, and that he was vain. Although she could have surmised the same about both men from the voluptuous young women who approached, draping themselves on Kiran and Paul's arms and bowing their heads in deference to Cane. Women who were at least as young as their own daughters. Cane raked his eyes over the women, lingering on their curves, then he dismissed all four and dragged Maria farther into the room.

The guests eyed Maria speculatively, whispering salaciously behind fans when they were sure Cane's attention was elsewhere, simpering about how inspired Cane's choice of outfit for Maria was to his face, delighting in the opportunity to share a joke with their leader. Maria ignored them. She saw them for exactly what they were: desperate sheep.

A few guests kept themselves apart, standing back at the edges of the room, a hint of disapproval about the set of their shoulders. Maria took strength from them, even though she had no way to tell if their censure meant support for her and Elex or otherwise. Maria was studying a particularly po-faced older woman who reminded her of her mother, when a second hush fell over the room, and everyone stared at something over Maria's shoulder.

Cane wheeled them around, and the crowd parted to give them a clear view of Opal standing in the entrance, one hand on her cocked hip, a demure smile on her lips.

'What the fuck?' Cane said under his breath, dropping Maria's arm and taking a single step forward before collecting himself.

Opal wore a sheath of pure white silk that wrapped around her neck and flowed all the way to the floor. Aside from a thigh-length slit that revealed one leg and her bare arms, her whole body was covered, a luxury Cane hadn't allowed either of his wives—or Maria—at a single public dinner since Maria had arrived.

A headdress of fluffy white feathers arranged in a fan shape adorned Opal's head, and her long hair streamed over her shoulders, finishing level with her nipples, which formed obvious peaks through the fabric.

'Happy birthday, my darling husband,' Opal gushed, stepping towards him, swinging her hips provocatively.

Cane hesitated, glancing left and right, seeming unsure. The tension in his jaw told Maria he dearly wanted to beat his wife for her disobedience, but he could hardly do that in front of the people he most needed to keep onside, including Kiran and Paul. Despite treating his own partners the same way, Paul regularly left dinners where Cane became overly amorous with Opal, and it was plain for all to see the man disapproved of the skimpy outfits Cane forced his daughter to wear, so to publicly annihilate her would be pushing his luck, even for Cane.

Cane was so preoccupied with his wife, he seemed to have forgotten Maria entirely, and she wasted no time before letting the crowd envelop her. She wove backwards, heading for the edge of the room, as far away from Cane as she could get, everyone else pushing forward to get a better view.

'Thank you, my dear,' said Cane, striding to Opal's side and sliding his arm around her waist. Opal winced, then covered it with a smile, and Maria had no doubt that Cane had pinched her. He leaned his head down to her ear, and a flash of something hateful crossed Opal's features. What had he said? And why had she defied his orders for the sake of a dress? It didn't make any sense.

Arms slid around Maria from behind, and she squirmed, trying to get away, then stilled as a familiar woodsy scent washed over her. She sagged in relief—Elex—then half turned and kissed him, needing the feel of his lips against hers, trying to banish every last trace of Cane.

'Thank the Goddess,' she breathed, sliding her hand across his face, tears pooling in her eyes.

She started shaking, and Elex lowered his chin, resting it on her shoulder, holding her tighter. 'You're cold?'

She shook her head. 'I ...' But what could she say? If she told him what Cane had done, Elex might do something stupid, and she couldn't bear to be parted from him for even a second. 'Later.'

'Maria, what happened?' he pressed, trying to look into her eyes. 'Why are you crying?'

She was crying? Maria turned her head away and brushed the tears from her face. She couldn't fall apart. Not here. Not now. Not yet. 'I met the mother of the woman you've been looking for, the one who let your enemies through the gate,' she said, her voice high-pitched and strained. She had to tell him everything in case the guards pulled them apart. Given Cane's mood, he would be delighted to have a target for his wrath, seeing as he couldn't publicly punish his wife. 'She's Kiran's mistress.'

Elex stilled. 'Kiran's? You're sure?'

'Yes.' She gripped his arm, turning her head. 'Why?'

'Because the women in Kiran's brothel swear they know no one meeting her description.'

'Maybe they never met?'

Elex blew out a breath as he considered it. 'I suppose it's possible.' He held her tighter. 'But that's a problem for tomorrow. Tonight, we're getting you out of here.'

Maria's heart leapt, and a fresh stream of tears flooded down her cheeks.

He kissed her temple. 'It's going to be okay, sweetheart. It's almost over.'

Maria nodded, not trusting her voice. She was never like this, and her grandmother's face filled her mind's eye, telling her to grow a backbone. It helped not at all, only making her feel worse.

'There'll be a ruckus,' Elex whispered. 'Be ready to run as soon as the guards leave their posts.'

She sniffed and wiped away the tears. She had to concentrate. 'What about the gate?'

'My friends are waiting,' he said soothingly. 'Just run, Maria, that's all you have to do.'

Maria's breaths became shallow, her heart beating wildly. This was it, finally. No more confinement and having to watch Cane fuck his wives and being treated like a pawn in someone else's game. No more whiling away endless hours with nothing meaningful to occupy her time. She could write to her family, hear their news, and that of Celestl ...

But she mustn't get ahead of herself. The road to escape was fraught with danger, especially given Cane's mood. She took a deep breath and tried to center herself, but although the tears dried up, she couldn't make the shaking stop entirely.

'Cane's furious,' she told Elex. 'Erica's missing. She's planned a surprise for Cane's birthday and changed the outfits he ordered for tonight, but I can't work out why. Why risk his wrath? For what? He'll surely punish her.'

Elex hummed an exhale.

'Do you think she's working with her father?' Maria asked. 'That Kiran could be planning something else? Another coup?'

Elex moved them a little closer to the exit. 'I don't know, but it's almost time for us to leave.' He cast an eye towards where two servants headed for a group of women, each approaching from an opposite side and carrying a fully laden tray of drinks. The tray-bearers were being careful to avoid looking at each other as they maneuvered through the crowd, and Maria held her breath as she watched their progress from the corner of her eye.

Would the servants collide with each other or with the group of women in floor-length dresses? The party-goers were watching Cane and Opal from behind their fans, so enraptured they passed only occasional words back and forth between them. Maria tensed as the servants closed in, perhaps fifteen paces apart. Ten. Five.

Elex gave Maria a reassuring squeeze, and then a fanfare cut through the room, Maria unable to tell from where the sound originated. Some of the women spun around, forcing the servants to divert.

'No,' Maria whispered.

'What the fuck?' said Elex. Maria could feel him scanning the room for the cause of the disturbance, just as she was, and then Maria's jaw dropped open.

'Goddess,' she whispered. 'Is that ...'

'Erica's birthday surprise?'

Four servants wheeled Erica into the hall from the kitchens. She was standing on a platform next to a tiered cake so high it was taller than she was. The icing was snowy white, just like Erica's dress, which matched Opal's aside from the neckline, Erica's a daring, low-cut v.

'Happy birthday, my darling husband!' Erica cried as she came to a stop before him. 'May this year be your most prosperous yet.'

Cane's eyes were wide, his mouth literally open—just like many of their audience—and it appeared as though he had no idea what to do. 'Thank you, wife,' he said haltingly, and Maria wasn't sure if he was furious or delighted.

Erica jumped down and grabbed his arm, tugging him away from Opal. 'Come! Come!' she coaxed, pulling him up onto the platform. Cane looked awkward and unsure as Erica bent her knees and cast her arms wide, one up to the ceiling, the other to the floor, framing Cane. Then she moved her hands to his face and kissed him deeply.

The room went still, unsure how to interpret her bold behavior, and Cane faltered once again as Erica pulled back, a slight flush on his cheeks. Erica reached for a long, vicious-looking dagger that was propped up on a stand beside the cake. 'My birthday gift to you, my darling,' she said, holding it out to him, the enormous rubies along the hilt glinting as they caught the light.

Cane took the weapon from her hands, then pecked her on the lips. 'You're lucky I love you, wife, because you know how I hate surprises.'

'Cut the cake, darling!' she trilled. It was a strange choice of knife to cut a cake, and certainly a task far beneath the station of the dagger.

'A beautiful present from my *most* beautiful wife,' said Cane, turning it back and forth in his good hand. He looked over his shoulder at Opal. 'I hope yours is as pleasing, wife.'

'Oh, it is!' Opal giggled, lifting her shoulder and turning her face into it, covering her mouth with her hand. The shy gesture made her seem so young that Maria felt sorry for her anew, and Maria wondered what gift could possibly compete with Erica's song and dance.

Cane smiled, and it seemed genuine. Apparently Erica's show was lifting the dark cloud over his head, and Maria could not have been more thankful. A happy, relaxed, distracted Cane was exactly what she and Elex needed.

Cane held the dagger aloft, and Erica gasped, bringing her hands to her chest as he attacked the cake, slicing through three layers before withdrawing the blade and holding it up once more. The crowd cheered, and Erica took the dagger as he lowered it, reaching for a cloth to wipe it clean. Cane waved to the crowd as they continued to cheer, making eye contact with his most important subjects, his hand moving in a rolling motion.

And then he just ... stopped, his arm dropping to his side, confusion drawing his features down, melting his smug smile. Erica pulled him back against her and whispered something in his ear. He turned his head and tried to push her away, but she was too fast, her arm up, drawing the dagger across his throat in a blink.

Maria gasped, the breath whooshing from her lungs in an instant. The place erupted as Erica let Cane fall to the floor, her white dress covered in blood.

'Goddess, Erica ...' Elex whispered, pulling Maria back so they stood right beside the exit as every guard in the room rushed forward, guests scrambling to get out of their way.

A barrel of a man in a commander's uniform stepped up in front of Erica, protecting her and ordering the other guards to stand down.

'What the ...?' said Maria, wondering who he was as the guards slowed, then stopped, most seeming unsure. Was he one of Kiran's men? Or Paul's?

The commander offered Opal his hand as she approached the platform, helping her up, then drawing the dagger from his hip and presenting it to her. Opal didn't hesitate, snatching it and stabbing her dead husband's chest four times before she took pause, blood splattering her pristine white dress and the cake.

'Alright, daughter,' chuckled Paul, positioning himself in front of the platform, 'calm your emotions.'

Opal bowed her head and did as she was told, moving to stand behind her father, while Erica stood behind Kiran, who'd moved to Paul's side.

'They're all working together?' whispered Elex.

'Here is what will happen,' said Kiran, bringing his palms wide as he addressed his gob-smacked audience. Most of them seemed to be frozen in shock, their eyes glued to the spectacle, just like Maria and Elex. 'We are the new leaders of Oshe Blade, and you will swear fealty to us tonight.'

'What the fuck?' spat Elex. 'We have to get out of here.'

Maria would have gone willingly, but new guards blocked the exit. 'This must have been their plan all along.'

'But the Goddess has returned!' cried a man near the front. 'The Oshe line must continue or we will have no sacrifice!'

'Worry not,' said Paul, showing the room a relaxed, reassuring smile. 'Our daughters each carry a child. The Oshe bloodline will continue.'

Maria's guts churned. Did these people see her that way? As a commodity? Someone whose worth was only in breeding?

Kiran turned, scanning the crowd, then fixed his eyes on Elex as though mention of the Oshe line had reminded him of Elex's presence. 'You shall go no farther, Elex.'

The guards in the entranceway took a step closer, puffing up their chests. *Fuck, fuck, fuck.*

'Yes, stop!' Erica called in a high-pitched tone, her outfit a riot of crimson and white. 'You wouldn't want to miss the best part.'

Maria and Elex shared a look that said they would fight rather than be taken, and Maria squeezed her eyes closed for a beat, collecting herself, preparing for what she might have to do. But then Erica and Opal let out twin shrieks, and when Maria turned her attention back to them, she found they'd each knifed their own father in the back.

Cries and gasps came from the crowd, and Maria's eyes flew wide, but then she and Elex moved in unison. If they were to make an escape, now was their moment. Elex floored the two guards blocking their way in a single movement, and then they ran.

Chapter Twenty-Three
Sophie
Six Weeks After Dromeda Started Spinning

Sophie instructed her maid to wake her early—long before sunrise—and she rode for the Inner Circle, determined to get there in time to watch Nicoli and Hale's inspection, whatever that meant.

The ride was liberating, her horse keeping up a fast canter while the wind stole wisps of hair from her sensible updo and whipped them around her face. She passed the lake, the ground still deeply scarred, but the first signs of healing were making themselves known, some of the holes having been filled, shoots of grass in the divots.

She couldn't remember the last time she'd been truly alone with no guard or maid hovering nearby. Hale cared so little for her wellbeing that it had been a trifle to get a horse and ride away, the gate guards barely batting an eye as she passed. It was the first time in her life Sophie had felt truly free, like she could go anywhere and no one would notice or care, the thought surprisingly scary, as though she stood on the edge of a precipice, nothing between her and a deadly fall.

She'd never known anything but a cage, and now the door was open, her instinct was to pull the bars shut and hide away inside. It was strange, seeing as she'd always thought of herself as independent, fiercely so. But the cage felt safe, even better if it was a cage of Hale's making, especially if he was prowling around on the inside …

What a fool she was. Had he not told her many times how much he loathed her, how little he thought of her, how no part of him wanted to be her husband? And yet still she wanted him. Why? Was the Goddess punishing her? Sophie had come to Alter with the intention of using the first son to get with child and then committing mariticide, after all.

Not that she was planning to do that any longer. But what was she planning? A long and unhappy marriage to a man who used her like an emotional punching bag? Or perhaps after their wedding, whatever was causing his cruelty would work itself out, like a kink in a rope pulled taut or the unpicking of a particularly stubborn knot.

Stubborn was about right because in the moments when Hale let his guard down, they seemed to get along just fine. Better than fine, in fact. If only he would meet her halfway.

She put the fanciful thoughts from her mind as she dismounted, leaving her horse at a tavern, then hurrying on foot the last hundred yards to the top of the Inner Circle. Sophie found the route down that she'd bribed out of a stable girl, but swallowed hard when she surveyed the steep, rocky descent.

She took a deep breath, then stepped onto the path, knowing she had no time to dally. She almost slipped more than once, glad she'd selected sturdy boots and the style of dress favored by Maria—little more than riding breeches covered by a split skirt. Sophie had scoffed when she'd first seen Maria in the get-up, but now she understood the outfit's practical value—not something Sophie had ever needed to think about when selecting clothes before, seeing as she'd never done much that was practical.

Sophie slid down the last section, landing squarely on her backside as her feet went out from under her, glad no one was around to witness her humiliation. She got gingerly to her feet and dusted herself off, trying to ignore the blunt pain in her lower back as she moved as quickly as she could across the open scrub towards the tree line.

She reached cover just in time, male voices floating down from above as she dove behind the trunk of a large oak tree. When she peered around the bark, she found Nicoli and Hale scrambling athletically down the incline, racing one another to the bottom. Hale won, pipping Nicoli by leaping the final eight feet to the ground, a move which made Sophie's heart still in her chest.

'You always were a filthy cheat,' laughed Nicoli, shoving Hale as he joined him at the bottom.

'And you were always a sore loser, my friend,' Hale retorted, clapping Nicoli on the back. The sight of Hale so relaxed and clad only in shirtsleeves and breeches made Sophie's heart flutter. Had his forearms always been so ... like *that*?

Nicoli took off at a sprint, shouting, 'Last one to Dromeda forages breakfast!'

'Who's cheating now?' Hale cried, pelting after him, disappearing from Sophie's view in seconds.

'Damn,' Sophie said under her breath, scurrying along behind their crashing feet, but less than a minute had passed before she lost their trail. 'Damn, damn, damn!'

Sophie jogged towards Dromeda as fast as she could, desperate not to miss all the action, but jogging was not an activity she was used to—or liked—and she was soon out of breath, sweaty, and had a painful stitch in her side. The stitch forced her to walk, and she clutched her belly as she wheezed deep breaths into her lungs. 'Fucking perfect,' she muttered, walking as fast as she could despite the discomfort and looking up often to ensure she was still heading in the right direction. 'Just *perfect*.'

She trudged on for what felt like endless minutes, careful to avoid the tree roots and brambles, straining her ears for voices, although it was difficult over the loud thuds of her heart. But then ... Wait ... What was that? She stopped dead and listened hard. Had she heard a noise, or had it just been her foot coming down at the same time as——No, there it was again, a deep scraping noise that reminded her of stones grinding flour. And the ground felt like it was ... Was it ... moving? Shaking? It was ... *Shit!*

Sophie didn't waste any more time trying to work out the details. She turned and sprinted back the way she'd come, although she didn't make it far before she had to hobble, her stitch back in full force. 'Shit!' she breathed, as the ground shook harder, fear wrapping its way down her spine.

She staggered on, tears filling her eyes as she searched desperately for any glimpse of the cliff. She was fairly sure she'd retraced her steps, but what if she hadn't? What if she came out in the wrong place and couldn't find a way to the top?

She ran again as far as she could but soon had to bend double to catch her breath, clutching her side. The ground shook even harder now, and Sophie's eyes scanned the path for fractures, wondering if the whole place would crack apart. Was the Goddess angry there were people near her domain? Would she take their lives as punishment? Would she finally refill the Inner Circle with water?

The thought put a vice around Sophie's lungs, and she gasped harder, desperately trying to inhale enough air as she forced herself onwards. She would not die. She would get to the cliff and climb to safety. She would be fine. She would. She had to be.

Sophie suddenly broke through the tree line, and three things hit her all at once. One, hope because she was so close, maybe she could make it before the place imploded. Two, Nicoli and Hale were already at the base of the cliff, starting the climb. And three, that a great, terrifying, rushing noise had filled the air.

'Hale!' she screamed, but he didn't hear her above the noise. She ran for them. 'Hale! Hale! Nicoli! Hale! Wait!'

They turned, whether because they'd heard her or because of the fearful noise she didn't know, but the moment Hale's eyes found Sophie, they locked on and didn't leave. Hale grabbed Nicoli's arm, shouted something into his ear, then jumped back down, sprinting as soon as his feet hit the ground.

He raced for her, covering the ground impossibly fast, and she ran towards him with renewed strength, her heart hurting. Surely the Goddess wouldn't be so cruel as to end their lives here, like this?

Hale slung her over his shoulder the moment they came together, then turned back to the cliff without pause, her weight seeming to trouble him not at all as he ran. Sophie could have cried with an equal mix of relief and mortification. Perhaps she would have if the rushing hadn't become louder, if Hale's feet hadn't been swept out from under him. They went down hard and had not even a moment to catch their breath before a furious torrent of water swept them at breakneck speed towards the cliff.

CHAPTER TWENTY-FOUR
AVA

AVA THREW OFF THE bedding as she woke, too hot under the down filled duvet and blankets, especially with Kush's warm body beside her. She hadn't felt him join her, but she loved that he had, that he wanted to be close to her as much as she did to him.

'Morning,' Kush murmured, kissing her neck as he stirred.

Ava let out a soft huff of surprised pleasure because he'd never done that before, and she really really liked it.

'I love you, Ava,' he said, kissing her shoulder, and she felt his voice as much as heard it, rumbling from his chest into her back.

She squeezed him tighter, her heart feeling like it might burst. 'I love you, too.' She closed her eyes as he kissed behind her ear. 'But, Kush,' she said, and he stilled, presumably hearing the hesitation in her tone, 'what will Var do when he finds out you've been helping me?'

His taut body relaxed, and he stroked her shoulder. 'He'll already know. Billy was right when he said Father has spies everywhere.'

'Will he hurt you?'

He huffed out a breath that hit her ear. 'He's unpredictable.'

'And mean.'

'He can be. But he can also be kind, Ava. I know you've never seen it, and Billy hates him, but Father's been good to me ... in some ways, at least.' His hands tightened on her skin. 'I'm a bastard. He could have disowned me. Could have left me in Santala and never thought of me again. There are those in the Clouds who refuse to acknowledge my existence, who mock me, but he's always stood by me. He brushes them off and acts as though the joke's on them.'

'Kush ...'

'I know he has a dark side, but he wants what's best for the Federation, truly. Everything he does is to protect it, and for that, we need fresh blood, new trade relationships, more energy. That's why he sends me to unfederated worlds, why he's willing to take the risk, because it's so important for everyone.

'The other Gods care about marriages and producing heirs and parties, but Father doesn't pay attention to any of that. He only wants to keep the web healthy.'

Ava had a hard time believing Kush's words. From what she'd seen of Var, he was monstrous, but she didn't doubt that Kush believed them. 'What's it like in the Clouds?' She was sure the Gods couldn't live on the fluffy white things that streamed across the sky and broke apart into whisps.

Kush shrugged. 'It's ... grand and formidable. Beyond that, I don't really know. As I said, the Gods don't like me, so I've never had much chance to explore.'

She sat up a little, looking him in the eye. 'Then where do you live?'

He shrugged. 'I move about. Sometimes I live in the enforcers' barracks, sometimes I stay in one of Father's apartments in the Atlas Tree, and my friend Hunter lets me stay at his a lot, too.'

'Is he a God?'

He shook his head. 'A bureaucrat, but his eyes are set on bigger things. He's always been like that.'

'What are his eyes set on?'

'Novak's job.'

'Master of the House?'

He nodded, but she gave him a perplexed look, so he continued. 'Novak might have been disgraced and kicked out of the Clouds, but now he runs every portal in the tree. He has more power than most Gods.'

'How so?' Ava thought it strange that the Gods would be happy with such an arrangement.

'Each family in the Clouds has responsibility for something in addition to their federated worlds—balance, the map, the development of alcoholic drinks—Novak's role is similar, but more arduous. He oversees all trade between worlds, both legitimate and otherwise. He has incredible freedom.

He keeps ledgers and reports numbers to the Gods, of course, but no one ever checks them. No one apart from Hunter, who runs the Trove.'

'What's the Trove?' she asked, rolling over to face him, propping herself up on her elbow.

He mirrored her, going up on his elbow, too. 'It's where goods are documented and stored so the Gods can collect taxes.'

'And Novak's swindling the Gods?' He certainly had reason to, seeing as they'd treated him like scum for his whole life.

'Hunter says so, but he doesn't have any proof, and it might just be wishful thinking.'

'Or it might be a way to get Novak to talk to us ...'

Kush frowned, sliding his free hand into her hair and caressing her temple with his thumb. 'Why would we want to do that?'

'To see if Billy's lying to us. Novak was there back then. He knew my parents, was a close friend of my mother's, and he was the only one who didn't want to be a God. Why?'

'Hmmm,' said Kush, his lips pursed as though holding back some thought.

Ava shifted, and as she did, something sharp dug into her ribs. 'Ouch!' she squealed, lifting up to see what it was. Kush grabbed it and held up what looked like a small, golden pin. 'What is it?'

'One of the many priceless things I discovered with Billy last night,' he said, a vague smile on his lips.

Ava took it and turned it over in her hands, tracing her fingers over the three circles bisected by a straight line, trying to work out what was so special about it. 'This is priceless?'

Kush raised his eyebrows. 'This means you are a member of the Cloud Synod,' he said, sliding his knuckles across her cheek. 'It means you are a God with a seat at the highest court in the web.'

She sucked in a sharp breath. 'Kush, I'm not a God!' At best she was a demi-God, which still seemed ludicrous. 'I'm not immortal, and I don't want any part of what goes on in the Clouds.'

'All Cloud children descended from two magical parents call themselves Gods these days, regardless of whether your mother split their souls or not.'

'So I should pretend to be something I'm not, too? Just go along with the deception?'

'No, it's not like that. It's ...' Kush's features turned thoughtful, as though trying to find the best way to explain. 'Of the fifty or so Cloud families, thirty had kids around the same age as our parents. All of those—aside from Novak—jumped at the chance of eternal life, but like Billy said, most others were skeptical of your parents' claims. And by the time everyone was convinced, your parents were dead, and no one else knew how to perform the magic.'

'So the others started calling themselves Gods because they were jealous?'

He tilted his head. 'Sort of, but it's more complicated than that. The long-lives need the others to produce heirs or the magical families that have dominated for centuries will die out. It's a delicate balance.'

'Because soul-splitting messes with reproduction?'

He nodded. 'And now they're all obsessed with having kids and value highly those who can provide them.'

'Oh.' Ava tried to wrap her head around this new world she was somehow a part of. Not that she had plans to attend a meeting of the Synod any time soon. 'But you and me ...'

He shrugged. 'There are a few others like us, born to parents with split souls, but they hide away in the Clouds, wrapped in cotton wool and encouraged to breed.'

'Then why didn't they do the same to you?'

Kush moved his lips to one side. 'I only have one magical parent. My mother is a common temple woman.'

'But—'

'I represent everything they fear they'll have to become, Ava. If they can't keep their families going with two magical parents for every child, they'll have to dilute their bloodlines with non-magical blood. They can't think of a worse fate.'

His words were snappish, but she still didn't understand, and she needed to. 'But if Var doesn't care ...'

'He does care.'

'But you said—'

'He doesn't shun me like the others do, but I'm not his heir.'

'Var said that?'

'It's ... complicated.' He turned his eyes downward. 'And it hardly matters, he'll outlive me anyway.'

Guilt flooded Ava for having upset him, so she squeezed his arm and asked brightly, 'Did you find anything else last night?'

Kush paused for a moment then exhaled a sigh. 'We found plenty. Magical objects, notebooks, jewelry, but nothing as important as that pin, and not the Atlas Stone or anything referencing the missing souls. Billy wasn't happy, so he drowned himself in a bottle of *Wit's End*, then passed out on the floor.'

Ava laughed, even though it wasn't really funny.

Kush shook his head slowly. 'You still don't get it, do you?'

Ava's lips formed an amused pout. 'Get what?'

'How important you are. How powerful. How much of a threat you are to the ruling Gods.'

She gave him a slow smile because the whole thing seemed ridiculous, but she was also desperate to cheer him. 'Am I more powerful than you?' she said jokingly.

He caught her hand, his features serious. 'I'm nothing next to you. I'm—'

She shoved him playfully, and he tipped onto his back. 'You're a demi-God! You have a whole world at your fingertips!'

He smiled indulgently, grabbing her arm as she tried to prod him, surprising her by pulling her down so she lay half on top of him.

'Kush!' she squealed.

Her hair cascaded around them, cocooning them, his eyes inches from hers, boring into her. 'You could have all the worlds you desire, Ava.'

His statement was too big to comprehend. Too big to be real, so she cocked an eyebrow and said quietly, 'Can I have other things I desire?'

He stilled, then swallowed, holding her gaze for a long moment. 'Like?'

She tilted her head down, gathering her courage as she walked her fingers over the hard ridges of his abdomen, then looked up at him from under her lashes. 'You,' she whispered.

His gaze moved from one of her eyes to the other, then he gently pushed a lock of hair behind her ear. 'We shouldn't, Ava ...' he said in a low, intense voice.

Disappointment crashed through her, and she turned her head, unable to meet his eyes, beginning to roll away. 'Sorry, I thought ...'

He put his hand on her lower back, halting her retreat, hugging her to him. 'It's a bad idea,' he said, as though trying to convince himself, his body stiff as his fingers slid back and forth across her spine, melting her insides.

She pressed herself more firmly against him and slid her hand down his torso, needing more of him, wanting to feel every part of him and for him to touch every part of her. Her fingers paused as they snagged on the tented front of his taupe pajamas and all moisture left her mouth. Kush became stone still, even his chest locked in place as he held his breath, but he didn't try to stop her as she slid her hand under his waistband. 'Why is this bad?' she whispered, taking his hard length tentatively in hand.

He exhaled and tipped his head back into the pillow. 'You're all I have,' he said, lifting his hips and pressing himself further into her grip.

'And you're all I have, Kush. You're all I want, but I want all of you.' She stroked up and down with light fingers while his hand moved to her backside and squeezed. Her breath caught, and she hooked her leg across his, pressing her core against his thigh, tilting her hips.

'Ava ...' He said her name as though about to reject her, but his hand was still on her hip, holding her in place.

'Kush,' she breathed, squeezing him harder. 'You think I don't feel like this, too?'

He pulled her hand away, and shame filled her, so she buried her face in his chest, too humiliated to look at him. He was denying her. He didn't want her. He—

He took hold of her jaw, forcing her eyes up to his, and then he reached down and caught the hem of her nightgown, drawing it up her legs, his fingers tracing the backs of her thighs as he slid inexorably higher. Ava's breathing hitched at the heat and pressure and skittering bolts of energy that pooled in her core, and still he continued, uncovering her backside, his fingers dipping tantalizingly close to her most sensitive flesh, circling teasingly before skirting away.

Ava lost herself in Kush's deep blue eyes as he bunched the fabric around her waist, then he gently held her hip and pushed her backwards onto the bed until she lay looking up at him. Ava was surprised to find she didn't feel vulnerable under his hungry gaze, even when she lay sprawled near naked beneath him, her most private flesh exposed. She felt seductive, desirable, powerful.

He ran his fingers across her lower belly, pressing gently before moving higher, skating his fingers under the thin fabric of her nightgown. He cupped her ribs, then her breast, and it was like her skin was too tight, like she might rip apart at any moment. She moaned as he squeezed her and gently teased her nipple, her hips moving of their own accord, pulsing up and down, some urgent energy she'd never felt before dictating her movements.

'Kush,' she breathed, digging her hand into his hair, but before she could pull his lips to hers, they were already on her, kissing and sucking and nipping. His fingers journeyed back down her body in a series of featherlight touches, and she forgot to kiss him back—forgot to breathe—as he passed her waist.

Kush ran his nose down hers before pulling back a little and watching her face as he slowly skirted her jutting hip. He inched lower, and she needed his fingers to hurry up, to stop teasing her, to touch her before her body imploded or she died of desire.

'Kush,' she whispered. 'Please.'

His lips twitched as he dipped his fingers lower and lower, and she bucked at his first delicious ghost of a touch against her core, pure sensation overtaking her. Ava pulled his lips back to hers, kissing him with deep, rhythmic movements as he caressed her, but it wasn't enough, her body screaming for more. 'Kush,' she moaned, scrabbling at the waistband of his pants.

He pushed her nightgown higher, Ava sitting a little so he could slide it over her head, and then he lifted his hips, helping her remove the fabric in her way. He rolled atop her, pinning her beneath him, forcing her legs apart so he could lie between her thighs.

'I love you,' he breathed, but Ava could barely focus on his words, her whole being attuned to the way his naked flesh slid across hers, her center hot and tight and demanding with his arousal between her legs, the feel of so much skin on skin scrambling Ava's brain until she wasn't even sure which way was up. And then she felt him against her entrance and she froze, holding her breath, scared to move in case he changed his mind.

But he didn't change his mind. He slid inside her, grunting as he reached his hilt, and her body pulsed around him, stretching to accommodate the new, perfectly full feeling. They lay motionless for a moment, and then Kush lifted his torso, looking down at Ava with hooded, reverent eyes, watching her as he pulled out and then slid in again and again. His hand went to her breast, his thumb flicking back and forth across her hard, aching nipple, and Ava's eyes rolled back in her head, her head tipping back on a moan.

She writhed beneath him, lifting her legs and wrapping them around his waist, her hips pulsing in time with his thrusts, her body somehow knowing what to do, what it wanted, driving her half mad.

She grabbed a handful of his hair, her other hand gripping his shoulder, and Kush's arms settled around her, pressing more of his body against her, the feel of his skin sliding over hers intimate and erotic as he breathed garbled words into her ear.

She held on for dear life as their movements became smaller, faster, harder, Ava's moans turning feverish as their bodies aligned so he hit her exactly where she needed him every time. They crescendoed together, climbing higher and higher towards some invisible summit, and then suddenly Ava tipped over its peak, tumbling, flying, her body clenching around him, sensation ripping through her in powerful, pulsing waves that had unintelligible sounds pouring from her lips.

Ava's body arched wildly as Kush grunted and went rigid above her, but still they clutched onto each other, Kush pushing into her a handful more times as though not willing to admit it was over, each thrust sending a fresh shiver of pleasure through Ava's insides.

Kush finally stilled, bowing his head to look down at her, then gently moved her mess of hair out of her eyes before kissing her tenderly.

Ava finally understood why the women of the Cleve giggled together about *intimate relations* when they thought no one was listening. They would have laughed hard about how long it had lasted, but Ava didn't care.

What was there to care about when it finally felt like Kush belonged to her, like they belonged to each other.

The kiss went on and on, sweet and devoted, a silent conversation between them, confirming how much they meant to one another, how this shared physical act had brought them even closer. Kush wouldn't run back to Var, not when it felt like his very being now wrapped around her, enveloping her, tying them together in a tight, aching knot under her ribs.

Kush rolled them so Ava rested half on top of him, wrapped in his strong, smooth arms, her body fitting perfectly against his, their naked limbs entwined, but then Kush tensed, and a flutter of panic took flight in Ava's chest, shattering the listless moment. 'You won't get with child,' he whispered. 'I'm sorry, I should have ... I take a potion. Father insists on it. I think he's terrified someone non-magical is going to seduce me, and my bastard child will cause an even bigger scandal than I did.'

Relief chased away Ava's panic, and her limbs released the tension holding them tight, so she molded against Kush once more, but oh, Gods, he was right. Her monthly bleeds were anything but regular, her malnourished body probably not even capable of growing a baby, but she'd been the one to get herbs for the dancers in the Cleve. She should have at least stopped to consider that her actions might have consequences.

Ava raided her mother's wardrobe, selecting a fawn-colored rollneck top, a long, dark green skirt, and brown leather boots. The outfit was warm and demure and comfortable like her clothes had never been before, and it made her feel different, especially when Kush attached her Synod pin, his fingers lingering on the shimmering metal for a beat before stepping back. She slid a thick jacket over the top, hiding the pin from view, then tied her long hair in a ponytail while Kush dressed in a shirt and relaxed pants that had belonged to Rupert.

His eyes lingered on her as they finished dressing. 'You look so ...'

'Old?' she asked on a laugh.

He shook his head. 'Sophisticated. Powerful.'

She gave a shy smile. 'Well that tallies, seeing as my mother was both of those things.'

Kush took her hand and leaned close. 'You are both of those things.'

They found Billy on the floor in the library, arms splayed, eyes staring upwards at the image of the Atlas Tree on the ceiling. He rolled his head towards them as they entered, doing a comical double take when he saw them. 'Jumping cracklejacks!' he cried, scrambling to his feet, his lip curling into something that might have been a snarl. 'You look just like her.'

'Um ...' It didn't sound like a compliment.

Billy stepped menacingly forward. His eyes were red and puffy, his features drawn, and he looked like he was shivering, too. 'You are just like her, aren't you. A weasel. Just like Polly. Just like your grandmother. Just like—'

'Enough, Billy,' said Kush, stepping between him and Ava.

'Ha!' Billy spat. 'She's got you wrapped around her conniving little finger, and you can't even see it. She's got two stones now. Hers and yours. Two out of three. What do you think Var will do when he finds out, huh?' Billy's eyes bulged as he turned towards Ava. 'You have it, don't you.'

Ava shook her head slowly. 'No, I ... Billy, are you okay?'

Billy grabbed handfuls of his hair, then ran on the spot, stamping his feet. 'Where is it?' His voice was high-pitched and frenzied. 'You've got us both where you want us, haven't you, you wretch. Pretending to be some poor little victim, to be *innocent*. You planned it all, didn't you. And now you're hiding two stones!'

'I'm not!' said Ava, stepping back. 'I never ... I ... I only have Kush's.' And perhaps she should give it back. It was upstairs in her old dress along with her other treasures, and it seemed unfair to keep it after ... everything.

'B told me what you're like! She told me Novak left a package for you, that she gave it to you on your eighteenth birthday. She never opened it because she wanted nothing more to do with the Gods, and she could feel the magic radiating from it. It held the Atlas Stone, didn't it? Didn't it!' He tried to lunge towards Ava, but Kush caught him and pushed him back.

'Come one step closer and you'll regret it,' Kush growled.

'Didn't it!' Billy shrieked, bending double and clutching his head.

The house shook. A small vibration, but all three of them froze.

'What was that?' Ava asked, a shot of fear coursing through her blood.

Billy pulled himself up to his full height. 'Answer my question,' he demanded.

'No,' she said, 'I don't have the stone. The package had other things inside, but not that.'

The house shook again, harder this time, and Ava worried it would shake her off her feet.

Billy squatted, his hands on the floor, eyes looking up at Ava. 'I don't believe you.'

'Then leave,' said Kush. The shaking stopped. 'No one invited you here. Ava's telling the truth, of course she is. Why would she lie?'

'Then what?' said Billy, rocketing to his feet and stalking towards Ava. 'What was in the package?'

The shaking came again, as Kush blocked Billy's advance towards Ava with his arm.

'A wooden thing,' she said, her voice trembling a little, Billy scaring her, but she didn't want him to leave, not when there was so much she needed to learn from him. 'I don't know what it is, but it has different strands twisted together. And there was a knife—a scalpel—and a drawing of the Atlas Stone. That's how I knew where to go when I escaped Var. It took me to the place where you found me in the tree. I'll show you.'

But before she could leave the room, the door banged shut, and the package appeared on the round table by the window, making a loud *thud* as it landed. Was the house angry? Why? Because she was showing them? Revealing her secrets?

Billy raced to the table and picked through the contents but soon pushed away with a hissing exhale.

'Novak gave B the package,' said Ava.

'You think B has the stone?' asked Kush. 'Or Novak?'

Ava shook her head. 'I don't know, but Novak must have at least looked inside because he knew exactly where I would land on my birthday. It must have been from the coordinates depicted in the package.'

'Maybe he created the drawing,' suggested Kush.

The house vibrated so hard, the chandelier shook, and Ava's shoulders came up to her ears as she eyed it swinging crystals warily.

'It's got to be the house,' said Billy. 'It's hiding the stone.' He rounded on Ava, his eyes bulging. 'Ask for it.' The house went deathly still, and a shiver ran down Ava's spine. 'Ask for it. Ask for it! If you truly have nothing to hide, then ask for it.'

Ava scowled as the stillness turned dangerous, like the air was charged and might ignite at any moment. But she was curious, and if the house did have the stone, she wouldn't hide it from Billy and Kush. 'House, if you have the Atlas Stone, please give it to me now.'

The house vibrated so hard, books fell from the shelves and a crack appeared in the ceiling, but no stone materialized before them.

'See?' said Kush, stepping towards Billy, whose eyes were darting wildly around the room. 'Perhaps you and B already have it and are trying to throw us off the scent.'

Billy scoffed. 'If I had an Atlas Stone, I would be far away from here.' He turned back to Ava. 'Ask the house to show you what's in the cubbies by your parents' bed. Perhaps there's a clue in one of those.'

'No,' said Ava. The stone was one thing, but whatever her parents had hidden in their most secret places, she'd rather discover on her own.

He screwed up his features, balled his fists, and leaned towards her. 'Yes!'

'No!'

The house shook once again, and something about the intensity of it finally made Billy back off, or perhaps it was the unwavering look in Ava's eyes. 'Fine,' Billy said with a flounce, then he folded dramatically forward. He swept his hands from the floor to the sky, inhaling a long breath, holding it, his eyes closed, face angled towards the ceiling for a count of five before he pulled his hands down to his heart with a loud exhale. He tipped his head slowly from side to side, stretching, and when he opened his eyes, they were clearer, more lucid, less scary. 'Right, well, now we've got that out of the way, you need to practice travelling via stone, and I need breakfast.'

CHAPTER TWENTY-FIVE
MARIA
SIX WEEKS AFTER DROMEDA STARTED SPINNING

ELEX GRABBED A CLOAK from a cubby near the exit and slung it around Maria's head and shoulders, covering her skimpy outfit. 'Keep your face in shadow,' he murmured as they passed under an archway and out into the crisp night air.

They made a beeline for the gate, which was devoid of life, suspiciously quiet, at least until three men popped out of the guardhouse, two of them great, looming statues, the other short and wiry. 'Thank the Goddess,' said the short one, then all three moved towards the pedestrian side gate, quickly ushering Elex and Maria through.

Maria breathed a sigh of relief as they swung the gate silently closed behind them, but then the others froze, and icy fingers of dread crept down Maria's spine as she realized she'd celebrated too soon. Figures began to appear from the shadows before them, dressed all in black, slithering like venomous serpents into the light of the flaming torches around the gate.

'Thought we might be seeing you,' laughed the man in the middle of the newly formed semi-circle of soldiers. Maria counted twenty of them to their five, and she didn't know how to fight. They were not favorable odds, especially when the enemy were such formidable looking creatures, but she could see no way out, nothing but a stone wall and a return to captivity at their backs.

Maria wanted to cry. They'd got so close to freedom she could smell it.

Elex turned towards her and put his hands on either side of her face. 'You have one job, my little hell cat,' he said in an urgent whisper. 'Do not let them take you.'

Maria nodded, her eyebrows pulling together. They would fight, then.

'Keep us between you and them,' he continued, pressing the hilt of a dagger into her hand. 'And don't let them get behind you. Stay close to the wall but remember guards might come through the gate.'

She barely had time to nod again before he whirled away.

'Touching as that was—' said the leader, but he never got to finish his sentence because Elex pulled a dagger from his cloak and let it fly in a movement so seamless the man didn't have a chance. He went down hard, his surprised mouth gaping wide, but as his knees hit the ground, the rest of them charged.

Elex sent two daggers quickly after the first, felling two more men, but the others didn't even check. One of Elex's friends pulled out twin axes, taking out two of the enemy with rapid left-right blows, while another of Elex's group cut a sword back and forth, ending three more.

Maria gawked. *Eight.* They'd killed eight ferocious men in the blink of an eye. But twelve remained, and now the men in black were wary, respectful, cautious. They circled instead of rushing in, and some cast quick glances Maria's way. She shied back, but the lights from the walls made it impossible to hide.

The last of Elex's friends, this one smaller than the other two, dashed forward and pulled two daggers from the bodies of the dead. He held one out to Elex, who took it and released in a single fluid movement, another of their enemy going down.

The small man let out a merry cheer, then cried, 'One of your finest yet, brother!' The sound drew the attention of a few of the circling men, and the axe and sword wielders used the distraction to launch a coordinated attack, each of them taking out another two men before Elex threw the second dagger.

Fourteen. Goddess. They'd killed fourteen men in what must have been less than a minute. Only six remained, but those six wasted no time, striking together with a roar.

Two locked their eyes on Maria, and she let out a whimper, looking left and right for an escape, but she had nowhere to go, and ... *Fuck!* The gates were opening.

'Elex!' she screamed. 'The gates!'

The small man who'd retrieved Elex's daggers raced to Maria's side and grabbed her hand. 'With me,' he said calmly, then tugged her along the wall.

'Elex said not to—'

'I know, I know, but sometimes we have to get creative. I'm Zeik, his brother. You can trust me.'

Zeik yanked her a little farther along the wall, Maria having to jog to keep up, and then he came to an abrupt halt as he reached into a shadowy recess between two stones and pulled out a loaded crossbow. He pointed it back the way they'd come and fired without hesitation, the thud of a man hitting the ground filling Maria's ears, much too close for comfort. Zeik immediately continued their retreat along the wall, and Maria followed, but she'd made it only a handful of steps before a weight barreled into her from behind, and solid arms closed around her, dragging her to a stop.

'No!' she screamed, kicking and hitting and flailing. 'No! Let me go!'

'Can't do that I'm afraid,' the man grunted, his grip as strong as a constrictor's.

'Maria, be a dear and play dead,' said Zeik, holding up another crossbow. 'Now.'

He was so commanding, Maria didn't think. She let her body go floppy, acting as though she'd fainted, her dead weight so hard to hold, she slithered through the man's grasp far enough that Zeik had a clear shot.

The crossbow mechanism made a loud *click* as it released, and Maria's body fell heavily on top of the man as he flew backwards, driven that way by the impact of the arrowhead.

'Very good,' said Zeik. 'Now up, quickly, it's time to go.' He held out a hand and hauled Maria to her feet, then pushed her towards an alley. She registered the sounds of loud boots behind them and shouts demanding they stop, but Zeik didn't slow for a second, guiding Maria through tight turns, up narrow steps, and even through a basement and out the other side.

After what felt like an eternity, Maria's heart thundering, her bare feet ripped and bleeding, Zeik yanked her into a thin, dark side street and pressed her back against the wall, listening carefully before opening a door in the ground used for rolling beer kegs into tavern cellars. Maria climbed quickly through, but lost her footing, the steep incline taking her by surprise. She slid, grazing her leg and side, then landed heavily on the straw covered floor.

Zeik jumped down beside her. '*Smooth*, but don't worry, no one saw. Oh, wait, no, the whole gang's already here.'

'You could have warned me,' she groaned, rolling over to find three sets of eyes watching her, one of them belonging to Elex. He helped her to her feet, wrapping her in a tight embrace as soon as she was upright.

'It was a stressful situation!' Zeik retorted. 'And anyway, you jumped straight in, you left me no time.'

Maria winced as Elex pulled back, his arm brushing the rash of grazed skin across her hip.

'Shit,' said Elex. 'You're hurt?'

He tried to take a closer look, but Maria batted him away, pulling the cloak more tightly around herself. She was done with strange men ogling her bare flesh, and she'd never been so close to death as she'd been tonight or had to run for her life. 'What the fuck just happened?' she snapped, full of pent-up emotions that needed an outlet. She leaned against a barrel, shaking hard as she tried to collect herself, trying to block out the pain of her torn skin and the shock of ... everything.

Elex stepped closer, but she scowled at him, halting him in his tracks. 'Who were those men? Cane's or Erica's?' Her teeth started chattering, and Elex's gaze burned with concern, but he didn't try to approach.

'I don't know,' he said quietly.

'Uh ... What?' demanded Zeik.

Elex quickly relayed the events of the night to the others, from Erica stabbing Cane to both Erica and Opal killing their fathers.

The one who'd fought with the sword whistled through his teeth. 'Fuck.'

'So it was them all along?' asked Maria, squeezing her upper arms with her hands as though that might stop her quivering. 'Opal and Erica working together? They planned everything?'

Elex shrugged.

'It doesn't matter,' said the axe-wielder, his voice deep and purposeful. 'What matters is what will happen next.'

Zeik made a dismissive noise. 'What matters is getting the quarter back.'

'Or at least the water,' said the sword man.

'The quarter,' Zeik insisted. 'Anything less is ... What's the word ...'

'A complete fucking shit show?' said the axe man, heading for the stairs.

The others trooped after him until only Maria and Elex remained. Maria tried to follow, but Elex stopped her, holding an arm across her path. 'Sweetheart,' he said, 'you're shaking.'

'I'm fine. I'm just ...' She bit the insides of her lips together, trying to stop her chattering teeth.

'You're in shock.'

'I'm fine. I'll be okay in—'

'Let me help.' He stepped closer, and she leaned her forehead against his chest, something she hadn't wanted to do with the others watching or while adrenaline still poured through her veins. But now it was just the two of them, she could let her guard down, be vulnerable, accept help. He breathed a loud sigh of relief as he wrapped her in his arms, and his warmth and the press of him helped instantly, bolstering her strength, fortifying her soul.

'I can't believe I'm really free,' she said into his chest. 'That we got away. I thought ... Those men outside the gate ...'

He rubbed soothing circles on her back. 'I didn't get my reputation for nothing, my little hell cat, and you ran like the wind even with no shoes on. You did your bit.'

She let out a choked laugh, nodding against him but still not feeling herself.

'Are you two coming?' Zeik called from the top of the stairs.

'Maria needs warm clothes and hot food,' Elex snapped.

'Just a moment!'

Maria pulled back. 'He just saved my life, he shouldn't be running around after me. I can—'

'He's not running around after you, sweetheart,' he said, cupping her cheek, a roguish look in his eye. 'He's running around after me.'

Maria couldn't help but smile. 'He shouldn't be running around after you, either.'

'Yes, he should. What else are younger brothers for?'

'Normally I'd take issue with that,' said Zeik, clattering down the stairs, a steaming mug of soup in one hand and a pile of clothes slung over his arm, 'but he also pays my wages, so I'll let it slide.'

Oh.

'It's nicer upstairs,' Zeik said encouragingly. 'When you're ready.'

Maria nodded. 'I just need a minute. Thank you, though.'

'Dressings, too, please,' Elex said to his brother's retreating back.

Zeik waved his hand. 'Already on it.'

Maria took a sip of the thick vegetable soup, and as the delicious savory liquid traveled down her throat, it warmed her from the inside out, making her strangely emotional. She took another long sip, then put the mug on a beer barrel and pulled on the soft pants, cotton shirt, and chunky woolen jumper Zeik had provided. They were all too big and designed for a man, but it was blissful to be warm and covered in modest, loose-fitting clothes. She felt free, like her body was hers again because no one else could see it.

'Better?' asked Elex, pressing the warm mug back into her hands.

She gulped down the remaining soup. 'Much,' she said, savoring the mug's residual warmth for a moment, then, not allowing herself to think too much about it, heading for the stairs, limping a little on account of her damaged feet.

'I can carry you,' said Elex, at her side in a heartbeat.

'No!' she cried, giving him a chastising look and holding him away with a hand on his shoulder. 'You can't *carry* me up there in front of your friends. What will they think of me?'

He smiled furtively.

'What?' she demanded.

His smile grew wider. 'It's nothing.'

He tried to turn away, but she held his arm, scowling. 'Tell me!' He laughed as he swept her up into his arms, and she gave a little yelp of surprise. 'Elex!'

'I'm just so glad I've got you back, that's all.' He kissed her, then carried her to the top of the stairs and set her gently on her feet. Before she could think of a reply, Elex opened the door and they spilled out into a cozy taproom, a fire blazing in the hearth, the flickering light like a warm hug after the cold, dingy cellar.

'Here,' said Zeik, placing a basin of warm water in front of an armchair by the fire. Maria hobbled to it and flopped down, dipping her feet into the water, wincing against the sting. Tension melted out of her for the first time since she'd entered Oshala, which was strange given the squadron of guards most likely combing the streets for them right at that very moment.

'Do you have any thyme oil? Or tarragon? Or clove?' she asked Zeik.

He shook his head. 'You'll find standards a little lower here than inside Elex's quarter.'

'Salt or cider vinegar?'

'That we can do,' he said, jumping up.

'And she'll take some more soup while you're at it,' Elex said from where he stood by the fire.

The other two snickered from their respective armchairs, but Zeik didn't blink. He disappeared through the door behind the bar and returned moments later with a tray filled with more soup, a hunk of bread, a pat of creamy yellow butter, a bottle of vinegar, and a ramekin filled with salt.

'Thank you,' said Maria, tensing as she sprinkled salt and vinegar into the basin. It stung like crazy, but if it stopped her wounds from turning bad it was worth more than a little pain. She pulled her feet out, drying them on a clean, pressed square of cotton, then moved to a sofa and stretched out along its length with the tray on her lap.

She appraised Elex's other friends, both big men with white-blonde hair and something about their brown eyes that seemed to match. 'Are you two brothers?' she asked, after downing most of her soup.

'Cousins,' said the sword wielder. 'I'm Tallin.'

'And I'm Sol,' said the other.

Maria gave a small smile. 'Nice to meet you, and thank you for ... you know ... saving my life.'

'Ah, don't mention it,' said Tallin. 'You did us a favor, actually.'

Maria's features scrunched. 'I'm sorry?'

Tallin chuckled while Sol said, 'We haven't had a fight in a while. It was good to stretch our legs.'

'Practice makes perfect,' agreed Zeik, handing out tankards of beer, and although it wasn't Maria's drink of choice, it had a malty sweetness that was comforting. She put aside the tray and rested against the cushioned arm of the sofa, surprised to find she felt almost at home with these men.

'So what now?' said Tallin, who Maria had immediately warmed to. Where Zeik was quick witted and mischievous, Tallin seemed solid and stable, his easy smile sincere and reassuring but with a twinkle in his eye that said he didn't take himself too seriously. Sol, though, she couldn't figure out. He was quieter and more intense, and she wasn't sure if he liked her or not. Or maybe she was reading too much into his absence of freely flowing words and lack of boyish smile.

'Will Erica and Opal be able to take over?' asked Maria. 'Do they have that kind of support?'

'Tricksy little minxes,' said Zeik, as he finally took a seat in an armchair.

Tallin clapped a hand on his leg. 'Got to hand it to them, no one saw it coming.'

'Especially not their sires,' Sol agreed darkly.

Elex pushed off the mantelpiece. 'Erica's always been ambitious. She'll want to lead.'

'But Maria's right,' said Zeik. 'Does she have the support?'

Tallin cocked an eyebrow. 'And will she share with Opal?'

Elex tipped his head, looking at Maria. 'What do you think? You've been around them far more than we have.'

The weight of their attention pressed down on Maria's shoulders, and she shrugged as she considered it. 'Opal and Erica never let me in. They seemed distant from each other most of the time, although they presented a united front of devotion to Cane. Erica seemed jealous of Opal, but maybe it was all a lie. Maybe Erica was protecting her from Cane by drawing the brunt of his attention.' Elex shifted, and Maria quickly continued, not wanting to discuss Cane's foul ways with a room full of men. 'Opal pretends to be shy and naïve, clawless, but after what she did tonight ...'

'Perhaps Erica groomed her,' said Sol.

'Or maybe they planned the whole thing together from the start,' said Zeik.

Maria considered both suggestions, but the truth was she didn't know. They'd hidden their plans so completely, it was impossible to tell if any of her conversations with them had been real. 'Who was the commander? The one who called off the guards?'

'One of my father's men,' said Elex. 'One of his most loyal.'

Maria frowned. 'Then why would he help kill Cane?'

Zeik mimed stroking a beard. 'Hmmmm, it's a mystery.'

Maria hurled a cushion at him, and he yelped as the others laughed. 'Then which one of them is he fucking?' she said.

Zeik waggled his eyebrows salaciously. 'Why not both?'

Tallin chuckled and shook his head. 'Never ends well.'

Sol nodded sagely. 'Especially not for Cane ...'

'It would be what they're used to with Cane, though,' said Maria, her cheeks heating a little as they all turned to look at her, their laughter dying on their lips. Had Elex told them what Cane had made her witness?

'I suppose we'll find out soon enough,' said Tallin, breaking the awkward silence before it could properly settle.

'Alas, Erica is far smarter than our late brother,' said Zeik, in an overly bright tone, 'and she's a premier bitch. Now we'll really have to watch our backs.'

The others snickered, and Maria joined in, feeling almost like her old self again, like she was joking with her siblings at home. When had she last laughed? It was such a tonic. She twisted her head to look at Elex. 'Well, you were right about one thing.'

'Oh?' His eyes shone with intrigue. 'Just one?'

Maria's lips quirked. 'Oshe is nothing like Alter.'

CHAPTER TWENTY-SIX
SOPHIE
SIX WEEKS AFTER DROMEDA STARTED SPINNING

SOPHIE SMASHED INTO THE cliff, her shoulder taking the brunt of the force, the impact knocking the air from her lungs. Water rushed over her head and into her mouth, and she scrabbled for the surface, coughing and spluttering, trying to get her feet under her. The saturated fabric of her dress made every movement a weighty struggle, and panic stole all sensible thoughts from her brain.

Her hands found the bottom and she pushed desperately upwards, sticking her head in the air, and found, to her immense surprise, that it was enough to break the surface. She sucked in a mouthful of air, then tried again to get her feet on the ground as she searched frantically for Hale. Where was he? Was he dead? Had he hit his head on the rocks? Had the Goddess taken him?

The Inner Circle would fill to the brim, and Sophie had never been a strong swimmer. Her dress would drag her down, she would surely die! She couldn't get her skirts out of the way of her legs ... She——

Hands were suddenly hauling her to her feet, lifting her from under her armpits, and as she came upright, she found herself chest to chest with Hale's strong body, his fingers sweeping back her sodden hair as he searched her eyes. 'Are you okay?' he asked urgently. 'Can you climb?'

Climb. Of course, they could climb to the top! Why hadn't she thought of that? 'Yes,' she breathed, and Hale stepped back, giving her a full view of his impressively ridged torso through his sodden shirt.

'Come on,' he said, wading through the knee-high water towards the path. 'It seems to have stopped rising for now, but I don't know how long we'll have before the next wave.'

'Then she's truly returned,' whispered Sophie, more to herself than to Hale.

'Looks that way,' he agreed, waiting for her as he found the place where they would start their climb. It would change everything, the Claws having their own water.

Sophie reached Hale's side, and he started tugging at the laces of her dress.

'Hale!' she squealed, trying to stop him.

'It has to go,' he said, refusing to stop. 'You can't climb in it, it's too heavy.'

Sophie growled a resigned exhale. 'Fine.' She shoved his hands away and pulled at the wet fastenings herself. She stripped off the top layer and dumped it unceremoniously into the water, which left her standing before him in breeches, boots, and a sodden brassier.

'That will do,' said Hale, then boosted her up the start of the climb. 'Go slowly. Be sure of every step. Your boots are wet, and you don't want to slip.'

'Hmm, hadn't thought of that,' she said under her breath, but if he heard her sarcastic words, he didn't rise to her bait.

She climbed, but the route seemed endless, her limbs shaking from the effort mere moments after she started. Or maybe from the cold. Or the shock. Or all three.

She focused on putting one foot in front of the other, testing every hold before committing, telling herself it wasn't that far, that she just had to keep going.

'Nearly there,' said Hale, close behind her but not crowding her movements or rushing her. 'Not far now.'

Her fingers and toes had gone so numb she couldn't feel the ends, her arms and legs shaking so hard she worried they would give way. Tears gathered in her eyes. What if she didn't make it? What if she fell?

'Stop, Sophie,' said Hale's rich, commanding voice. 'Rest here.' They'd reached a plateau big enough to hold them both only ten yards from the top.

'No,' she said, shaking her head. 'We have to get to the top. We have to keep going. The water ...'

She put her foot onto the next step of the climb, but he pulled her back with a light touch on her arm. 'Sophie, just for a moment. The water level hasn't changed.'

Sophie shook from the cold, and she worried if she stopped her limbs would seize up, that she wouldn't be able to continue. But it was as though Hale had read her mind because he stepped up behind her and wrapped his arms around her waist, pressing himself against her back so his body heat seeped into her frigid skin.

'Oh my Goddess,' she breathed.

'Give me your hands,' he said into her hair. She complied without hesitation, and he held them between his, then lifted their joined hands to her mouth. 'Breathe on them.'

'Hale ...'

'It'll help.'

She did what he asked, feeling a little stupid as she blew air between his thumbs, but between that and his body heat, she stopped shaking, and that made her feel like she had a fighting chance of reaching the top again.

'Okay, let's go,' she said, taking a deep breath.

'You're sure?'

'The water could start again at any time.'

He released her after a reassuring squeeze of her upper arms, and she continued up the incline, glad she'd listened to him and given herself a rest. She could feel her fingers again, and her legs had stopped shaking, at least until she reached the final few steps of the path, where it branched into two.

Hale took the steeper path, hopping over the edge with ease, then turned back to face her. He looked ... dazzling, in his element, his wet hair slicked back, his muscles bulging after the climb, a roguish smile on his lips, and Sophie grew suddenly conscious of what she must look like. Perhaps worse even than the first time they'd met after Nicoli's stunt at the lake.

She ran a hand through her hair as she put her foot onto the final step, then reluctantly reached forward towards Hale's offered hand. But as she pressed all her weight down, her toe slipped and she fell hard against the path. She started sliding, her hands clutching for holds, panic flooding her because if she fell from this height, she would surely die.

Hale's eyes went wide. 'No!' he cried, diving to the ground and grabbing her arm. For a second, it looked as though Hale had gone too far over, that her weight would drag him down, but then Nicoli dove onto Hale's legs, using his full weight as an anchor, and it was enough to stop their fall.

Sophie's breaths came in short gasps, her legs flailing as her body shook anew. How long would Hale be able to hold her? Shock and fear had her in their jaws, stealing her ability to think, to——

'Sophie, feet back on the path.' Hale's voice was strained, his words clipped.

Right, the path. She scrabbled for purchase, but her feet slid again and again before she finally found some, and then Hale released her, shimmying back with Nicoli's help.

Hale jumped to his feet and offered Sophie his hand once more, but she couldn't move, even though her head and shoulders were now above the top, her folded arms resting on the lip.

'Sophie?' said Hale, crouching before her. 'It's just one more step.' He peered over the edge. 'There's a ledge by your right thigh.'

She shook her head, shivering again. 'I can't ... I can't ... I ...'

'One more step, that's all you have to do.'

'What if I slip again?' she said in a rush, avoiding his eyes.

'You won't.'

'I—'

Hale abruptly stood, looking at Nicoli. 'We'll pull you up.'

'No, I ...' But she couldn't think of a reasonable objection. It wasn't like she could stay there indefinitely, and Nicoli and Hale were already getting into position, one on either side of her.

They slid their hands under her armpits, and then Hale looked at her, his lips quirking up at the edges. 'Are you planning to help us or are we doing all the work?'

She scowled, feeling safer with their warm, strong hands supporting her weight, so much so that her fear all but evaporated. 'It's not funny,' she hissed, feeling for the hold Hale had told her about with her right foot.

'Maybe not to you ...' Hale countered.

Sophie launched herself upwards, standing hard on the ledge and throwing herself over the lip, taking them by surprise.

'Whoa, wait!' shouted Nicoli.

'Sophie!' cried Hale, staggering backwards. Nicoli maneuvered lithely out of the way, but Hale tripped over his feet and plummeted to the ground, Sophie landing half on top of him.

'Oof.' The air flew from his lungs as her weight hit his chest.

'Oops,' said Sophie, feeling a genuine pang of guilt considering he had just saved her life.

'Goddess,' breathed Hale. 'That was close.'

Sophie accidentally dug her elbows into his stomach as she tried to get up, and he inhaled sharply, grabbing her and holding her still.

'Thank you, Nicoli,' she said, looking up at him. 'Both of you. I—'

Nicoli peered over the edge, ignoring them completely. 'The water's stopped. It isn't rising.'

'What?' said Hale. 'Still?' He lurched upwards, rolling Sophie to the side so her bottom hit the ground hard.

'Ow!'

'It's stopped,' Nicoli repeated. 'It's only ankle fucking deep.'

Sophie joined them at the edge and looked down. 'But ... why?'

Hale shrugged. 'Why does the Goddess do anything?'

'It's not enough,' said Nicoli.

Sophie shook her head. 'It is enough. It has to be.'

Nicoli continued to stare downwards, unblinking, his jaw working back and forth in tiny movements. 'Fuck!' he screamed at the sky, then turned to face Hale. 'Why would she do this to us? Why return and give us a few meagre inches when we need the whole fucking thing?'

Sophie shook her head. 'It's knee deep,' she said encouragingly.

Nicoli's features turned murderous, and something about the expression made Sophie want to laugh. She tried to stifle it, but a noise like a bark broke free, making both men look at her as though she'd lost her mind. She clamped her mouth shut, but their joint incredulity made it even worse, and quick beats of laughter oscillated back and forth inside her. Then she caught the crinkle at the corner of Hale's eyes, which had gained a playful sparkle, and a giggle broke through the barrier of her sealed lips.

Nicoli scowled, and Sophie wheezed a half-hearted, 'Sorry,' as she tried to get herself under control. The situation was so utterly preposterous.

They'd run for their lives, Hale had thrown her over his shoulder like a sack of potatoes, and then Sophie had almost fallen to her death evading a flow of water that amounted to little more than a puddle. And once again she looked like a drowned rat in front of her betrothed.

It was ... funny.

Hale's lips twitched as he watched her. He bit his lip, and then he chuckled.

'Oh, for the love of the Goddess,' snapped Nicoli.

But his words only made Sophie laugh harder because it was the Goddess who had done this to them, and Hale's chuckle turned into a full laugh.

Nicoli's whole face scrunched. 'For fuck's sake. This is fucking serious!'

'We thought we were going to die!' cackled Sophie.

'You have to admit,' wheezed Hale, 'it is ...' He trailed off as another bout hit.

Nicoli squared up to him. 'You think it's funny that the Claws don't have enough water?'

'No!' breathed Sophie.

'Of course not,' said Hale.

'But Hale nearly threw himself off a cliff!' Sophie doubled over and clutched her ribs.

'And you,' cried Hale, clapping his hands and looking at Sophie, 'fell flat on your face and thought you would drown!'

'My dress is still down there,' agreed Sophie, inching towards the edge to try and see it.

'Oh no,' said Hale, pulling her back by the waist, his warm hands shocking against her bare skin. 'I'm not saving you a second time.' He led her to his horse and retrieved his cloak, which he flung around her bare shoulders, and their laughter finally ran out of steam. The wool immediately warmed her, and she inhaled the salty smell of him as he fastened the clasp then tugged the cloak straight, their eyes meeting for a lingering moment before he stepped away.

Sophie swallowed. 'Thank you. Really, both of you.' She turned to look at Nicoli, who was mounting his horse, a dark look on his face. 'If you hadn't grabbed Hale, I would have died, and Hale would have—'

'But the fate of my people is *funny*?'

'No!' Sophie said with as much sincerity as she could lace into the word.

'Come on, old friend,' Hale cajoled. 'We nearly died. People react strangely to such things. It says nothing about our feelings towards the Claws. And Sophie's right, thank you.'

Nicoli shook his head impatiently. 'But has the Goddess returned or has she not? Will the water rise farther or will it not? So much hangs in the balance, and nothing is in our hands.'

'Will the Toll Bells chime or will they not?' Sophie added quietly. All of this was uncharted territory. Perhaps that meant the old rules no longer applied. Perhaps it meant her life would soon be forfeit.

Nicoli scoffed. 'Should the Toll Bells chime, the Goddess would claim the lives of four of our most privileged, that is all. Thousands live in the Claws.'

'Of course,' said Sophie, 'I didn't mean—'

Nicoli kicked his horse into a canter, riding off towards Arow Claw without a backward glance.

'I'm sorry, Nicoli!' she shouted after him, then closed her eyes and pinched the bridge of her nose. 'Why did I do that?' She turned questioning eyes on Hale. 'Why did we laugh?'

Hale held open his hands as though it was obvious. 'Relief, Sophie. You nearly got us both killed.'

She covered her face with her hands.

'Come on,' he said. 'We should get going before you freeze or faint from shock.'

She scowled. 'I'm not going to—' His victorious smile at having successfully goaded her shut her up. 'You're so annoying.'

He grinned as he helped her up onto his horse, then surprised her by swinging up behind her, not walking alongside as she'd assumed he would.

He shunted her forward in the saddle as he slid into place, then pulled her back against him. Their bodies seemed to touch everywhere, his arms encircling her as he took the reins and asked her where she'd left her horse, the stubble on his chin rasping her cheek.

She told him, and after a few strides, she let her rigid spine soften, relaxing against him as they swayed with the rhythm of the horse. She resolved to take full advantage of Hale's warmth and smell and comfort because there was no telling when she might have access to him again.

'It was a nice dress, by the way,' he said into her hair.

She tensed. 'I didn't think you noticed such things.'

He squeezed her just above her hip. 'I notice everything.' Her insides pulled tight, and then he slid a hand inside her cloak and traced his thumb down the curve of her naked waist. 'This outfit looks good on you, too.'

Sophie tipped her head back against his shoulder and exhaled a light puff of air, every part of her focused on the slow slide of his thumb. He cupped her hip, and she had to bite her lip to keep from moaning as desire pooled tight in her belly.

'Untie your horse, Sophie,' he murmured in her ear.

'Um ... what?' she said hazily, opening her eyes, which she'd apparently closed. 'Oh.' They'd reached the tavern where Sophie had left her horse, and Hale had maneuvered them close to her mare. She swallowed, then nodded a little, trying to clear her head as she leaned back, preparing to swing a leg over his horse's neck to dismount, but he grabbed her hips, stilling her.

'Lean forward and untie her,' he said slowly, his voice husky.

'You ... don't want me to ride her?'

He slid his hand up and cupped her ribs, his thumb sliding back and forth across the ridge below her breast. 'You're freezing, and we can't risk you getting hyperthermia on the ride home now, can we?'

She exhaled a disbelieving, off-kilter, breathy laugh. *Fuck, no.* No part of her wanted to ride alone, not when the alternative was whatever Hale was doing.

She leaned forward—which only served to press her backside more firmly against Hale's crotch—and unhooked her horse's reins. Hale wheeled them away almost instantly, one hand still petting her beneath the cloak, and Sophie leaned back, closed her eyes, and soaked it up, kept in place by his powerful thighs, no idea at all what it meant.

Chapter Twenty-Seven
Ava

The world was shabby, plant life sprouting from the cracked and broken pointing in every stone wall, patches of moss and bright yellow dandelions growing in the middle of the track that led to what Billy assured Kush and Ava was the best breakfast in any world.

'It's owned by a lesser God,' Billy explained, as they approached a building that amounted to little more than a shed at the edge of the sand dunes overlooking a wind-swept beach. 'She's very old and neglectful. Never had kids. Keeps herself to herself, but she does have a thing for good food, so the place is a veritable treasure trove of culinary delights, and with beverages to match. They license my family's recipes, naturally. How I first came across the place, actually.'

They pushed through the wooden swing door into a welcome refuge from the biting wind and took a seat by one of three enormous picture windows overlooking the sea. The place was practically empty, only two of the twenty or so tables occupied, and the occupants barely even looked up when they entered the shabby wooden room.

An ancient looking stove in the corner kicked out enough heat that Ava shucked off her mother's thick blazer before sitting, hanging it over the back of her chair.

'*Fucking Atlas ...*' Billy breathed, his tone causing Ava so much alarm that she almost jumped back to her feet, her eyes flying to the door, searching for the threat. 'One fucking day knowing who you are, and you think you're a member of the Synod? I bet you don't even know what those circles stand for.' He swiveled his head dramatically towards Kush. 'Either of you.'

It took Ava a few moments to realize what Billy was talking about, her face creasing into a frown, but then she remembered the pin, the one that made her a member of the Cloud Synod, the one Kush had attached to her shirt. *Shit.* Ava covered the symbol with her hand, gripping it as though it might give her the answer to Billy's question. She had seen it before, every time she'd passed the entrance to the temple in Santala because it was emblazoned above the door, but of course he was right, she had no clue what it stood for.

'Keep your voice down!' Kush hissed in alarm, looking around to see if anyone was listening.

Billy gave a dramatic eye roll, then sat rod-straight in his seat and lifted his hand, touching the tips of his fingers to the tip of his thumb, making a ball shape. He muttered a word Ava couldn't make out as he flicked his fingers violently apart, then threw himself against the back of his chair. 'Happy?' he demanded.

Ava leaned in. 'What was that?'

Billy lifted one shoulder as though it was no big deal. 'Now they can't hear us.'

Her mouth fell open in awe. 'But, how?'

'Magic,' he said impatiently, then he shifted forwards, screwed his hands into fists, and rapped them hard on the table. 'Well? Anyone know what the circles mean?'

'They represent the Atlas Stones,' Kush said defensively, although something unsure tinged his answer.

'Ha!' Billy pushed himself back so hard, his chair tipped up on two legs. He tilted his head as it reached its apex, then grabbed the table's edge and pulled, slamming the chair's front two legs back to the ground. 'Some think so, but anyone who knows the truth knows that's not true. Anyone else?' He rounded on Ava and at the same time called the server over with an extravagant flick of his arm.

A bored looking boy strutted over, Billy ordered for the table, and then the server hurried away. 'Well?'

Ava shrugged, while Kush looked towards the sea as though it might offer escape.

Billy huffed, propped his chin on one palm, then played the table with his fingers, pursing his lips into the silence. He sat back and huffed again. 'The circles represent the three fundamental principles of the Atlas Web.

The three laws the Synod is supposed to protect.' He threw up a hand and made a tsking noise. 'The same Synod you now think you're a member of.'

The server returned with steaming, sweet-smelling drinks and plates laden with waffles, kippers, eggs, and marmalade. Ava sipped her frothy drink and almost hummed in delight, her stomach sending pleasure signals all around her body.

'Gods,' scoffed Billy, picking up his own mug, 'you'd think you'd never had hot chocolate before!'

'Then you'd be correct,' said Ava, taking another long sip, her chest lifting with joy. This was her life now. Hot chocolate and waffles and someone else bringing it to her while she just sat there doing nothing. Well, while she sat there being berated by Billy.

'What are they?' she asked, after swallowing an enormous mouthful of her magnificent breakfast. 'The three principles?'

Billy slowly picked up his mug and cradled it in his hands as he fixed his eyes on Kush. 'I can't believe Var didn't teach you this.' Kush shrugged, and when it became clear he had no intention of responding with words, Billy took a long, deep breath, then said, 'One: Take what you give. Give what you take. Two: Time is not a constant. Three: Balance is binary. Not that you'll understand what any of that means, of course.' He set his mug down and picked up his cutlery.

Ava leaned towards him, an incredulous look on her face. 'We will if you tell us.'

'And why would I do that?'

She glared. 'Why wouldn't you?'

'Oh, I don't know. Perhaps on account of missing half my soul?'

Ava was planning her retort, searching around for the most cutting rebuke she could find, when Kush put a hand on her arm. 'Please,' he said to Billy. 'I know you have no reason to trust us, but we have to find a way through this, and perhaps if we understood more ...'

Billy scoffed, but Kush continued unperturbed. 'You're right, they teach us hardly anything these days, and me less than most on account of my *questionable parentage*. If it's your soul you want, helping us is the best chance you have, seeing as Ava's the only one who can access her family's things. Not to mention, as a member of the Cloud Synod she has access to—'

Billy barked a laugh. 'What exactly do you think they'll give her access to? They hide the bits of the past they don't like—Var's orders.'

'Like what?' said Ava. 'What do they hide?'

'Oh, you know, the origins, the principles, balance, proper portalry,'—Billy gave Kush a meaningful look—'not the newfangled crap Var peddles. Back when I was young, we couldn't just take from the pools, we had to consider the principles first, but, of course, that didn't last ... Now it's nothing but take take take.'

Ava's head swam as she tried to grasp each of the threads he'd dangled in front of her, desperate to know more, but she couldn't quite keep up, like he was a pace too far away. Ava took another sip of her drink, but her arm was weary, everything so heavy, and she had to concentrate hard on swallowing.

'*Shit.* We need to go,' Billy hissed urgently, leaping to his feet and throwing a handful of coins onto the table. 'Now.'

'Kush,' Ava breathed, turning imploring eyes on him, but he wasn't looking at her, he was searching for whatever had alarmed Billy. She tried again to say his name, but her throat wouldn't comply, and then she slumped forward, her face landing noisily on her empty plate, the cutlery digging painfully into her skin.

Chapter Twenty-Eight
Maria
Six Weeks After Dromeda Started Spinning

MARIA PANICKED, THRASHING AROUND as she struggled to get free of the weight pinning her in place. Her eyes flew open, finding the ceiling had peeling paint, the curtains were made of thin yellow fabric, and the place smelled of ... of ...

'Maria, it's okay,' said Elex, the weight lifting off her waist. He held up his hand placatingly, as though approaching a wild animal. 'You're safe. You're with me.'

Maria clutched her chest as she flopped back onto the bed, trying to still her racing heart as her memories returned and relief flooded through her. 'Sorry.'

Elex stroked the hair off her forehead. 'You have nothing to apologize for. Are you okay?'

The others had sent them to bed after only one drink, had refused Elex's offer to take a watch shift and told him to look after Maria instead. If their words had contained inuendo, Maria hadn't detected it, and she'd silently thanked them for their kindness. 'I'm fine. Good. I slept well.' She'd slept like the dead, actually, even if she'd woken up dreaming of Cane. 'What about you? How do you feel about ... well, everything? Your brother ...'

He stroked her cheek. 'I have you back in my bed. How do you think I feel?'

She placed her hand on his forearm and squeezed. 'Who owns this place?' she asked, looking around at the shabby room with its threadbare rug and sparce furniture. The pictures on the walls were of horses and dogs, all old and faded, one with a broken frame.

'Are you asking if we'll be disturbed?' He gave her a rakish smile. 'The others will leave us alone ...'

Her cheeks heated, and she averted her eyes, trying to cover that he'd flustered her. 'That's not what I meant.'

He leaned down and kissed her shoulder, his movements tender and exploratory.

'How do you know them?' she asked, her eyes fluttering closed as his lips reached her neck.

He pulled back and looked down at her, tracing the line of her jaw. 'Zeik's my bastard half-brother. I have many, but Zeik's the only one worth knowing.'

'I'm sorry.'

He shrugged. 'It makes little difference to me. And I've known Tallin and Sol my whole life. Their fathers were both commanders in my father's army.'

She grabbed his hand, halting the slide of his fingers down her neck. 'They're trustworthy?'

His forehead pinched as he looked deep into her eyes. 'Beyond a doubt. Why do you ask?'

She gave a little shake of her head. 'Just checking.' She slid a hand into his hair. 'They seem nice.'

He grinned, then kissed the hollow above her collarbone. 'Exactly the description they'd hope for, I'm sure.'

She huffed a laugh as she stroked his hair. 'It was good to meet them. To see a real part of your life. I mean, we're married, and yet I know nothing about you.'

He stilled, then lifted his gaze. 'What do you want to know?'

She looked from one of his eyes to the other, a mischievous smile on her lips. 'What's the worst thing you've ever done?' She wasn't sure why she wanted to know that first.

He tilted his head and slid a thumb across her rib, making her shiver. 'You really want to know?'

She nodded, she really did.

His lips pulled up on one side. 'Aside from killing my own father?'

Her eyes flew wide. 'Oh, Elex, I'm sorry. I didn't mean—'

'I stole Cane's favorite pony when we were kids and sold it to a man in Osp Claw.'

She gasped. 'You didn't!'

'Cane never saw Dusty again, and he never got over it.'

'Elex!'

He chuckled, then rolled on top of her, caging her in his arms. 'You wanted to know ...'

She tipped her head back, and as he kissed her, she savored every press and slide, worried that at any moment she would wake up and find herself back in Cane's clutches.

He pulled back, wickedness sparkling in his eyes. 'What about you?'

She thought for a moment, then grinned. 'I once slipped John a tincture that made him miss his own birthday ball.'

Elex's eyebrows shot up. 'You little fiend!'

She lay her head back and looked at the ceiling. 'In my defense, he had been particularly obnoxious that whole week and had sworn to tell his best friend I had a crush on him.'

'Did you?' he asked too quickly.

She slowly batted her lashes as she returned her eyes to his. 'Are you jealous?'

He cocked an eyebrow. 'Desperately.' She giggled, then shrieked as he pinched her waist. 'Well?'

She grinned. 'No crush, and John never got the chance to spread his vile lie.'

He dropped a kiss on her lips. 'Then justice was served. Do you regret it?'

She snorted. 'Not for a second. Do you regret selling Cane's pony?'

He chuckled. 'Nope.'

'What about killing your father?' she said slowly, tracing her finger over his bottom lip. 'Do you regret that?'

Elex caught her hand, and her eyes went wide at his sudden intensity. 'He was a conniving, wicked, sadistic piece of shit, so no, I don't regret it. He did more harm that I can begin to describe ... to me, my mother, my siblings, Oshe, Celestl ... and he was only becoming more ambitious in his plans.' He paused for a beat, his gaze fiery. 'Does that change things between us? Do you wish for me to repent?'

She flicked her gaze back and forth between his eyes as she considered her feelings. 'No,' she said, not sure if the word was true before she said it, but in saying it, she found that it was. 'You never tried to hide who you are. I won't pretend I understand this bizarre land you call home, or your people or customs, but I trust you have reasons for all you've done. You're not cruel. You're fair and level and your friends stuck by you when they could have easily fled to Cane's side. I'm sure your father earned his fate, and it saddens me to think of all you endured.'

'Don't give him that power,' he said, shaking his head and rolling off her, sitting beside her. 'What he did to me and my family—beatings and games and fights and *challenges*—it shaped me ... taught me what not to be. I'm not glad of it, but I'm glad of the lessons I learned.'

She pushed herself up onto her elbow, wincing as she leaned on her grazed skin, and nodded slowly, understanding a little because of what she'd had to endure at the hands of her uncle—placating and coddling him, running his errands—but it was not the same, it was nothing in comparison.

Elex slid down beside her and pushed her hair behind her ear. 'What did Cane do to you last night, my little hell cat?'

She bowed her head. 'Elex ...'

'It was bad, then?'

She closed her eyes. 'No. He just ...' She looked at Elex's bare chest, unable to meet his gaze. 'It was the same as before. Humiliating, belittling. But he made me stand closer. He was angry because Erica wasn't there. He grabbed me and made me look into his eyes as Opal ...' She choked, then bit her lip, tears sliding free as she closed her eyes. 'I was powerless. That was the worst of it, that there was nothing I could do.'

Elex pressed his forehead against hers. 'I'm so sorry, Maria.'

'He's dead,' she whispered.

He cradled her face. 'I should have sent spies ahead of us before we came to Oshala. I shouldn't have brought you here ... Should have kept you safe.'

'It's not your fault.'

'It—'

She shoved him away. 'Stop, Elex. We're together now. It's over. Your brother is dead. Do not dwell on things we cannot change.'

He kissed her, and her eyes fluttered closed as she urged her mind to soak in the moment, to imprint the feeling of comfort and love on her memory, so even years in the future she could look back and feel that same way any time she liked. It was a futile hope because feelings never felt the same after the fact, but she wished for it anyway.

Elex gently kissed her jaw, her cheekbone, her temple, her neck, worshiping her with each tender press of his lips and stroke of his fingers. She surrendered to him completely, running her hands down the muscular ridges flanking his spine, then letting them fall away, lying pliant and languid, soaking up the love he lavished on her, its healing power seeping into her soul.

He sucked and kissed and stroked, soothing her with his hands and mouth but never pushing for more, backing off anytime he came close to her especially sensitive places, and careful to avoid the broken skin from her slide into the cellar. He kissed his way back to her mouth, pressing his lips to hers as though Maria was sun on light-starved skin, his being drawing her inside. Maria's chest pulsed with intoxicating feeling, her mind whispering that Elex's arms were exactly where she was meant to be, that the Goddess was rewarding them after all they'd endured, that perhaps the Goddess had crafted Elex and Maria especially for one another. But then a clatter sounded from the stairs, and their door flew open, and Zeik careened into the room.

'They're charging for fucking water!' he cried, pacing to the window and throwing open the curtains, acting as though he hadn't noticed that Elex was atop Maria in bed.

Elex gave Maria a final, lingering kiss, his hand cupping her head, then he pressed his forehead to hers, taking several steadying breaths before reluctantly rolling onto his back. 'What are you talking about?' Elex asked, propping himself up so he could look at his brother.

Zeik spun violently around. 'Erica and Opal! Announced it by pinning a piece of parchment to the gates of your quarter. *Everyone will henceforth be subject to a water tax. Anyone who can't pay will accrue a debt that must be settled within three days. No exceptions.*'

'Shit,' said Elex, running a hand through his hair.

Zeik stomped closer. 'We need to retake your quarter. Now!'

Maria sat and looked from Zeik to Elex and back again, her brain taking a moment to kick in, addled by Elex's attentions. 'We can't just retake the quarter. It's not that easy!'

Zeik scowled. 'Well, we can't just lie around in bed all day. We have to *do* something!'

'And we will,' Maria said calmly, throwing back the covers, 'but first, we need Nicoli.'

CHAPTER TWENTY-NINE

SOPHIE

SIX WEEKS AFTER DROMEDA STARTED SPINNING

SOPHIE RELUCTANTLY STRAIGHTENED AS they neared Hale's home, and he pulled his hand out of her cloak. But he didn't remove it entirely as she'd expected. Instead, he wrapped his arm around her on top of the heavy fabric and held her close, the intimacy of that somehow greater than what had come before.

But what did any of it mean? He hated her one minute, then shared his horse and coddled her the next. Why? What were his true feelings? Or was it all just a game to him?

She filled the comfortable silence with daydreams, images of them living out the remainder of their days like this together. Riding horses before breakfast, sharing tender moments. It was not like that for most in the first families, given their matches were always political, for advantage and breeding, but rarely accompanied by affection.

She cautioned herself harshly because Hale likely felt none of the fondness for her that she did for him. The way he'd spoken to her in the library suggested he cared for her the same way Sophie's father cared for her mother——which was to say not at all——yet despite that, her parents had had no issue conceiving children. Perhaps Hale had merely decided to be pragmatic in the face of his forced betrothal, deciding that sex with Sophie was preferable to finding some other woman to bed. Perhaps he saw Sophie as nothing more than an object to be used. She should probably have tried to find out, but she didn't want to risk souring the moment.

The courtyard was abuzz with activity when they rode under the arch, presumably because word had spread about the water in the Inner Circle, but a stunned hush settled when they set eyes on Hale and Sophie riding together.

'Please draw Sophie a bath in her quarters,' Hale said in a loud voice, dismounting, then helping her down, careful to immediately put a respectable distance between them.

A maid approached, wringing her hands. She curtseyed low. 'Begging your pardon, but the communal bathing areas have just been filled. It will be a half hour at least before we have enough water boiled for another bath.'

Hale nodded reluctantly. 'Very well, the communal bathing area will suffice.'

'Hale!' squealed Sophie, her voice at least an octave higher than usual. She couldn't *bathe* with the servants.

'We'll clear the women's bathhouse right away,' said the maid, who scurried off without another word.

'Hale!' Sophie hissed. 'The servants will hate me for this.'

He shrugged. 'If that's all it takes, then we should get new servants.'

We? Sophie pulled up as though a poisonous reptile had appeared in her path. Hale smirked, then strode from the courtyard. Sophie hurried after him, and when they reached the women's bathhouse, it was quiet and tranquil and blissfully empty. The space was full of lit candles, a stack of fluffy white towels waited on a stool, and the water was scented with fresh, fragrant oil.

Steam rose into the air of the cedar-clad room, swirling around them, this not at all what Sophie had expected. It was more akin to her mother's private bathing room back in Laurow than a servants' washroom. It was warm, ethereal, and heady, the mist seductive and indulgent.

Sophie pulled the pins out of her ruined updo, expecting Hale to leave now she had everything she needed, but he showed no signs of moving, watching her from a pace away as she let her hair cascade down her back. She shook out her long locks, and it felt good, pushing the strands back and forth until her scalp no longer tingled, but not quite as good as the feeling gathering in her chest as she held Hale's curious gaze.

Neither of them moved for several long moments, then Sophie lowered her eyes, looking down at the clasp on her cloak. She slid it apart, returning her eyes to Hale's as she let the fabric slide slowly off her shoulders, revealing her skimpy outfit below. Hale's eyes darkened, and he stepped towards her, hooking a finger into the waistband of her breeches and tugging her so close that only inches separated their skin.

Hale hesitated as though knowing he was about to cross a line he could never step back from, teetering on the edge of a precipice, Sophie willing him to fall. They shared each other's breaths, staring into each other's eyes, everything inside Sophie pulling tight, her skin tingling in anticipation of his touch, her open lips silently begging him to close the tiny distance between them. He lowered his head and drew her flush against him, his hands on her backside as his rough, stubble-covered cheek slid against hers, the shock of it making her nipples go hard. 'Hale ...'

'Mmm?' he said lazily, then lightly bit her earlobe.

Sophie gasped, and she lifted her hands to his waist, grabbing the bunched fabric of his still damp shirt as she pressed her temple to his.

He twisted his head and captured her lips, and she met him willingly, kissing him back without hesitation. His first kisses were light, exploratory presses, and Sophie was half worried he would change his mind and pull away, but then he slid one hand into her hair and the other around her waist and deepened the kiss. She exhaled a moan as she opened her mouth to him, their tongues mating as he pushed his leg between hers, the contact of his hard thigh against her core making her pull her shoulders back so her body arched into him, desperate for more.

She pulled his shirt from his breeches, then slid a hand beneath his waistband, her fingers finding the hard muscles of his backside and squeezing as she rocked against his leg. He abruptly broke the kiss and stepped away, Sophie reeling as Hale coughed and turned his back, the loss of his touch a physical pain, her body screaming at him to return. 'I'll ask the servants to bring you fresh clothes,' he said in a tight voice.

Hurt slammed through her as he retreated. 'Wait, Hale,' she demanded, her words halting him by the door. 'What is this?' She waited for a reply, but he didn't oblige. 'You're blowing back and forth faster than a fickle wind and it's making me nauseous.'

He stayed where he was for a few furious heartbeats , then left without another word, and she balled her hands into fists before ripping off her clothes. Why did *stupid* men have to be so Goddess-damned *stupid*? He hated her one minute, then kissed her the next ... What was *wrong* with him?

She climbed the three shallow steps that led to the wide, deep pool tiled all around with swirling patterns in lilac and white, and just as she reached the top, the door re-opened.

'Uh,' she said, covering her most intimate areas with her hands as she turned to see who was there. 'Hale?'

He closed the door with a click, his eyes roaming over her naked flesh as she stood on a pedestal in the flickering candlelight. He seemed frozen in place, and she cocked a challenging eyebrow as she removed her hands, then stepped slowly backwards into the deliciously hot water, shivering as gooseflesh rampaged across her, pulling her skin tight.

Hale said nothing. Just continued to stare.

She swirled the water with her fingertips, inhaling the smell of eucalyptus into her lungs. 'Don't pretend you've never seen a naked woman, Hale.'

His lips parted and his chest expanded as he sucked in a breath.

Sophie tipped her chin down. 'We don't frown on nudity in Laurow the way your people do.'

'That is because your father keeps a harem of whores,' he snapped.

Sophie flinched as though he'd slapped her. His words were true enough, but still they stung. She turned and sat on the shelf below the waterline, facing away, only her head poking out above the rim.

'I'll leave you to your bath, then,' he said in a strained tone.

She quickly spun. 'Why did you come back?' she asked, desperate to keep him with her, knowing this might be all she'd get of him for days ... weeks, even. What if he went back to hiding himself away? She had to prolong their time together, to show him they were two individuals who could coexist peacefully—constructively, even—convince him to spend time with her. Not to mention, if she didn't have the company of someone other than her maids soon, she would go mad.

He faltered, half turning, and she rested her arms on the side of the pool. As soon as her nakedness was hidden, his features smoothed, and Sophie inwardly mocked the prudish ways of Alter.

'I brought you this,' he said in a husky voice, holding up a tortoiseshell comb and padding to the steps. He placed it on the pool's edge, then seemed to weigh his options before exhaling heavily and dropping down to sit on the middle step.

Sophie barely dared to breathe, wishing she knew his inner thoughts, or anything to give her a clue about what he wanted.

Hale scrubbed his face with his hands. 'I must speak with my advisors about the Inner Circle.'

He wanted her council? A sounding board? Someone to share his burden? 'What will you say?'

He leaned back, resting his weight on his arms. 'I will tell them a little water has filled the Inner Circle. They will ask me what that means. I will tell them I do not know. They will grumble. I will placate them by saying we will investigate and that we should be on our guard. I will advise my people to stay out of the Inner Circle.' He paused for a beat. 'But all we can really do is wait.'

Sophie inched closer to him as she mulled over his words. 'What about the Claws?'

He turned his head. 'What about them?'

She shrugged. 'If they can get the water they need from the Inner Circle, the power dynamic shifts.'

'And?'

Sophie fought the urge to roll her eyes. 'The other Blades won't like it.'

'I couldn't care less what the other Blades like or don't like.'

This time she did roll her eyes. 'Well that's great because Spruce, Oshe, and Laurow couldn't care less what *you* think, and neither do they care about the Claws.'

He shifted, angling his body towards her, scowling hard. 'You're pretending to care about the Claws now?'

She leaned closer and scowled right back. 'You've never asked for my thoughts on anything, but I suppose I am a *woman*, so you probably think I don't have any of my own.'

He recoiled. 'No, that's not ...'

'Yes?' She batted her eyelashes, letting the façade she'd used on his brother take possession of her features. If he wanted a dumb vassal, she would show him the reality of that, and make him face the damage it did to smart women like her.

'Don't,' he snapped.

'Don't *what*, my most clever and accomplished future husband?' She pouted and looked up at him from under her lashes, then giggled behind her hand.

'Stop it.'

'Or what?' she asked breathily.

She bit her bottom lip, and his eyes snagged on the movement, then he violently turned his head away. 'I would like to know your thoughts.'

She froze. 'About the Claws?'

'About all of it. The Claws, the Goddess, the Blades, our marriage ...'

Their eyes met and held, and Sophie thawed a little as she stared into the depths of his unusually tender amber orbs. 'Why?' she asked, the word a whisper.

He said nothing for a beat, and it seemed as though he would refuse to answer, so she began to pull away, chastising herself for her stupid hope. But he stopped her, placing his hand over hers, the fabric of his shirt soaking up water as he leaned against the bath's wide lip.

'Because you are to be my wife,' he said, staring at their joined hands, 'and I want to know you. The real you.' He met her gaze once more. 'To understand what you think ... *How* you think.'

Her breath caught in her throat. 'Do you mean that or is this just some game to toy with me?'

He shook his head. 'I mean it,' he said roughly.

She traced the fingers of her free hand along the strong line of his jaw, her fingers rasping against his stubble. 'Then why are you so vile to me?'

He slid his thumb across her knuckles, his expression full of guilt but containing no sign of remorse. 'You hurt my brother.'

She exhaled an incredulous breath. 'You don't even like—'

He squeezed her hand. 'He's still my brother, and I suppose, if I'm honest, I don't like the idea of my wife and John having had ... intimate relations.'

She nodded slowly.

'And you only want me for my title ... What I represent.' The words seemed to remind him that getting close to her was a bad idea, and he lifted his hand from hers, sitting up so he faced away.

If only he knew the truth. Of course Sophie had to marry some member of an influential family——there was no getting away from that——but she wanted him for him, not because of his title. She was intrigued by him and attracted to him and was desperate for his attention. She wanted to learn about his childhood, and what he thought of Maria's match, and to know his dreams. She'd never wanted any of that with John. With John, she would have been content to live a life of separate bedrooms, smiling sweetly and gritting her teeth anytime he called for her. 'It was that way to start,' she said quietly, mainly so he might believe what she said next. 'You know how the first families operate. People like me rarely get to choose our own paths, but I had hoped ...'

He swiveled his head, his expression urging her to continue, but she chickened out, still not trusting that he wouldn't use her words against her, so she turned her back and leaned her head against the bath's edge, racking her brains for a way to break down the barriers between them. He'd said he wanted to know her. Did he mean that or did he really want information to use against her? But they had to start somewhere ... She thought for a moment, blowing ripples across the water. 'Do you realize your library contains not a single storybook?'

'Uh ...' She felt his eyes on her, and a smile pulled at her lips, but she didn't look at him, staring resolutely at a guttering candle.

'It's a travesty. And I hate politics. I loathe the fighting and back-stabbing and plotting of the Blades. I don't know the Claws, so I neither like nor dislike them, but they're people just like us, and it seems unfair for them to be downtrodden and exploited simply because their lands have no water, especially after all they've done for Celestl.

'I don't much like my father, but I feel loyalty to my parents and my Blade. They gave me all I have, made me who I am, taught me all I know. I've had an easy enough life when compared to those who know real hardship, but that's not to say I've had it easy.' She trailed off, thinking of the training she'd had to endure at her mother's hands.

'I believe the Goddess has returned,' she continued, 'and I'm increasingly worried that the Toll Bells will ring, partly because I fear stepping through the Toll Gate, but also because——' She stopped her runaway words. She'd given him plenty to be going on with and it was unwise to give him too much more.

She could still feel his gaze on her skin, could see a little of his intrigue from the corner of her eye. 'Tell me,' he breathed, his voice low and enticing.

A sick feeling filled her stomach. 'No.'

'Please, Sophie.'

She exhaled the breath she'd clamped tight inside her chest, hardly believing she was about to let down her guard with this man after all the horrible things he'd said. 'I don't want to go through the gate, Hale, because I want to know what my life will be like with you.'

A loaded silence descended, and she closed her eyes, refusing to fill it.

'The bells won't ring,' he said eventually.

Disappointment cratered her chest. That was all he had to say? 'Speaking those words won't make it so,' she said matter of factly. 'Anyway, it matters not because it's beyond our control. Will you continue to support the Claws? To share Alter's water in secret?'

He turned away again, then his elbow appeared beside her head as he leaned back on his arms. 'I won't let them suffer when we have enough to go around, and I hope they can pump the water from the Inner Circle, that they can grow their own crops again and return to strength.'

'You would like that?'

'The Claws pose no threat to my people.'

'The other Blades will stop them.'

'Perhaps. Perhaps not.'

Sophie shook her head. 'And you'll do what? Just wait and see?' It was ludicrous, wasting the opportunity to get ahead of what might turn into a crisis.

'For now,' he agreed, 'which will give me the time I need to unpick my uncle's affairs, and to tour Alter Blade and take stock.'

'You're leaving?' Her chest lurched and she held her breath, not sure she wanted to hear his answer.

'You could come ... The people of Alter will want to meet my future wife.'

She flipped over, staring at the top of his head as though she might find answers in his thick curls, still not sure if she could trust him. 'Is this the real you or will you blow cold again at any moment?'

He huffed a laugh. 'I'm never not the real me.'

She narrowed her eyes. 'And yet you regularly lurch from loathsome to ... this.'

'This?' he asked, flirtation in his tone.

She huffed, then dug her wet hands into his hair. 'This,' she breathed, gently scratching his scalp.

He tipped his head back farther, his eyes falling closed as she continued to massage his scalp and temple, tugging on small locks of his hair. 'You're good at that,' he murmured, and she moved her fingers to his ears, then his neck. She refrained from telling him she was good at it because she'd had intensive instructions aimed at her taking advantage of exactly this sort of moment.

'What do you want from me, Hale? From our marriage.' She unbuttoned his shirt and slid her hands in firm strokes across his muscular chest.

'Mmmm.'

She withdrew. 'Hale ...'

He opened his eyes, looking up at her face above him, and if her nakedness phased him now, he didn't show it.

He blinked. 'I suppose I don't know. I've never given much thought to the topic. I'd planned to avoid marriage for as long as possible ... Until your mother forced my hand by finding my darkest secret.'

Sophie hissed, the sound a surprise even to her—she was usually so good at keeping her emotions in check.

He sat in a swift movement and turned to face her, and she ducked below the water, hiding her breasts, feeling unusually vulnerable under his scrutiny. 'Sophie ... I didn't mean ... I just ...' He looked down at the tiles as he collected his thoughts. 'This morning, when the water knocked us over, and then again when you slipped at the top of the cliff, you nearly died, and it felt like I'd ...' He huffed out a breath. 'Like I'd nearly lost something.'

It was a peace offering of a kind, but a sinking feeling dropped through Sophie's vital organs as she realized once again that she'd been a romantic fool. *That he'd nearly lost something?* Like she was some possession, perhaps akin to a favorite quill or dagger, an object he was fond of but would put from his thoughts easily enough.

She forged a protective iron wall between them in her mind, one she would not let him penetrate, then she cocked her head seductively. 'Would you like to know *my* darkest secret? I'm not sure you can truly know a person until you know that, and I know yours, after all, which is, as you so gallantly reminded me just moments ago, the only reason you're marrying me.'

He pulled back a little, shaking his head in confusion, this clearly not the reaction he'd expected.

She covered his hand with hers. 'I'll tell you in return for an answer of my own.'

'Sophie …' He tried to put space between them, but she held tight to his hand and inched closer, her eyes boring into his, daring him to look away because unlike before, where she'd shown him tenderness and fragile hope, this time her stare was a cold steel blade. A fuck you.

'Did you do it?' she whispered coquettishly. 'Did you work with Nicoli and John to kill your uncle?'

He shook his head at the floor for a moment, then yanked his hand from her grip. 'Why do you even care?'

'Because just like you, I want to know the person I'm being forced to marry.'

He held her gaze for a long moment. 'Story books are for children,' he said harshly, pushing to his feet. 'It makes sense now why you seek them.' He stormed away, and she waited until the door slammed shut, then ducked her head under the water and screamed.

CHAPTER THIRTY
AVA

THE HERIVALE DIDN'T TASTE normal as it hit Ava's tongue, the flavor mingling strangely with the bits of kipper still in her mouth, that all Ava had time to think before rough hands slid under her arms and yanked her upwards. She registered the cold gust of a briny sea breeze, an uneven road beneath her feet, and then Kush and Billy's urgent whispers.

'Do it!' Billy hissed. 'Now!'

'No! Anyone can see us! And Ava isn't back to herself yet.'

'Better watched than captured. They're coming, Kush!'

Ava felt a sudden yanking sensation, then snapped back to full consciousness as they landed in the library of her parents' house. Kush tried to lower her into a chair, but she shoved him off, already feeling fine.

'What happened?' she demanded.

Billy stalked to the shelf where he'd left two bottles of liquor the night before, swigging straight from the bottles, one after the other. 'A man was watching us from the beach.'

Kush shook his head. 'You think he was a spy?'

Billy set the bottles down with a thud. 'I need to speak with Ava. Alone. Now.'

Kush looked from Ava to Billy and back again, and Ava wasn't sure what to say. Kush gave a slow, disappointed shrug. 'I'll be in the solarium if you need me.' He pointedly slid the Atlas Stone into Ava's hand before leaving the room, and Ava's chest tugged at the sight of him walking away.

'What if it was him?' said Billy, pacing frantically. 'What if he tipped someone off?'

Ava half laughed in disbelief. 'When could he have?'

Billy grabbed the back of a chair. 'When we got there, perhaps.'

'But *you* chose the destination! And we both put our trust in you when we agreed to that, I might add.'

Billy dropped into a seat, elbows on his knees, drumming his fingers on his cheeks.

'Billy, it's fine. We're safe now.'

He turned sharp eyes on her. 'We'll never be safe, Ava. Not with Var ...' He folded his arms and bent forward as though in pain.

'Billy?' she breathed, sitting next to him, placing a tentative hand on his shoulder. 'Are you okay? What's going on!'

He slowly lifted his head, looked her dead in the eye, and went abnormally still. 'He'll betray you, Ava. He will.'

Ava frowned, not understanding.

'Kush!' Billy said insistently. 'His loyalty is to Var. And Var does unnatural things ... Terrible things. None of them ever cared about the rules, not really. And when they split their souls, they thought themselves above such things. They thought they'd somehow won, that they'd overcome the very foundations of the web by understanding some hidden meaning in the principles. But they were wrong, and balance is binary ...'

Ava shook her head in frustration. 'I don't understand, Billy.'

He jumped to his feet. 'No,' he hissed, 'and that is the problem!'

'Then help me! Teach me. If Var is the enemy, then we need to work together!'

He scoffed and threw up a hand. 'It won't make any difference. Even if I teach you all I know, you're not your mother. B was right, I see that now, and Kush will always report on us like a good little lapdog.' Billy picked up both bottles of liquor, then lay on the floor, his eyes trained on the map painted on the ceiling.

Ava exploded to her feet. 'So that's it? Your solution is to lie down and get drunk?'

'As good a solution as any that's presented itself.'

Ava gritted her teeth and headed for the door before she said something she would regret, aggravation bubbling through her veins. She wanted to lay into him, to chastise him for running to a bottle every time anything got difficult, but perhaps he was right, perhaps it was as hopeless as he made out and they should all take comfort where they could. Either way, she needed him. He was her only source of information and the only God who was likely to speak to her, to teach her anything useful, which meant she had to find something she could tempt him with to make him cooperate.

She headed to her parents' room and put her hand over the section of wall the house had refused to open for Billy. 'I'd like to see inside, please,' she whispered, and after what felt like a reluctant pause, lines appeared in the shape of a rectangle, and a panel swung open.

She gasped, magic still so alien to her, regardless of how casually Billy used it. She stared for a beat and then she pulled herself together and examined the contents.

A leather journal sat inside, along with a ream of dog-eared letters tied up with string, and Ava's heart raced as she reached for them. Were they her mother's or her father's? And why had the house refused to let Billy see them?

She sat on the bed and opened the journal, flicking through the pages, desperate to find any reference to the Atlas Stones or soul splitting. It contained endless diagrams with scrawled notations she couldn't decipher, and her eyes snagged on several drawings depicting lengths of wood twisted together, reminding her of the one in the package B had given her on her birthday. But she continued to the end without pause, then closed the journal because she found no obvious mention of anything Billy would care about.

Ava set the journal down, then untied the letters. They were all addressed to her mother, and all written in an identical untidy hand. She pulled one open, and her heart lurched when she saw it was from Novak. He and her mother had had a close friendship, but then she'd treated him badly ... or so Billy had said. Part of her felt she should put the letters back and let her mother's private business stay in the past, but that wouldn't help her get Billy on side, and she was itching with curiosity, so she began to read, her progress painfully slow, seeing as she had to sound out most of the words.

Polly,
Polly, Polly, Polly. Come to the party with me. You know I'm the most fun.
Also, I've been thinking about how the trees keep the portals open, a little mental exercise I'd never entertained before you dropped your cryptic ques-

*tion. And the short answer is: I don't know. I can't work it out. Will you tell
me?*
Novak

Ava put the first letter down and moved straight on to the next one.

Pol,
You went to the party with him. *WHY? Don't worry, I understand why, but
does he really have to sit with us in class? He stares at you. It's disturbing.
Surely we can agree on that?*

  *I enjoyed our one dance, and the blush on your cheeks said you did, too,
although I wish you'd had time for more ... and that Rupert hadn't watched
us like a hawk. Again, unsettling, no?*

  *So this whole roots-twist-the-portal-open thing, I'm going to need more on
that. It doesn't make any sense. Meet me for a study session? Somewhere
public, so a certain somebody doesn't get upset. Surely he can spare you for
longer than the length of one dance? He's a Blackwood, for Atlas' sake. He's
not scared you'll run off with someone like me ... is he?*
Novak

Ava's cheeks heated as she read. The words weren't meant for her eyes, and
she feared what she might find, yet nothing could have torn her away from
this window to the past she so sorely wanted.

Polly, Polly, Polly,
He damn well is *scared you'll run off with someone like me. Hilarious (although I'm game if you are?)! I'm not sure he understood your explanation
about quilliam portals and the quarter eight shift, but I did, and my mind
is exploding with questions. When can we meet again? And this time, can
you please ditch the side piece?*

  *Remember, when you marry him (because judging by the
who-would-have-thought-it-possible increase in spine-chilling staring intensity, he most certainly plans to propose—maybe soon—and of course you'll
say yes because he's a Blackwood and you'd be kicked out of the Clouds if you
didn't), that you are better than him in every possible way.*

And I'm not just saying that because he's a jerk and I happen to love you (have done for a while). But please, just remember he needs you more than you need him. And referencing the aforementioned running off ... just say the word, Princess Pol.
N

Ava sat heavily on the bed and dropped the letter into her lap. Had her mother returned Novak's feelings? Had she only married Rupert because she'd had no other choice? Then again, perhaps Novak's feelings had been unrequited, or Polly had loved both men, or perhaps she'd loved neither, a mere object for others to fight over.

Urgh. She picked up the next letter and read on.

Pol,
Please don't do this, I'm begging you.
Do you think we'll be able to spend more time together outside the Clouds? That we'll have more freedom? Is that what this is about? We won't, P, Rupert won't allow it. And my Cloud and non-Cloud relatives are separate for a reason.
Please, Polly. Please leave it be.
Novak

Pollyana,
You're a bitch. You're worse than that, but I don't want to waste my time thinking of better words. You should work with Rupert from now on. I'm sure he'll be a great sounding board for quadrative twists. Or perhaps B can assist. Good luck with that.
Novak

Ava sucked in a ragged breath. What had happened? What had Polly done? Novak's hurt was a palpable thing. She tore into the next letter, wishing they had dates.

Pol,

I'm sorry for your loss—Celia was a force—and congratulations on your marriage. Perhaps I can be Godparent to your firstborn ...

And please don't worry. The unnatural portals, as you call them, continue to work well. Var assures me they function the same as the natural versions, and up close they truly seem to. No hexacles to worry about, either. What is it you don't like ... aside from the obvious?
Novak
P.S. Perhaps we should talk.

Was Novak Ava's Godfather? But if he was, why hadn't he looked after her when her parents died? Why had he dumped her on B? Perhaps because he hated her mother, just like Billy seemed to?

Polly,
Once again I find myself writing to beg you not to do something. I'm sure the result will be the same as last time, but at least my conscience will be clear.

No, I do not want to split my soul so I can live forever. The span of one natural lifetime is quite enough, especially without you. Why would I want more? No one should take more than they've been given, including you. What will you give to counteract taking this much? It's unnatural, and I will remind you of your disdain for unnatural things ... of the danger ...

You ask for my silence, and you have it because I love you, but it will get out, Pol. Not by my lips, but you know it will.
N

Pol,
My cousin? Really? And Billy? You used them for your experiment? Do you care nothing for anyone but yourself?

I knew it was too much to ask that you heed my warning, but now, to save B, to clean up your mess, I've lost my place in the Clouds. And do you know why B did it? Why she told them about your discovery? It's poetic, really. She did it because she doesn't like the way you treat Rupert and me. Doesn't like your power over us, the way we fawn over you ... By Atlas, you must think us pathetic.

Remember when I begged you to stop? None of this would have happened if you'd just listened for once. But that's you all over, Princess. *You ate B up then spat her out, all the while pretending you cared. I once thought Rupert's staring sinister, but now I know I was wary of the wrong half of your twisted love affair. You were the villain all along.*

Perhaps you'll take some perverse comfort in that while you're splitting the souls of every young person in the Clouds. How many more lives will you ruin with your schemes? What of the cost? How long before it catches up with you ... with all of us? Don't you ever wonder about that?
Novak

Ava shivered. Billy had been right, Novak hadn't wanted the long lives of the others, had known it would end badly.

P,
You shouldn't have come. The dress, the mask, the club, the ... everything. You weren't yourself, and neither was I. It can't happen again.
N

Pol,
You're with child, and B is beside herself. Everything's changed. Everyone's changed. You're the reason, I feel it in my bones. But this is ... It's too much to bear. It's cruel, even for you. B wants what you have. Desperately. Please, if you ever felt for me at all, give back her soul.
N

Polly,
I witnessed something tonight. I need to see you. Come, please. Use the stone. Tell no one.
Novak

That was it, the last letter, and now there was even more Ava didn't understand. The letters seemed to corroborate Billy's story, but what had B wanted? And what did Novak mean about the cost of her mother's actions, and the danger of unnatural things?

Ava shoved the letters back into the hidden compartment and closed the door. They were useless in her quest to convince Billy to help her.

She huffed a disappointed exhale, but she would get Kush to show her the location of the other places the house had refused to open for him and Billy; perhaps one of those would contain something useful. But as she tried to get up, her arms and legs refused to budge.

'Shit.' *Stone sickness*, she realized, but, thank Atlas, unlike every other time, she could still use her voice, and she still had enough control to keep herself upright.

'Kush!' she yelled, but he was too far away. *Shit, shit, shit.* And then she remembered the house. 'House, please amplify my voice like you did to Kush's the other day.' She paused, waiting for a change, but nothing felt different. 'Kush!' she screamed, and this time, her panicked voice echoed through the whole place. 'Stone sickness!'

A door crashed open downstairs, then came the slap of wet feet on wooden floorboards, the creak of weight on the stairs, and then he was there, wearing nothing but a towel, dripping water on the floor, a vial of Herivale in hand.

'Thank you,' she whispered, her volume back to normal, the house apparently knowing she no longer wanted her voice to boom in every room.

Kush cradled her face and administered the cure, checking her eyes to make sure she was okay. 'I thought you were with Billy ...'

She shook her head. 'Billy preferred a bottle, but the sickness wasn't as bad this time. It's getting better.'

'Good,' he said, sounding relieved. 'Find anything?' He nodded to the journal still on the bed.

'Nothing much. Just that and some letters from Novak to my mother. He loved her, but she chose Rupert, and then she fucked everything up just like Billy said.'

He squeezed her shoulder. 'I'm sorry.'

She balled her fists in frustration. 'I need Billy's help. He's the only one who can teach me anything useful. If I can just give him something he wants first, get him to trust me ... Or barter with him.'

Kush pulled back, looking down into her eyes as though trying to find the right way to say whatever was bothering him. 'What do you want out of all this?' he asked eventually.

Her brow furrowed. 'What do you mean?'

'You have more wealth than it's possible to imagine, a magic house, and an Atlas Stone. You could do anything, go anywhere.'

Panic flared in her chest. 'You think I should leave?'

'No! But ... you could, if that's what you wanted.'

She scowled. 'Why would I want that?'

'Why wouldn't you want to get away from this mess?'

'Like you, you mean?' she asked cynically.

He growled a little as he breathed out. 'It's different for me.'

'Why?' she demanded.

'My father is very much alive. I don't have the freedom you do.'

She tilted her head and pursed her lips, taking a moment to slow the conversation, to consider his suggestion. She gave a long sigh. 'Where would I even go, Kush?'

'Anywhere!'

'I'd be alone.'

'You'd be free.'

'I'd be hunted,' she snapped.

'No.' He shook his head. 'Father would leave you alone eventually, just like he did before.'

'After how many years of my life spent in hiding? Looking over my shoulder. Terrified. Wondering every day if I would be discovered.'

Kush bowed his head.

'You've had enough of me already, is that it?' She tried to make the words light, jokey. She failed.

He shook his head. 'I love you, but if that means letting you go, then—'

She surged to her feet. 'I'm a part of *this* world whether you like it or not. And if I can learn magic, maybe I can be useful. Maybe I can change things. You said it yourself, I have a seat on the Synod. You think I should walk away from that? From the ability to fight for the people who weren't born in the Clouds? People like the girl I was until a few days ago. What would it have been like if someone had fought for me?'

Kush ran a hand through his hair. 'You don't understand what you're up against. And I suppose ...' He turned away, shaking his head a little. 'I wish I had the possibilities you do.'

'Why?'

He whirled back to face her. 'My father controls every aspect of my life.'

'He's not controlling you now.'

'And I'll pay for this time eventually, unless I can convince him I was somehow working with him.'

She flinched. 'You'll go back to him, then?'

'No! But you have to understand, Ava, he is everywhere! Unless I live inside these walls for the rest of my life, his enforcers will catch me and haul me back to him eventually.'

'Will they even need to haul you back?' she asked quietly. 'You said it yourself, you *believe* in his goals ... in what he's trying to accomplish.'

Kush paused, going very still and looking down into her eyes as though trying to work out if she'd just laid a trap. 'I believe in some of it,' he said carefully. 'The Federation, stabilizing the portals ...' A haunted look pulled at his features. 'But not all of it. Not the killing and taking what he likes when he likes. Not the plotting or the way he treats me and my mother. Not his friends. Not his plans for you.'

She straightened. 'What are his plans for me?' He'd never told her that.

Kush bit his bottom lip, then let it slide free. 'He wants his soul, and he wants all the other souls, too. You're the only one who can give him that.'

Ava let out a disbelieving huff of laughter. 'He wants to hold the other Gods' souls hostage just like my parents did to him?'

Kush lifted one shoulder.

'And what will he do with me once he has what he wants?'

Kush looked at the floor and shook his head.

'Kush!' she laughed his name incredulously. 'He wants to *kill* me.'

'He doesn't.'

She rubbed her face with her hands. 'And why are you so sure his intentions for the Federation are good?'

'They are,' he bit out.

'Why do you think that?'

'I just ... I know they are.'

'How?'

'Ava.' He said her name like a curse and a bolt of panic stabbed sharply through her chest because he'd never spoken to her like that before, like he might hate her.

'I'm sorry,' she breathed, terrified he would go back to Var—he'd said it himself, it was a question of when, not if—and he thought she should run away and live without him. But she couldn't lose him. She needed him. He was all she had. 'Kush, look at me.' She took his hands, meeting his eyes, showing him only softness. 'I love you. I didn't mean to upset you.'

He pulled her close, and Ava almost cried. 'My father is complicated, Ava. It's hard even for me to understand sometimes, but he wants the Federation to succeed. And if you trust nothing else, trust that his own fortunes and those of the Federation are closely linked. If the Federation fails, the Gods lose most of their power, most of their wealth and status. I trust in that. In their greed. But also, they feel pride when they visit the federated worlds, when they see people prospering who otherwise would have floundered. It gives them a sense of accomplishment they can't get elsewhere.'

She didn't want to fight with him, but she'd seen firsthand that the Federation wasn't good for everyone. 'I lived in Santala and barely survived, Kush. The Federation did nothing for me; I didn't even know it existed.'

He squeezed her harder. 'It was better than the alternative.'

'What is the alternative?' she asked gently.

He cradled her head, holding her face to his chest so she could feel his words rumbling through him. 'Closed borders, no trade, no access to the temples and their healing waters.'

'None of that made a difference to my life in the tavern,' she whispered.

'It did, you just didn't know it.'

Ava pushed off his chest and paced to the window, hiding her frustration. 'Maybe.' Or maybe Kush was almost as clueless about her past life as she was about his. 'I'm not running, Kush,' she said in a firm, even tone. 'I want to understand the Atlas Web, the principles Billy spoke of, the Clouds, and I want to learn magic, which means I need Billy, unless you know someone else who can teach me?'

'*Why*, Ava? Why not leave the past in the past and live your life?'

She spun to face him. 'Because this is my life. The one I was born into. This is about who I am, who my parents were, and I want it. All of it. Just like you want your legacy, I want mine.'

'You're wrong. I want no part of any of this, but unlike you, I have no choice.'

'I'm sorry.'

He squared his shoulders. 'It's not for you to be sorry about,' he said in an aloof, clipped tone.

Long beats of silence stretched between them, and Ava began to panic that she'd pushed him too far. 'Will you show me the other places the house wouldn't let you see?' she asked quietly.

He seemed conflicted, avoiding her eyes.

'Please, Kush. Maybe the house is hiding something that could help us both.'

He gave a long sigh, then shrugged in defeat. 'If it's what you really want.'

Chapter Thirty-One
Maria
Eight Weeks After Dromeda Started Spinning

'I've already sent messengers to Nicoli,' said Elex, as he and Maria gratefully accepted plates of eggs, bacon, and pancakes from Tallin.

Zeik sat heavily on the opposite side of the square table in the taproom. 'But Nicoli hasn't responded.'

Maria swallowed a delicious mouthful, her stomach gurgling appreciatively, the cuts and scratches on her feet aching a little from the walk down the stairs. 'I'll write to him.'

Zeik's eyes flicked to Elex, who shrugged and pressed his leg against Maria's under the table. 'Maria and Nicoli have been friends for years. He didn't answer my request, but maybe he'll answer my wife's.'

'Your wife!' laughed Zeik, holding up his coffee mug and saluting Elex with it. 'How strange that is.'

Maria scowled, still a little annoyed about Zeik's untimely intrusion into their bedroom not ten minutes before.

'Strange but wonderful, I mean,' Zeik amended.

'You're a marvel, is what Zeik meant to say,' said Tallin, from the next table over, 'and we're very glad you're with us. It's just unexpected for Elex to be the first of us to wed.'

Maria side-eyed her husband. 'Is that so?'

'Thank you,' Elex said with finality, his eyes flashing in warning at his friends.

Zeik and Tallin laughed.

'It could have gone differently,' Maria said cheerlessly. 'It nearly did, and my brothers were not so lucky.' A poignant silence settled over them, but Maria would not let sad thoughts bring her down, not when she was finally free of Cane and back with her husband. She snapped them out of it with a sharp inhale. 'So, what shall I ask of Nicoli?'

Zeik nodded and slid his cutlery together on his empty plate. 'To move water from the lake below up to the city, we pump it into a reservoir just beneath the surface, and from there, it's piped throughout Oshala.'

Elex pushed away his own empty plate. 'The pumps and the main water outlet are in my quarter.'

'Erica and Opal's quarter,' corrected Zeik.

'Not for long,' Elex countered darkly.

'If we can redirect the water, either on the way into the reservoir or the way out,' said Tallin, 'then we take half their power.'

Maria nodded slowly, turning it over in her mind. 'I understand what's in it for us, but what's in it for Nicoli? Why would he help a Blade after everything that's happened?'

Zeik drummed his fingers on the table three times, then stopped. 'Because it's the strategic move. We want to help Nicoli, to treat the Claws as our equals, but we can't do that until we take back control.'

Maria looked at her husband. 'And if he refuses?'

Elex shrugged. 'Then we'll have to work it out ourselves.'

Maria's eyebrows shot up. 'And risk all the water?'

He shook his head. 'No, not that. I would never risk doing anything to the water supply without help from Nicoli. I meant we'll overthrow Erica and Opal. It will be easier if we control the water, but we'll do it either way.'

'It will be bloody if we have to fight our way in, though,' said Tallin.

'I'll write to Nicoli,' said Maria, 'but I don't know if he'll come. We've been close for years, but we're not on the best of terms right now.'

Elex slid his hand over hers. 'Thank you.'

She squeezed his fingers. 'Even if he refuses to help, the people inside your quarter are ready to rise up. They're loyal.'

'How do you know?' asked Zeik, a tinge of suspicion in his words.

'Zeik ...' Elex growled in warning.

Maria put her hand on top of Elex's, sandwiching it between her two. 'It's fine, Elex. He's right to question.' She turned her head to Zeik. 'Because I made friends with the servants. I gave them bath oils to gain their trust, and eventually traded those for information. I met with a midwife whose daughter was the one who distracted the gate guard the night you lost the quarter. The midwife was furious, embarrassed, hated Cane. I also met the woman whose son opened the gate. He was just a naïve child. They want to make it right. They told me they're ready, that the whole quarter is.'

Zeik tapped his cheek, humming thoughtfully. 'It's not a lot to go on.'

Elex nodded in agreement. 'No, but it's something.'

'And let's face it, we're going to give it a go either way,' Tallin said jovially, leaning back and resting his feet on the table, 'so at least we have a midwife and a grieving mother with us, if no one else.'

Maria turned pensive as the reality of Tallin's words washed over her. More fighting, unknown odds, certain death for many. She sent a silent prayer to the Goddess that her husband would not be among those who fell. How many more would have to die before they could live in peace? She wondered how the other Blades fared. Were they in turmoil also? Were her siblings in good health?

'What are you thinking about?' Elex asked as Zeik went to fetch parchment and ink for her letter to Nicoli.

She sighed and sat back in her chair. 'I was just wondering about the other Blades, and hoping my siblings are well. I don't even know if Pixy, my sister, married the first son of Spruce like she was supposed to.'

'We'll send a messenger,' he said quickly. 'We'll do it today.'

Her chest swelled. 'Thank you.'

'It's a simple thing. I just wish it was as easy to find out about my sister. Father said she ran from Laurow, but ...'

'Where would she go?'

He lifted his hands. 'She's always had secrets.'

Tallin's feet thudded to the ground, and he noisily cleared the plates.

'Does she have friends in Oshe?'

'Probably, but I don't know who they are.' Elex cast a glance Tallin's way. 'I've always respected her privacy, and she did the same for me. We weren't close, but we had a kind of understanding.'

Tallin made a growling noise as he cleared his throat, and Maria frowned at him as she put a supportive hand on Elex's leg, wondering why Tallin was being so insensitive. 'Maybe she's lying low until everything settles down.'

The taproom door swung open, and Sol appeared in the entryway, something like awe on his face as he strode inside. 'Water,' he breathed.

'What?' Tallin demanded, abandoning the plates on the bar.

Sol looked at each of them in turn as though about to convey words laced with magic. 'The Inner Circle's filling with water. It's only ankle deep so far, but the Goddess ... she must truly have returned!'

Tallin and Sol clapped each other on the back and made gleeful noises, but Maria remained frozen in place, the news making her blood run cold.

Chapter Thirty-Two
Sophie
Six Weeks After Dromeda Started Spinning

Sophie fidgeted with the collar of her dress as she followed a servant to Hale's quarters for dinner. The stairs were endless, and she was nervous after what had happened in the bathhouse. Not that she regretted her words. Obviously no one ever called Hale out on his insensitive bullshit, but she would not pander. She was to be his wife, and she would start as she meant to go on.

But this damned dress was so restrictive, the collar so high it practically severed her airway. The fashion in Alter was strange, that was for sure, but Hale seemed to prefer it to the styles of her homeland, and this was to be her home now, too, so she would make an effort.

She wondered, as she trudged up yet another staircase, if Hale was the kind of man to hold a grudge. Would he be angry about the way she'd spoken to him earlier? Would he punish her? Was that why he'd called her up here? That was the way they did things in Laurow. It seemed different in Alter, but maybe they just put up a better façade.

Well, Sophie wanted to punish *Hale* for the way he'd treated her, for what he'd said, but it was more important to build than to win, so she would swallow her pride and convince him that they should forge a pragmatic partnership that worked for them both. After their conversation in the bathhouse, Sophie had resolved to put her silly notions of finding a love like Maria and Elex had behind her, but there was no reason why she and Hale couldn't be happy enough … just like one was when one used a favorite quill or dagger.

But she would have to be careful, to guard her heart. He changed so fast it gave her whiplash. Perhaps it would always be that way with him, perhaps that was who he was, and she would have to learn to deal with it, but she dearly hoped that wasn't the case.

The corridor hit what looked like a dead end, but then Sophie's eyes found a spiral staircase in the gloom, and up her escort went, Sophie following a few steps behind. She briefly wondered if this remote part of the mansion was where Hale's family kept their prisoners, but before she could run for her life, the servant knocked on a sturdy, bottle green, circular door, then retreated.

Hale opened up almost immediately, looking divine in casual pants and a pressed shirt, his sleeves rolled up to his elbows, no shoes on his feet, his face freshly shaven. Sophie felt almost overdressed.

'Hi,' he said, moving back to let her in. He seemed almost nervous.

'Hi,' she replied, tentatively stepping past him into a breathtaking space. 'Oh ... wow.' His arm brushed hers as he closed the door, and she quashed the zing of awareness that travelled through her, focusing instead on the shear marvelousness of the room.

It was large and round with a domed glass ceiling, decked out in a strange, mismatched style. Some items screamed luxury—the sofas and circular table in the corner laid for dinner—but a hammock hung from two of the wooden struts of the dome, and navigation charts had been pinned haphazardly to the walls, overlapping one another. The desk was a mess of notes and rough sketches—of what she couldn't see—and she caught a glimpse of what looked like his bedroom through an open door on the far side of the space, which seemed to be a smaller version of the first room, complete with its own dome.

Clinking sounded from overhead, and Sophie jumped, then looked to Hale to see if there was cause for concern. He smiled reassuringly, slipping his hand into hers and tugging her farther into the room, the shades covering the glass sections of the dome sliding down a little, revealing more of the sky.

'They open and close of their own accord,' he said, leaning towards her. 'It's ingenious. Hugely complex, but Nicoli helps maintain it. One of his ancestors created it for one of my ancestors, and without the shades, it would be unbearable up here at midday.'

'Oh,' said Sophie, interested to a point, but far more intrigued by Hale's handholding and volunteering of information.

'It's a little bizarre to have these circular structures hidden away up here, but I've always liked them, and my grandmother keeps me company next door.' He pulled her to a window through which she could see another domed structure. This one was directly below the Toll Bell, and Hale's grandmother was reading in an upholstered armchair by a window made of many small panes.

Their movements must have caught her eye because she looked up and waved, and Sophie couldn't help but chuckle as she waved back. She'd only met the woman a couple of times, but Sophie had warmed to her, drawn in by the twinkle in her eye and the way she'd stood up to Danit. She seemed not to be cowed by anyone.

Hale stepped away from the window, and Sophie took a moment to scan the room as she tried to get her head around the shift in him from earlier. Why had he invited her into his private space, especially after how things had ended in the bathhouse? Her eyes snagged on a low bookshelf beside a worn armchair, and it drew her in. What did Hale fill his head with?

She crouched beside the wooden shelves and ran her fingers over the spines as she read the titles. Nautical navigation books mainly, with the odd tome on the falls of Celestl, the history of the Inner Circle, and inter-Blade relations. *Scintillating stuff.*

'Don't you read anything fun?' she asked, standing and finding Hale watching her.

His lips twitched. 'Nautical navigation is fun.'

'The doing of it perhaps, but reading about it ...?'

He moved to his desk. 'Well, I have time for nothing but the documents and ledgers in Danit's office these days.' The words were dry but something about the way he said them made them seem playful.

She smirked. 'I suppose the scandal found there is its own kind of entertainment.'

He smiled wryly as he picked up a small, leatherbound book from a short stack on the floor beside his desk, then held it out to her.

She took it warily, half expecting it to be lessons on decorum, but her eyes flew wide when she read the spine. '*Tales from the Tree*?' Her hackles immediately rose. 'You said story books are for children.'

He raised an eyebrow. 'Not that one ...'

Her cheeks heated, wondering just what exactly he'd given her.

'And I said a lot of things you should probably ignore.'

Interesting. She looked up, meeting his gaze. 'Go on.'

'Danit had a whole collection of these books hidden at the back of his office. I was always told such things were foolish fancy, but—'

'Whoever told you that was lying?' Hale grinned, and Sophie softened a little. 'Do you want to know what I was told about such things?'

'Yes,' he said without hesitation.

'I was told books like these contained clues about our past, our present, and our future. They tell stories of magic and heroes and great battles and travel between worlds.'

'And they speak of many Gods and Goddesses, but we only have one,' he countered.

'Perhaps it was not always so.'

'Or perhaps they're just stories.'

She scowled. 'Aren't you curious?'

His smile widened. 'Endlessly.'

The word brought her up short. 'But ...'

He shrugged. 'We have no evidence one way or another. I'm merely saying either option is possible.'

She blew out a frosty breath, mostly because she had to concede that he was right.

'The books are yours if you want them,' he said gently.

She thawed, gratefully accepting his peace offering. She'd been going out of her mind with no good books to read. 'Thank you. I do want them and I look forward to reading them, even if you still secretly think they're childish.'

'I don't—'

'Yes, you do!'

'Sophie, I——'

'Perhaps you should read them. Maybe then you'll see.'

He cocked a victorious eyebrow. 'As it happens, I already have one on my nightstand.'

She regarded him carefully, searching for any hint of a lie but discovering not a whisper, and that turned her speechless.

Hale moved to the table and picked up a bottle, a deep popping noise filling the air as he flipped the lid. 'Drink?'

'Thank you,' she said, joining him at the table and accepting the glass of gently fizzing yellow liquid he offered. He pulled out a plush, cushioned chair, and she cautiously sat, on edge, still uncertain of his intentions and worried his tone might change at any moment, just like it had many times before.

He slid onto the seat beside her and held up his glass in salute. 'I wanted to apologize.'

'Oh?' said Sophie, straightening and wondering what she was missing.

'I'm sorry, Sophie,' he said, leaning forward, his eyes capturing hers, something about the way he said her name sending gooseflesh flying across her skin. 'We got off to a bad start, and I'd like to try and explain. I know I've been ...'

'An arsehole?'

A laugh broke through his lips. 'Changeable?'

'Oh, you mean how you cornered me in the corridor one minute and treated me like a traitor the next?'

He sat back in his seat and appraised her. 'Well, yes, if we're being blunt about it.'

She nodded. 'Your honesty is refreshing if nothing else.'

He leaned forward again, this time with an intensity she hadn't seen in him before. 'From the first moment I saw you, I wanted to hate you. John was obviously head over heels, and I didn't want anything to come between my brother and me, much as he's a ... What did you call him?'

'A limp fish.'

Hale smirked. 'Much as he's a limp fish sometimes. But I also wanted to stay out of the pact. I didn't want to be a part of it, but neither did I want to jeopardize it.'

He paused, and she waited for him to continue, holding back the cutting remarks that fought to be set free.

He took her hand. 'I can't stop thinking about you, Sophie. You invade my dreams and my waking thoughts. When I saw you in the Inner Circle today, for a second I wondered if I'd conjured you from my mind, and then I was gripped by a fear stronger than I've ever known. I couldn't bear the idea of losing you.'

Sophie sat back, stunned. She wanted to believe him——and his words seemed genuine——but she didn't know if she could.

'I'm sorry for the way I treated you ... For the things I said. I know how to command a ship full of rowdy sailors, but you ... This situation ...' He ran a hand through his hair and then got to his feet, pacing a few steps away before turning back and meeting her gaze. 'My brain counsels caution, whispers that maybe you're playing with me, that you and your mother are a team, some scheme between you. It's driving me insane, and ... I want you, Sophie, but can I trust you?'

The agony on his face was like an arrow through Sophie's heart because he was right not to trust her. Then again, if she told him the truth, it might shatter any hope of there ever being trust between them.

'Did you work with Nicoli to kill your uncle?' she asked, her words flat and quiet.

He turned his face away and balled his hands into fists, silence stretching between them. 'No.'

She nodded, believing him, and if he was willing to be truthful with her, then she would offer him the same in return. Perhaps this was the start of something pragmatic between them, if he didn't kick her out when he learned the truth. 'For there ever to be trust between us, Hale, there's something you need to know.'

She spun her glass by the stem, watching it as it moved on the table, building her courage, and when she looked up, Hale's expression had turned guarded. 'My mother sent me here to seduce and marry the first son of Alter, get with child, and then poison my husband in his sleep. I had no feelings for John, but with you ...'

His body seemed to turn to stone as he processed her words. 'Why are you telling me this?'

She sat back in her seat and took a gulp of her drink, then shrugged. 'A deal's a deal. I promised you my darkest secret in return for your answer, and by telling you, it means my mother can never use it against me, which she would do in a heartbeat when she finds out her goals and mine no longer align.' She took a deep, steadying breath, ignoring the churning in her guts, forcing her shoulders down. 'I want you, too, Hale, more than I care to admit, but ... Does what I just told you make you hate me? Has it made you change your mind, knowing you were right not to trust me? Knowing I'm a liar?'

He went to her side and pulled her to her feet, cupping her face in his hands. 'Sophie, I've always known you were a liar. How could a woman like you ever love my brother?'

She barked a laugh of surprise. 'Knowing I'm a killer, then?'

'Have you ever actually killed anyone?'

She shook her head. 'Have you?'

'No.' He kissed her hungrily, and Sophie sank into the kiss, letting it consume her, letting herself believe the fantasy that everything would be okay now, that their lives would be simple, that they could live happily ever after.

He devoured her, then slowed, learning her, his fingers in her hair as she lifted her hands to his torso. He moved them backwards, Sophie cursing her dress as it wrapped around her legs, then he lowered her onto the wide, flat hammock, holding the edge to stop it from swinging away.

She sighed as he rolled in beside her and sucked on her neck with barely a pause. She clutched at his hair, using him as an anchor as the gentle rocking combined with his touch and threw her senses off kilter. She felt as though she was flying and falling and flying once more, and she needed ... She needed ... 'Hale,' she breathed. 'Lie on top of me.' That's what she needed. Weight. Grounding. Him.

He did as she asked without hesitation——albeit a little awkwardly given the slight curve of the sturdy fabric beneath them——and she let her head fall back as her body drank in the contact and compression. 'That's ... yes ... stay there,' she commanded, her eyes closed, arms wrapped around him.

He pressed his lips to her jaw, then her mouth, where he sucked and nipped before kissing up the contour of her cheekbone, making her shiver as he moved to her ear and tugged on her earlobe. He nuzzled his way up and down her neck, taking his time, his movements unhurried as though savoring every kiss and taste.

It made her listless, her muscles turning slack until he hit a particularly sensitive spot, which had her back arching of its own accord. He shifted to the side so he could kiss her collarbone, but she eased him off her and onto the canvas, then did to him what he'd done to her, exploring his face and neck with her lips. But when she walked her fingers lower, he caught her wrist, halting her progress.

She looked down into his hazy eyes, asking a silent question.

He slid his hand to her waist and drew her down on top of him. 'We're not doing that tonight. It's not why I asked you here.'

She pulled back a little, frowning at the sincerity of his features. 'You're serious.'

He stroked the curve above her hip. 'We should wait until after we wed.'

She rolled away, huffing with frustrated disappointment. 'How honorable,' she said dryly.

'You're wrong.'

She turned her head back towards him. 'Oh?'

His lips quirked at her hopeful expression. 'It's self-serving, actually.'

She narrowed her eyes. 'Go on.'

'The longer we wait,' he said, sliding a tantalizing finger along the underside of her breast, 'the better it will be.'

Fresh desire skittered out from his touch, and she moved closer. 'When do you suggest we wed?' she asked, caressing the hollow at the base of his neck.

'Oh, I don't know ... in a month or two?' His features were teasing, and she grabbed his hand and lightly bit the fleshy part of his thumb. He groaned, and she smiled like a vixen.

'Tomorrow's good,' she said, then bit him again. 'Or tonight.'

'Tonight is almost over,' he countered, sliding his thumb across the pulse at her throat, 'and I wouldn't want you to get married in any old thing. I know how you love to dress up for an occasion.'

'How kind,' she deadpanned. But despite her desire to have him, she found she wasn't against his game. He was right, it would heighten things. It already was, the swipe of his thumb positively erotic. She exhaled breathily, and he pulled her lips to his, part of her wondering if she could combust from a kiss alone.

She rested her head on his chest, enjoying the way his fingers scratched her scalp, his other hand arranged casually on her hip, the position feeling so natural it was as though they lay like that often.

'We should eat,' Hale said eventually, swinging his legs over the side and hopping down.

Sophie wasn't hungry and thought about protesting, but she knew never to get between a man like Hale and his stomach, so instead she ran a hand through her tousled hair, then shimmied to the edge. His hands closed around her waist, helping her down, and she made sure to slide her body against his as she descended to the floor.

'Fuck,' he said on an exhale.

She smiled coyly and pulled away, sashaying ahead of him to the table, giving him a good view of her swinging hips.

Sophie refilled their glasses as Hale removed the silver cloches that covered the platters of food. The spread was simple: cold meats and cheeses, crackers studded with fruit and nuts, chutney, pickles, and small orange tomatoes. They grazed as they talked, covering all manner of topics from management of the mansion to Hale's proposed tour of Alter Blade to how they could bring the other Blades around to the idea of being fair to the Claws.

'You really want to help them?' said Hale, before sliding a sliver of hard yellow cheese into his mouth. 'I thought ... Well, before, you said ...'

'I said what I needed to say to impress your brother,' she replied, holding his gaze. 'And I believe he said some of the things he did because he wanted to impress Danit. Truthfully, I've never thought much about the Claws. My life has been sheltered. I barely ever left my home, and when I did, it was never to visit the Claws.

'I'd never seen their plight before coming here or heard much about them. But I have no reason to dislike them, and it's unfair, the way we treat them.'

'Hardly an enthusiastic commitment to their cause,' Hale said wryly.

'You want me to lie?'

He smiled as he shook his head. 'No lies between us from now on.'

Sophie's stomach convulsed because she still hadn't told him everything. 'I'm sure I'll become more dedicated as I get to know them.'

'Because you're so kind and tender-hearted?' he teased.

She barked a laugh. 'Like you'd know what to do with someone like that.'

He leaned towards her, his expression suddenly penetrating. 'You think I know what to do with you?'

She bit her lip at the dark look in his eyes. 'You're not off to a bad start.' She sat back and picked up her glass, swirling the wine before taking a sip.

A comfortable silence settled over them, and Sophie luxuriated in it. She'd been prepared to kill her husband but had never considered what it might be like to coexist with him.

'Another drink? Perhaps something stronger?' he said, interrupting her thoughts.

She shook her head, dread filling her. 'There's something else I haven't told you, Hale.'

He froze, his glass halfway to his lips, then he threw the contents into his mouth and put the glass down, looking at her expectantly, waiting for her to continue.

Her lips moved left and right, knowing if she told him this now, there was no going back; it was a full betrayal of her people and her mission. But Hale was to be her husband, and she couldn't keep it from him forever, especially if he wanted to help the Claws. He had to know who they really were before devoting himself to their cause.

'Laurow Blade also has an agreement like the one Alter has with the Claws,' she said quickly.

'For water?' Hale asked, sitting back.

She shook her head. 'For food. I don't know the details, but I know the Claws pay Laurow, and my parents keep it a secret.'

Hale nodded slowly, his eyes unseeing as he processed her revelation. 'Do you think all the Blades have similar agreements?'

She shrugged. 'I don't know, but I suppose it's possible. Please just ... Please don't tell anyone. I don't want my people to suffer because of this, but I also don't want secrets between us.'

Hale huffed an incredulous laugh. 'Your mother acted so high and mighty, so shocked and offended. She used it to——'

'To force you into marrying me,' Sophie finished, looking down at her hands. 'If you want to call it off, then you have a way to do that now.'

Hale faltered, his features turning guarded. 'That's what you want?' He stood abruptly. 'Is that why you told me?'

She shook her head and pushed to her feet. 'No! Of course not! That's not what I want.' He was infuriating and changeable and might very well hollow out her insides and leave her a husk of her former self, but even if that happened, she wanted it, the alternative going back to Laurow with her tail between her legs. And despite trying to convince herself otherwise, she wanted him, had never met a man she wanted more. Perhaps she shouldn't have trusted him so easily, shouldn't have put her fate so squarely in his hands after a single pleasant evening, but her fate was in his hands anyway, and at least this way it gave them a chance to build a life together on foundations made of something solid.

The seconds stretched, Hale's jaw working as the cogs inside his brain whirred. 'I want to marry you, Sophie.' He closed the distance between them and slid his hand into hers, entwining their fingers. 'I've never met a woman like you.' He smirked. 'I've never wanted to fight so much with anyone.'

She exhaled a breathy laugh, relief and hope flooding through her, the thickness of it filling her up and bringing tears to her eyes. He kissed her, a kiss that held the promise of something unwavering between them, a partnership, a connection that, if not yet strong, at least wouldn't break in the first stiff wind.

Sophie buried her face in the crook of his neck, breathing him in, and he wrapped his arms around her, stroking her back with slow, soothing strokes, resting his cheek against her hair. Sophie felt as though she was living a daydream.

She pulled back, and he brushed the hair off her face as she looked up into his eyes. 'Is this real, Hale?' she breathed, not stopping to worry if the words would offend him, somehow knowing he would understand.

He gave her a long, appraising look, then nodded. 'It's real for me.'

She exhaled a shaky breath, then reluctantly detangled herself from his grip. 'If you're not going to let me stay, I suppose I should go to bed. It's late.'

He seemed conflicted, and an impish smile slid across her lips as she wondered how hard it would be to break his will. She picked up the book he'd selected for her, and as she tucked it under her arm, an idea took hold in her mind. She acted without thinking, taking off towards his bedroom at a sprint.

'Sophie, what are you ...'

A wild laugh escaped her as she raced towards her target, her blood flowing high and bright in her veins, her lungs working hard, making her breathless.

She plunged through the door and scanned Hale's bedroom, her eyes roaming over the enormous, comfortable-looking bed with crisp, white sheets and pillows that looked like they might swallow a person whole, and then she located the nightstands. *Bingo.*

She launched herself at the single book, grasping it and holding it high like a prize as she turned and found him standing in the doorway.

'Satisfied?' he asked, leaning against the doorjamb, arms folded across his chest.

'Not even a little bit.' She wanted to crawl out of her skin at the sight of him, rugged and shoeless, his broad shoulders taking up considerable space, blocking her exit. Which was fine by her because she didn't want to exit. She wanted to dive under his bedsheets and stay forever.

She cleared her throat, then scanned the book's cover. '*The Chronicles of the Sea Lord.* Not a surprising choice.'

He cocked an eyebrow. 'You were hoping for something else?'

'*The High Lord and the Maiden of Magic,* now that's a good one.' She moved towards him as she spoke, tossing both her book and his onto his bed. 'Or perhaps, *The Portal Pirate Meets his Match.*'

Hale pouted a little. 'Sounds interesting. Is this pirate an affable and dazzlingly handsome sort of chap?'

She laughed. 'That's how you see yourself?' she asked as she stepped into his arms, which he closed around her.

'I'm more interested in the *Maiden of Magic*.' He kissed her, slow and deep, like he was savoring her ahead of a long absence.

'I could stay,' she said as he pulled away, not wanting to let him go. 'We don't have to——'

He kissed her again, sliding a hand to her backside, then turned them so her back was against the wall, moving his hand slowly down her thigh. He lifted her leg and hooked it over his hip, pushing her dress out of his way so her stockinged thigh rested against his clothes. He drew a few light circles atop the sheer fabric before moving his hips forward and rocking unhurriedly against her. 'You think you can?' he asked, his voice husky. 'Stay and not give in to temptation?'

'Or we could give in,' she breathed, sighing as he squeezed her breast. 'This game was your idea, not mine.'

Hale seemed to consider her words for a moment, and then his features turned feral. 'I suppose I could give you a taste of what's to come ...'

She swallowed hard, nodding slowly as he moved his hips back and began to tug the rest of her dress upwards. He tucked the fabric behind her, his eyes going wide and dark as he studied what lay beneath, and she was glad she hadn't abandoned all the clothing of her homeland.

He dipped his hand between them, his fingers starting at the edge of her stocking and walking up the lace of her suspender belt, his progress achingly, torturously slow. He hit the hem of her underwear, and her eyes fell closed as he skirted light fingers down the seam of her leg towards her core, her nipples pulling tighter with every passing inch.

Hale stroked the edge of the fabric at the apex of her thighs, and Sophie tipped her hips, trying to force him to touch her where he knew she wanted him.

He chuckled. 'Patience is a virtue, Sophie.'

'Not one I have,' she countered, reaching for the bulge in his breeches, but after only the lightest of touches, he grabbed her hand and forced it away.

Hale moved his face close to Sophie's, his eyes boring into hers. 'Do that again, and playtime is over.'

Sophie pouted as she reluctantly complied, moving the offending hand to his neck, stroking her thumb up and down, then drawing his lips to hers.

He allowed that, although the kiss was punishing. He returned his fingers to the edge of her underwear, and Sophie writhed, desperate to find the friction she so sorely needed.

Hale removed his touch, looking chastisingly into her eyes as he waited for her to still. He delayed for a few moments after she'd obeyed his silent command, then finally slid his thumb over the fabric of her underwear, his touch light and taunting. 'Hale,' she moaned, rubbing her cheek against his, her hands on his neck.

'Yes, *darling*?'

'Please,' she breathed, biting his earlobe.

'Please what?' he growled.

'Touch me.'

'I am touching you.'

'Harder.'

He pushed her underwear to one side, then withdrew his fingers, and Sophie nearly died of anticipation, knowing instinctively that if she did anything to rush him, he would deny her, but her body didn't want to listen. Her body was pulsing with need, crying out for all kinds of things she knew Hale wouldn't give her tonight.

And then Hale stroked his thumb against her, and her legs nearly gave out at the rush of feeling, her body chasing more—more pressure, more movement—and this time Hale obliged, sliding two fingers inside her. Sophie gasped in surprise, her body undulating against him, her moans becoming higher pitched the closer he drove her towards release.

But then a knock cut through the moment, and Hale froze.

Sophie's eyes flew wide, her hips still moving. 'Don't stop,' she begged. 'Hale, please, I'm so close, I'm—'

He watched her with an absorbed expression as he pressed down with his thumb, and she combusted around him, crying out and clutching onto him as she rode the fierce waves of pleasure. She was still coming down from the high when the knock came again, and Hale frowned.

'The servants?' she asked, her breathing ragged.

He withdrew his fingers as he shook his head, then dropped one last kiss against her lips before lowering her leg and rearranging himself. He washed his hands in a basin, then tugged Sophie back into the main room just as the door creaked open. Hale pushed Sophie behind him, shielding her from the potential threat, seeming shocked that anyone would dare enter his domain without waiting to be invited inside.

'Hale?' said a woman's voice, and a pang of jealousy hit Sophie square in her release-addled chest. Her body wasn't even done sending aftershocks yet, and she was about to come face to face with one of Hale's past lovers. Who else would so brazenly wander into his rooms late at night? Sophie wished she could see the woman's face.

'Mother?'

Oh.

'I hope I'm not interrupting?' His mother's tone was cutting and highly judgmental.

Oh shit.

'You are, actually,' said Hale, apparently over his initial shock, 'but I'm sure my future wife and I will forgive you.'

'Your ... what?'

Fuck.

'It's very nice to meet you,' said Sophie, quickly smoothing her disheveled hair and drawing herself up tall before stepping around Hale's considerable frame. And it was then she realized she didn't know her future mother-in-law's name. 'I'm Sophie Laurow.'

'And this is my mother,' said Hale, his lip twitching in amusement, perhaps on account of Sophie's pleasure-flushed face. 'Bianca Alter.'

'I heard you refused to marry her,' said Bianca, turning accusing eyes on her son. Sophie prickled at the woman's cheek.

'Then your news is out of date,' said Hale. He slid an arm around Sophie's waist and pulled her close, dropping a kiss on her temple.

Bianca was tall and sturdy, her long, dark hair streaked with grey, the lines on her face deep with what looked like exhaustion or perhaps worry. She closed the door behind her and moved to a sideboard where a handful of bottles stood on a tray and filled a tumbler with a measure of tawny-colored liquid. She took a sip, then strode to the table and raked over the remaining food, selecting a cracker and taking a bite.

'Shall I send for more?' asked Hale, drawing Sophie with him to the table, where they each took a seat.

Sophie was intrigued beyond measure at the frosty interaction between Hale and his mother. They hadn't seen each other in years, and yet there was no warmth in the greeting, no affection, just a kind of hostile wariness.

'Your sister is being held hostage by Spruce Blade,' said Bianca, as though she hadn't heard his offer. 'Pixy refused to wed their first son after everything that happened with the falls. Many died, and it impacted her badly.

'Spruce told the administrator to enter the marriage into the register regardless ... I'm not sure if he did or not, but in the eyes of Spruce, Pixy is theirs to use as they wish. They held us both prisoner until I bribed my way out.' Bianca threw an olive into her mouth and looked her son dead in the eye as she chewed, a layer of steel sitting just below her obvious exhaustion. 'You need to get her back.'

'You heard about Danit's death, then?' said Hale, giving nothing away. 'That's why you came to see me?'

Bianca gave a reluctant half nod. 'And Cane's, too.'

'Cane's?' Sophie blurted. 'He's ...'

Bianca turned her hostile stare on Sophie. 'Stabbed in the back by his wives during his birthday celebration. They put on quite a show, apparently, then killed their own fathers, too.' She gave a long exhale. 'These are turbulent times.'

Hale leaned forward across the table. 'What about Maria? Does Elex now lead Oshe?'

Bianca scowled. 'Elex didn't stab his brother in the back.'

'Then ...' Hale's features scrunched in disbelief. 'Erica?'

'You know, Hale,' Bianca snapped, 'you would think with a mother like me you might have learned that women are capable of much.'

Hale pulled back, hitting the padding of his chair as he threw his mother a look of disdain. 'I never said otherwise.'

Bianca dropped into a chair, finally giving into her weariness. She took a long sip of her drink, then carefully set the tumbler on the table before her eyes flicked up to find Hale. 'When will you go for Pixy?'

Sophie stifled a gasp because Bianca seemed to think it a foregone conclusion, but Hale couldn't just ride to Spruce and demand they hand over his sister. It was insanity.

Hale's forehead pinched in thought. 'Tomorrow. I'll treat with them, but will also take a show of force.'

Sophie nearly fell off her chair. 'You can't! It's too dangerous.'

He turned towards her, softening. 'Sophie ...'

Her mouth set into a hard line. 'Yes?'

'I can't let this stand.'

'And you can't just ride off into battle at the drop of a hat, either!'

'I can, and I—'

'Well, you shouldn't if you want to win.'

He gritted his teeth but held his tongue, presumably because he knew she had a point. His mother looked between them, confused and irritated perhaps, but she had the good sense not to comment.

Hale took Sophie's hand. 'We can marry before I go. You did say tomorrow would be convenient, if memory serves.'

'Hale!'

'Yes?'

Sophie's mind went blank. 'I don't have an outfit. I ...' He couldn't be serious!

'It will take a few days to ready our troops,' said his mother, intervening before Hale could say anything more, 'and you should invite Sophie's family to the wedding. They'll consider it a snub if you don't, and it will take time for a messenger to ride to Laurow and to bring back their reply.'

Sophie couldn't work out what game Bianca was playing. Was she hoping to buy enough time to convince Hale not to marry Sophie or was she truly concerned about keeping Laurow on side?

'In the meantime,' Bianca continued, 'write to Spruce and ask them to return Pixy to us. They'll no doubt turn down your request, but diplomacy should always precede intimidation.'

Hale closed his eyes and bowed his head. 'You pen the letter, Mother. You know them better than I, and it seems I have a wedding to plan.'

She inclined her head, then pursed her lips, her eyes flicking to Sophie and then back to Hale. 'We should speak alone, Hale. There is much to discuss. Things you do not know but should ...'

Like helping the Claws to steal water, Sophie thought but didn't say.

Hale inhaled deeply, and the sound sent a trickle of disappointment down Sophie's spine. He was sending her away. 'Sophie,' he said, pitching his tone low, sounding almost tender, 'do you mind?'

She held his gaze for a moment, then loudly pushed back her chair and stormed from the room.

'Sophie!' he called after her, but she didn't stop, and he didn't follow, unlike Bianca's words, which struck like poisoned arrows as they sailed down the stairs behind her.

'What the fuck are you doing, Hale?' Bianca hissed, and then the door slammed shut, and Sophie could hear no more.

CHAPTER THIRTY-THREE
AVA

AVA EMPTIED EVERY ONE of the house's hidey holes she could find, but it was futile. They contained magical instruments, rare herbs and minerals, texts, notebooks with scribblings about portals and indicators of balance, seeds, a chipped mug, a hairbrush ... but nothing that would convince Billy to teach her magic. After several long hours, she was fractious and hungry and had nothing to show for her efforts.

'Something will turn up,' said Kush. 'Maybe the notebooks will be enticing enough to get Billy to help you.'

'Hmm,' Ava said skeptically, as they headed downstairs, but she paused before descending the final steps, her mouth dropping open. She stopped so abruptly, Kush nearly knocked her down the remaining few stairs.

'Oh wow,' he said.

'Indeed,' she breathed, unable to tear her gaze from Billy, who was ... drunk.

Billy held a bottle in one hand and a long silver spoon in the other. He'd selected the biggest, most ostentatious hat he could find from the coat closet and set it on his brow at a jaunty angle, a fat feather bobbing and swaying in time with Billy's dance. If a dance was what it was. He circled and undulated, heading first one way and then the other, then he bumped into the stairs and sat heavily on the bottom step.

He took a long swig from the bottle, then stood again, noticing Ava and Kush for the first time. 'Ahhhh,' he cried, throwing his arms wide. 'I'm having a party!'

'I think he has a problem,' Ava whispered as Kush moved onto the step beside her. 'He doesn't seem well.'

'No. Really?'

Billy waltzed into the drawing room, and Ava and Kush followed, Ava concerned he might hurt himself. When they entered the room, Billy was studying a small portrait on the mantel, caressing it with his thumb.

'Billy?' Ava said tentatively.

He turned his head. 'You look so much like your mother.' He sighed dramatically. 'I miss her, the devious little swamp witch. It's just not the same without her sass, her wit, her endless theatrics ...'

Ava folded her arms across her chest. 'I ... Um ...'

Billy took a few steps towards where Ava and Kush hovered by the door. 'I need dumplings,' Billy said urgently, his voice low, little more than a whisper. '*Now.*' Billy leaned towards them, his eyes taking on a frightening intensity.

'Um,' Ava said apprehensively. 'Why?'

'Because I do!' Billy stamped his foot. 'Don't question me!'

'Ah ... okay?' Ava sent Kush a wide-eyed look. 'We could—'

'No!' Billy cried. 'Not you. You have to stay here so I can tell you a secret.' He leaned back and put his hands on his hips, the feather on his hat bobbing wildly.

'I could ... go and buy dumplings?' Kush suggested, his eyes looking questioningly at Ava.

Ava froze. That meant giving Kush the Atlas Stone. It meant trusting him not to run back to Var. Trusting him to return.

Billy raised an eyebrow, his weight resting on a single leg, his cocked hip mocking her from across the room. 'Good idea,' Ava said brightly, narrowing her eyes at Billy as she dug her hand into her pocket and pulled out the stone. She dropped it into Kush's palm, then wrapped her arms around him, clutching onto him for dear life as though the harder she squeezed the more likely he was to return.

Kush's body seemed to engulf her, and from the way he held her, she somehow knew he'd come back, that it would be okay. 'I love you,' he whispered, then kissed her temple. 'I won't be long.'

He was gone in a heartbeat, and when Ava turned back to Billy, his features were scornful. 'You're playing with fire with that one. The Cloud-dwellers look down on Kushy-Kush because of his lowly mother, but Var's one of the few with a child, so they're also *deeply* jealous. It's a ticking timebomb.'

Ava had no idea what he meant. 'What's the secret?'

'Come again?'

'You said if Kush went you'd tell me a secret.'

'Oh, that. Yeah ... There isn't one.'

'You lied?'

'I wanted dumplings.'

'But you just ... lied!'

Billy rolled his eyes, then lowered himself into a velvet chair, throwing his legs over the arm and leaning back in a dramatic stretch, one hand on his hat, holding it in place. When he came upright, he leaned towards Ava as though about to let her in on something scintillating and highly salacious. 'I once kissed a man called Hunter, and he totally liked it. There,' Billy purred, leaning back and stroking the feather on his hat, 'obligation fulfilled.'

Ava shook her head, wondering if she was in some bizarre dream. 'The Hunter who runs the Trove?'

'Ha! Ha!' Billy removed his hat and flung it high in the air. It landed somewhere on the floor behind him. 'One and the same.'

Ava threw herself into a chair, it was hardly a secret that was useful. Billy wiggled his shoulders in time to a silent tune, and Ava wondered what else she might be able to get out of him in his current state. 'Billy?'

'Mmmmm?' The sound pitched up at the end, as he turned his eyes on her.

'Why don't you like the Federation?'

Billy kicked his legs up, then swiveled them to the floor, leaning forward and slapping his hands on his thighs. 'Well, one must give what one takes, and it takes too much. Balance is binary.' He waggled his eyebrows as though she should know what he meant. She didn't.

'Can you please just talk plainly?'

He scowled. 'Most worlds similar to Santala willingly signed up to the Federation, the magical families having sold them on the supposed benefits, and people trusted that the Cloud Synod would be fair—idiots. Really the Federation means money for the decision-making few. That's always been the case, but then your parents became too powerful, broke *all* the rules, stole our souls, Var did his thing, the Clouds neglected their duties until everything was wildly out of balance, and then your parents died—were killed—same same.'

She gave him a perplexed look.

He threw up his hands. 'The whole thing is out of whack,' he said slowly, as though she wasn't a native speaker of his language. 'The Federation works for the Gods, makes them richer, but is dangerous for everyone else because it's sucking the web dry.'

Ava nodded slowly as she processed his words. 'Thank you ... for that,' she said eventually, 'but I don't understand why the system is out of balance. How is the Federation sucking the web dry? And what does that mean?'

Kush appeared in the doorway, carrying a stack of bamboo boxes whose contents smelled divine. 'I'm back.'

Billy rushed over to him, shivering like an excited dog. 'Kush-Kush!' he gushed, 'is this what I think it is?' Billy swiped the top two boxes then circled away. 'Little glutenous parcels stuffed with meat and herbs and just the right amount of gravy?'

'Uh, yes,' said Kush, handing a box to Ava. 'I wasn't sure which flavor you'd like, so I got one of everything.'

The house vibrated as Billy began to pry the lid off one of his boxes, the other box teetering on the edge of the sofa where Billy had perched it.

'Kitchen,' said Ava, 'don't you think?'

Billy paused, looking around the room with nervous eyes. 'Yes,' he agreed, then picked up his food and ran.

Ava followed him at a more leisurely pace, and Kush dropped a kiss on her lips as she reached him. 'Everything okay?'

'Fine ... Sort of ... He's not making much sense.'

'Delicious!' Billy cried as they entered the kitchen, holding a dumpling between his fingers.

'We have cutlery,' Ava snapped, needing an outlet for her growing angst. She had so many unanswered questions.

'And who are you? My mother? These were made to be eaten with the hands.'

'No, they weren't,' countered Kush.

Billy waved dismissively. 'What else have you got?' He reached for the boxes in Kush's arms, making quick work of placing them on the table and pulling off the lids. 'Ooh, yellow cinder fish, yes? Tell me I'm right.'

'You're right,' Kush said on a weary exhale, 'but those are for everyone.'

Ava slid into a chair and helped herself to a yellow cinder fish dumpling, nibbling at the corner, but she cast it aside, practically gagging on the potent fishy flavor.

Kush pushed a pot of smaller dumplings towards her. 'Try these.'

Ava smiled weakly, preoccupied by all the things she didn't know about her new life, while Billy reached over and snatched a dumpling out of the pot in front of her. 'Ava, darling, *lighten up*.' He shoved the dumpling into his mouth whole, then said around the food, 'You have no idea how hard it is to get these things without an Atlas Stone.'

'I ... I just ...' She pushed a dumpling around the pot. 'What did you mean when you said the system is out of balance?'

Billy wiped his mouth on a napkin the house had helpfully provided. 'I told you, I have no interest in being your walking encyclopedia.' He grabbed a bottle of liquor from the island and poured himself a liberal quantity.

Kush banged his fist on the table. 'If you won't teach her, then get out.'

Ava had to bite her lip to stop her protest. If Billy went, then she had no one to teach her, but worse, it meant if Kush abandoned her—like Billy insisted he would—Ava would be alone. The thought probably made her pathetic. How many times had she seen women in the tavern pander to men who weren't good for them, wondering why they did it. And now here she was doing the very same. But she couldn't imagine anything worse than being alone.

'Urgh!' Billy said with a flounce. 'You're no fun.' He sat back, rubbing his hands rhythmically over his stomach, seeming to be gathering his words. 'Well, you see, it all comes back to the three principles—you'll find most things do.'

Wait, what? It was that simple to get Billy to cooperate? A single threat?

'The first principle is self-explanatory, no? *Give what you take, take what you give*. But just in case you've failed to understand, it means you can take what you please from the Atlas Web, just so long as you give an equal amount in return. But not too much. If you give too much—or, more accurately, if the system as a whole has too much—the web will also fall out of balance.'

'Take what, though?' said Ava, frowning in frustration.

Billy shrugged. 'Magic, that's the simplest description, and it can manifest in many ways: in raw materials, healing, sunlight ... You get the gist. But it all must stay in perfect balance, otherwise things go sideways.'

'Sideways how?' Ava still had very little idea what he meant.

Billy shoved another dumpling into his mouth, then spat it into the lid of a pot and shuddered. 'Urgh, yuck. Gross. No thank you. Why did you get those?' Billy scowled at Kush as he swilled his drink around his mouth.

'Sideways how?' Ava repeated.

Billy lifted a shoulder, then surveyed the other dumplings. 'Well ...' He picked up a dumpling and carefully sniffed it. 'The Atlas Tree starts to fail. It's happened once or twice over the years. Bits have died off, roots turned black, terrible creaking, cracking noises, a couple of portals snapping closed leaving people trapped on the wrong sides.

'But the times before now, when your ancestors realized the crazy shit correlated with their taking too much from the web, they decided they would have to start managing things properly, so they divvied up responsibilities to different Cloud families—back when the families could be relied upon to do their bit. The Blackwoods took responsibility for overall balance, the Vars,' he said, looking at Kush, 'were in charge of maintaining the portals, and spotting early warning signs of imbalance.'

'And your family were in charge of alcohol?' asked Ava, remembering what Kush had told her.

'Potions,' Billy said wistfully. 'Anyway, the problem with the web is that balance is binary. It is either in balance or it is not, and maintaining it is no easy task, especially since the creation of the Federation. It's a constant struggle, a constant tipping of the scales one way or another, and Rupert cared more about Polly's experiments than doing his job. Things got bad for a while, until others stepped up in Rupert's absence.'

'Who?'

'Novak, mainly.' Ava's heart gave a tug. She almost felt sorry for Novak now she knew more about his life, although he'd still abandoned her ... 'But your mother gave it a good go first, which was, of course, disastrous.'

'What do you mean?'

Billy flicked his eyes up to the ceiling. 'Declared she'd mastered principle two.'

Ava's features scrunched as she tried to remember. 'Wait, what was that one?'

'Time is not a constant,' said Kush.

Billy inclined his head. 'Look at you, Kush-Kush! They taught you something at least.' Kush scowled, but Billy didn't seem to notice. 'Polly thought, if she could manipulate the balance of the web using time as a controllable variable, she could ensure balance no matter how much everyone took.'

Ava leaned back in her chair, still no real idea what he was talking about. 'I'm guessing she was wrong?'

Billy tipped his head from side to side and pursed his lips. 'She died.' He shrugged. 'So who knows if she'd theoretically found a way, but all indicators point to *no*. Unnatural things have consequences we never understand until it's too late. The tree created portals and maintained balance for who knows how long before people came along and ruined it all. If you ask me, we should shut it all down and leave the tree to its own devices.'

'Bit late for that,' said Kush.

Billy sneered hard. 'It's never too late. Not while the place is still standing.'

Ava balked. 'You think it might not be one day? Is it in balance now?'

Billy chuckled. 'Is it in balance?' He shot forward and slammed his hands on the table. 'No, Ava, of course it's not in balance, that's what I've been telling you! Your parents took more than they gave. The Gods and people of the federated worlds continue to do the same. Var's panicking, frantically trying to find new worlds to shore things up, but the system demands too much.'

'Now Novak's Master of the House, he'll be expected to do more. The formal line is that he *assists* the Gods, but really he runs that little hell hole, and that means when eventually the cracks we see around the edges turn to fissures—'

'You're a liar,' Kush breathed, his hands balled into tight fists. 'The whole point of the Federation is balance.'

Billy went still, like a cat who'd spotted prey. 'Did Daddy tell you that? He's quite attached to his unnatural portals and temples and healing pools and *adoring temple women*, is he not?'

'Billy!' Ava snapped. Kush looked about ready to hurl himself across the table.

'The portalry practiced by your father is a cancer infecting the web. It benefits no one but the Gods. He forces his way into other worlds using resources that do not belong to him, costing lives ...'

Kush's jaw worked, his eyes fixed on the table. 'The Federation benefits everyone.'

Billy's mouth quirked a little at the corner. 'There are whispers of unrest. Shouts in some quarters. How do you account for those?'

Ava thought of the echo chamber, what they'd heard. It certainly hadn't sounded like everything was rosy. But it felt like a betrayal of Kush to side with Billy. 'It must do *some* good,' she hedged, 'otherwise it would have failed long ago.'

Billy fixed her with a look that could have withered flowers. 'The Federation was developed by a few enterprising Cloud families as a way of extracting cash and resources, despite what Kush has been brainwashed to think. And no one is *happy*. Believe your boyfriend if you wish, but I speak the truth. Why would I lie?'

'I'm not calling you a liar,' said Ava, 'but—'

'Kush is a big boy.' Billy turned his condescending smile on Kush. 'Aren't you Kushy? He can take a little criticism.'

'None of this is about me,' Kush ground out.

'Which is just the way your father likes it.' Billy pouted and pushed back his chair. 'Now, I do believe I put aside some absolute gems last night. I have a date with some of my family's most brilliant creations.'

But if Billy wanted her liquor, he could damn well learn some manners. He couldn't speak to Kush that way. 'Your family may have created them,' Ava said, rising to her feet and bracing herself against the table, 'but they belong to me. You can only have them if you agree to be civil to us both, and to teach us everything you know. About the past, the web, magic ... everything.'

Billy blew out a petulant breath, then waved his hand glibly. 'Seems like a fair trade.' He sang a triumphant tune as he headed for his prize.

A bitter scoff escaped Ava's lips as she dropped heavily back into her seat, while Kush made a noise of disgust. Ava had been looking for a carrot, and it turned out all she'd needed was a stick.

Chapter Thirty-Four
Maria
Six Weeks After Dromeda Started Spinning

Elex ushered the midwife towards Maria and Sol, who stood hidden in a shadowy alley, the hoods of their cloaks drawn over their heads. They'd heard of a difficult birth nearby and knew she would come, seeing as she was the most sought after of all the midwives in Oshala.

So they'd watched as she'd entered the well-maintained residence of a mid-level trader, and had waited all night until the woman's work was done. When she'd finally reappeared, looking weary but satisfied, Elex had pounced.

'What's this about?' the midwife asked, casting wary eyes over Maria and Sol as she pressed herself into the shadows of the alley, hiding from the road. It was early morning and the streets were dead, but she was smart to be careful.

'We've been hearing strange reports from my quarter,' said Elex, 'but we have no way in or out to verify them.'

She gave them each a skeptical look, one after the other. 'You want information, is that it? And you're desperate enough to have to ask me?'

Elex gave a low chuckle. 'Oh, come now, Noranda, you and I both know you're one of the best-informed residents of my quarter.'

Noranda put her hands on her hips. 'You think you can win me over with flattery?'

Elex opened his hands. 'Just stating a fact.'

Noranda raised her eyebrows and cast her eyes up toward the sky in a gesture that made Maria think Elex was indeed winning her over.

Noranda folded her arms over her chest and cocked her head defensively. 'You want a report? Those wenches have increased taxes on everything.

They've put guards on the water fountain—charging for every drop—and their *wedding* ... a farce if ever I've seen one.'

'Their wedding?' said Maria, casting a glance at Elex, whose expression told her he was as much in the dark as she was.

'You didn't know?' Noranda asked, seeming surprised.

Maria and Elex shook their heads.

'They're styling themselves as the joint Queens of Oshe.'

'But what of the commander?' asked Maria. 'The one who helped them take over.'

'Oh, he's a clever one, that one,' said Noranda. 'Sneaky and hard to his core.'

Maria's mind whirled, trying to piece it all together. 'Did they wed him also?'

Noranda raised her eyebrows. 'No.'

Maria nodded slowly. Then their theory about the commander had been completely wrong. 'But Celestl doesn't have royalty. It only exists in fairy tales. The Goddess—'

'The Queens say the water in the Inner Circle is a sign that the Goddess approves of their rule,' Noranda snapped irritably. 'Endorses it, even.'

Elex exhaled heavily. 'And what do the people think?'

'The people will support you more now than ever, my dear. Why don't you attack?' She gave him an encouraging nod. 'Take back what's yours, eh?'

Elex gave a cheerless shake of his head. 'I wish I could, but the place is a fortress. One way in and one way out. If I gather an army, I'll spook them and they'll stay cooped up behind their walls, but if there's no obvious resistance, they'll be forced to come out eventually. If they don't, they'll look weak, and they won't have a hope of holding the city, let alone the whole of Oshe.'

'You're lying in wait.'

Elex nodded. 'Gathering intelligence, so we're ready when opportunity strikes.'

The midwife scowled. 'Sounds like doing nothing to me.'

Sol snorted a laugh. He'd been so quiet, Maria had all-but forgotten he was there.

'Now, I must go. I have mothers to check on, and babies wait for no man. Not even you, my dear.' She patted Elex on the arm as she passed.

'Thank you,' said Elex, 'and know we will prevail.'

'I don't doubt it, and I'll be waiting, but the longer you leave it, the more damage you allow those terrible women to do.'

That night in the tavern, Maria played over what they'd learned in her mind many times, curled up under a soft woolen blanket in an armchair. No way into the quarter, no way to raise an army without spooking the so-called Queens, and still no word from Nicoli, either. Perhaps he would refuse her request. Perhaps he never wanted to see her again.

'We still have people inside,' said Tallin, after they'd relayed the details of their meeting to him and Zeik. 'We could find guards willing to open the gates, just as they did when the quarter was taken from us.'

Elex moved to his usual spot by the fire. 'But that only worked because we were all away,' said Elex, 'and they used troops who were already stationed in the city. They had the element of surprise and had people ready to pounce when our defenses were light. But even if we could open the gates, we don't have enough soldiers.'

'Noranda is convinced your people will rise up and support you,' said Maria.

Elex shook his head. 'And I hope she's right, but I'm not willing to risk our lives on a hope.'

'Curious about the commander,' said Zeik, sitting at the table where Tallin and Sol were playing cards. 'What's in it for him?'

'Proximity to power?' suggested Tallin. 'And not everyone wants to rule.'

Zeik tapped his fingers on the tabletop. 'Perhaps ...'

'Force is the only thing the people of Oshe truly respect,' said Sol, 'meaning the Queens' power comes from their army ... From the commander.'

Tallin put down his cards. 'So what's your point? You think the commander is playing a long game? Waiting for the right moment to pounce?'

'Oh, stop,' snapped Elex, running a frustrated hand through his hair. 'This is all just speculation. Nothing we can work with. Assuming Erica and Opal took over their fathers' business operations, they're not without means. Their wealth and influence are considerable, and someone has to pay the army. Can the commander do that without them?'

'Hmm,' said Zeik, on a defeatist exhale. 'And still no word from Nicoli.'

Maria's stomach dropped, while Tallin scowled and shoved Zeik hard. 'It hasn't been that long,' said Sol.

Elex turned and braced his hands against the mantel. 'We can do little but watch and wait and gather intelligence.'

'They're still using your masseuse ...' said Zeik.

'And your cook ...' said Tallin.

Elex sent a skeptical look over his shoulder. 'So what? Your plan is to massage them all to death?'

Sol cocked an eyebrow. 'Or poison them.'

A pregnant silence settled.

'No,' said Elex. 'We—'

'We could,' said Maria. 'I have poisons in my repertoire.' And the thought of working a still again made her want to cry with joy.

Elex shook his head. 'They have food tasters.'

'I'll make it slow acting.'

Elex turned fully. 'No. It's reckless. Foolish. Has too high a chance of going wrong.'

Zeik waggled his eyebrows at Maria. 'One to keep in our back pockets, then.'

CHAPTER THIRTY-FIVE

HALE

SIX WEEKS AFTER DROMEDA STARTED SPINNING

HALE ACCEPTED THE FLAME torch his mother handed him and held it high as he approached the end of the jetty where his uncle's body floated on a pyre. Memories flooded Hale's mind's eye, some bringing a smile to his lips, but most reminding him what a manipulative snake Danit had been. It gave Hale comfort, knowing the man was gone.

The pyre bobbed at the head of the river flowing out of the lake of Alter to the sea. It would burn, and the ashes would sink long before it got that far, which brought Hale comfort, too, because it meant Danit's remains wouldn't pollute Hale's true home, the ocean.

He shook off his reverie and lit the four torches on the pyre, two on either side of the body. They would burn down and light the wood upon which Danit lay, and then Hale would truly be rid of the man.

Hale unhooked the rope securing the pyre to the jetty just as the Midday Fall began, thundering out of the sky, and he gave the pyre a solid shove with his foot, ensuring it would float far enough out to be caught by the stream. He doused his torch in the water, then moved back to where his mother and Sophie waited.

Word would spread quickly, and many would turn out to pay their respects and throw flowers at the pyre, but there would be no celebration of the man's life at Hale's table.

Hale stood close to Sophie, but she refused to meet his eye, and had refused to speak with him past pleasantries and single-word answers since he'd asked her to leave his rooms the night before. He wished he'd sent his mother away instead, especially as she'd told him nothing he didn't already know, and they'd never been close, not after she'd let Danit take over Alter, a role that should have been Hale's from the moment of his father's death.

Hale wished he could send everyone away now, that he and Sophie could be alone, that he could apologize, but Hale's mother and his army's most senior commanders flanked them, and this was not a time to show weakness. These were the leaders Hale needed to support his rule and to help save his sister. They had to believe in him, in his strength. So he stood motionless and stoic, wishing his dammed uncle would float faster.

After what felt like a lifetime, Danit's pyre finally rounded a bend in the river, and their party broke up, Hale's mother heading immediately for her horse.

'Sophie,' said Hale, halting her rapid retreat.

She reluctantly turned to face him. 'Yes?'

'A word, please?'

She lifted her head, and their eyes locked as they waited for the others to move away, Hale so lost in her gaze that he became oblivious to everything around them. He moved closer, so close he could smell her delicate honeysuckle scent, but before Hale could form words, Nicoli suddenly appeared at his elbow.

'I have an idea,' said Nicoli. Hale didn't even look at him, while Sophie watched Hale with interest, narrowing her eyes a little as she waited to see what he would do. She was enchanting in her high-collared purple gown. She'd taken to the style favored by his sister, and it truly suited her, making her look imperial and resplendent, her hair pulled back in a severe chignon, gold knots studding her ears. Hale wanted to peel the clothes off her, to worship her for days, and the fire in her eyes made him even more determined. 'I must speak with you, Hale,' Nicoli insisted.

Hale finally flicked his eyes to Nicoli. 'Find me later.'

Nicoli scoffed. 'No.'

Sophie folded her arms across her chest. 'You'll have to excuse Hale,' she said, her tone a sugar-coated spear. 'He's distracted by his plans to march on Spruce.'

Fuck.

Hale turned in time to see Nicoli flinch. 'Your ... what?'

Sophie stuck out her hip, clearly enjoying tormenting him. 'He's changeable like that.'

Hale shook his head, needing to find a way to turn the conversation around and not lose his chance to talk to Sophie. 'They're holding Pixy against her will.'

Nicoli's expression turned incredulous. 'She married their first son! There's no undoing that.'

'She didn't agree to the marriage,' Hale ground out. 'It doesn't count.'

Nicoli scowled. 'So you'll start another war when we finally have a chance at peace?'

'I'm honor bound.'

'Only if you want to be,' said Sophie, issuing another stab. Hale gave her a wide-eyed, questioning look, not quite a plea, but certainly an appeal.

'And what of your duties here?' asked Nicoli. 'To your Blade? To Sophie? To the Claws? Are those not enough?'

Hale screwed up his features. 'So I should abandon my sister? Would you abandon your cousin if our roles were reversed?'

'Who will step up if you fall during this foolish endeavor?' said Nicoli. 'John? Or have you put a bastard baby in your future wife? You think either of those will lead to stability?'

'Careful, Nicoli,' Hale growled.

Nicoli laughed. 'Or what, friend?'

'We're to be wed tomorrow or the next day,' said Sophie, tilting her head to one side. 'So it wouldn't really be a bastard.'

'Sophie!' Hale couldn't believe the change in her since last night. He wanted the soft, pliable version she'd shown him then.

Nicoli hissed. 'You fucking people. Maria requested my help. Perhaps she still cares about the plight of the Claws even if Alter does not. There is little I can do about the madness you propose in Spruce other than to council you against it, but maybe there is something of value I can do in Oshe.'

Hale didn't even glance at Nicoli as he retreated because a terrible thought had taken hold of his mind. There was no way Sophie could be carrying *his* bastard child, but what if ... 'Tell me,' he said, unable to drag air into his lungs, feeling as though he was drowning.

She scowled and shook her head, then turned her back on him. 'I need to rest.'

'Sophie, please.' He chased her, thankful no one else had lingered within earshot. 'I'm sorry about last night. I shouldn't have asked you to leave. I ...' He stepped in front of her, barring her path, horror gripping his chest. 'Tell me, Sophie, please.'

'Tell you what?' she snapped.

Hale recoiled in confusion. 'You said ... A bastard child ...'

'Hale!'

'You're not ...'

'Of course not! I was being facetious.'

He kissed her, his lips crashing into hers as the overwhelming relief almost sent tears to his eyes. 'What the fuck are you doing to me?' he whispered, crushing her to his chest. 'I ... The idea that ... That ...'

'We never even slept together,' she said, her tone still frosty, but she didn't pull away.

Hale's relief was a visceral thing, and he kissed her again, then pressed his forehead to hers.

She turned her head away, hiding from him. 'This isn't fair, Hale. I thought ... Last night ...'

He pressed his lips to her hair, inhaling her. *Fuck!* When had she become so thoroughly wedged under his skin? Why did he care so much about hurting her? He'd only agreed to marry her because her mother had found Alter's dirty secret, but now he wanted to rip himself apart for causing her pain. 'I'm sorry about last night. I shouldn't have asked you to leave.'

'Don't go to Spruce,' she whispered into his collar, her hands gripping the stiff fabric of his uniform.

He stroked her hair, wishing he could do as she asked. 'I have to.'

She pulled back, looking up at him with imploring eyes. 'Treating with them won't work, and we can't have another war.'

He shook his head slowly. 'She's my sister, Sophie.'

'And by the time you go, I'll be your wife, but if the Goddess comes for me, you'll have no choice but to let me go. This is the same, it's—'

He lifted both hands to her face, cupping her jaw. 'If the Goddess comes for you, she'd better bring an army because I won't stand by and let you go.'

Sophie grabbed his hands and yanked them off her skin, scoffing as she threw them away. 'Don't make promises you can't keep, Hale. You can't be so selfish as to threaten our whole world for the sake of my safety.'

His heart gave a loud thud because she still didn't understand. He tugged on her chin until she finally relented and looked at him once more, his chest nearly fracturing at the doubt he saw there. 'Darling, please don't underestimate how selfish I can be.'

Chapter Thirty-Six
Ava

Despite drinking himself into oblivion, Billy was up early the following morning, and he didn't hesitate before pulling Ava out of bed. The bed she was sharing with Kush.

'Billy!' she squealed, extremely glad she was wearing a nightdress.

He didn't seem to register her embarrassment, pulling back a little with a frown on his brow. 'You don't want to learn?'

'Of course I do, but—'

Billy closed his eyes and took a long inhale as though smelling something lovely. 'The hours when the sun is coming up are my most productive. If you want to learn, then this is when the action happens.'

'Urgh, fine.' Ava looked around for clothes, running her fingers through her bird's nest hair. 'I'll be up in a minute. Just let me get dressed.'

Billy spun for the door. 'Tick tock!' he said, then made a popping sound with his lips as he passed through the doorway.

The house helpfully provided a simple shift dress, hold ups, and slippers, and she hastily pulled them on. When she'd finished, Kush yanked her back onto the bed, and she squeaked in surprised delight as he kissed her.

'Morning,' he breathed, pushing her hair behind her ear.

She slid her hand to his neck and kissed him again. 'Morning.'

'Tick tock!' Billy's irritated voice rent the air around them, even though he was crashing about in the attic above their heads.

Kush gave her a final reluctant peck, then slid his thumb across her lips. 'Have fun.'

She froze. 'You're not coming?'

His features became carefully neutral. 'You want me to?'

'Of course!'

He swallowed. 'I don't have any magic, Ava. None to speak of, anyway.'

She frowned in confusion. 'So?'

'You don't care?'

She gave an incredulous laugh. 'Why would I?' She dropped a playful kiss on his lips. 'And anyway, I happen to think you're quite magical.'

A slow smile crept across his features.

'And if anyone can bring out your inner magic, it's probably me.'

He stroked her jaw. 'You think you can succeed where many others failed?'

She stood, looking cockily down at him. 'You doubt me?'

He threw back the covers, revealing his sculpted body in all its naked glory. 'Well in that case ...'

'Oh my Gods ... Kush ... I ...' She couldn't tear her eyes away.

He smirked, then kissed her again. 'I'll see you up there.'

She hesitated, but Billy screaming, 'Tick tock!' had her racing for the stairs, although she paused at the door and took one more look.

When Ava made it upstairs, she found Billy rearranging furniture in one of the many attic rooms. He'd pulled a desk in front of a chalkboard, and was dragging two uncomfortable looking wooden chairs in front of that.

'Sit,' Billy commanded, just as Kush joined them. Kush and Ava dropped into the chairs, while Billy completed a whole-body shimmy. 'By Atlas, this is taking me back to my youth. Might even be fun, playing teacher.' He flung notepaper and pencils at them, then launched into a stream of consciousness while pacing back and forth.

The morning passed in a haze of information, Billy unleashing one fact after another, and Ava wished her writing was good enough for her to scribble notes like Kush. Instead, she would have to rely on her memory.

'So there's magic,' said Billy, 'the natural kind like portals and healing pools and medicinal plants, and then there's physic, where we take our knowledge of magic and manipulate it. The simplest forms are things like heat and light stones, the most complex are portals, but there are also navigators and watches and any number of other objects that have been imbued with magical power.

'Your mother had quite a penchant for inventing physic objects, and your father was obsessed with all the things she created—with the social capital they brought him. He endlessly wanted more, and she was vain enough to thrive on his flattery, but *more* always comes at a cost.' Billy looked wistfully down at the desk, as though replaying some memory in his mind.

'You mean in terms of balance?' asked Ava.

Billy clapped his hands so loudly Ava jumped. '*Precisely*. Very good. Physic sucks energy, either when objects are created, or when they're used, or both. On a small scale, it doesn't do much harm, but physic objects have been manufactured and sold across the web, and on that scale, it's another story.'

'Objects like the navigator you wear,' Kush sniped.

'Yes, yes, I'm not perfect,' said Billy, leaning against the desk and entwining his fingers in a controlled movement, then dropping them against his leg. 'None of us are. Not to mention, the Federation facilitates the trade of physic, which means the Gods' interests are conflicted. On the one hand, they're supposed to ensure balance, while on the other, their wealth comes from trade. Anyway,'—he threw up his hands and shot away from the desk—'that's not the point.

'If you want to wield magic, you must always consider the type of magic you mean and what you intend to use as a source: natural magic or physic. Physic uses natural magic ultimately, of course, but it's a middleman if you will, a conduit, and in some cases, a store.'

Ava leaned forward in her seat, hungry for more. 'Which do we start with?'

Billy chuckled. 'Well, you've already been using physic by talking to this house.'

Ava looked at Kush. 'And Kush gave me a heat stone when I lived in the tavern. He showed me how to make it work.'

'Kushy Kushy,' said Billy, drawing out the words as he turned salacious eyes on Kush. 'You dark horse, you.'

'Why?' Ava asked quickly, worried she'd said something she shouldn't have.

Billy raised one eyebrow. 'The God of Santala—our mutual friend, Var—tightly controls the flow of magical objects in his worlds.'

'To ensure balance,' Kush bit out, 'as is his *duty*.'

'Mmm-hmm?'

Kush's entire body tensed, frustration rolling off him in waves.

Billy snickered.

'Can we focus?' Ava snapped.

'Yes yes.' Billy shimmied his shoulders. 'Well, using natural magic is easy. One just has to lie in a healing pool or eat a medicinal herb or walk through a natural portal, and using physic objects most people get the hang of without too much trouble, but creating them is an entirely different thing.'

A prickle of excitement ran down Ava's spine. 'Why?'

'For *so* many reasons!' Billy clapped his hands on his thighs. 'There's the craftsmanship of the objects—magic is picky and it doesn't like to live just anywhere—then there are the principles to consider, the source of the magic, how one will use the object, how long it should last. It's complex and intricate. Requires careful planning and precision and patience.'

'Can we make something today?' asked Ava, leaning so far forward she almost fell out of her seat.

'Ha!' Billy barked a laugh, then searched the bookshelves, humming to himself as he traced his finger along the spines. He picked an enormous tome, slid it off the shelf, then slammed it down on the desk. 'Come see me when you've finished that.'

A weight dropped through Ava's stomach. 'But my reading's terrible!'

'Then I guess it will take you a while.' Billy sashayed from the room, and Ava sighed, disappointment leeching through her. It would take days to read that book, maybe even weeks.

Kush reached for her hand and squeezed it reassuringly. 'I can read it to you, and if you follow the words as I speak them, it will help your reading, too.'

She nodded, thankful he was there with her, even if her insides squirmed with embarrassment.

They headed to the kitchen where they made tea and toast slathered with butter and marmalade, then settled in the solarium, lying together on a lounger, Ava cradled between Kush's thighs so they could both see the writing. They barely moved from that spot for days, distracted only by meals, sleep, and brief intervals of stretching their muscles.

After a while, Ava began reading small sections aloud, although it took her so much longer than Kush, and her cheeks heated when she stumbled over words. Kush was patient and encouraging, but it made Ava want to curl up inside, feeling like a failure.

When they finally neared the end of the first book, Billy dumped five more on the table beside them.

'You can't be serious!' Ava whined, sitting bolt upright and staring him down.

Billy waved his fingers in front of his nose. 'Does this face look like it's joking?'

She collapsed back against Kush as Billy skipped away. 'At least he's cooking for us,' she said under her breath, that the only silver lining she could find.

Kush rubbed her arms. 'And giving us the reading order.'

'True.' Kush was right, they wouldn't have had a clue where to start without Billy.

The books explained the cycle of magic in each world. How it flowed, passing from plants to animals to the soil to the sky, and how the trees held everything together, sucking magic from the air, then transferring it through the roots into the soil and vice versa. And then, how the roots had found their way into other worlds, and with the roots, the magic.

The books told of the flow of magical power through the web of linked worlds, the origins of physic, which began with simple uses and storage of magic, developing over time into complex objects like navigators and eventually unnatural portals.

Kush became increasingly irritable as the days wore on, his interest in the subject matter waning the more technical it became, and then Billy dropped a tome called *The Puzzle of Time* in their laps, and Kush's eyes glazed over completely.

'I'm going for a swim,' he said, as Ava peppered Billy with questions about why time moved faster in some worlds and slower in others.

'It's all about dilation,' said Billy.

Ava squeezed Kush's hand as he got up. She knew she should probably go after him, see if everything was okay, but instead she said, 'So the bigger the world, the faster time moves?'

'Exactly,' said Billy, shoving Ava until she made space for him, then sitting cross-legged on the lounger beside her. 'Bigger worlds dilate the web more, meaning the magic has farther to travel.'

'Because the speed of magic is constant, not time.'

Billy gave her an almost proud smile. 'There's hope for you yet, my dear.'

'And that's how the Gods have long lives, because their souls are tied to other worlds where time passes more slowly?'

Billy nodded sadly.

'So the souls must be tied to really small worlds, right?

Billy raised his eyebrows, seeming impressed, and Ava's chest swelled with pride. 'Certainly a lot smaller than the world of the Atlas Tree.'

Ava hadn't thought of the tree as a world, as such. 'But the Atlas Tree isn't that big.'

'Oh, it's bigger than it looks. The tree is at the center of a veritable forest.'

Ava puffed out a breath, then lay back. There was still so much she didn't know.

'Buck up, my dear,' said Billy, slapping her thigh.

'Ow!'

'Tomorrow you become a physic.'

Her heart leapt. 'Wait ... what?'

Billy surged to his feet, standing on the lounger. 'Let's celebrate!'

Chapter Thirty-Seven
Maria
Six Weeks After Dromeda Started Spinning

Maria flicked pieces of bread off the table onto the floor, seeing how far she could make them fly, casting periodic looks at Sol and Tallin, who were playing chess at a table in the corner. Zeik and Elex were out, and she was bored. So very very bored. This had never happened to her before. She'd always had places to explore or books to read or people to trade with for information, but here, there wasn't even a library.

It had been two days since they'd seen the midwife in the street, and they'd heard nothing useful since. The others were combing the city for information about the Queens and the commander, but seeing as Maria didn't know anyone in Oshala, she couldn't even help with that.

Maria loudly pushed back her chair and headed for the chess game. She hadn't played in years, but she remembered how.

She studied the board over Sol's shoulder, but neither of the men even looked up. Ordinarily, the minor slight wouldn't have concerned her, but in her fractious mood, it got under her skin. 'He's going to take your knight with his queen, and that will be check mate.'

Tallin looked up with a severe frown, and it gave Maria a rush, a thrill swelling her chest, knowing she'd riled him as he had her. It was petty and childish and probably mean, but the waiting was sending her out of her mind, and she needed a release for the anguish that felt like it might burst through her chest and tear her apart.

The door banged open, and Zeik swaggered into the room, a broad smile on his face. Maria's heart leapt. 'What is it?' she demanded, hope spiraling up inside.

'We're in luck, my friends,' said Zeik, milking the attention with a dramatic pause. 'Now they are wed, Erica and Opal are coming out of Elex's quarter and taking over Barron's old home by the bridge.'

'Idiots,' said Sol.

Tallin nodded in agreement. 'That place is full of holes.'

'They had no choice,' said Zeik. 'Their trading partners are becoming bold, taking liberties and spreading rumors of the Queens' weakness. If they stay put, they play into those claims. They must make a show of strength, to be visible to their people.'

'When?' Maria asked breathily.

Zeik raised an excitable eyebrow. 'Today.'

'So, what?' said Maria. 'We strike?'

Elex strode into the room holding a piece of parchment with a wax seal. 'We wait.'

'Urgh.' Maria wanted to punch something.

'Everything okay?' asked Zeik, his tone sliding up at the end as though her reaction was somehow funny.

'No,' she snapped, 'everything is not okay. It's alright for all of you, roaming the streets and keeping watch, but I cannot stay cooped up in here with nothing to do any longer. I'm going insane!'

Elex shoved the parchment into his pocket and slid his hands up and down her arms. 'Not much longer my little hell cat.'

'No!'

'Maria ...'

'No, Elex. I can't. I need something to do.'

He shook his head and pulled back a little, retrieving the parchment and sliding a finger under the seal.

'Who's that from?' Maria demanded, angry that he'd practically dismissed her.

'The Queens.'

'What?' Maria snatched it from his fingers. 'It could be poisoned.'

'Unlikely.'

Panic flooded her as she carefully pulled it open, checking for moisture or residue. 'Do they know we're here?'

'No,' Elex said reassuringly. 'They sent out many copies, distributing them to shop owners and inn keepers, although no one knew the contents, and we couldn't get a copy from a trusted source, and then I tripped over this one on the way in.'

Alarm pulsed in her veins. 'But how did they ...?'

'This is a tavern, remember?' Zeik said disparagingly. 'They shoved it through the letter box.' Zeik snatched it from Maria's hand, then danced out of reach.

'Hey!'

'Fuck.' Zeik turned suddenly serious.

'What?' asked Elex.

Zeik sat at a table and put the parchment on the wooden surface. 'The Queens have requested your presence at a special celebration tomorrow afternoon. It's at the bear pit. They have your sister and will be *displeased* if you don't attend.'

Tallin's jaw clenched, his shoulders suddenly rigid. 'Shit.'

'Just me?' asked Elex.

Zeik shook his head. 'You and Maria. Alone.'

'No,' said Elex, finality in his tone.

Tallin launched to his feet, a sneer on his lips. 'You'll turn your back on her?'

'He's right,' said Maria, 'we can't.' If they had Pixy, she wouldn't hesitate.

Elex looked away, his jaw working, and Maria could practically see the cogs in his brain whirring. 'They could be bluffing.'

Zeik huffed a cynical laugh. 'Unlikely.'

'We'll find out,' said Tallin, looking at his cousin. 'Come on.' Sol stood without hesitation and followed Tallin from the room.

'Wait for me!' called Zeik, sending an infuriating look Maria's way, reminding her of the kind of look her own brother would use to stoke the fires of her annoyance. 'Good luck, brother,' he muttered as he followed the other two.

The moment the door closed, Maria rounded on Elex. 'What was that about?'

'I won't put you at risk,' he said numbly, refusing to meet her gaze.

She stepped up in front of him, forcing him to look at her. 'That is not your choice to make.'

He cupped her cheek. 'It's dangerous, Maria, even more so now than before. Cane pushed the boundaries, but Erica and Opal ... Anything goes in their court. The reports we've been hearing ... If they kidnap you ...'

She shoved his hand away. 'Like they've done to your sister?'

'So I should let them have you both?' he snarled.

Maria hated to admit he had a point. She took a breath, forcing herself to think. 'Why do they want us there? What's the purpose?'

He stared into her eyes as he considered his answer. 'Legitimacy, and to display their dominance. Holding onto control will be far easier if it looks like they have my family in line.'

'Why not just kill us all?'

'They can't. If the Goddess has truly returned and the Toll Bells ring, they need a female sacrifice from the Oshe family, and all they have right now are babies in their wombs.'

'If that story is even true ...' Maria deflated, not wanting to think about the Goddess or Toll Bells or what it might all mean for her and her family. 'So that's why they've locked up your sister?'

He shrugged. 'Or they're using her as bait to trap us.'

'You think they would?'

His eyebrows raised. 'Don't you?'

She growled a frustrated exhale, then balled her hands into fists. 'I will not sit here doing nothing any longer.'

He shook his head. 'I won't lose you again.'

Maria's mouth set into a hard line. 'We're going.'

'We're not.'

'You can't stop me.'

He stepped closer, crowding her. 'I can, actually.'

'How, Elex? Will you lock me up? Chain me?'

He slid his hands to her neck. 'I think I would like that,' he said, squeezing gently, 'because right now you're driving me crazy.'

'Same,' she whispered, refusing to yield under his dangerous touch.

He squeezed again, and she reached for his waist, holding on to keep herself steady as a rush of relief cascaded through her blood. After days of inaction, she was surprised to find this was just what she needed, the bite of his fingers taking the edge off her torment.

He kissed her, his lips bruising, his thumbs on her pulse points, and every nerve across her body came alive, like fireflies furiously batting their wings against her skin. 'I can't wait to rule Oshe with you, my little hell cat. To give you what you deserve.'

But it seemed so far away. Too far away. A distant dream that might never come to pass. First Maria had been trapped by Cane, and now she was trapped in the tavern, but here she couldn't even go outside without fear of discovery, nor could she trade her oils or do anything useful. Elex wanted her to rest, to recuperate, but life in the tavern couldn't provide Maria with either of those things. She needed a fast gallop or to hunt for triffles or to climb a tree. At least the invitation from the Queens meant she could escape for a few hours, breathe some fresh air and see more of this strange city she now called home.

Elex squeezed harder. 'We're not going, Maria.'

She gripped his shirt, soaking in the relief for several long beats, then pushed him away. 'Yes, Elex, we are.'

Chapter Thirty-Eight
Ava

AVA LAY HER HEAD in Kush's lap, looking up at him with wide, unfocused eyes as they sprawled on a sofa in the drawing room.

Kush took small, clipped sips of his drink, everything about him tense, whereas Ava had never been so relaxed. 'Billy's not good for us,' Kush said in a low, strained voice.

'Not good, but necessary,' she countered, and found that funny for some reason, so she giggled.

'What are you two love birds whispering about?' Billy demanded. He stood on a circular table near the drinks cabinet that was definitely not designed to support his weight. The tabletop listed dangerously to one side, and Ava wondered if his sock-clad feet would slide right off. She giggled again.

Kush squeezed her arm. 'We could find someone else to teach you, especially now you know the basics.'

Ava swiveled her eyes back to his. 'Who?'

Kush shook his head. 'Someone. I could ask around.'

'What?' Billy shouted, even though it was just the three of them in the room.

Ava pushed up onto her arms, resting them on Kush's thighs. 'Come closer,' she whispered, leaning towards Billy as though about to let him into their confidence.

Billy inched a little more towards the edge of the table, and with a great creaking snap, the top gave way and Billy slid to the floor, landing on his feet without spilling a drop of his half-full drink. Ava cheered as Billy bowed, saluting them with his tumbler.

Ava fell back, howling with laughter, wondering if the pink *Bubbles and Doubles* liquor Billy had plied her with all night was the cause of her uncharacteristic frivolity.

Kush huffed and pushed Ava upright, then stalked to the table to assess the damage. Billy catapulted himself into Kush's vacated spot, crossing his legs and nudging Ava conspiratorially with his elbow. 'Someone's in a grump.'

'Hmm,' she said, leaning back and watching Kush. There was definitely something he wasn't saying, something he was holding back.

'Either of you planning to fix this?' Kush asked, scowling hard.

'Ha!' Billy, threw his head back. 'DIY isn't my thing, my dear Kush-Kush.' Then Billy sat forward as though he'd had a great idea. 'I could do an illusion!'

Kush scrubbed his face with his hands. 'Yes, Billy, that's exactly what we need.'

Billy pouted. 'Sarcasm is beneath you, dearie, and an illusion would fix the eyesore.'

'Can't the house fix it?' asked Ava. 'Please, house, will you fix the table?'

The house vibrated, but the table remained in two pieces, and then the door slammed shut.

'I think we annoyed the house,' said Ava, feeling a tinge of remorse. 'I'm sorry, house.'

'Oh, for Atlas' sake,' said Billy. 'It's only a table!'

The house shook again, this time so hard, even Billy shrank a little. 'Oh, fine. I'm sorry for breaking the table.'

'We appreciate everything you do for us,' said Ava, thinking back to the cleaning and sheet-changing and tidying she'd had to do at the tavern. She'd barely lifted a finger since getting here. 'Truly. And I'm sorry we broke the table.'

The table snapped back together so fast, Ava almost missed it, and Kush took a hurried step back in alarm. Then the table jumped a foot in the air before slamming to the ground with such a loud bang, Ava jumped, spilling her drink all over herself.

'Thank you,' Ava whispered. 'And sorry again.'

'You know what,' Kush said pointedly, 'I'm going to bed. You two have fun.'

'Kush!' cried Ava, moving to get up, but Billy put a hand on her arm.

'Don't go running after him, that's exactly what he wants!'

She shook Billy off, but something about his words kept her on the sofa. 'Kush! Don't go!'

'Ava!' snapped Billy. 'Don't *chase* him. What would your mother say?'

'I don't know, seeing as she was killed when I was like, six? And,' she said, rounding on him, Kush already out of view, 'while we're on that topic, what exactly did you have to do with her murder?'

Billy crossed his arms and angled himself away, tapping his foot.

'Well?' she demanded, all remnants of her levity diving for cover ahead of the wrath cresting through her veins. 'Who killed my parents? And why?' She'd been sitting on the question since the day Billy had arrived, telling herself to believe he hadn't been involved, that maybe it didn't matter. But it did matter, and now the question was out, she couldn't believe she'd waited so long to ask again. 'Kush said it was you and B.'

Billy shook his head. 'No.' Although he didn't quite commit to the word, and he was fidgeting all over.

'Liar.' The word slipped out before she'd had time to consider if saying it was a good idea, but as it hung between them, she found she had no desire to reel it back.

His head moved violently towards her. 'I did not kill your parents, but I didn't stop it from happening.'

'Could you have?'

He shrugged. 'Maybe.'

'Was it B?'

Billy closed his eyes and bared his clenched teeth.

'Billy? Was it?'

He nodded, the movement quick and jerky. 'I think so.'

Ava folded forward, clutching her stomach against the physical pain. 'Why?' she whispered, rocking back and forth. It made sense now why B had treated Ava like shit her whole life. Was that why B had taken Ava in, the opportunity to exact revenge on her parents even after they were gone?

Billy lowered his head. 'Because Polly ate her up, spat her out, then ground her to a pulp under her heel.'

Ava considered his dramatic words. 'By stealing her soul?'

He leaned forward, then said accusingly, 'Your mother hijacked B's life, used B for her own purposes, and then stole her hopes of having children, all while flaunting you, wounding Novak, using Rupert as a puppet, and refusing to make things right.' Billy brought his legs up and wrapped his arms around his shins. 'She had it coming.'

His words stole the righteous wind from Ava's sails. 'B wanted children?'

'Desperately. And she had someone she wanted to have them with, too.'

'Oh.'

'She wanted her old life back. Her normal life. After B outed your parents' soul-tying secret to Var and the rest, she became a pariah. Var was glad to be rid of her, Novak's family lost their place in the Clouds, but your mother ... she was furious. She went out of her way to treat B like shit ... and me, even though I didn't *do* anything.'

'Do you ever do anything aside from getting drunk?'

'Oh, please,' he spat, giving her a condescending look.

'You said it yourself, you didn't stop B when perhaps you could have.' The thought made Ava's heart hurt.

'The other Gods wanted revenge, but they still hoped one day to get their souls back. B knew that would never happen, that your parents would continue to destroy the web, to take too much and give too little. B was the only one with the guts to go through with it. She wanted me to help her, but I ... I suppose I had more to lose than she did.'

'Or maybe you were just a coward.' Ava stood and made for the door, going after Kush—what she should have done all along.

'He'll leave you,' said Billy, his tone unusually somber. Ava paused and looked back to where Billy had stretched his legs out along the cushions and rested his head against the arm of the sofa. 'When the chips are down, his loyalty is with Var and Var alone.'

'You're wrong.'

'And once Kush gets what he wants from you, Var wants you dead. Maybe Kush will even be the one to do it ...'

'No,' she whispered, refusing to believe his vindictive words. She went in search of Kush, feeling as though she walked on shifting sands. Her whole life in the tavern was a lie. B had known who she was, who her parents were, had killed them! Ava clutched at her chest as she climbed the stairs, wishing the truth wasn't quite so hard to bear.

Chapter Thirty-Nine

Sophie

Six Weeks After Dromeda Started Spinning

Sophie's parents had demanded a minimum of two weeks before the wedding to give themselves time to organize their affairs and travel to Alter. Hale had reluctantly agreed——much to Bianca's horror——and he'd treated Sophie like a goddess for days on end, unwavering in his affections, at least during the short stints when she got to see him. He spent most of his time holed up with his commanders, strategizing about the best way to rescue his sister, who, if you asked Sophie, was well past rescuing. And even if they could get her out, the best way was by stealth, not combat.

But Hale hadn't been receptive to her ideas, and his commanders were gleefully filling his head with battle plans, so there was little Sophie could do aside from using the time alone to get to grips with running the mansion. She met with the housekeeper, cook, maids, and gardeners, the seamstress and the stable hands, while doing what she could to avoid Hale's mother, who was a weasel, plain and simple.

His mother, however, did not want to be avoided. She seemed to lurk around every corner, offering to take any and all household duties off Sophie's hands. So Sophie's heart fell when she entered the library that evening to find Bianca and Hale's grandmother already seated, crystal tumblers in hand, the housekeeper before them.

'Yes, ma'am,' said the middle-aged woman. She had pasty skin, her greying hair tied back in a bun. 'But you see, Hale gave me a direct order to take *my* orders from Sophie. I really must insist you speak with him. It's putting me in a very difficult situation, ma'am, I'm sure you understand. My hands are tied.'

Hale's grandmother, Dio, said not a word, watching the interaction like a hawk, which seemed to be her way.

'The years I spent running this place count for nothing, then?' said Bianca, her tone turning dangerous.

'Ma'am,' said the housekeeper, 'I'm sorry, but you must understand the decision is not mine. My personal feelings are not relevant.'

'I gave you this job, and I can take it away.'

Sophie coughed loudly, her blood beginning to boil, and the housekeeper's head whipped around. The woman bobbed a curtsey, then hurried from the room with a quiet, 'Good evening, ma'am.'

'Good evening,' said Sophie, heading for the drinks stand, doing what she could to delay having to talk to Bianca. She added a few cubes of ice to a crystal tumbler, then helped herself to a measure of walnut liqueur before saying, 'Please stop harassing my housekeeper,' with her back still facing the other women.

Her words sucked the air from the room, and a smile tugged at Sophie's lips. She turned to face them, swirling her drink over the ice. 'Our housekeeper is right. If you're angry at anyone, it should be Hale or me. I appreciate this situation must be difficult for you after so long—'

'You know nothing of my life,' spat Bianca. 'And you and my son are not yet married. You should not count your chickens before they have hatched.'

Hale entered the room at that moment, his eyes lighting up when he saw Sophie in her demure purple gown. 'Good evening,' he said, casting his gaze over the other women, seeming oblivious to the heavy atmosphere as he moved to Sophie's side. She turned her face up to him, and he pressed his lips to hers. The kiss was too long and deep for Alter society, but was par for the course in Laurow, so Sophie didn't give two hoots, and when Hale pulled away, she slid her hand into the crook of his arm for good measure.

Bianca appeared ready to blow a gasket when Sophie and Hale sat side by side on the empty sofa, their legs pressed together, but a sly smile played around the edges of his grandmother's lips. Sophie couldn't get an exact read on the woman, but she certainly seemed to be an ally, siding with Sophie whenever an opportunity arose, and she had a soft spot for Hale.

Dio asked Bianca a question, drawing her into conversation, and Hale bowed his head towards Sophie's ear. 'I missed you,' he whispered. It had been twenty-four hours since she'd last set eyes on him, and she didn't want to admit how much she'd missed him, too. A small frown appeared on his forehead. 'I saw the housekeeper. She said my mother isn't settling into her new role graciously ...'

Sophie shook her head in shock. 'She said that?'

He smirked. 'I read between the lines. Are you okay?' He stroked his thumb across her cheek.

She nudged his shoulder with hers. 'She's nothing I can't handle, but I doubt we'll ever be the best of friends.'

He cupped her face. 'She'll get used to her new position eventually.'

'It's been lonely without you,' Sophie said, changing the subject, wanting to keep him to herself for as long as she could. 'I've had nothing but books for company at night.'

He smiled wolfishly. 'Then perhaps tonight—'

'What are you two muttering about?' demanded Bianca. 'It is rude to whisper.'

Hale dropped a resigned kiss on Sophie's forehead, then pulled back with a sigh.

'I was just thanking Hale for my reading material,' Sophie said sweetly, answering before Hale could. 'He has stories in his library I've never read before.'

'Stories?' Bianca's mouth fell open.

Hale awkwardly cleared his throat. 'I found them in my study. Turns out Danit had quite a collection.'

'Wonderful stories,' Dio agreed with a clap of her hands. 'Which is your favorite?'

Hale's eyes went wide. 'You've read them?'

'Of course! It's only recently they were removed from the main library. I read them as a girl and nobody batted an eye, but my late husband—Hale's grandfather—didn't like them at all. It wasn't a battle I cared to pick, so off they went to his study. I still smuggled them out under a scarf every now and again.'

Sophie smiled broadly. 'Which is *your* favorite?'

'The love stories,' she said scandalously.

'Hale's too,' said Sophie, not missing a beat.

The old woman barked a laugh. 'I can believe it! Along with the tales of voyages across the endless seas.'

Sophie grinned as she turned her head to tease her future husband. He pinched her leg. 'Ow!' she laughed. 'It's not my fault your grandmother knows you so well.'

Bianca's scowl deepened. 'What of Pixy's rescue? Has there been time to plan that alongside all this make believe?'

Why Bianca had insisted on *intimate family drinks* ahead of their wedding tomorrow, Sophie couldn't fathom, especially not if she wished to talk only of war.

'Everything is planned,' said Hale. 'We'll ride out the day after tomorrow. I don't want to leave so soon after my wedding, but Pixy's been trapped long enough as it is, and I'm sure Sophie will cope without me for a week or two.' He squeezed her hand, but it wasn't in the least bit reassuring.

'And she has me to help her run the house,' said Bianca. 'We'll be fine. Even better when Pixy is back at home.'

'What of the wedding?' asked Dio, tapping her cane on the floor. 'I think I'll come along, you know. Be a dear and tell the stables to prepare an extra carriage.'

Hale's face lit up. 'Of course! We'd love you to come.'

She nodded, settling the matter. 'Now, tell me all the details. Who's coming? Anyone I like?'

Hale outlined their plans for a simple wedding, and Sophie studied Bianca, taking the opportunity to truly catalogue the woman while she was distracted by her son. But Bianca must have sensed the scrutiny because she flicked her icy gaze to Sophie, her features flat and unreadable, a look that would have made most cower given the older woman's position. But tomorrow, Sophie would become the First Lady of Alter, a role she had been trained for since she was a child, and she wouldn't let a small thing like a disgruntled mother-in-law stand in her way.

Chapter Forty
Ava

Ava had apologized to Kush about the table incident, blaming her stupid behavior on the alcohol and promising to swear off it for a while. He'd accepted the apology, and they'd stayed up most of the night exploring one another, but Ava still felt like there was something he wasn't saying.

They waited in the attic room where Billy had delivered his first and only lecture several weeks before, Ava excited in a way she'd never been because today she would become a physic.

She kissed Kush as they waited, and he happily kissed her back, pulling her onto his lap and caressing her lips with unhurried, luxurious movements. With Billy set to show up at any moment, it couldn't go any further than a kiss, and that made it somehow sweeter, the kiss an end in itself rather than the start of something more.

Ava lost herself in his soft, delicious lips. Lips that chased her lingering doubts away because if he was loyal to Var, if he had plans to sell her out, surely he couldn't kiss her like this? Sincere and devoted and as absorbed in her as she was in him.

As the kiss went on and on, even those thoughts fell away, Ava caring only about their joined mouths, the way his hand rested casually on her hip, and the transcendent place inside herself he transported her to.

They might have stayed like that all day, nipping and licking and pulling, but eventually Billy joined them. 'Okay,' he said in his most officious tone, and Ava jumped because she hadn't even heard him come in. Billy waggled his fingers. 'Physic.'

He didn't mention their kissing, nor did he wait for Ava to climb off Kush before he began his first explanation of the lesson. It was like he hadn't even noticed, and although she dearly wanted to learn the things

Billy planned to teach them, for a moment, all Ava could focus on was her swollen lips, Kush's strong legs under hers, and his spicy smell.

Kush pulled her back and kissed her one final time, unhurried and deep, before helping her slide onto the chair beside him. She didn't want to end the moment, but Billy was definitely saying something interesting, and she could kiss Kush again as soon as the lesson was done, which was exactly what she intended to do.

'All magical objects draw power,' said Billy, 'either from the user or from the web, but nothing comes from nothing. Whatever power they use must be repaid.'

'Give what you take,' said Ava.

'Principle one,' agreed Billy. 'But to keep things in balance, we must also take what we give, either through using magical objects or healing pools, and some even claim to have managed it in echo chambers. The problem is,' he said, tipping out a basket of magical instruments—watches, navigators, light stones, heat stones, knives, and many more—'when one multiplies these instruments by the great number of people who use physic objects all across the Atlas Web, the system becomes strained.'

'The system is not strained,' Kush countered with an exasperated exhale.

'Beg to differ,' said Billy. 'Now, how does one give back?'

'Ummm.' Ava tried to think of an answer, but Kush's scowl was scrambling her brain, making her worry he might leave the lesson, and she wanted them to do this together.

Billy huffed and crossed his arms. 'When we die, our bodies rot, and the magic within us finds its way back into the web. But we can also create magic though living—interacting with others, dancing, singing, fighting, even. The higher our emotions, the more we make, and the surplus goes back to the web.'

It all seemed very opaque to Ava. 'But ... how?'

'Through healing pools and the like—as the women of the temples are regularly expected to do—or, in less potent fashion, through the air. It leeches out of us, and the trees suck it up and pass it along through their roots. Plants give off magic, too, as do animals ... anything living, really, and even some rocks, but that's another story.'

Ava's forehead creased. 'So it just ... flows around?'

'Mmm-hmm, until it's embedded into something or a person. Polly was working on collection devices before she died, vessels in which to store larger quantities of magic, things that could be used as regulators, but as far as I know, she never succeeded. Magic wants to flow, you see. It doesn't like to sit idle.'

Ava shook her head as she considered his words. 'But it must sit still in some cases. In the Atlas Stones and light stones and all these instruments.' She waved her hand over the pile on the desk.

'Well, yes, fine. But those are small quantities, not large ones, and they'll run out of magic eventually.'

'Even the Atlas Stone?' said Kush.

Billy flicked his eyes to the ceiling. 'Who knows. But probably not. The Atlas Stones are special. We didn't create those; we found them inside the tree.'

'But we find some heat and light stones already imbued with magic, too,' said Kush, 'so what's the difference?'

Billy shrugged. 'If only we knew. Needs more research, but Var doesn't like research he doesn't control, so it's not easy these days.'

A swirling gust of interest pushed up through Ava's chest, making her sit straighter in her seat. 'There are researchers?'

'Naturally.'

'Who?' asked Kush, leaning forward with interest. 'Where?'

'Nice try,' said Billy, wagging his pointer finger back and forth. 'Even if I did know, I would never tell you.'

'Billy!' cried Ava, putting her hand on Kush's arm. 'We're all on the same side.'

Billy folded his arms and cocked his head at a probing angle. 'And what side is that, exactly?'

'Well ...' Words deserted her. *The side against Var?* No, that wasn't quite right. Kush certainly wasn't against his father. But he wasn't exactly for him, either. *The side of good?* But what did that mean? What side was she on? Her own side? The side of—

'Can we just move on?' snapped Kush. 'You don't trust me, and I don't trust you. Let's leave it at that and get on with what we're here for.'

'Hmmm,' said Billy, pausing for a moment and staring Kush down, but then he slowly unfolded his arms and produced three round stones from his pocket. He beckoned Ava and Kush over to the desk, set one stone in front of each of them, and placed his hand on the smooth grey surface of the one he'd kept for himself. He inhaled a long breath, closing his eyes, then exhaled with an accompanying *haa* sound. 'Calighto caroumium magnila installia.' Nothing obvious happened, although Ava thought she might have detected something faint in the air, like a gentle ripple against her skin or maybe that was just wishful thinking. Billy passed the stone to Ava. 'That is now a heat stone. Say the words Kushy-Kush taught you.'

Ava scowled. Why did he have to constantly bait Kush? She said the words, '*Infernon mynon,*' anyway, and the stone heated in her hand. She laughed and almost dropped it in astonishment. 'That's it? It's really that simple?'

Billy leaned towards her. 'That, my naïve little cracklejack, was anything but simple. Very few have the gift of channeling magic, and that is truly what sets the Cloud families apart—aside from their greed—they're physics, and most others are not.'

'Which is why they're obsessed with bloodlines?' asked Ava.

Billy popped his lips. 'Bingo. Now, your turn.'

Ava grabbed her stone. 'What were the words again?' she said in a rush.

Billy rolled his eyes almost indulgently as he slid an open book under her nose. Her reading was almost fluent now, seeing as she'd been putting in so much practice, and she quickly found the right place.

Ava took a deep breath like Billy had—without the noise on the exhale—then said the words. Nothing happened and she felt no ripple. 'Did it work?' She looked left and right as though the answer might be hanging in the air beside her.

Billy threw his head back and barked a delighted laugh. 'See! Harder than it looks.'

'What did I do wrong?'

Billy shrugged. 'Probably a lot of things.'

Ava slid the book so it sat between her and Kush, encouraging him to give it a go, too. Billy stilled, watching Kush closely, and Kush lowered his head, the air suddenly thick. Ava looked from Billy to Kush and back again, wondering what could possibly be going on.

Kush pushed back his chair. 'I'm going for a swim.'

'Kush! No!'

He turned and met her eyes, his expression carefully blank. 'Stay, Ava. You want to learn this stuff, but it's not for me.'

He seemed to mean it, and she didn't detect bitterness or anger, only something melancholy, so she did stay, turning questioning eyes on Billy as soon as they were alone. 'Well?' she demanded, when he wasn't forthcoming.

Billy folded his arms and leaned his hip against the desk, his expression unusually sober. 'That is why physics care greatly about their bloodlines.'

'Oh, shit ...'

Billy raised his eyebrows.

'Kush's mother isn't from the Clouds ... Doesn't have magic ...'

Billy batted his hand back and forth in the air. 'Everyone has some magic, and the temple women especially, but not enough, apparently. Perhaps Var thought his own magic would be sufficient to ensure a magical child, but it was not, and Kush's lack of ability is the real reason the Cloud families rejected him. Could you imagine if he impregnated one of their offspring?' Billy held a hand in front of his open mouth, and Ava wasn't sure if he was being sincere in his considering the idea scandalous or not.

Ava's cheeks heated at the thought of Kush impregnating anyone. She bent forward over her stone, unable to imagine how hard all of this must be on Kush. Her obsession with magic, with understanding her parents' work, and being here with Billy—someone who flaunted his magical abilities but did absolutely nothing with them—while Kush had no real magic of his own.

'All very upsetting, I'm sure,' Billy said with absolutely no compassion, 'but first impressions indicate your magic is also unimpressive, so you're going to want to practice.' Billy swayed, clutching the desk. 'Meanwhile, I'm off for a lie down ... Not as well practiced as I used to—' He crashed to the floor.

'Billy!' cried Ava, rushing to his side, but he was out cold.

Chapter Forty-One
Maria
Seven Weeks After Dromeda Started Spinning

Maria's headdress sat heavily on her brow. It was not the custom in Alter to wear such things on any occasion, but in Oshe, Zeik had assured her, all the wealthy ladies would have them perched atop their heads.

And he wasn't wrong. As they entered the first family's box suspended over the bear pit, she was glad of the ostentatious gold creation that splayed out like a fan across her head. If she hadn't had one, she would have been out of place among all the women sporting tall, broad, sparkling pieces, many of which had rows of gems dangling beside the wearers' faces.

Maria's dress was equally opulent, layer upon layer of silk, which rustled as she walked, cinching her in so tightly she could barely breathe, her chest heaving up and down at the top of her light blue gown from the exertion of climbing the stairs.

The bear pit was a large stone amphitheater in the middle of the complex of buildings Elex's father had once called home. The stairs were inside, which meant the crowd hadn't been able to ogle them as they'd ascended, but they were ogling now, a hush falling over the place as Elex helped Maria down the two shallow steps into the Queens' domain.

Elex squeezed Maria's fingers, holding on for a moment too long before reluctantly letting her go. He'd finally relented and agreed to come only hours earlier, when Zeik had produced an outfit and Maria had made it clear she was going whether he joined her or not. He'd brooded for the entire walk across the city, then had refused to set foot inside until she'd promised that if things took a turn for the worse, she would get herself out at all costs.

Maria smiled reassuringly at Elex, then made a show of beaming at the Queens, who stood and turned as one to face them, wearing matching headdresses, although one was silver and the other gold. Each had five prongs poking upwards, the middle prong shorter than the others, an enormous light blue gemstone at its tip. Their dresses, however, were entirely distinct, Erica's skimpy and provocative, Opal's understated and demure, both in the light blue color of their Blade.

Opal approached with open arms, pulling Maria into an embrace. 'It is good to see you, friend.'

'Ahhh … You too,' Maria replied, taken aback by the public display of affection.

'Have you met Rosalind?' asked Erica, waving her hand in the direction of a woman who had not dressed up for the occasion. She wore no head-dress, and her outfit was a plain smock that finished just above her knees with long pants beneath. Her dark hair was tied back in a rough bun, not a scrap of kohl around her eyes or rouge on her lips. She was attractive although not pretty, and her whole demeanor screamed, *fuck off*.

Maria beamed at her. 'It's a pleasure to meet you.'

Rosalind gave a curt nod, then said, 'You too,' in a clipped tone.

'I hope you are well, sister?' said Elex. They both seemed a little awkward, and Maria assumed it was on account of their large audience, the eyes of the entire place still glued to the box.

'Hmm,' said Rosalind, who quickly returned to her seat in the second row beside the same barrel-chested commander who'd helped the Queens take over. Was he Rosalind's guard, there to ensure she didn't escape?

'She's always like that,' murmured Elex, bending so his lips brushed Maria's ear.

Maria glanced behind them and found the influential families of Oshe much closer than she'd realized, dressed up in all their finery, staring back at her, doing nothing to hide their interest. The poorer members of the Blade were higher up still, separated from the rich and powerful by a railing and walkway.

'Come, sit with us, Maria,' said Erica, indicating that she should take the chair between the two Queens in the front row. Elex stiffened, but it wasn't as if Maria had any choice, so she gave a polite smile and joined them, while Elex seated himself in the chair on Erica's right.

The commander kept leaning into Rosalind's space, touching her arm and whispering in her ear. Maria could see them out of the corner of her eye, and Rosalind seemed angry, her body stiff like a wooden board, but then, she'd seemed that way from the moment Maria had laid eyes on her, so maybe that was how she always looked. Elex kept turning to observe them, too, but like his sister, he was giving nothing away.

'It's just like old times!' gushed Opal, drawing Maria's attention.

Erica leaned forward, her usual cat-like smile on her lips. 'But now we have our clothes on, and Opal and I have no man to boss us about.'

Maria couldn't help the shocked laugh that huffed out of her. 'Those were troubling times.'

Opal hummed her agreement. 'Over now though.'

'And today we will have some fun!' Erica waved to a man below who sported a greasy ponytail, and the crowd roared, making further conversation impossible as two men built like bulls entered the arena through a gate that reminded Maria of the dungeons at home.

'We have much planned!' Opal squealed as the crowd quietened, the men moving to opposite sides of the arena. 'Singers and dancers and all kinds of wonderous things.' She clasped her hands in glee. 'And a special announcement.'

The words made Maria's blood run cold. The last time the two women had planned something special, three of Oshe's most prominent figures had wound up dead. She felt a little nauseous as she wondered if she and Elex would be next.

Erica leaned towards Maria, dropping her voice. 'The best thing about today is that all the performers are here to work off their water debts.'

Maria looked blankly back, taking a moment to understand Erica's meaning, then doing her best to hide her disgust. These people couldn't afford the water they needed now the Queens had started charging for every drop.

'It makes me so proud,' said Opal. 'Our fathers would have taken a finger.'

'Or an eye,' added Erica.

They both looked at Maria, obviously expecting her agreement. 'Cutting off limbs certainly seems barbaric,' she hedged.

She sensed movement behind her, and turned to find Rosalind leaning forward, her eyes like shards of blue ice fixed on Maria. 'Although this one,' she said, nodding towards where the men in the arena were now circling each other, 'is a good old-fashioned fight to the death.'

Rosalind sat back, and Opal scowled. 'We have to give the people what they want!'

The crowd roared as the men came together, the larger of the two knocking the other onto his back. It was over in an instant, the man on top repeatedly stamping on the other's head. The crowd did indeed seem delighted, although the Queens were less impressed, while Maria wanted to vomit.

'Make them last longer!' Erica screamed at the man below.

The man hesitated, seeming unsure about how to do that.

Opal let out an impatient growl. 'Do a group one next!'

The group fight lasted much longer, but also resulted in far more death, five out of the six poor souls taking their final breaths before a roaring crowd.

'Ooh, this one should be good,' said Opal. She shuffled forward to get a better view of the three figures entering the arena—two men and one woman—as guards dragged out the dead. The men seemed nervous, the woman less so.

'In this one,' said Erica, leaning in conspiratorially, 'the woman must choose one of the men to marry. The man she rejects will be our slave for a year.' She chuckled cruelly. 'Isn't it marvelous?'

'Do they know each other?' asked Maria, her guts churning at the thought of being in any of their places.

'No!' Opal enthused. 'That's what makes it even better. The woman will ask them questions and then she'll decide.'

Oh, Goddess. A year of slavery or a lifetime shackled to a stranger, a steep price indeed for water.

The woman asked the men questions about their backgrounds and livelihoods and families. One was already married, a tanner with five children to feed, while the other had no employment at all.

'I'd go for the tanner, wouldn't you?' asked Erica, not taking her eyes off the action.

Maria recoiled a little before catching herself and covering the movement. 'But what about his wife?'

'They'll find a way to happily co-exist, I'm sure.'

Maria shook her head. 'But they still won't be able to pay for their water.'

'Oh, don't worry about that. We're giving them free water for a year!' said Opal, waving a dismissive hand. 'We are nothing if not fair.'

'You're barbarians,' said Elex, gritting his teeth.

'Careful, darling,' Erica purred, putting a hand on Elex's thigh and squeezing as she leaned into his space, 'or we'll make *you* fight.'

The thought made bile rise from Maria's stomach, stinging the back of her throat.

'Don't fret,' said Opal, patting Maria's hand, 'you're safe. Cane punished you enough, and you've already had to marry against your will once, poor thing.'

Erica raised a salacious eyebrow. 'Although fate dealt you a man decidedly more enticing than our late husband ...'

Maria couldn't argue with Erica there.

The woman in the arena chose the tanner, and strangely both men seemed relieved, but as the trio were leaving, the crowd began chanting, 'Kiss! Kiss! Kiss!'

Erica giggled and clapped her hands with glee. 'Yes!' she squealed, conveniently forgetting that this was exactly the kind of abuse she'd suffered at Cane's hands. 'Kiss!' she cried, and guards immediately barred the trio's exit.

The tanner shook his head and tried to leave, but the guards pushed him back, using more force than was necessary. It looked for a moment like the tanner would fight, but then he bowed his head, presumably remembering where he was and that he had no choice and no power.

The woman paled but didn't fight as the tanner placed a brief kiss on her lips. The crowd went wild, then started chanting, 'Hold her hand! Hold her hand!' The tanner did it without waiting to be forced, then quickly yanked her from the arena.

'Such fun!' said Opal, looking around with bright eyes and a beaming smile. 'What's next?'

It was endless, although at least the more brutal activities—assault courses with open pits of vipers, packs of hunting dogs, and street children forced to fight with knives—eventually gave way to the singing and dancing Opal had promised.

Refreshments came and went—of which Maria sampled none, not trusting her hosts—and then finally, Erica and Opal stood and addressed the crowd.

Dread pooled in Maria's guts as she considered that attending this charade might not have been a good idea after all. Elex had been right, they were sitting ducks with no way to defend themselves, and the Queens were brutal, terrifying women with motives that made no sense to Maria. They'd seemed different when Cane had been in charge, showing the world muted versions of themselves, lying in wait, playing a part. Maria didn't know these women at all, and it made her nervous.

All Maria could think about was getting out, and how they could take Rosalind with them. There hadn't been a chance to even speak with her, let alone plan an escape, and she was so damned cold and aloof, Maria wondered if she even wanted to be rescued.

The Queens droned on about how brilliant and fair and wise they were, how much in love, how they were delighted to have Elex and Maria with them—which eased Maria's worry a small amount—and then they finally got to the punch line.

'As you know, this is a special day for us,' said Opal, pausing as she surveyed the crowd with a knowing smile. 'Not only because this is our first public entertainment, but also because we have a *very* special announcement.'

The Queens looked at each other for a beat, building suspense, while Maria held her breath, her body rigid.

'It is with the greatest of pleasure,' Opal continued, 'that we have given our permission for Commander Winn, a cherished member of our chosen family, to wed Rosalind Oshe, a cherished member of our late husband's.'

Maria froze. *What the fuck?* She looked sideways at Elex, but it was as though he hadn't heard, his features still fixed in an expression of irritated boredom.

Erica smiled a victorious smile as she looked back at those sitting in their box. 'With their union, and the union of Elex and Maria Oshe—who have joined us here today—we have further secured the future of our great Blade. Together, we will provide heirs for the Goddess, as we—your Queens—rebuild this place we call home.'

The applause was tentative at first, but it grew into a swell, and then erupted when attendants started throwing free skins of water into the crowd.

Commander Winn's hand was on Rosalind's back as he guided her to stand beside the Queens. He was shorter than Maria remembered, only a hair taller than his wife to be, and although his strength was obvious, he had the beginnings of a paunch around his middle and jowls around his chin. Perhaps the life of a court diplomat was new to him, leaving less time for the sparring ring than he was used to.

The commander took Rosalind's hand in his and raised their joined fingers high. The cheering swelled, but Rosalind's expression was still entirely unreadable. How she felt about the marriage, Maria couldn't tell.

Finally the true purpose of today's show was clear. The Queens were demonstrating to anyone considering a move against them that they alone controlled the Oshe family line. With the return of the Goddess, that was more important than ever because if the Toll Bells rang, the prosperity of all Celestl would rest upon each Blade offering up the required sacrifice.

Was Winn's real duty to guard Rosalind in case Oshe ever needed her? How did she feel about her new arranged marriage? She'd escaped one in Laurow only to be forced into a different partnership in her homeland, but still, her expression gave nothing away.

Maria's role was obvious: to provide a legitimate baby girl with Oshe's blood and name so the Queens wouldn't have to sacrifice one of their own children if it ever came to it. Today was a master stroke, seeing as Elex, Maria, and Rosalind sitting in pride of place alongside the Queens implied their support for the women's plans.

'But what about the peace pact?' Maria asked in a quiet voice. 'What will Laurow say?'

Erica waved a dismissive hand as she turned and headed for the exit, suddenly all business now the entertainment was over. 'The pact is dead and buried. Old news.'

'See you at the wedding!' trilled Opal, following Erica.

'Rosalind,' said Elex, reaching for his sister as she passed, but she shrugged him off, refusing even to look at him.

Winn stepped close to Elex, staring at him with a gaze that promised violence. 'Do not touch my future wife again.' He left, but Maria found her shoulders up around her ears because something about the interaction felt unfinished, and they were entirely unprotected.

Maria laced her arm through Elex's and pressed close to his side, hurrying to follow the others down the stairs. 'I'm sorry Rosalind blanked you,' she whispered. 'Maybe she has no choice.'

He squeezed her arm. 'It's so unlike Rosalind not to put up a fight.'

'You think she wants to marry him?'

'No, but ...'

'You think there's something in it for her?'

He shrugged. 'We certainly found out what's in it for the commander. My father would never have consented to their match.'

'Perhaps she's biding her time like Erica and Opal did with Cane.'

They emerged into the sunlit courtyard at the base of the stairs, and the Queens peeled off to the left without a backward glance.

'Or maybe they knocked the fight clean out of her,' said Maria, her eyes watching the Queens' retreating backs. 'Sorry ... That was ...'

Elex shook his head. 'If they did, it would have taken a lot, and Rosalind looks well enough.'

Rosalind and Winn made to follow the Queens, but as they turned the corner, a man dashed out of the crowd and wrenched Rosalind away, holding her back to his chest with an arm wrapped across her shoulders.

Maria blinked a few times because her eyes must have been deceiving her. 'Shit, that's ...'

'Tallin,' Elex breathed, pulling Maria to a stop a safe distance from the ruckus, Winn looking ready to commit murder.

Tallin whispered something in Rosalind's ear, and Rosalind turned her head sharply, meeting Tallin's gaze. He released her, sliding his thumb along the line of her jaw before dropping his hand. Rosalind turned fully to face him, but Winn yanked her away, then whirled back towards Tallin, his dagger drawn. But Tallin was already gone, melting into the crowd so effortlessly, Maria had lost sight of him, too.

Elex pulled Maria quickly towards the gate out of the Queens' new home. 'What the fuck was that?' she hissed, struggling to move at speed in her ludicrous outfit.

'Tallin and Rosalind have a complicated history,' he said reluctantly, Maria falling a pace behind.

'They were in love?'

'They had a deep friendship, but they both knew it could never be more.'

'Why?'

He sent her a look over his shoulder that said he was surprised she had to ask. 'Their difference in station. The same as with Winn, my father would never have allowed the match, not to mention, Tallin's always been loyal to me. Father would have seen their relationship as a threat, would have assumed we were working together to move against him. And then there was the peace pact, obviously, but by then they'd already moved on.'

Maria cocked an eyebrow. 'You're sure about that?'

'They've each had plenty of flings. I'm sure they still care for one another, but that's all it is.'

Maria turned her face away as they ducked into the safe house where Tallin had left their clothes, not wanting Elex to see her skeptical expression. They quickly changed into drab, worn clothing, shoving their finery into the waiting packs, then slipped out and took a convoluted route back to the tavern. When they arrived, they found Tallin pacing, head down, hair disheveled. It was so unlike the mellow, kindhearted man Maria had come to know, and her heart squeezed at his obvious pain.

Zeik and Sol wore matching forlorn looks as Maria and Elex entered, but Elex tossed his pack angrily aside and rounded on his friend. 'What the fuck was that about?' he demanded.

'Oh Goddess, that feels good,' said Maria, trying to deflect Elex as she placed her pack carefully on a chair, seeing as hers contained a priceless headdress. She stretched her neck, tilting her head from side to side. 'Those packs are torture, not to mention the headdress ...'

'Well?' Elex pressed, refusing to be nudged off course.

Tallin stopped pacing and glared. 'I told her we'd find a way to get her out, that she should be ready, not to give up on us. It's not like *you* gave her any hope, so someone had to.'

Elex crossed his arms defensively. 'She doesn't need hope.'

'Everyone needs hope! She just doesn't know how to show it.'

Elex took a menacing step forward. 'You think you know her better than me?'

Tallin scoffed. 'You barely know her at all.'

'Whereas you know her *intimately*?'

'Stop it,' snapped Maria. 'You're acting like children. We need to find a way to get her out, and fighting among ourselves won't help anyone.'

Tallin punched a cushion with such force, Maria moved instinctively closer to Elex. Tallin was so mild ordinarily that it was a shock to see him this way, a reminder that he was a soldier first and foremost ... that all of these men were.

'Ideas?' she said, with more confidence than she felt. 'We could poison the commander ...'

'Poison is still too dangerous,' growled Elex.

Zeik thought for a moment. 'We could snatch Rosalind off the street.'

'We could assassinate the commander a different way,' Sol said darkly. 'That would buy us time, and we could do the Queens for good measure.'

Elex considered that idea the longest. 'We'd need to learn their patterns, plan meticulously. It would take too long.'

'I *would* say we should seize the water,' said Zeik, 'but Nicoli seems reluctant to join us, soooo ...'

His words made Maria feel nauseous, but she shook it off as best she could. She didn't want to dwell on the fact that her best friend in the world had ignored her plea for help. 'How did you acquire your quarter in the first place?' asked Maria, thinking maybe they could do the same again and secure the water that way.

Elex sighed, then perched on the arm of an armchair. 'My great uncle gifted it to me. It's tradition for the second son of Oshe to control the water. It moderates the first son and forces balance.'

'Well, then we're back to poison,' Zeik said flippantly.

Maria nodded encouragingly. 'It's quick; I can make it in a day. And aren't they still using your chef?'

Elex clenched his jaw, his eyes on Maria although he didn't really seem to see her, his mind processing hard.

'We can make poison work,' Tallin agreed, 'and it's easy to slip into the Queens' new residence.'

Elex's eyes focused. 'What would you need?'

Maria took a breath, delving deep into her memory to recall the ingredients. 'Leaves from the Pappas shrub, Cumulous berries, and a still.'

'Easy enough,' said Zeik.

Elex bowed his head, silence stretching as they waited with bated breath for his answer. 'If we're going to take a risk this big,' he said eventually, 'it has to be about more than rescuing Rosalind.'

Tallin scowled and kicked a chair, but Sol sat up straighter, his face splitting into a slow smile. 'You mean ... we're doing it?'

'We'll need soldiers,' said Elex, meeting Sol's gaze, 'lots of them, and to get word to the people of my quarter, telling them to be ready.'

'*Brother* ...' said Zeik, his tone full of mock scandal.

Maria looked questioningly at Elex, open-mouthed after his endless insistence on biding their time, not sure she fully understood.

Elex nodded slowly. 'If the Queens birth their babies, and either of them has a girl, they will have no need for us or Rosalind any longer. And they're getting complacent, think they're untouchable, are convinced that they have us exactly where they want us. If the Queens are with child, the closer they get to delivering their babies, the tighter their security will become. We would be foolish to wait until that happens before we strike.'

'Wait,' said Tallin, 'are we ...?'

Zeik grinned. 'We're going to end this once and for all.'

Elex's expression was grave, but he nodded, resolute. 'We're going to take back what's ours.'

CHAPTER FORTY-TWO

AVA

WEEKS PASSED, AND AVA managed to imbue precisely zero objects with magic. Billy told her to focus, then not to focus, then to try it while walking, then while eating, then before bed, when she woke up, while in the bath, cooking ... Nothing worked. And given he'd blacked out the first time, Billy refused to demonstrate again. 'I need to work up to it,' he insisted.

Ava became increasingly scared and frustrated, terrified she had no magic, but also because her relationship with Kush had a hairline crack right down the middle, not big enough for anything to seep through, but visible if you looked closely. They hadn't talked about his lack of magic or what that meant, but now Ava worried if the same was true of her. Her mother had had no shortage of magic, but her father's family had become lackluster. Maybe they hadn't passed enough on.

While she endlessly attempted to become a physic, Kush swam a lot and gardened—the one thing the house didn't seem able to do. He set up an impressive irrigation system, getting the water to flow in ingenious ways, weeded and planted, and had it all looking spick and span in no time, so a serene, contented feeling spread through Ava whenever she went outside.

Kush went often to get them food, Ava's guts still pulling a little tight every time he left, some deep part of her brain worried he wouldn't return ... or that Var would find him. Sometimes they went together, and occasionally Billy tagged along too, needing to get out of the house.

Kush showed Ava all his favorite parts of the Federation, but although some were flat, some hilly, some mountainous, some with fields full of crops, some wooded, some with great quantities of water, others bone dry, they all seemed much of a muchness to Ava. Markets, houses, people, all the same as they were anywhere, some rich and clad in luxurious silks, others poor and wearing rags, but life was life was life, or so it seemed to Ava, and she found none of it inspiring. Kush, conversely, found endless wonder in each new surrounding, and that made her happy, at least when she wasn't consumed by thoughts of magic.

She liked the great healing lake in Kush's own world, although it seemed ludicrous to call it *his*. It belonged to its people, not to some demi-God from the Atlas Tree. Not that she voiced her thoughts because Kush seemed so flat all the time, she didn't want to drag him down farther.

Ava greedily sucked up Kush's heat as they lay curled up together on a lounger after a swim in the chilly healing lake in Xonia, Ava finally able to enjoy it now her stone sickness had abated. But despite the restorative swim, she was preoccupied by her lack of magical progress, so she finally gave voice to the words she'd been so frightened to say. 'What if I have no magic, Kush? What happens then?' She pressed her face to his chest, too scared to look at him.

He tensed, and she panicked because she didn't want him to think she was judging his own absence of magic. 'I just mean ... will the Gods try to kill me if they think I can't help them? That's the only reason they want me alive.'

He relaxed a little, sliding his hand across her back in soothing strokes. 'It won't come to that, and it takes time, even for powerful sorcerers.'

'But I've managed nothing, not even a single heat stone.'

He tugged gently on her hair until she looked up at him. 'It'll come; I know it will.'

She rested her lips on his collar bone. 'How?'

He traced his fingers down her spine, making her shiver. 'Because I can feel the magic in you.'

She looked up with desperate hope in her eyes, while her brain told her he was probably just being nice. How could he feel the magic in her when he had no magic of his own? 'Really?'

He pinched her chin, his features downcast and resigned. 'I can. You're more powerful than you know. More powerful than your mother, even, I'd bet.'

'If that's true,' she said, still not letting herself believe it, 'why do you make it sound like a bad thing?'

He turned his eyes to the water, shaking his head a little. 'Because I love you, and I'm selfish.'

'You're not selfish, Kush.' He looked down into her eyes, something there she couldn't read. 'You're the opposite of that.' He kissed her, rolling on top of her, and suddenly it was hard to think about anything but him.

He nuzzled her neck. 'I don't want to lose you.'

She gave a little gasp. 'You won't, Kush, ever ...'

He stilled. 'You can't promise me that, Ava, and I would never ask you to.'

She forced his head up and held his cheeks in her hands, looking deep into his eyes. 'I love you. We were meant to be together. Whatever happens, I'll never stop believing that. I don't care who your parents are or if you're a God or whether you have magic. I only care about how we feel. If I make you happy. If you want to be with me.'

'You make me delirious,' he whispered. 'I'll never not want to be with you, no matter what. Your magic will show itself and then you'll see just how powerful you are, but even if it never does, you have power over me, Ava.' He pressed his forehead to hers. 'My heart is yours.'

Chapter Forty-Three
Maria
Seven Weeks After Dromeda Started Spinning

Maria commandeered the barrel room in the basement where she'd landed the first time she'd entered the tavern. She carefully cleared the straw and anything else flammable from her work area, then used stones to build a raised platform in the fireplace big enough for her still.

She took a deep, fortifying breath, then ignited the wood beneath the copper base, not allowing herself to dwell on what she intended to create.

While the water heated, she slapped the Pappas leaves Zeik had procured for her against the edge of an enormous stone mortar, then tossed them into the first of two wire baskets she would place above the water in the still. Then she gently split the Cumulous berries with a stone pestle, careful not to mash them too hard.

She transferred the berries into the second of the wire baskets, and contentment washed over her in a wave. She loved stilling, the ritual of it, the familiarity, the need to focus and shut out the world. She'd never actually made this—or any—poison, but using her hard-won skills made her feel capable and useful and happy. She was good at this, and she felt light for the first time since arriving in Oshe.

She adjusted the leaves and berries in the baskets, spreading them out, then hooked them over the still's edge before meticulously sealing the lid in place. This was her still from Alter which they'd brought with them on their journey, and she knew its various quirks. She triple-checked the joins, the contraption old and dented, but it was a loyal and dependable friend if treated right.

When she was fully satisfied, she stepped back, ran her hands down the front of her apron, then tied a cloth over her mouth and nose. She watched and waited, nervousness making it hard to breathe as she carefully managed the fire, ready to tamp it down just before the water came to a boil. That moment was always tense, and like usual Maria half wondered if it would work, if she'd forgotten something. But then she heard the drip drip drip of liquid falling into the glass bowl she'd placed under the pipe attached to the lid, and a broad smile spread across her lips.

She quickly used a poker to pull some of the fuel out from under the still, sliding it to the other side of the generous fireplace. If the fire burned too hot and the water boiled, she would end up with too much water in the mix, and the poison would be useless.

She continued until the drips slowed, then replaced the first glass bowl with a second, letting it run for a few minutes more before taking the still off the fire completely.

Maria opened the small sack of salt Zeik had provided, and carefully spooned it into the first glass bowl, continuing until the salt had soaked up all the liquid. Then she tipped the mixture onto a large ceramic tile to dry.

It was agony waiting for the others to return from their duties, Maria itching to test the poison, but later that evening, she held up two vials, one with the liquid from the second bowl, and one with the poison-laden salt.

'Did you get the rats?' she asked Sol, the others following her movements as she strode into the tap room, but not one of them said a thing, their mouths hanging open in what Maria assumed was disbelief.

Sol nodded to a crate in the corner, and she picked up a discarded crust of buttered bread from Zeik's plate as she made her way to it. She sprinkled a little of the salt on top of the crust, so it stuck to a smear of butter, then poked it through the slats.

The rats grabbed at it greedily, fighting each other, and the victorious animal ate it down. 'It should take a minute or two,' she said, as much to herself as the others. Their plan required the poison to take a little time to act. 'But it'll work faster on rats than people, obviously,' she added, anxiety filtering into her tone because the rat was still very much alive and kicking.

She dipped a second piece of bread into the liquid version and fed it to another rat, mainly as a distraction. *Please work. Why isn't it working?* Had she remembered the recipe correctly? Had she forgotten a step? Had she misjudged the potency? It would be embarrassing beyond belief if it failed.

She had one single contribution to their plan, but without the poison, the plan was dead. Could they procure poison some other way? But if they did, it might raise suspicions. The risk would be great ...

Maria felt the eyes of the room boring into her back, and she stopped breathing entirely, the pressure and worry and fear dizzying. So she almost didn't notice when the second rat fell sideways, twitching for a moment before going still.

Zeik clapped his hands. 'Yes!' he cried, joining her just as the life leached out of the first rat, too.

Maria breathed a deep sigh of relief. She'd done it! It had worked. The poison worked!

Elex took hold of her shoulders and dropped a kiss on the top of her head. Now all she had to do was produce another thirty or so batches, enough for any plan they might concoct. She would have got straight to work, but she needed more ingredients, and that had to wait until morning, so instead she tucked up with Elex near the fire, feeling proud and hopeful, like they might actually have a chance.

Chapter Forty-Four
Ava

The next few days were more frustrating for Ava than any she'd had before. Billy was irritable, having finished several of the liquors he coveted most, Kush was like a puffer fish, ready to throw out his spikes at the barest provocation, and Ava was a tinder box set to explode. She'd still made no progress, and Billy was refusing to help her. He said there was nothing he could do until she'd figured out the first step, but Ava was truly beginning to believe she was a lost cause, that she had no magic despite what Kush insisted.

'You're useless!' Ava screamed, balling her hands into fists to stop herself from hurling a glass across the kitchen at Billy. 'I need more help!'

'Oh, please, find someone who cares.' Billy selected a spice-covered nut from a bowl and popped it into his mouth.

'Of course! I'll just wander out into the street. Or I could use the Atlas Stone and go searching in the Clouds. Maybe the real Gods would help me.'

'But what would your little Kushy-Kush say? Running to the people who treat him like an outcast.'

'Oh, fuck off.'

Billy tossed another nut into his mouth, but then almost immediately spat it out again. 'Help,' he wheezed. 'Help me. That was ...' Billy fell sideways off his chair, but Ava ignored him, sure it was a trick. 'Ava ...' he breathed, begging her to pay attention, and something about the pure desperation in his tone made her comply. She slowly rounded the table and looked down at him.

'The stone,' he croaked, each sound a struggle. 'Give me the ... stone.'

It really didn't seem like a joke. Billy's face was going purple and there was real fear in his eyes, so she dug the stone out of her pocket.

'The house gave me agrimanne. Poison,' Billy said in a forced whisper.

'What? Why?'

He reached for the stone, set the dials, then handed it to Ava to spin, grabbing onto her with both hands. 'Hurry.'

Ava did as he asked because his life truly seemed to be in danger, and much as she hated him for not helping her more, she still needed him. The stone jolted them through the web, then deposited them in the middle of a room crammed full of benches covered in physic objects. Three surprised faces looked up from their work.

'Billy, what—' Ava began, her heart hammering in her chest as she tried to work out where he'd brought her. Were they in danger? Had he made a mistake? Was he kidnapping her? Rough hands grabbed Billy from her grasp.

'What is it?' demanded a woman with green eyes and short purple hair.

'He said ... um ...' Ava wracked her brain, her eyes snagging on the roots that formed the walls, finding them familiar.

'Tell me!'

'Um ... agrimanne? He said—'

'Shit.' The woman rolled Billy onto his side on the floor, then ran to a cabinet at the back of the room and unlocked it with steady fingers despite her obvious haste. She grabbed a bundle of leaves, then raced to where a copper pot of boiling liquid sat atop a pile of heat stones and shoved the leaves inside.

One of the other two—an older woman—poured a little of a bluish liquid into a beaker, then heated it over a flame. The first woman fished the leaves out and shoved them into the blue liquid, grabbing the beaker and swirling it around a few times, then mashing the leaves with a metal rod before pulling them out.

The purple-haired woman hurried back to Billy, who was barely breathing at all now, and held his head in a surprisingly gentle manner. She tipped a little of the mixture into his mouth, then a little more until it had all disappeared down his throat.

'He'll be fine, dear,' said the older woman, patting Purple Hair on the shoulder.

'Always is, that one,' said the third person—an extremely short, dark-skinned man with wrinkled skin. He hopped down from his stool and waddled a little as he walked to Billy, then grabbed him by his lapels and hoisted him up and down a few times in a ferocious shake. He lifted each of Billy's legs in turn and shook those, then his arms, and then, finally, Billy opened his eyes.

'See,' said the man. 'Right as rain.'

'Not sure we would go that far,' groaned Billy, not moving from his position on the floor.

Purple Hair exhaled an irritated breath, slid Billy's head off her lap, and pushed to her feet. 'What are you doing here?' she hissed. 'And more to the point, what were you thinking, bringing *her*?'

Billy rubbed his eyes under his round glasses, then gingerly raised himself up on his arms. 'Her house forced my hand. It's a long story.'

'One we have no desire to hear,' said the older woman, tidying away the beaker. 'Time to be on your way.'

'But ...' They couldn't leave again so soon, not when this place looked like the answer to Ava's dreams. 'You're physics? Sorcerers? What are you working on? Who are you?' Ava turned in a slow circle, taking in every detail she could find. Shelves packed with books, beakers, and ingredients, animal specimens pinned to boards hung on the root-covered walls, tools and stones and watches scattered on the benches. The place had the slightly damp smell of a forest but mixed with something sharper, reminding Ava of the raw alcohol she'd used to clean tavern tables after someone had vomited all over them.

'That's none of your business,' said Purple Hair, folding her arms, at the same time as the short man said, 'So many things.'

Ava whipped her head around to look at Billy. 'Are we inside the tree?'

Billy lowered his gaze to his legs and shook his head regretfully.

'You have to leave,' said Purple Hair.

'Cool your potatoes,' said Billy, getting unsteadily to his feet and dusting himself off. 'Var doesn't even know how to find this place.'

'And we'd like it to stay that way,' said the older woman.

The man frowned. 'Last I heard, this one and Kush were an item.'

'They are,' said Billy, 'but don't worry, Ava won't blab.'

Purple Hair narrowed her hazel eyes, something about them familiar, but Ava could tell the woman was about to send them on their way, so before she could, Ava said in a rush, 'I want to learn. Billy says the web is out of balance, and I want to help.'

Purple Hair sneered, then said sarcastically, 'I'm sure you do.'

'I do!'

Purple Hair tilted her head in challenge. 'How?' She was young, perhaps the same age as Ava, and a stab of jealousy ripped through Ava because Purple Hair had spent her childhood learning magic while Ava had been cleaning sticky floors and changing soiled sheets.

'I don't know,' Ava admitted, but she refused to back down. This was her chance.

'What can you do, child?' the man asked almost kindly.

'I ...' She trailed off because the truth was she could do nothing. She could barely read, had no apparent magical ability, and the only things going for her were her house, Kush's Atlas Stone, and her dead parents' belongings. 'I'm learning, but I'm sure if you gave me a chance I could do something useful. I *want* to help.'

'Go home,' said Purple Hair. 'Our lives are hard enough without having to babysit you.'

'But ...'

Billy put his hand on Ava's arm, and she stilled, gritting her teeth. They wouldn't listen, not yet, not until Ava gave them a reason. She set the coordinates on the Atlas Stone with clipped, frustrated movements, looked at the three of them one more time, then spun the disc between her fingers.

'Who were they?' Ava demanded, not even giving Billy time to draw breath as they landed back in the kitchen. 'What are they working on? Are they physics?'

Billy took the remaining nuts from the table and tossed them into the fire beneath the stove, then looked up at the ceiling, 'That was dangerous you stupid house!'

'Billy!'

He glowered at Ava. 'Your house tried to kill me!'

'It did not.'

'It poisoned me!'

She folded her arms. 'Probably just chivvying you along a bit, seeing as you don't seem to want to help me.'

He put his hands on his hips. 'Well, perhaps you should learn to help yourself.'

'I'm trying!'

He quickly tipped his head from left to right. 'Evidently not hard enough.'

'Urgh! Just tell me!' She had to fight the urge to stamp her foot. 'Who were they? Why are they angry with you?'

Billy fanned himself with his hand. 'I need a lie down to recover my strength. Such an ordeal.'

She forced herself to be calm, taking a deep breath. 'Billy, please, just … help me. Tell me who they are.' Because if they truly were physics, maybe they could teach her what Billy had failed to. Maybe they could help her find her magic.

'Leave it alone, Ava, and focus on your work, for their good as well as yours.'

Ava shrieked. 'You're so infuriating!' She spun and flew towards the garden.

'Ava!' Billy called after her, and something in his voice made her pause—a tone she hadn't heard from him before—and he'd never come after her during a fight. 'If you tell Kush what you saw, he will tell Var.'

Ava opened her mouth to protest, but he held up his hand to stop her.

'He will do it with the best of intentions, but if Var gets wind of what you saw today, their lives will be in danger, and believe me, you don't want their blood on your hands.'

A cold chill slithered down Ava's spine. It was the most serious she'd ever seen him, the most somber.

'You won't be able to live with yourself, and nor will I,' he said in a sad, quiet voice, and then he turned away.

Ava punched a pile of washing, then headed out into the sunlit garden with a storm of emotions warring inside. Arguments with Billy had become daily occurrences, and she felt like she was standing still, not learning anything, the stagnation slowly driving her mad. And now she had to lie to Kush. She never lied to Kush. She didn't want to.

Ava wondered how much longer they could all stand living like this, on the inside of a powder keg set to explode, Billy drunk and depressed, Ava frustrated and itching for movement, and Kush kicking his heels, cycling from irritable to feverish to bored. It had to end, and soon, if Ava continued to make no progress, but a voice inside her head whispered that when it ended, she would once more be alone.

She forcefully shook off the thought and stomped towards where Kush was tinkering with his irrigation system, Ava preoccupied by thoughts of the three people hidden somewhere in the Atlas Tree that she wasn't allowed to mention. Something about Purple Hair still nagged at her, something she couldn't quite put her finger on.

She reached Kush and looked down into one of the many small pools of water he'd connected to the planters, but before she could open her mouth to regale him with her usual complaints about Billy, realization hit her like a bolt of lightning. Ava knew why Purple Hair had seemed so familiar, and it sent a ball of lead plummeting through her stomach, dragging her down.

CHAPTER FORTY-FIVE
MARIA
SEVEN WEEKS AFTER DROMEDA STARTED SPINNING

THE NEXT MORNING, MARIA and Elex were finishing breakfast when the taproom door slammed open. Maria jumped, her heartrate rocketing as she turned her head to see Tallin storm in. 'We have three days,' he said tightly. 'Three fucking days.'

Tallin brandished a piece of parchment, which Zeik took and read aloud: *'The Queens of Oshe require your presence at the marriage of Commander Nigel Winn to Rosalind Oshe three days hence in the bear pit at the time of the Midday Fall.'*

'They're all over the city,' Tallin snarled.

Zeik dropped the parchment onto a table, then rubbed his hands together. 'Well, nothing like a deadline to focus the mind. I'll get to the market for ingredients.'

Sol stood and clapped his hand on Tallin's shoulder. 'We'll rally the troops and spread the word.'

An electric energy spread like wildfire across the city, filling Maria up so she barely even felt the long hours at her still and lack of sleep.

The others came and went, Zeik dutifully recording every piece of information, coordinating the plan, and keeping Maria in raw materials. It felt good to have a goal, a purpose, and to finally be taking back what was Elex's by right. They were all buoyed by it, and none more so than Maria. This was what she'd always wanted, to feel part of a team, to be valued and respected.

She stowed her latest batch of poison on a shelf in the cellar, then washed her hands in the waiting basin. She closed her eyes and breathed deeply for a moment, exhaustion finally catching up with her. She'd heard of people falling asleep standing up and wondered if she would if she worked much longer.

But the scrape of the door behind her fired a bolt of adrenaline into her blood, and she whirled towards it, her heart singing when she saw Elex coming down the stairs. She hadn't seen him all day.

'Elex,' she said as he strode towards her. He kissed her without a word, drawing her against him, and Maria sank into him, her tired body glad of the support. The wedding would take place the following day, and even if she'd wanted to spend the remaining hours making poison, she had no ingredients left, so she let him tug her towards the stairs.

'Everything's ready,' said Elex, as they entered the taproom, the delicious savory smells of roasted meat and gravy filling Maria's nose. 'Our soldiers, my chef, the people inside my quarter.' Maria almost moaned as she sat at a table in front of a waiting mound of sliced meat, roast potatoes, and steamed vegetables, the others already seated, waiting for them.

Zeik poured tankards of beer for Maria and Elex. 'Let's hope the Queens don't make any last-minute changes.'

It was the worry that had plagued Maria, too, because the Queens were unpredictable, and it was the kind of thing they'd do just for fun.

'They won't,' Elex said with confidence. 'There's no time.'

Sol picked up his beer and saluted them all. 'And even if they do, we're committed. There's nothing we can do about it now.'

Maria gave a small nod of agreement, lifting her beer alongside the others, and then she filled her mouth with the biggest forkful of food she could manage.

Chapter Forty-Six
Ava

Ava froze, not hearing Kush's question, barely registering his concerned hand on her back a few moments later.

A strange ringing started in Ava's ears as she looked down into the pool of water once more. There they were again, Purple Hair's eyes staring back at her. Her own eyes.

What did it mean? Whose eyes were they? Polly's? She glanced back at the house, wondering if Billy would tell her if she asked. He wouldn't, not in his current state. He'd need to drink their argument out of his system, sleep for at least ten hours, then pretend it hadn't happened first. But would he tell her tomorrow? Certainly he wouldn't in front of Kush ...

Did this mean she had a family? Oh, Atlas, she hadn't stopped to think that she might have living relations. Did Ava have an uncle? Cousins? *Oh shit* ... A sibling of her own? Perhaps she had a whole boatload of relatives ...

Ava sank onto a planter, her head between her legs, her breaths short, ineffectual pants. Kush was saying words but they didn't register. She looked up at him and tried to concentrate on his lips, to understand, but that didn't work, either.

She had to find Purple Hair. Had to ... To what? Proclaim them related based on their eyes? The thought sobered Ava, calmed her, turned off the ringing in her mind with a sharp click. She was being ridiculous. They were just eyes. Plenty of people had eyes that looked like hers. Her eyes were a perfectly common shade of hazel.

'Ava!' Kush said loudly, alarm laced through his tone. 'Can you hear me?' He was crouching in front of her, holding both her hands in his, and she shook her head, swallowed, then nodded.

'Sorry, I think ... I ... I just ... I'm better now.'

'Did something happen?'

'Yes,' she breathed.

'Another argument?'

And then she remembered she wasn't supposed to tell him. 'No,' she whispered, as a voice in her head screamed at her to tell him the truth. Not to let anything come between them. To trust him. The words were on the tip of her tongue as she looked up into his eyes and searched for ... what? Evidence she could trust him? Reassurance he wouldn't tell Var everything?

'Well ...' She looked down at her hands. 'It was a little different to the others. I don't think he wants to help me, and I think he's angry with my lack of progress.'

Kush squeezed her fingers. 'He's a frustrated drunk. He's trapped here just like we are, and it's a lot for us all. You need a break ... something to take your mind off the stress of trying to find your magic.'

She shook her head. 'I don't think I have magic.'

'You do.'

'You don't know that!'

He smiled so reassuringly, warmth spread through her chest despite her skepticism. 'Ava, you have more magic in your little finger than almost anyone I've ever met.'

'Kush—'

He pressed a finger to her lips. 'Just trust me, okay? And trust me when I say you need a break.'

She pulled his finger away, then entwined their hands. 'We've taken plenty of breaks, to the healing pool and the fish market and the silk weavers, and the—'

'Ava,' he said gently, hooking a finger under her chin and urging her eyes up to his, 'take a breath.'

She inhaled until her lungs could take no more, then held the air inside, and she hated to admit it, but as she exhaled she did feel a little better.

Kush pulled away, rolling to his feet. 'Will you help me with something?'

She nodded, and he tugged her towards a series of raised water butts at the far end of the garden where he was setting up another irrigation route. 'What can I do?'

'Hold this.' He gave her a copper pipe. 'Can you connect it at that end?'

Kush busied himself with something at the water butt end, while Ava did what he asked, but really *connecting it* just meant resting it in the holder Kush had already prepared along the front of a planter. 'Now what?' she asked, stepping back.

Kush gave her a wolfish smile, then launched to his feet and grabbed her hand. 'The water's going to flow along here,' he said, showing her how it tracked across the front of the vegetable bed. 'It will seep out through tiny holes in the metal, then it's going to flow down this spiral, which has a water wheel inside that will move this bird scarer,'—he gave a beautiful metal and glass sculpture a push with his finger, and it started turning in on itself then coming out the other side.

'Wow,' she whispered.

'I've put a few of these along the route,' he said, tugging her farther along the back wall of the garden and pointing out other beautiful sculptures. Some swayed, others spun, one was shaped like a tree with tiny jingling bells on each branch.

'The water sets them off?'

He nodded. 'And any water left at the end flows into the pond in the middle, just like all the others.' Ava watched the drips from the three other runs he'd already set up around the garden. She marveled, then felt guilty.

'You've done all of this yourself? It's incredible!'

He huffed a laugh. 'I had some time on my hands.'

She smiled and slid into his arms, squeezing him tight as he tucked her under his chin.

'But there's just one problem ...'

She spun to look at him. 'What?'

'There's no hole in the water butt.'

She frowned. 'Oh. We need a drill?'

His features turned mischievous. 'We don't have a drill, but we do have a physic.'

'Oh, Kush ... I ...' She bit her lip.

'Don't you want to see my inventions come alive?' he said with a mock pout.

She rolled her eyes and shook her head, but her lips pulled into a smile as a swell of excitement inflated her chest. It felt different to all the other times she'd tried to find her magic. She had no real desire to make a heat stone, but this ... She *wanted* to see the water flow, *needed* to help Kush. But she paused as she put her hand on the cool metal, disappointment crashing through her. 'Kush, I don't know the words.'

He waved a flippant hand. 'You don't need words. Just do what comes naturally.'

'I'm sorry ... You're an expert now?' she joked.

His expression turned coy. 'Humor me.'

'Kush—'

'Don't you want to see what happens when this sculpture turns?' he asked, moving to the first of the metal beauties and giving her puppy dog eyes.

'Kush!' But the answer was, *yes*, she really did want to make it move. Almost as soon as she'd had the thought, a wave of energy took off from her chest, rolled up to her throat, bowled down her arm, then flowed into the section of water butt under her finger, leaving her suddenly cold when it had gone. *Open*, she silently begged, *please. Make this work. Make Kush smile. Help me prove I do have magic.*

Ava was so engrossed in her silent pleading that she didn't realize it had worked until Kush gently pulled her finger off the metal. Water poured out, and Kush whooped and swept her up in his arms. 'Ava! You did it!'

Ava's eyes tracked the water flowing slowly along the half pipes. It hit the first sculpture, which began its inside outside spin, and then she batted Kush's chest, making him release her so she could dash along the whole route, following the flow.

'It's working!' she shouted, clapping her hands and dancing up and down. 'Kush, look!'

'I can see!'

'I did it!'

'You did,' Kush agreed, leaning against the water butt and folding his arms, following her progress with his eyes.

'You did what, exactly?' said Billy, surprising them both with his sudden appearance.

Ava twirled. 'I made a hole in the water butt!'

Billy narrowed his eyes. 'Which you did how?'

'I just sort of … willed it to happen! I can do magic, Billy! I'm not a lost cause!'

Billy's eyes darkened and he folded his arms across his chest. 'We started where we did with your magic for a reason.'

Kush scowled at Billy. 'Well it wasn't working, and you were driving her crazy.'

Billy bent forwards from his hips, his arms still locked across his torso. 'I was building a respect for magic,' he snarled.

Ava stopped in her tracks and tore her eyes from the water. 'I do respect magic,' she insisted. 'Just look at what marvelous things it can do!'

'She just needed something a little more inspiring,' said Kush, still leaning against the metal butt. 'More interesting, motivating …'

Billy sneered, then pulled himself inward, curling his arms around himself as though someone had punched him in the gut. 'You have no idea what you've done.'

CHAPTER FORTY-SEVEN
MARIA
EIGHT WEEKS AFTER DROMEDA STARTED SPINNING

MARIA LOWERED A NEW headdress onto her head as she prepared to leave for the wedding with the others, a host of butterflies beating their ferocious wings in her chest. 'You cannot be serious,' she said, aghast.

'Sorry,' said Zeik, as one of the dangling strings of her headdress's gemstones swatted Maria's cheek, 'it was the best I could get at such short notice.'

At least he'd done a better job on the dress this time, which was less tight given the tie fastening, more demure, and purple—the color of her homeland. Strangely, it boosted her confidence, like part of her had forgotten she was a first daughter, that she'd had a life before coming here. That her name carried weight.

Elex threw his cloak around his shoulders, then raised his hood. 'Ready?' he asked, itching to move, just like they all were.

'Ready,' said Sol, while Tallin nodded solemnly. He'd become a different man over the last few days, and Maria hoped he would turn back into his old self once the day was through. Perhaps even a happier version, if Rosalind still returned his feelings. Maria knew that was too much to hope for, that she shouldn't be greedy, and the truth was, if they ended the day free, she would be more than content. Anything else would be icing on the cake.

'Ready,' she said, accepting Zeik's help to raise her own hood, then following the others out of a new safehouse onto the street, her heart hammering in her ears. She gripped Elex's arm so hard, it was a wonder his blood made it to his hand, and he periodically patted or stroked her, doing his best to calm her fraying nerves.

Tallin, Sol, and Zeik soon slipped away, Zeik to the kitchens with the poison, while Sol and Tallin headed for a warehouse near Elex's quarter where their troops were quietly gathering. The two sides of the plan were almost entirely independent, meaning even if one side went awry, the other could still succeed. 'Hold the quarter at all costs,' Elex said as he gripped Sol's arm in farewell. 'Do not yield, even if Maria and I are taken.'

Sol nodded. These were not new orders. 'Good luck, my friends. We will celebrate our victory by the Sunrise Fall. I swear it on the Goddess herself.' Elex clapped his friend on the arm, and then Sol followed Tallin and Zeik down a side street.

Maria and Elex walked on in silence, making their way slowly through the buzzing streets. They were already thronging with people, the crush of humanity growing denser as they approached the bear pit, until they were shoulder to shoulder with the masses of Oshala.

'Whatever happens, I love you my little hell cat,' Elex whispered in Maria's ear, almost getting swatted by her swaying gems.

Maria hesitated, not wanting him to talk that way, not wanting any thoughts of failure to slip into their minds. 'I love you, too, but have faith, the Goddess is with us, and so are your people.'

He gave a small nod, then maneuvered them to the left-hand side of the street, to where four burly guards stood at the entrance to a roped off path. Maria and Elex lowered their hoods, and the guards stepped immediately aside, Maria breathing more easily as soon as they were on the spacious track reserved for Oshala's well-to-do.

From that moment, she felt eyes on her from every angle, people watching for signs of treason or weakness or merely because they were curious. So she pulled her shoulders back and projected an air of quiet, unshakeable confidence, showing them the powerful, privileged first family member that the people of Oshe would respect.

But when they entered the bear pit, Maria's confidence faltered because guards guided them into the arena itself, not into the stands, and it was all Maria could do not to gasp at the scene.

A long banquet table had been laid out in the middle of the oval space, covered in crisp white linen and laid up in a decadent style with rows of gold cutlery, creeping floral displays, and the finest silver goblets Maria had ever seen.

Two thrones sat side by side in the middle, but despite the table's great length, only four other places had been laid, the chairs less opulent than the thrones, but still splendid, covered in gold leaf and with deeply cushioned pads the light blue color of Oshe.

The table was an arresting sight, but what stopped Elex and Maria in their tracks was neither that nor the fact the table was empty. It was that on the far side of the arena, a woman had been tied to a post on a newly constructed platform. A woman they knew.

'The midwife,' breathed Maria, unable to tear her eyes away, her hand covering her mouth. She quickly dropped it because the seating was filling with spectators, and all eyes were on them. Apparently Maria and Elex were to be the entertainment, at least until the Queens and the happy couple arrived.

'We don't know her,' Elex muttered, leaning casually towards Maria and offering her his arm.

He was right, it was the safest course for them and the midwife, at least until they found out what in the name of the Goddess was going on. Maria gave him a dazzling smile and slid her hand into place.

'But where will they wed?' asked Maria, scanning all around in case she'd missed something. There was no obvious location for Rosalind and Winn's nuptials aside from the platform, which wasn't screaming romance and fairytales right at that moment, given the woman tied to a stake.

Elex gave the smallest of shrugs. 'Where shall we sit?' he asked, leading her towards the table. One side had only two chairs, while the other had four—the two thrones flanked by two more.

'The side opposite the thrones?' suggested Maria, smiling sweetly as they sauntered along, pretending to have not a care in the world.

'But then we'll have to look the Queens in the eye.'

'It will split Rosalind and the commander though, so your sister won't have to endure him during the meal.'

'Either way, it will be near impossible to get a message to Rosalind.'

Maria's stomach dipped. He was right. The walk to the other side was acres long, and the table was far too wide to lean casually across.

'Then we should wait here,' said Maria, pulling Elex to a stop by the head of the table. 'Let the Queens direct us when they arrive. They'll enjoy the power, and it will give me a chance to hug Rosalind and warn her about the poison.'

Elex nodded minutely, then drew her close and looked down into her eyes, and the crowd whooped.

'Elex ...' she breathed, terrified of what he might do, not wanting to share an intimate moment between them with any kind of audience, let alone one this big.

A cad-like smile ghosted his lips, and then he kissed her. The place erupted into raucous, ribald applause, so Maria's face was flushed when he pulled back only a heartbeat later.

'The people of Oshe love you already,' Elex murmured, running his nose down hers, then dropping one more peck on her lips before pulling properly away.

'Don't tell me you're an exhibitionist,' she chided, doing her best not to melt into a puddle of embarrassment at the insistent calls for more.

He gave a nonchalant shrug. 'Just giving the people what they want, and nothing's more compelling than a love story.'

'You're manipulating them?'

He smoothed a stray strand of hair off her forehead, looking down at her with an adoring smile. 'I'm showing them who we are in case this all goes to shit and we need them on our side.'

Oh. He was right, it was a good plan, even if it made her uncomfortable. This was their first proper introduction to his people, and first impressions mattered.

A sudden silence rippled across the crowd, and Maria's skin prickled. Elex squeezed her hand, and she took a long, centering breath as a fanfare blared out across the pit. *Show time.*

Maria turned as the Queens strode into the arena, their headpieces nearly identical to the five pointed crowns they'd worn last time, their Oshe-blue dresses sweeping out behind them.

A pace behind, Rosalind and Commander Winn followed, Rosalind's arm linked through Winn's, her dress white as the bells of Maria's favorite flower.

'That's a bit rich,' Elex whispered. 'Rosalind is anything but pure.'

'Is white traditional in Oshe?'

'Not for at least two hundred years, and it wouldn't have been Rosalind's choice.'

The gown gave Maria flashbacks to the night the Queens had stabbed Cane, visions of their pure white dresses splattered with his blood flashing before her eyes.

The Queens reached where Maria and Elex stood, coming to a halt beside them. 'Elex,' said Erica. 'Maria.'

'Erica,' said Elex, nodding politely. 'Opal.'

Rosalind and Winn stopped a pace behind the Queens, and Maria flung herself at Rosalind's stoic form. 'Sister!' Maria pulled Rosalind into an embrace and whispered, 'Eat nothing past the first course,' in her ear. Maria moved back and caught the slightest widening of Rosalind's eyes, a small freeze in her movements, and then nothing but a smooth, blank mask, the reactions gone.

'She may still be your sister by marriage, but she no longer shares your name,' Erica said with a smug smile.

Maria tried not to look too confused. 'But the nuptials—'

'The nuptials are already done,' said the commander, with the air of a smug child.

'Oh!' cried Maria, clapping her hands as though the news was an absolute delight. 'Congratulations!'

'Congratulations, sister,' Elex said formally. 'Commander.'

'We are brothers now,' said Winn.

Elex gave a curt not. 'So we are.' Maria took comfort from the knowledge that they would not be brothers for long.

Erica clapped impatiently. 'You two,' she said, pointing to the newly-weds, 'far side. You,' she said to Elex, 'next to me.'

Maria fell in beside Opal as they walked to the middle of the table, Maria still entirely conscious of the thousands of eyes watching them as though they were performers in a play. Did the Queens enjoy being in the spotlight or was it simply making everyone else uncomfortable that they relished?

They took their seats, and Winn wasted no time at all before nuzzling into Rosalind's neck. Maria's stomach sank because they had no way to stop him. Rosalind would have to endure his fondling until the main course was served, although Rosalind's face was characteristically blank, so if she found the commander's ministrations distressing, Maria couldn't discern it from her features.

Rosalind even put her hand on the back of the commander's head, seeming to hold him to her. Was that an act for the crowd? A show of dominance? Elex had assured Maria time and again that Rosalind could look after herself, so maybe she planned to fix her own problem and knife the man in the back before their meal was through, to do what the Queens had done to their own husband and shove the forced marriage in their faces …

Six servers leaned over and poured wine from glass carafes into their goblets, then they set the carafes on linen-covered tables a few paces back from each chair. Apparently every diner was to have their own supply of wine, the servers lingering, their eyes trained on the goblets as though their lives depended on it.

Two servants stepped forward and lifted the Queens' goblets from the table. They took a taste, then another, then they set the drinks down. When the tasters didn't keel over, Opal lifted her goblet and raised her voice high. 'To Rosalind and Winn!'

The crowd parroted the toast, and the diners dutifully took sips of wine, Maria testing the bold, fruity flavor with the tip of her tongue, searching for any hint of poison. It would be so easy, seeing as each of them had their own carafe, but she detected nothing out of the ordinary, so took a shallow sip, doing little more than wetting her lips just in case.

'A good vintage,' said Elex, raising his goblet in toast before setting it down.

Erica pouted. 'Only the best for the first family. Isn't that so, my love?' She took Opal's hand and kissed her knuckles.

'Since the beginning of time,' Opal agreed too sweetly, her tone setting Maria on edge. Maria suddenly felt too hot, a trickle of dread creeping down her spine. The Queens were playing with them, and her eyes flicked involuntarily to where the midwife stood on the stage.

'Pitiful, isn't she?' said Opal, following Maria's gaze.

'Who is she?'

'Ha!' laughed Opal. 'You met her, did you not? When you lived with us.'

Of course the Queens would have interrogated her guard. 'She's the midwife?'

'She is.'

Maria didn't like being at such a stark disadvantage. 'But why's she here?'

'All in good time,' said Opal, with a flash of her eyes.

Six new servers placed plates of smoked eel with bacon and apple before them, and Maria knew she had to eat, to keep the Queens' minds off their food, but her stomach roiled. What was she missing?

The food tasters stepped forward once more, and after they'd done their work, everyone lifted their cutlery, Maria chewing slowly, worried she might not keep the food down.

Across the table, Winn moved Rosalind onto his lap, and Maria's fork paused halfway to her lips. It was a regular custom in Oshe for couples to sit that way, but usually they waited until the end of a meal. She wished she could see Elex, that she could take his hand and reassure him, but Rosalind didn't seem unhappy, and Maria hoped Elex would take comfort from that.

'I can't wait to fuck my new wife,' said Winn, his eyes directed at Elex.

'Now now, Commander,' said Erica. 'Let's keep things civil.'

'At least until we've finished our meal,' said Opal, with a laugh that bordered on a giggle.

Maria nearly remarked on it, the words almost out before she'd had time to think, then a feeling almost like homesickness washed over her. She frowned at her plate in confusion.

'Everything okay?' asked Opal, leaning close, her eyes shining with intense interest.

'Yes. No. I'll be fine.'

Opal chuckled knowingly.

What the fuck was going on?

Opal waved at the guards blocking one of the many side entrances into the pit. 'Time for a little light entertainment, I think.'

'Hmm, yes,' Erica agreed, a smile tugging her lips wide.

A server cleared Maria's plate just as two guards led a young, beautiful, dark-haired woman towards the stage.

'Traitor!' screamed the midwife, lifting her head fully for the first time since Maria and Elex had entered the pit.

The younger woman stopped, but only for a moment because the guards shoved her so hard, she almost fell forward into the sand.

'This suffering … This injustice … It is all by your hand!' the midwife cried.

'No, Mother,' said the woman between the guards, her voice loud but edged with fear, 'do not attribute more to me than is my due.' The guards forced her up onto the platform, and her eyes flitted wildly around, clearly searching for an escape. 'I was a pawn. We all here are pawns aside from those people at that table.' She spun and pointed, her eyes locking onto the Queens. 'Only they have the power to do anything of consequence.'

'You are wrong,' said the midwife, as the servers placed plates of roast guineafowl and crispy stacks of thinly sliced potato before the diners. 'I have done much of consequence in my life. I have brought countless babies into this world, including three of the souls at that table.'

The midwife's daughter laughed cruelly. 'You're as much a pawn as anyone, but you always had ideas above your station.'

Opal chuckled as she got to her feet. 'I'm so pleased to see your hatred for one another; it will make what comes next much easier and more enjoyable.'

The daughter hesitated for a beat, looking uncertain. 'My Queen?'

The guards unbound the midwife, then stepped down from the stage.

'Fight,' commanded Opal. 'First blood or to the death, whatever takes your fancy.' She sat as the food tasters finished their work, a drip of aromatic gravy falling onto Opal's skirt, but Opal didn't notice, or if she did, she didn't make a fuss.

Maria's mouth fell open, and then her brain whirled at a thousand resolutions a second. What did the Queens know? The midwife had helped with the plans to take back Elex's quarter. Had she told the Queens? Were Tallin and Sol at that very moment being slaughtered by waiting guards?

Opal raised her fork to her mouth, snapping Maria out of her spiral. She'd taken a mouthful, and Erica was chewing. Just a couple more …

Although perhaps one would work ... It would take longer. Ten minutes, maybe.

Opal took a sip of wine. 'Oh, stop judging us so hard and eat your food,' she bit out.

Maria turned her head. 'You're barbarians,' she whispered, the words spilling free of their own accord, beyond her control.

Opal barked a laugh and gave a little clap, Maria's insult seeming to lift her. 'Now the fun can really begin! The midwife was caught stealing water, she's no innocent, and her daughter—'

'Why?' Maria demanded.

Opal flinched, clearly irritated by the interruption. 'Why?'

Maria faced the midwife and raised her voice. 'Why was that woman taking water?'

The midwife and her daughter were circling each other on the stage, their movements tentative, wary. The blood drained from Maria's face. She couldn't imagine what it would be like to be in their place, having to fight her own mother for survival.

'I took water to birth babies, you evil witches!' the midwife screamed.

'See,' said Erica, opening her palms wide, 'she openly admits it.'

Maria felt hot and lightheaded, not at all like herself. Had the Queens put something in her wine after all? 'You're sick.'

'Ha!' laughed Erica.

Across the table, the commander seemed drunk, his fork swaying as it headed for his mouth, but Rosalind pushed his hand back to his plate, then looked Maria directly in the eye as she bent to whisper in his ear. Winn froze, but Rosalind covered it with a deep kiss, and panic gripped Maria's guts. Rosalind was working with him? Did she love him? Was their relationship real?

Rosalind had let the Queens eat the food, but perhaps she and the commander had plans of their own. Plans that might be dangerous for Maria and Elex.

Behind them, the women on the stage came together for their first tussle, each screaming a war cry. Maria couldn't bear to watch, and anyway, she had more important matters to consider, like if she and her husband were in mortal peril. But she couldn't make herself focus ... couldn't think.

'Have you done something to me?' Maria asked, not meaning to say the words aloud.

Opal chuckled, then took a long sip of her wine. 'Now your lips have sufficiently loosened, we'd like you to tell us the truth.'

Maria leaned forward and looked at Elex, whose brow was furrowed. Was he similarly affected or had he had the good sense not to taste the wine at all? But then again, perhaps they'd put something in the food. Perhaps the Queens had foiled their plans.

A shriek of pain stabbed through the air from the stage, but that only served to confuse Maria further. 'The truth?' she said, her mind latching onto those words through her confusion. 'You're an entitled bitch and I hate you. I used to feel sorry for you, but that's all worn off now. Were you two working together even before the pact?'

Opal leaned so close, Maria could see the little red lines in her eyes. 'What do you and the pampered second son have planned?'

'Your demise,' said Elex, saluting them again with his goblet. 'Today. Right now, in fact.' So they'd drugged him too then.

Maria wondered once again if the Queens had eaten enough food for the poison to work, assuming the poison had made it into the Queens' food. Opal instantly froze, then pushed to her feet and made a grab for Maria's hair, Maria realizing she must have said the words aloud. 'You bitch!' Opal hissed, yanking so hard Maria's chair tipped over backwards. 'We were kind to you.'

Elex jumped to his feet, as did the others at the table, and somewhere in the recesses of her mind, Maria could hear bludgeoning sounds coming from the edge of the arena. But she didn't have time to focus on that, not with Opal's heel aimed at her head.

Elex launched himself at Opal, tackling her to the ground, while Maria tipped herself sideways, rolling onto her stomach, then pushing to her feet, vaguely noticing that her cumbersome headdress was no longer on her head.

'You poisoned us?' Erica breathed. Her wild eyes found the food tasters who were still very much standing. 'It didn't work,' she added, her tone frantic. 'They're still alive! We're still alive. We didn't eat enough!'

'Maybe,' Maria said cheerfully, 'but maybe not. And you poisoned us, too.'

'We gave you truth serum,' spat Erica, clawing at Elex's arm and shoulder, trying to make him release Opal, 'because we knew you were devious and untrustworthy, yet we were willing to share our power with you!'

'You need us,' Elex grunted, fending off Erica while holding Opal down.

Maria shoved Erica, forcing her to release Elex, but then Erica squared up to Maria, her teeth bared in a look so ferocious, fear and adrenaline flooded Maria's blood. But just as Erica was about to launch herself at Maria, a noise like a sack of potatoes hitting the ground came from behind them, and they turned as one to find a food taster slumped on the sandy floor.

'No!' Erica shrieked, at the exact moment the second food taster fell. 'I have worked too hard for ... for...' Erica dropped to her knees, her mouth opening and closing like a fish out of water. 'You killed your father!' she bellowed, one last play for the sake of the crowd.

Maria frowned in confusion. 'My father died years ago, and it had nothing to do with me.'

'Not you,' she hissed. 'Him!' She pointed at Elex before collapsing onto her back.

Elex scowled. '*You* killed your husband,' he said, projecting his voice for the benefit of the crowd, 'not me.' Despite the chaos, Maria felt a swell of pride because Elex had found a way around the truth serum. Erica had killed her second husband, even if she hadn't killed the first, but that's not how it sounded.

'You ... killed ...' she choked out, but Erica never finished her sentence, the poison finally doing its worst.

Opal, too, had stopped resisting, and Elex lurched backwards as though her skin was painful to touch.

The bludgeoning noise came again from behind them, louder this time because every other person in the place had gone mute, the soft hush of twitching limbs the only other sound. Maria turned, and the appalling sight that greeted her almost made her vomit. The midwife had found a length of wood and was kneeling over her daughter, beating the life from her body. The woman raised the baton one last time and brought it down with a guttural shriek, then she threw it aside and stepped down from the stage, leaving her daughter's lifeless form behind.

'You're an idiot,' said Rosalind, suddenly in front of Maria. How she'd made it all the way around the table so quickly, Maria couldn't say—she must have gone over or under while the others were preoccupied. 'You've handed us the keys to Oshe.'

'Us?' said Elex, scanning the space for Winn. 'You're working with that fool?'

Maria found Winn's large form by the main entrance, holding back the guards, and as Maria looked around, she realized all the other exits were barred by iron gates. Icy dread slithered through her insides.

Rosalind huffed a laugh as realization dawned on Elex's features. 'My husband and I control the water, have the largest army, and I'm the only one left with the right to rule, seeing as you killed our beloved father, and that is an act of treason punishable by death.'

Silence stretched between them, and across the whole of the bear pit, nobody daring to move a muscle in the stands. Maria's mind went to Sol and Tallin, wondering how they were faring in their own battle. Tallin, who loved the woman before her and would be devastated by this news.

Winn shouted orders not to let Maria and Elex leave with their lives, and panic stole Maria's ability to think. This couldn't be it. Her time with Elex had been so short, and he'd been born to rule—the only one in his family who showed an ounce of compassion for his people.

Elex's eyes bored into his sister. 'Why?' he breathed. 'We always got along fine. I thought we understood one another, that we wanted the same things.'

She sneered and shook her head. 'That's the problem with people like you. You see what you want to see, not what's really there.'

'You think he'll make you happy?' asked Elex, tipping his head towards Winn.

She exhaled as though it was a ridiculous question. 'Happy enough.'

'What about Tallin?' Maria blurted. 'You wouldn't be happier with him?'

Rosalind turned poker sharp eyes on Maria, holding her gaze for long moments, but then the scraping, clanging sounds of metal on metal rang through the air, and a flash of worry crossed Rosalind's features before she whirled around to find the cause.

Elex quickly stepped to Maria's side, gathering his wits far faster than she did. 'You've made a few assumptions you'll find are incorrect, sister.'

Rosalind spun back to face him, clearly rattled, but also suspicious, as though she thought Elex might be bluffing. 'Such as?' Rosalind took a step back, moving out of her brother's reach.

'By the day's end,' said Maria, the Queens' drug still in control of her tongue, 'we will control the water, and you'll find our army is really quite big, too.'

Rosalind snarled, looking like she might launch herself at Maria, but the midwife, Noranda, chose that moment to prostrate herself at Elex's feet.

'Get up,' hissed Rosalind.

Noranda looked up into Elex's eyes. 'The true leader of Oshe is with us!' she bellowed. 'All hail Elex Oshe!'

A flood of guards broke into the bear pit, and the crowd hesitated, obviously not sure what was going on, and Maria was right there with them. She forgot to breathe as she tried to work out if the guards were friends or foes, but then she spotted Zeik among them, and a choked, relieved half-sob escaped her lips.

Maria met Elex's gaze, and tears welled in her eyes. Their plan had worked ... at least the part about poisoning the Queens and rescuing Rosalind, even if Rosalind didn't want to be rescued.

Elex wrapped his arm around Maria and tugged her to his side, and the crowd, seeming to sense what Maria just had, went wild, calling and chanting and cheering.

'Long live Elex Oshe!'

'To our leader!'

'Kiss her again!'

Maria closed her eyes against the barrage of noise, fighting to hold back tears.

'We have the quarter,' said a low voice, and when she opened her eyes, she found Zeik's delighted face alarmingly close.

'Losses?' Elex demanded.

'Very few,' said Zeik. 'The people of your quarter did most of the work before our army was even inside. Turns out they were eager to exact revenge for the water tax.'

'I told you,' said the midwife, finally getting to her feet. 'Your people were ready.'

Elex nodded slowly, seeming to be processing everything that had happened. 'I never doubted it for a second.'

'Pffft! If only that were true, we could have ended this before ...' Her eyes flitted to her daughter's dead form, and Elex put a hand on her shoulder.

'I'm sorry for your loss, Noranda,' he said, his tone gentle.

The woman squared her shoulders. 'Thank you, but I lost that one years ago. It's more ... Taking a life ... It ... It's not what I am used to.'

'And it is not a pleasant thing,' said Elex, 'but you had little choice. For what it's worth, I'm glad it's you standing here beside us.'

The old woman inclined her head, her lips moving from side to side as though fighting tears. 'Thank you.' She paused for a moment, collecting herself. 'And I am glad it is finally you who now rules Oshe.'

Chapter Forty-Eight

SOPHIE

EIGHT WEEKS AFTER DROMEDA STARTED SPINNING

TODAY WAS THE DAY Sophie had spent her entire life waiting for. Her parents had made it clear her only worth to them—or at all—was in her marriage. And this marriage was as good as it got.

Hale Alter.

She let herself feel proud for only a moment, soaking up the feeling she'd so rarely felt in her life, knowing that her parents would finally be thinking positive thoughts about her. Even if her mother would take all the credit for the match, having blackmailed Sophie's future husband into it.

That didn't matter to Sophie. She and Hale had a connection, a real one, and that made her happier than anything else ever could. But he would leave for Spruce tomorrow at first light, and Sophie would be trapped with Bianca Alter for who knew how long.

She exhaled, giving her shoulders a little shake. Once he'd rescued Pixy, Sophie and Hale would have all the time in the world and nothing hanging over them.

'Your parents will meet you at the bridge,' said Sophie's new maid as she brushed out Sophie's hair. Hale had assured her that this woman was trustworthy, so she'd sent the maid her mother had appointed back to Laurow.

'Oh,' said Sophie, her shoulders dropping in her lamplit reflection in the mirror, the world outside dark at this early hour. 'I suppose that makes sense.'

'It gives us more time to prepare,' the no-nonsense young woman said with a smile and a reassuring pat on Sophie's shoulder. Sophie smiled weakly and submitted to the maids' assured ministrations.

It was two hours later when Sophie was finally primped and preened to perfection, her hair swept back, half tied up, the rest flowing in undulating waves down her back. Long strings of dainty pearls dropped from her earlobes, and around her neck she wore a beautiful golden chain that Hale had sent to her room as a wedding gift.

Her dress was in Alter purple, in the buttoned-up style Hale preferred, although Sophie had insisted on showing a little cleavage, and on making the skirts lighter. She wanted to be able to move freely at their small celebratory banquet ... and later.

Hale had been slowly driving her mad with subtle touches, lingering looks, and one heated kiss, and Sophie was more than ready for him to make good on his promises.

'Everything okay?' asked the maid, as they reached the bottom of the staircase.

'Uh ... yes,' said Sophie, finding she'd come to an abrupt halt. 'Where are the others?'

'Hale's gone ahead to greet your parents, as has Bianca. You'll travel together with Hale's grandmother, and there's still no news from John.'

That was for the best, and Sophie gave a relieved nod. The last thing she needed was for John to show up at her wedding after everything that had happened between them. The memories of his hands and lips on her made Sophie angry now. Not at John for doing the things she'd encouraged, but at the circumstances she'd been forced into, and at herself for not being able to scrub the memories from her mind.

'You look charming, my dear,' said Hale's grandmother, who stood in the flickering light of a flame torch beside their waiting carriage, leaning on her cane.

'Thank you. And you look ... quite striking, actually, and a little formidable.' The older woman wore a kind of suit, with straight-legged trousers beneath a long jacket that fell to the top of her thighs. The outfit was white trimmed with gold, and over her left breast, she'd pinned an enormous purple star of Celestl, the stone shot through with veins of gold. Her short grey hair was slicked back, and her flat shoes were pointed.

Dio chuckled. 'Excellent. Exactly what I'd hoped for.'

Sophie barked a laugh, then followed Dio into the carriage. Dio's back was rod straight as they jolted into movement, her hands wrapped around the purple orb at the top of the cane she always carried, its tip pressed against the floor between her feet. 'So, tell me what it was like growing up in Laurow. I visited plenty when I was a girl, although I'm sure things have changed much since then.'

They chatted the whole way, so Sophie barely noticed the journey. It made her feel better about Hale's impending trip to Spruce because his grandmother would remain in Alter, and there was no question that Dio could help Sophie handle any tricks Bianca had planned.

Sophie was buoyant when she climbed down from the carriage, so she didn't even feel nervous as she stepped in front of her waiting parents to greet them.

'Daughter,' said her father, casting an appraising eye over her. He'd gained weight since she'd last seen him—weeks before her departure to Alter—and he'd been large even then. But now, his jowls were more copious and his blonde hair was greyer. He'd aged, and she wondered what troubled him. Was it her?

'What are you wearing?' hissed her mother.

'She's wearing a dress fit for the First Lady of Alter,' said Dio, stepping up beside Sophie, 'not the skimpy rags you sent her clad in. Oh, don't look so pug-faced, the other clothes didn't work on Hale as you wished them to anyway. These are far more effective in that regard.'

Sophie flushed, but her mother retreated, so she also smiled covertly at Dio and whispered, 'Thank you.'

'You don't have to thank me,' Dio replied, a mischievous twinkle in her eye. 'I've had a shortage of sparring partners of late.'

Sophie's eyes widened a fraction, a little scared about what that meant for her wedding day, but she accepted the lamp a guard held out to her, then followed the old woman who moved with surprising vigor and grace as she stepped onto the bridge.

Sophie's parents muttered complaints about having to walk so far, then discussed how they hoped the administrator wouldn't drone on, but they soon lapsed into silence, her father's breathing becoming labored from the unfamiliar exertion.

The walk seemed endless, the only sounds the click of Dio's stick on the wooden surface, and her father's ragged breathing. They could see little in the lamplit gloom, the air around them still full dark. Hale had suggested they wed before dawn so they could walk back along the bridge accompanied by the first rays of the sun, but also so they could spend a full day together before he rode away to Spruce. Sophie tried to put the unwelcome thoughts from her mind.

They strode on in silence, and to her surprise, Sophie found herself increasingly nervous with each passing step, which was ridiculous because even if Hale didn't in fact want to marry her—which he did, she was sure—he had no choice, so why did she feel as though her breakfast might resurface at any moment?

It wasn't like they would have a large audience, either, only Hale and his mother, the administrator, and those already with her on the bridge, so that couldn't be the source of her unease.

When Hale finally came into sight, Sophie had to press her lips together and tense every muscle in her face to keep tears from spilling down her cheeks, a well of emotion bubbling up inside, filling her chest.

Sophie looked at her feet, trying to blink the tears away, and Dio exhaled a sound somewhere between a huff of approval and a laugh. Sophie's eyes flicked up to meet Dio's, and she found an almost tender expression on the woman's face.

They paused for a moment, giving Sophie's parents time to catch up, and Dio slid her arm through Sophie's. 'You truly care for him, then.'

Sophie froze, not sure of the right answer and worried her parents would hear. 'I ... Well ...'

Dio patted her arm. 'Don't fret my dear, he'll be yours soon enough.'

The last few paces passed in a haze. Sophie did care for him. Was that the cause of her strange feelings? Did people feel so ... strange at moments like these? Did they cry? She'd never been to a wedding, so she really had no idea.

Hale gave a small smile when Sophie reached him, and she returned it as best she could, her lips wobbling a little. He took her hand and wasted not a moment before leading her to the spot under Alter's wand where the administrator waited.

'You're beautiful,' Hale whispered, leaning in, his breath caressing her ear.

Sophie closed her eyes and savored the moment, cataloging the goose-flesh cascading across her skin, the frantic beat of her heart trying to break through her ribs, and the euphoric sickness that held her stomach with an iron grip.

She inhaled air deep into her lungs, noticing the smells so every time she smelled his sweet, salty scent, she would remember the way the muscles corded in his neck as he straightened, the way his throat bobbed as he swallowed, the first time she'd seen his thick mass of dark curls tamed, making him look even more handsome than usual.

And then his amber eyes looked deep into her eyes, seeing past her outer shell and into the core of her being, seeing her scheming, rancid past, and, she prayed, the depth of her affection for him and hopes for their future.

The administrator began, and with a small twitch of his lips and squeeze of her hand, Hale turned his gaze away.

Sophie tried to focus, to listen to whatever words of wisdom the administrator was imparting, but all her brain could process was how marrying Hale felt too good to be true, that she didn't deserve him after everything she'd done, that it might all be snatched away if the administrator didn't get a move on. She could concentrate on nothing else, almost forgetting to speak when it was her turn, almost forgetting their audience when Hale finally kissed her, barely containing her gasp of blissful relief.

Hale clutched Sophie to his chest while the others began the journey back along the bridge, seeming happier that it was over than that Hale and Sophie were wed. All except Dio, who congratulated them heartily.

Hale kissed Sophie again, then stroked his thumb across her lips and looked down into her eyes. 'I love you, wife,' he said, and her chest almost imploded at the kick of feeling his words let fly.

'Fuck, Hale,' she said, closing her eyes and resting her forehead against his chest. That explained everything, all the bizarre emotions she'd been feeling, and the fact she kept almost bursting into tears. 'I love you, too.'

'I wish we were at home,' he murmured, his chest inflating under her as he sucked in a long breath, 'that I could have you all to myself.'

She looked up at him. 'We'll be home soon,' she promised, the word *home* swelling her chest because his home was now her home. She had a home where she was wanted, and for more than just her usefulness in other people's schemes.

He groaned. 'But we have a banquet to endure.'

'We can sneak away.'

'Not soon enough,' he said, kissing her cheek before pulling away with reluctant force. Hale took her hand, and they followed their relatives, moving slowly, savoring the intimacy of each other's company before they spent the rest of the day surrounded by guests.

The sky had begun to glow orange so they could just see the outlines of the trees poking up from the Inner Circle below. Hale wrapped his arm around Sophie, and she pressed into his side, wishing he wore only a thin shirt and not a thick doublet so she could feel him more easily under her fingers. 'Do you really have to leave tomorrow?' she said, her hands holding onto him reflexively, not wanting to let him go.

He stiffened a little. 'The sooner I leave, the sooner I can return.'

She nodded, trying to ignore the words echoing around her mind. *What if you never return?*

'I'm only going to treat with them. It could be over in a matter of days.'

'Or they might hold you hostage, too.'

'I have no plans to go into their territory. We'll meet on neutral ground.'

Sophie nodded. That was better than she'd feared, but she knew in her gut Spruce would never release Pixy without gaining something in return, and Hale had nothing to offer them.

Hale pulled her to a stop and looked deep into her eyes. 'Don't ruin today by dwelling on tomorrow, my love.' He cupped her face and kissed her. 'And I will return to you, I promise you that.'

But he couldn't promise that. It wasn't fair for him to say those words, although he was also right, she shouldn't ruin what little time they had. She nodded, and then he kissed her again, slow and deep and tender.

They eventually made it to the end of the bridge where their relatives milled, the sun almost fully above the horizon, and the Sunrise Fall began in the distance. The others were clearly annoyed at having been kept waiting, and Hale pulled away from Sophie, throwing his arms wide and approaching the group with a broad smile on his lips. He opened his mouth to address them, but before he'd uttered a single syllable, a loud, shrill, ringing noise cut him off.

They all looked around in confusion, trying to place the sound, and then a deeper, booming *thung* rang out across the air, and Sophie's stomach fell.

Hale turned to face Sophie, and he seemed to move in slow motion back towards her, even though he looked like he was running. Voices shouted, 'The Toll Bells! The Goddess! She's truly returned! She's demanding our sacrifice!' The words seemed drawn out to Sophie, as though time had slowed.

Sophie's parents turned their heads towards her at the same moment Hale reached her side, too much happening too quickly, Sophie's brain failing to make sense of it all as Hale took hold of her hand. 'But it's not Toll Day,' she whispered. 'It's not Toll Day. It's not—'

The world snapped back into real time as her mother's eyes fixed maniacally on Sophie. 'We have only one living female born of the main Laurow line.'

Sophie's father shrugged. 'My wife speaks the truth.' He looked at Hale and raised an eyebrow. 'But I'll be a good sport and let you and Sophie travel alone in a carriage on your way to our Toll Gate.'

The lurid words made Hale's lip curl, but he said nothing for a beat, looking as though he was wracking his brains for an escape.

But there was no escape from the Goddess. Sophie doubled over, unable to get enough air. This couldn't be happening! How could the Goddess be so cruel? How could she snatch away the happiness it had taken Sophie a lifetime to obtain when it had only been hers for a handful of minutes?

'We must get going,' her father said insistently. 'We have only until sunset to have our sacrifice ready on the bridge.'

'*Oh my Goddess*,' breathed Hale's mother. 'Spruce! Hale, they'll send Pixy to the Goddess!'

Hale supported Sophie as she straightened, wrapping his arm protectively around her. 'They can't. She's not born of Spruce blood.'

Bianca grabbed Hale's arm, pleading with him. 'They don't care about such things. They even joked about it while I was there.' Bianca had gone sheet white, and Sophie didn't doubt the woman's belief in her own words or her sheer terror.

'If that is the case,' said Hale, his voice calm but unwavering, 'I don't stand a chance of getting her back, and I also have a duty to my wife.'

'Hale!' his mother screamed, clutching his arm with both hands. 'Please!'

Sophie blinked, and silent tears cut channels down her cheeks.

Hale's features were drawn, his voice somber when he said, 'I'm sorry, Mother, truly, but all we can do now is pray.'

Hale pulled his mother's hands off his arm and led Sophie towards their waiting carriage. He leaned close, his lips by her ear. 'Do you trust me?'

'What?' She looked up at him with sharp eyes.

He held her tighter, keeping them moving. 'I need to know that you trust me, Sophie, that you'll follow my lead.'

She inhaled shakily, then nodded her head. 'I trust you.'

'I'll protect you. I won't let the Goddess have you unless she comes out and pries you from my hands herself. I love you, Sophie.'

She wanted to believe him, wanted to believe that love could be enough.

'We'll follow you to Laurow,' Hale called to Sophie's father. 'We'll take my carriage.'

'Very good,' the older man said in reply.

Chapter Forty-Nine
Ava

When Ava headed to bed that evening, the excitement of the day still hadn't worn off. Not only had she gone to the tree and met other physics, but she'd actually *done magic*. She had to pinch herself to make sure it wasn't a dream, but before she could, a bundle of leaves on her bed brought her up short.

She approached them with caution, wondering how they'd come to be there. *The house,* her brain supplied the answer immediately. Or, if the house hadn't put them there, it would have removed them by now if they were dangerous.

So she sat on the bed and picked up what was in fact not a bundle of leaves at all, but a leaf-covered notebook, the pages thick and fibrous and covered in a scrawl she'd come to recognize as her mother's. Ava held her breath as she flicked through the pages, reading intently but—as was the case with most of her mother's books—understanding little. It seemed to be a journal and notebook, a place to doodle, jot ideas, and write poetry, all in haphazard order.

Some pages had been ripped clean out—she could tell from the jagged edges that remained—while other pages had been scribbled over, but most were still legible ... sort of—Polly's handwriting was often scrappy.

One page was entitled, *Imbue An Object*, the next, *Imbue Oneself*, this underlined vigorously, and it read:

Grandmama taught me today that not only can one imbue an object with magic, but also oneself. The possibilities! I've started my exploration, as Grandmama indicated I should, so I can be proficient by the time we reach the Clouds. Grandmama is negotiating her new job, and from what I can tell, she'll start teaching in just a few short months ... if they agree to let me go, too.

Well, the whole world knew how that story ended. Ava flicked over to the next page and found an image of a bird, three lines of poetry underneath, then an image of a box that seemed to spiral down into the page—an optical illusion—but part of Ava felt as though, if she wasn't careful, she'd fall right down and lose herself in its depths.

Another page contained a description of a star that read: *Energy, fireball, magic, person, glittering rock ... depends on the universe. Intriguing and certainly something to explore.*

Ava turned the page to find a drawing that looked like a spider's web, but with tiny circles atop each place where the lines intersected, then farther down, two lines twisted together, then a horizontal wave, and finally, at the bottom of the page, a vertical line bisecting three circles, just like her pin. The caption read: *But what does it all mean?*

Ava shivered as the weight of those words settled on her shoulders. It was a good question, and one she hadn't considered deeply. Sure, she'd questioned her life in passing many times, usually after a particularly bad day at the tavern, something like: *Why did my parents have to die and leave me here in this horrible place without food and warmth and love?* But why did the Atlas Web exist? Why had Rupert's ancestors been the ones to find it? Was there any point to it all? Or perhaps there was no meaning. Maybe the Atlas Web was just a beautiful, random occurrence brought about by inquisitive trees.

Ava stayed up all night trying to decipher the notebook while Kush lay beside her reading a text on magical water systems, trying to find more ways Ava could help him. She would happily do anything he asked if it meant seeing the look of delight on his face she'd seen earlier.

The following morning, tired, bleary-eyed, and wondering if she and Kush should move to a bigger bed, Ava made her way to the attic. She hoped Billy would meet her there and teach her, as he'd said he would once she'd managed magic, but he was nowhere to be seen.

Ava practiced while she waited, starting with the pebble Billy had given her, recalling the feel of the magic in her chest from the day before, how it had rolled up and out of her, how it had felt like light and heat and a balmy fullness, and how, when it had left her, she'd felt a gaping emptiness in her chest.

The stone in Ava's hand warmed, even though she hadn't said the relevant words, and she dropped it in surprise. She laughed in disbelief, examining her hand for any obvious sign that she'd just wielded magic. There was nothing there, at least, not that Ava could see, but there was smoke rising from the desk.

'Shit!' Ava grabbed a bucket of sand from the corner and used a piece of wood to slide the stone off the desk and into the bucket, but the vicious scorch mark left behind filled her with fear.

'Billy!' she screamed, as she took the bucket and ran for the stairs. The stone was starting to look like a burning coal, its orange glow so hypnotic she kept glancing down. She headed for the kitchen, then the garden, screaming Billy's name and pleading with him to come.

Kush, who was fiddling with something near the water butts, looked up as Ava came flying along the path towards him, the bucket held carefully to one side.

'What happened?' he said in alarm, springing to his feet.

'I heated a stone. Perhaps a little too successfully? Get Billy!'

Kush looked from the stone to Ava's face, then paled. He threw down his gloves and ran for the house, screaming Billy's name.

Ava put the bucket down on the small stone patio in the back corner of the garden, a place that caught the evening light and was usually quiet and tranquil, but the presence of the glowing fireball robbed the nook of its serenity.

She folded her arms tightly over her chest as she watched, wishing she knew what to do. *Cool down*, she willed, trying to find the same feeling she'd felt before, trying to summon magic to her aid. But she couldn't locate the sensation amid the chaos of her frantic pulse, the rushing in her ears, the iron fist around her guts. She tried to breathe, to slow, to concentrate, but the stone was glowing white now, so hot it was beginning to melt the sand.

'Shit. Please stop,' she whispered. 'Please cool. I'm sorry, I didn't mean for this ... I didn't know this would—'

'What happened?' called Billy, his tone surprisingly nonchalant given he was sprinting the length of the garden.

'I heated a stone.'

'Using the words I taught you?'

Ava shook her head guiltily. 'I'm sorry. I was exploring my magic. I didn't think about the words, just about putting heat into the stone. Can you stop it? Cool it down?'

Billy shrugged, looking critically at the liquifying sand. 'No.'

'What?' Ava's voice was shrill. 'Why not?'

'I don't have the power for that. Not many do.'

'Then how will we stop it?'

'We won't,' he said simply, then turned to leave. 'Oh, but I'd take it off the patio. Seems a shame to ruin those perfectly lovely flagstones.'

Ava stared blankly, while Kush surged forward and did as Billy said. The stone dropped deeper into the sand as he carefully placed the bucket on a corner of the lawn.

'What will happen?' Ava asked Billy's retreating back. 'When will it stop?'

Billy ignored her, but Kush looked up from the bucket. 'When it runs out of magic?'

'When will that be?'

Kush gave a slow shrug.

Ava balled her hands into fists. 'Fuck!'

The stone clunked to the bottom of the bucket, and sand fell in from the top, covering it over.

'What do we do now?' Ava asked desperately, feeling sick and tired and scared. She could have burnt the house down!

Kush crouched over the bucket, poking the sand with a stick. 'I'm not sure there's much we can do but make sure nothing else catches fire. Unless you think you can take the magic back?'

Take the magic back? How? And even if she could, the notion filled her with terror. The stone was hot. Filled with boiling, raging, scorching heat. Would the magic be hot now too? What would happen to Ava if that inferno came back inside her? *No.* There was no way she would try that—it might kill her!

'Or add more magic to cool it?' Kush suggested.

'Yes,' she breathed. That might work. Ava tried, searching for the feeling in her chest once more, but every time she found it and tried to take hold, the hammering of her heart or a tremor of guilty remorse sent it skittering away. She shook her head. 'I can't do it. I can't keep hold of the magic.'

'Then I suppose we just ... wait.'

They did wait. And wait, and wait, and wait until eventually the sun began to set and Billy finally took pity on them and brought them food. Then the three of them sat in wooden garden chairs around what had become a glowing hole in the ground, and Ava could almost pretend it was a cozy bonfire, not an out-of-control fireball.

Despite herself, with the stars twinkling in the sky above, warm stew in her belly, and the shock of the day abating, Ava felt content and oddly at peace. Until Billy opened his mouth.

'I've decided not to teach you anymore,' he said, after a particularly long swig from a bottle named *Mettle*.

Kush took Ava's hand. 'Then Ava should throw you out.'

Ava huffed irritably, mainly because Billy had ended her contented moment, but also a little at Kush for jumping straight to battle.

'Hmm,' Billy said petulantly. 'Well, here's the thing, when I teach Ava, in order for her to learn, she actually has to listen to the words I speak, otherwise it's a waste of everyone's time. And today we've established that listening is a problem area.'

Kush sneered at him. 'That is not true.'

'Hey! I'm right here,' snapped Ava, pulling her hand free of Kush's grasp, 'and I'm sorry, Billy, I am. I promise to listen better.' Because Ava had no other teacher, and if today's incident had taught her anything, it was that she was a danger to herself and those around her without him.

Billy sat up straighter and shook himself off. 'Well, I'm not ready to re-commit quite yet, but maybe this will be a valuable lesson. Next time, when I give you words to direct your magic, perhaps you'll do us all a favor and *use* them.'

She nodded furiously. 'I will, Billy, I promise.'

Kush growled and slumped back in his chair, his gaze fixed on the fire.

Billy took another swig, then silence settled once more, although this time, Ava was anything but content, preoccupied by how she would fix things with Kush. Billy seemed equally deep in thought, sucking energy towards him like it was sand and he was the base of an hourglass as he stared at one of Kush's waterwheels. 'How did you make the water flow?' Billy asked, flicking his eyes towards Ava with uncharacteristic stillness.

'The water?' It took a moment for Ava to catch on. 'Oh, you mean the hole in the water butt? I don't know how I did it exactly. I just needed for there to be a hole, and my magic created one, the same as I did with the heat stone ... Well, kind of.'

Billy nodded as though disappointed, circling his nails through his hair. 'I thought ... The water ... Well, never mind. It was stupid. Water magic is rarer than the liquor I finished last night.' Billy pulled a book out of his jacket pocket and thrust it into her hands. 'Work your way through this—and only this—and then maybe you won't be quite such a danger to us all.' He got to his feet, heading inside. 'You're too much like your mother, you know. Just because you find you *can* do something, it doesn't mean you *should*.'

Chapter Fifty
Maria
Eight Weeks After Dromeda Started Spinning

Maria had to pinch herself, hardly believing that they'd won, and especially at so low a cost. Elex addressed the enormous crowd in the bear pit, announcing that the abhorrent water tax was thereby abolished, and that all crimes and punishments relating to it were forgotten. The crowd cheered so deafeningly, Maria subtly pressed her fingers to her ears, and then, when Elex finished his speech, there was a stampede for the exits.

'Shit,' Zeik breathed, 'this is going to be bad.' He ran off calling orders, while Elex instructed a handful of soldiers to stay as their bodyguards, and a handful more to move the Queens' corpses and lash them to the gates of his quarter. Maria wasn't sure how she felt about that, but she reasoned it would serve as a deterrent to any remaining dissenters.

Sol, Tallin, and Zeik joined them as they walked slowly through the city, winding their way towards their prize, their home. Only Tallin's spirits were low, his shoulders hunched, his eyes staring off into the distance. They'd told him about Rosalind—who had escaped in the commotion with Commander Winn—and he'd scarcely seemed to believe it.

'Good luck to her,' was all Elex had said, not bothering to set guards on her tail. 'She'll dump Winn soon enough and then she'll be back; it's what she's always done before.'

Maria wondered if this time would be different, part of her hoping Rosalind had found a man she was truly happy with—not that Maria should care after everything Rosalind had done.

It took them hours before they made it to Elex's quarter because it seemed like every soul in Oshala wished to thank and congratulate them, and to shake Elex's hand.

'Thank the people of my quarter,' Elex said time and again. 'If they had not risen up, the day might not have gone this way.'

'And Elex sat about on his arse for most of it,' muttered Sol.

'Always the way,' agreed Zeik. 'Elex takes the glory, and the three of us do all the work.' He looked at Tallin, trying to pull him into their banter, but Tallin refused to bite.

Maria leaned in so only they could hear. 'You're right, that poison you spent days stilling was fine stuff.'

Sol snorted, and even Tallin's mouth twitched before he said, 'Only needed a fraction in the end, though. Turns out twenty minutes would have sufficed.'

Maria swiped him on the arm, full of mock outrage.

'Oh, fine,' said Zeik. 'I suppose it will be us *four* doing all the work from now on, then.'

Maria's chest swelled so violently she thought she might burst. *Us four.* It was what she'd always wanted. She truly was one of them now, accepted by Elex's inner circle.

They reached the open gates of Elex's quarter and stopped before stepping through, taking a moment to savor their achievement. 'Congratulations, my friend,' said Sol. 'And I believe earlier than promised. We still have hours until the Sunrise Fall.'

Zeik eyed the two dead bodies hanging from the walls. 'Not sure about the new décor, though.'

Sol chuckled. 'I think it's tasteful.'

Zeik shook his head. 'That is why no one ever comes to you for advice.'

They stepped across the threshold, closed the gates behind them, then headed for Elex's home. All around them, the people of the quarter were clearing away debris and setting things straight, each of them nodding respectfully as their party passed. But as they neared the archway that led into Elex's residence, a guard approached, his uniform ripped and covered in dirt, a slight frown on his brow. Maria's heart sank. *What now?*

Their group paused, and the guard snapped to attention a pace in front of them. 'You have a visitor, sir.'

'Rosalind?' asked Elex.

The guard shook his head. 'It's—'

'It seems you've been busy,' said a lithe man with dark hair strolling out from under the arch, 'which presumably means my services are no longer required?'

'Nicoli!' Maria exclaimed. She ran to him and threw her arms around his neck.

He caught her and gave her a brief squeeze before pushing her away, and she frowned, confused by his expression, which contained little warmth.

'I've been to inspect the pumps,' he said. 'They're in need of maintenance, seeing as your father neglected them for years and refused to ask the Claws for help. I'll send a team, assuming you're happy to pay?'

Elex nodded. 'Of course, but come, let us go inside. I'm sure we could all use a drink.'

Maria would have liked to talk to Nicoli—she hadn't spoken to him properly since before he'd killed her uncle—but he strode on ahead with Elex. And that meant she had time to dwell on being back inside the same buildings where Cane had detained her. It was unsettling, although it helped that Elex led them into a parlor Maria had never been into before, the walls light blue and crammed with battered books, the seats patched and ragged and comfortable.

Servants hastily lit the fire and brought platters of food as Elex poured them all drinks, thanking them each individually for their help in winning the day.

'Ohhhh, now there's no audience he thanks us,' said Zeik, accepting his tumbler.

'You're so needy,' Elex gently mocked, handing Maria a drink, then taking the space beside her on a wide, low couch.

'To Maria!' said Sol. 'Without whose poison, the Queens would still be here.'

Maria gave a jaunty salute with her glass, but her stomach roiled at her part in the plan. She'd never intended for her skills to be used that way. She was glad the truth serum had finally worn off and her mind was once again her own or she might have told them just how guilty she felt.

Nicoli turned judgmental eyes on her. 'You made the poison?'

She looked down at her hands for a beat.

'She did what needed to be done,' said Sol, his tone edged with a warning.

'You're proud of your part?' Nicoli's gaze bored into Maria's, and it made her see red. Who did he think he was, lecturing her after everything he'd done?

'Are you proud of all the blood on your hands, Nicoli?' Maria's tone was cutting. 'You weren't here, didn't see them. You put an arrow in my uncle, yet Erica and Opal were just as bad ... perhaps worse. They made their people pay for water! Danit never did that.'

'Your brother is preparing to ride on Spruce,' said Nicoli, his change of direction throwing her off balance.

'He's what? Why?'

Nicoli spun his tumbler on the arm of his chair. 'Pixy refused to marry their first son, but the first son refused to take no for an answer. Spruce declared the marriage valid, even though Pixy never said the words, and are refusing to let her go.'

'No,' breathed Maria. Pixy, her beautiful, snarky little sister. It didn't seem fair, especially not when the pact had given her Elex.

'Your mother escaped, and now Hale plans to ride on Spruce just as soon as he weds Sophie Laurow.'

Maria's mouth dropped open.

'But he hated Sophie,' said Elex.

Nicoli shrugged. 'Things change.'

'Is he happy?' asked Maria. 'Does he like her now?'

Nicoli gave her a cynical look. 'Who's to say?'

Maria scowled at her oldest friend. Why was he being like this?

'We'll help him, of course,' said Elex, squeezing Maria's hand. 'Spruce will have a hard time fighting on two fronts, and we already know where their defenses are weakest.'

Maria shook her head, hardly believing her ears. War was the very thing the pact had been supposed to end, and now they were preparing to fight over how it was executed.

'And perhaps the Claws will join us?' said Elex, looking at Nicoli.

Nicoli screwed up his features. 'So that's it? With no more information than that, you'll march off to war?'

Elex went rigid. 'Of course not.'

Nicoli abruptly stood. 'If you'd be so kind as to provide me with a bed, I will go to it now. I plan to return home at first light.'

An awkward silence descended. 'Nicoli ...' said Maria, 'I'm sorry, we—'

'I'm tired, Maria, and I have a long journey in the morning.'

A beat of silence passed, and then Elex signaled to a servant. 'I hope you sleep well, my friend. If you need anything at all, please don't hesitate to ask.'

Nicoli gave a small incline of his head, then followed the servant, and Maria's shoulders slumped as she watched him go. She desperately wanted things to go back to normal between them, but maybe she was asking for too much ... Maybe she would have to accept the change in him and just be grateful she still had him in her life at all.

'I need a real drink,' growled Tallin, gripping the edge of his chair and propelling himself to his feet. He stalked from the room, a dark expression on his features, and Sol and Zeik looked at one another, sharing a silent conversation before heading wearily after him, wishing Maria and Elex a good night.

Maria pitied any poor soul who crossed Tallin tonight. His mood was a deep, shadowy black, and he'd spoken little all evening, his mind elsewhere.

'Poor Tallin,' said Maria. 'He obviously still loves Rosalind.'

Elex's brows pulled together a fraction. 'It's rarely so straightforward with him.'

'What do you mean?' Tallin seemed like the most uncomplicated of all of Elex's friends.

Elex shrugged. 'I gave up trying to read him long ago, especially when it comes to women. I'm almost always wrong about his motives.'

Maria frowned. 'But if he doesn't love her, then—'

Elex pinched her waist. 'That's his business. And if he needs to punch every low life in the quarter to work whatever he's going through out of his system, then so be it. So long as he turns up for work in the morning—'

'Oh, don't pretend you don't care.'

Elex raised his eyebrows, a faint smile on his lips. 'Of course I care, but he's not ready to talk about it—might never be, especially with me, seeing as I'm Rosalind's *brother*.'

Maria chuckled. That was fair enough. Maria would probably feel weird about it if Sophie wanted to talk to her about John or Hale.

'And Zeik and Sol are with him. They'll keep him out of trouble.'

Maria nodded, then turned to sit sideways, one leg up on the sofa, one on the floor. She squeezed his thigh. 'We did it, Elex.' They'd taken back the quarter and more, the whole of Oshe now theirs. It was surreal, and meant they could do so much good—for their people, the Claws, their families ...

A servant poked his head into the room, and Elex sent him away, telling him to go to bed and clean up in the morning. 'Congratulations again, sir,' the man said before retreating. 'We're all so glad you're back.'

'Thank you,' said Elex, as Maria's heart gave a tug of pride. Of course his people were glad; Elex was a fair leader, a just leader.

The door clicked shut, and Elex leaned back, seeming to relax for the first time in as long as Maria could remember, the tension melting from his muscles. He looked good enough to eat, his hair mussed, his shirt open at the neck, sleeves rolled up to reveal his sculpted forearms. He put his hand over Maria's. 'We did it,' he agreed, 'and Oshe finally has the First Lady it deserves.'

'Just think of all the things we can do!'

An indulgent smile pulled at his lips. 'What first?'

'The water,' she said without hesitation. 'We have to make sure everyone has enough, and then we have to make trade fairer, and I'm going to still as many medicinal tinctures as I can think of so the healers can help people without worrying about the cost.'

He hooked her hair behind her ear. 'Then you'll be needing a generously sized still room, my little hell cat.'

She smiled. A still room that was hers—really hers—without the threat of it being taken away. She bit her lip, then nodded. 'At least ten stills wide.'

He chuckled. 'Your wish is my command, sweetheart.'

She turned her head and kissed his wrist. 'And what's your wish, Elex?'

He dropped his hand to her waist, stroking his thumb back and forth, watching her for a while. 'I want to fill our house with little hell cats.'

Her stomach lurched. 'So we have a sacrifice for the Goddess?'

Elex shook his head. 'So we have a whole pack of mini Marias to work the twenty five stills you're planning.'

She grinned. 'Good point. And we could do with a few mini Elexs, too, so they can scare everyone into submission when we're not around.'

'Hey!'

He pinched her again, and she squirmed, then looked up at him through batted eyelashes. 'Obviously they'll be absolute pussy cats underneath.'

'Oh, you ...' He pinched and nudged and tickled her, not stopping until she landed in his lap. 'That's better,' he said with a self-satisfied smile, wrapping his arms around her. He buried his nose in her neck, then sucked just above her collarbone, and his touch against her sensitive skin made her spine arch. He sucked and kissed, and she ran her hands through his hair and across his back, then pulled away and climbed to her feet, standing before him, a coy smile on her lips.

He seemed a little confused, leaning forward as though about to follow her, but she shook her head and reached for the laces holding her dress closed, and he lounged back as understanding dawned on his features, his enraptured expression spurring her on.

He shuffled his hips forward, making himself comfortable as he followed where her fingers tugged, taking a sip from his tumbler, then resting the glass on the sofa's arm as Maria pulled her dress apart, releasing her breasts from their cage. Elex shifted in his seat, groaning in appreciation, and Maria gave a self-satisfied smile. She lifted her skirts and slid down her underwear, letting the scrap of fabric drop to her ankles, then kicking it aside.

'Unfasten your breeches,' she said, eyeing appreciatively the bulge that had appeared there.

Elex complied without hesitation, then ran his hand slowly up and down his impressive arousal, not taking his eyes off her for a second as Maria slowly lifted her hands to her breasts and squeezed. She moved forward with sultry steps, raised her skirts and straddled him, taking him in hand before sinking down onto his length.

He exhaled and gripped her waist, pulling her even farther onto him, while Maria retrieved the tumbler and dipped her finger into the amber liquid, lifting a single bead of moisture and dropping it onto her peaked nipple.

Elex didn't hesitate before lowering his lips, licking up the liquid, then sucking her into his mouth. Maria gasped and tipped her hips, her free hand sliding into his hair as he tongued her.

He lifted his gaze and dipped his own finger into the drink, then drew a trail of droplets down her other breast before lapping them up with his tongue. He took her breasts in his hands and squeezed them together, and Maria pooled a little of the liquid in the well he'd created, then lifted herself up onto her knees, bringing her flesh closer to his lips. Elex drank it up, rubbing the remaining moisture across her sensitive skin, then gasped as she sank back down, sliding his hands under her skirts and grabbing her hips, urging her to move them.

She didn't need much urging, and Elex leaned back and looked up at her as she rocked, her chest rising and falling with each slow undulation.

He drank her in with his eyes, and Maria spread her legs wider, pressing her hips lower, pulsing harder, reveling in his admiration. He slid a finger between their joined flesh and stroked, and she bucked and moaned, her head tipping back and her eyes falling closed, her hands on his shoulders. 'Yes ... Elex ... Yes ...'

His other hand slid to her backside, squeezing as he moved his hips in time with hers, his grunts of pleasure spurring her higher, his fingers stoking such wonderful, primal sensations inside her that she ground wildly against him, her movements frantic, erratic things, her moans high-pitched and breathy. And then her body contracted and she cried out, and Elex swore into her hair as he lifted her and pounded her down onto his length. 'Goddess ... Fuck ... Maria ...' he breathed, while pleasure barreled through her. Elex groaned, his fingers digging into her flesh as his movements became small, fevered thrusts, and she rolled her hips, wringing out every last ounce of pleasure before they finally stilled, clinging to each other, panting and sated and happy.

CHAPTER FIFTY-ONE
AVA

AVA READ THE BOOK Billy gave her from cover to cover. It contained a hundred or so spells to imbue objects with magic, and she got to work the next day, carefully following the instructions and checking in with Billy about how to pronounce each strange syllable. She hoped with each question she might entice him back to the attic, that he might help her in a more active fashion and speed her progress, but he didn't.

Kush, on the other hand, was only too happy to help. He still thought she was pandering to Billy, that she should lay down some ground rules, but he was also caught up in her excitement, and more buoyant than she'd seen him in weeks. He read the book, too, then set her endless little challenges, creating reasons for her to need to achieve each spell.

When she wanted to make a light stone, he locked her in the coat cupboard, sitting outside until she called triumphantly through the door. When she tried to make a compass, he told her he'd left her a present at the northern end of the garden, which she would only get if she found her way there with magic. That one she'd completed in record time, and she was both disappointed and overjoyed to find that her reward was a kiss.

'I feel cheated,' Ava whined, burrowing into his chest.

'The next spell detects food,' he replied cryptically, 'and if you can use it to find the right pocket in my coat, you'll have your real prize.'

Ava raced to imbue her hand with the spell, then traced it all over Kush's body. It buzzed pleasantly as she covered his right hip, and she reached inside his leather coat, finding a beautifully wrapped miniature box of chocolates. 'Oh, Atlas,' she gushed, marveling at the bright pink paper, the golden ribbon, and the divinely sweet smell as she pressed the box to her nose. 'You're the best.'

'Will you still say that if I make you share them?'

She swatted him. 'You don't even like chocolate.'

'I like these ones.'

'Really?' Ava clawed at the ribbon, impatient to see what was different about them. Inside the box sat four star-shaped chocolates, each seemingly identical to the next, aside from a small dot of color in the center, one purple, one blue, one green, and one red.

'Try one,' he said, although given his tone, she wasn't sure she should.

She looked at him suspiciously. 'Why did you say it like that?'

His face split into a broad smile. 'Because they're not what you think.'

She pouted and narrowed her eyes. 'What do I think?'

He chuckled. 'You'll like them, Ava!'

'You first.'

Kush's chuckle morphed into a bark of laughter. 'If you insist.' He selected the purple chocolate and carefully bit it in half, then held the rest out to her.

Ava was still deeply apprehensive, but Kush closed his eyes, and she could tell he was rolling the treat around his mouth, savoring it. His acting skills weren't that good, so she popped her half in her mouth, and then her own eyes fluttered closed as a feeling of pure calm washed over her.

And the taste ... It was buttery and chocolatey and smooth in a way that made her think of mountain fields filled with wildflowers swaying in the wind, or ... But she couldn't pin the thought down because the feeling was fading.

She opened her eyes and found Kush watching her with a lazy, contented expression. 'See?'

'The chocolate's imbued with magic?'

'Made by one of the Cloud families, and sold at a specialty shop in the Atlas Tree.'

A pang of panic hit her. He'd been to the Atlas Tree? Had he seen his father? Had he been recognized in the shop?

Perhaps sensing her train of thought, he continued, 'Or at least, that's where they started. They sell all over the federated world these days.'

Ava tried not to sag in relief, covering her reaction by saying, 'Which should we try next?'

He grinned. 'Blue's for cunning, green's for wit, and red's for passion.' He leaned in and kissed her. 'So we should save that one for later, seeing as we have plenty more spells to work through before we get there.'

'Spoil sport.' Ava drew him back for another kiss as he began to pull away, then selected the green chocolate and bit it in half.

Over the next few days, Ava imbued cogs and food and even a pillow. She'd expected to feel tired and drained because Billy had told her repeatedly that magic came with a cost, but instead, she was like a bottle with too much pressure inside. Now the magic had found a path out of her, it wanted to be free, wanted to expand and be used. She didn't feel tired, she felt exhilarated and full of possibility.

With Kush's help, Ava made rapid progress, reaching the end of the book Billy had given her in no time, at which point Kush found reasons for her to repeat each spell, forcing her to memorize each and every one. When she knew them backwards, Kush made her use the spells when she was stressed, teaching her to call her magic even with distractions or when her emotions were running high.

Every time it got hard and she thought about giving up, she would go to the hole in the garden created by her out-of-control heat stone. The stone had sunk deep into the ground, but the hole remained, the occasional whisp of smoke snaking out of the top. The stone had gone too deep to see, and Kush thought they should fill the hole, or at least cover it up, but that felt somehow wrong to Ava, and maybe a little dangerous. Billy said it would run out of magic at some point, but there was no telling how long that would take.

Eventually even Kush ran out of tasks for Ava, so she went in search of Billy to ask him what to do next. Unfortunately, he was passed out in a drunken stupor. Instead of trying to rouse him—from experience, an impossible task—Ava turned her attention to the many books, scrolls, and notebooks around the house. She was most drawn to those that had been annotated by her mother, and to help her find them, she imbued a feather with a seeking spell that shook whenever it touched a tome with her mother's handwriting inside.

Kush helped her search, and once she had a large pile, she settled down and devoured them from cover to cover, while Kush busied himself in the garden, swam in the pool, or went out to buy food. Kush regularly had to remind her to eat and sleep and exercise, but now Ava had a basic understanding of magic, she could decipher so much more of what she read, and she wanted to know it all.

What Billy filled his time with, Ava didn't know. He seemed to sleep a great deal during the day because he stayed up late into the night, always with a bottle in his hand, and he seemed to have decided to avoid Ava and Kush, not even eating with them, instead cooking his own meals at odd times.

He was often in the library, lying on the floor or on a sofa, staring at the original map of the Atlas Web on the ceiling. He would blabber to himself about how remarkable it was, how the map should never have been moved from the tree, how he might become a web wanderer and lose himself for all time. Then he would make up a song or find a dress to dance around in or manically scribble on a piece of parchment until every last space was filled. In the morning, another bottle or two would be empty—although never the few bottles he'd cast aside the first day when he'd entered the house, which made Ava wonder what they would do to a person—and he would ask Kush to procure more of specific varieties.

After a while, Kush refused to buy any more, and when Billy realized Kush meant it, he started slowing his consumption to eke out the remaining supply. That was probably why Billy finally made it to the attic one day because he'd had a decent night's sleep and his head was clearer than it had been in weeks.

'What are you doing?' he asked, coming into the room so quietly, Ava jumped a foot into the air.

'Fuck! Billy!'

Billy snorted. 'Sorry, couldn't resist.' He stalked around the room, bending to look at the model of a portal she'd constructed, then flicking a few pages back and forth in an open notebook. He bent over so his elbows were on the desk, his chin on his hands, looking up at her with an expectant gaze. 'So?'

Ava's mouth pulled to one side as she considered what to tell him. 'I'm exploring ... experimenting.'

He straightened, then hesitated, seeming at a loss for words.

'Not by myself! I promise. I've learned my lesson.'

Billy cocked a hip, frowning in confusion.

'I'm following the instructions in Polly's notebooks. She was so brilliant. Some of her ideas ...!' Ava scrubbed her hands over her face, then stretched out her back, trying to remember when she'd last moved. What time was it?

'Wellllll,'—Billy folded his arms—'there are *instructions* and instructions, my gullible little cabbage. Your mother's are the former, whereas mine are the latter. Mine should be followed to the letter, whereas hers should be treated with the caution you'd apply to a raging forest fire. She did, after all, split many a soul in two and hide them from their hosts. That's the road you're on if you follow her lead.' Billy reached his arms up into the air then bent forward, touching his toes.

'What are you doing?'

'Stretching.'

'Why?'

He reached his hands forward on the floor, then lunged one leg between them. 'Because you just did, and it reminded me that I haven't in a while. I think I might have been on a bit of a rampage, and I've decided this is the moment to pull up from my dive. Time to tone things down, to swing the needle back the other way? Prevent you from creating some catastrophe that could bring us all to ruin.'

Ava leaned back and crossed her arms. 'Now you want to help me?'

'Better to steer the wrecking ball than let it swing in whichever direction the tornado takes it, and anyway, I'd be lying if I said I wasn't bored.' He windmilled his arms up into the air and turned his body sideways. 'Gods that feels good!' He bent backwards, arching his spine farther than seemed wise, Ava staring in fascination. 'And if you keep going with that particular potion,'—somehow he managed to nod towards the desk—'you're going to hurt yourself, or me, or blow the whole house up.'

A shot of adrenaline rushed through Ava's blood as she quickly reread the notes. 'But I'm following the instructions to the letter!'

Billy circled his arms to the ground, switched legs to lunge on the other side, then fixed her with a look. 'As I said, dearie, *instructions* and instructions.' Billy repeated his stretch on the second side, which looked equally improbable, mostly because Ava wasn't sure how his corded trousers had so much give, and then he returned his hands to the floor and exhaled loudly. 'You're even more like your mother than I thought,' he said, rolling slowly to his feet and pulling back his shoulders, 'and that's a colossal fucking problem.'

Ava flinched, then scowled. 'If you're going to—'

He rolled his eyes. 'I mean, you make magic by using magic.'

Ava's indignation evaporated. 'Ummm ...' The idea seemed impossible.

Billy tucked one foot into his groin, then reached for the ceiling with both hands. 'Some people make magic when they socialize or when they dance or sing or draw. Some need peace and quiet or sex or walks in the woods. You, though, when you use magic, it fills you up, and that makes more magic. You're a perpetumot. Rare and wonderful. Dramatic and dreadful. *Dangerous.*'

'I'm ...' Had Billy just called her *rare and wonderful*? She felt her cheeks heat.

'It's good and bad,' he said, switching legs. 'Others will inevitably be scared of you—they always are of things they don't understand—or will try to use you for their own gain ... If people find out, that is. If you want to keep it under raps, you'll have to be careful.'

'Just to make a change,' she deadpanned.

Billy gave a half shrug, the corner of his lip pulling up just a little. 'Variety is the spice of life, after all.'

CHAPTER FIFTY-TWO
MARIA
EIGHT WEEKS AFTER DROMEDA STARTED SPINNING

'DO YOU REALLY HAVE to leave so soon?' asked Maria, as she helped herself to apple slices slathered with ground peanuts.

Nicoli sipped his thick black coffee—the variety favored by the people of Oshe. 'Yes. I have nothing to keep me here.'

Maria threw down the slice of apple in her hand. 'No, you're right, your oldest friend is nothing at all.'

'My oldest friend is quite settled in her new land. I'm sure she has much to keep her occupied.'

'You sit there judging Hale for threatening Spruce, and Elex for taking back what's his, and me for brewing poison, but you kill and brutalize and jeopardize the whole of Celestl, and think yourself somehow superior? That your acts of aggression are different to ours? Well, my friend, they are not. You are stubborn and pig-headed and we are all as bad as one another.'

'I am not the same as you,' hissed Nicoli, leaning forward. 'Your pact makes that clear.'

Maria leaned in too, fury in her stare. 'It was never *my* pact, as you well know, and *we* want to help you.'

Nicoli sat back and looked away. 'I am honored indeed,' he said, his words dripping with sarcasm.

'You'd rather we didn't?' Maria bit out. 'You want us to treat the Claws like my uncle did?'

Nicoli sneered, meeting her gaze once more. 'I don't want your charity or pity or to feel beholden to you. I don't know why the Goddess has teased us with only a puddle of water in the Inner Circle, but so help me, I will find a way to fill it up.' He shook his head disparagingly. 'And what good are you in that endeavor?'

Elex gave a small cough as he entered the room, his eyes meeting Maria's, checking she was okay. 'No good at all, most likely,' he said disarmingly. 'You're the genius, we just got lucky with our family names. But whatever you need from us, we will help you, and not because we pity you or think of it as charity. Hale, Maria, and I want the Blades and Claws to be equal. We know what you've done for our world, that you deserve it, have earned it, that we would all have perished without you when the Goddess deserted us. And when we defeat Spruce—if it comes to that—it will only be Laurow left to convince that the Claws should have a seat at the table.'

Nicoli cocked an eyebrow. 'Will you assassinate the leaders of both Blades to get what you want?'

'Nicoli!' snapped Maria, slamming her hand on the table. 'You assassinated Danit!'

Nicoli looked at her with the same cantankerous eyes he'd used since they were children when he didn't want to give in.

Maria took a breath, taming her rage, then said quietly, 'Then what would you have us do?'

His lips curled into a snarl. 'We don't want to have to bow and scrape for water.'

'Then work with us!' said Maria. 'Without you, we can't repair our water pumps. Without you, the turbines would have seized. We've been friends since we were children, you know how I think of you and your people, and Elex feels the same. So I ask again, Nico, what should we do?'

Nicoli stood abruptly, then braced his hands on the back of his chair, his head angled towards the floor, and for several long moments he stayed like that, Maria holding her breath.

'Who wed between Oshe and Spruce as part of the pact?' Nicoli asked, his head still angled downward.

Elex hesitated. If he was anything like Maria, he was dizzy from Nicoli's sudden change of tack.

'My father's second wife married the leader of Spruce's brother,' said Elex. 'I believe it went ahead.'

Nicoli looked up. 'And where are they now?'

Elex's brow furrowed in thought. 'I don't know. I haven't looked for them since returning. They were to be wed here in Oshe, but neither wields much power.'

Nicoli scoffed. 'The man lived in Spruce all his life, at the right hand of their leader, and you don't think he's valuable to you? You don't think you should ask him about his brother's motives? You'll blunder blindly into war on nothing more than the word of Maria's mother?'

Maria loved her mother, in a strange sort of way, but Nicoli had a point because she wasn't always the most objective source.

'You're right,' said Elex, 'we'll find him ... Gather intelligence.'

Nicoli straightened and gave a curt nod. 'You ask what I want?' he said, turning his gaze on Maria. 'I want you people to start using your heads and stop rampaging about like idiots.'

'Nicoli, for fuck's sake!' said Maria, throwing down her napkin and pushing back her chair. 'We're on the same side!'

'So you say, but your actions tell a different story.'

'You want a fight, is that it? You always did have that streak in you, needing—'

But just as Maria was sinking into her rebuke, her words were cut short by the deep, dreadful ring of a bell pealing out from somewhere overhead.

Maria froze. 'What is that?' she breathed, looking at Elex for some kind of reasonable explanation. But Elex's face was sheet white, and Nicoli had devastation in his eyes as he looked at her.

It was then Maria realized the whole room had gone silent, the guards and servants still as statues, and everyone was staring at her.

Shit.

'The Toll Bells?' Her voice was breathy and frantic. 'Is that ...?'

Elex nodded slowly, but he didn't seem entirely present, like he was in shock or trying to work out their next move.

Which was exactly what she should have been doing. The sacrifice. They had to find a sacrifice by sunset, but Rosalind was the only remaining member of the Oshe line, and she'd disappeared. So there was no sacrifice. They had no sacrifice! Which meant what, exactly? What would the Goddess do when no one walked through the Toll Gate?

'We have to get you out of here,' said Nicoli. He rounded the table and tried to pull her towards the door.

'What? No! I'm not going to Alter. They ...' *They have Dio.* The only female blood member of Maria's family still in Alter Blade.

'He's right, Maria,' said Elex, suddenly at her side, too. 'We have to get you out of here.'

'But ...' She still didn't understand.

'Maria,' said Nicoli, staring intently into her eyes, 'you're the closest thing Oshe has to a sacrifice. Unless you think Elex's sister will hand herself over at sunset?'

No. They couldn't! Maria wasn't of the Oshe line.

Elex's movements slowed, then stopped, his eyes vacant, his mind clearly working. 'But who will we send?'

Nicoli shook his head. 'There's no time for that now. Where can we take her?'

A commander approached. 'Sir, we must find Rosalind.' His tone was high-pitched and scared.

Elex nodded. 'Yes. Take as many as you need, but do not hurt her.'

The commander gave a sharp incline of his head but stayed in place, looking sheepish.

Maria placed a hand on Elex's arm. 'Elex, she's your sister. You can't ...' But she trailed off because if not Rosalind, then who?

The commander's eyes flicked to Maria. 'And if we can't find Rosalind?' A shiver of fear scurried down Maria's spine.

Elex took an aggressive step towards the commander, who shrank back. 'Maria is not of the Oshe line.'

'She's of a first family,' said a second, ashen-faced guard.

A third guard took a tentative step forward. 'Probably all the same to the Goddess. And surely better than no sacrifice at all?'

Maria felt the walls closing in, nowhere to run. They were right—she was the obvious choice—and this was the justification for the privilege of the first families. They lived in luxury and ruled Celestl, and in return, once in a hundred years, they sacrificed one of their own.

Maria met Elex's tortured gaze. 'I have to do it,' she whispered.

'No,' he said, resolute.

'You'll lose everything if I don't.'

'I'll lose everything if you do.'

She closed her eyes, trying not to waver. 'We have no choice.'

'What of cousins?' asked Nicoli, never one to lose his head in a crisis.

Elex shook his head.

'Not even someone distant?'

'Perhaps,' said Elex, 'but would that work? Would the Goddess accept someone so far removed?'

Nicoli exhaled loudly. 'Bastards?'

Elex shrugged. 'All male.'

Nicoli clenched his teeth, even his great mind running out of options.

Elex looked around the room, perhaps hunting for inspiration or an escape, but he found neither. Even if they tried to run, they wouldn't make it out of Oshala, and anyway, Maria was no coward, and she would not shy away from her duty.

'I'll do it,' said Elex. 'It can't be you. I won't let it be you.'

Maria screwed up her features. 'What? No! Celestl needs you.'

'And it has to be a woman,' said the commander. 'Everyone knows that.'

Elex snarled at the man, who retreated a few paces, and Maria squared her shoulders. A long and happy life with Elex had always been too much to hope for. She would be grateful for the short time they'd had together, enjoy the time they had left, and do what had to be done.

'I'll remain here,' Maria said to the commander. 'Leave however many guards you deem appropriate, and if you can't find Rosalind before sunset, I'll take the Oshe wand through the Toll Gate. Perhaps I'll see my grandmother on the other side, and maybe even my sister.' Because as far as Maria could remember, Spruce had no living female of the first family's blood either.

'Maria ...' said Elex, but no words followed because there was nothing more to say. Unless they could find Rosalind before sunset, or think of some other option, Maria would be Oshe's sacrifice.

CHAPTER FIFTY-THREE
SOPHIE

SOPHIE CLIMBED INTO THE carriage, Hale a pace behind her, but before he could step inside, the door slammed shut. Sophie panicked, her eyes flying wide, her hand on the door handle, but then Dio's muffled voice filtered through the door. 'Before you go galivanting off into the sunset,' she snapped, presumably at Hale, 'you must state who from Alter will be our sacrifice.'

Sophie strained to listen, a struggle given the rushing in her ears, so she almost didn't notice when the door on the other side of the carriage swung open, and the face of a female guard came into view. The woman held a single finger across her lips, then beckoned for Sophie to follow her.

Sophie refused to budge. 'What's going on?' she whispered.

The guard huffed, then said, 'Dio's rescuing you. Hale will obviously try to do the same, but he'll likely botch it, and then you'll end up as Goddess food. This way, you get to run, and Hale can never be blamed because he's out there in clear view of everyone. This is your ticket to freedom, Sophie. But if you want to use it, we have to go now.'

Of course! If she stayed hidden until after the Sunset Fall, her father would have to send someone else through Laurow's gate—some cousin or bastard daughter. She'd never met any, but didn't doubt one existed. It would be embarrassing for her parents, but they'd get over it, and then Sophie could be with Hale.

Sophie's chest lightened as she took in the gaggle of mounted guards a few paces away. She jumped down from the carriage without further thought, accepted a leg up onto a waiting horse, then threw the offered cloak around her head and shoulders.

As soon as she was mounted, the guards formed up around her, ordering her to duck so they could hide her in their midst. She did as she was told, bending low over her horse's neck as they trotted away, their gait slow enough not to attract suspicion. 'What happens when they see us?' Sophie asked no one in particular.

'Dio will tell them she sent us to fetch another carriage, so Bianca can go to Spruce if she wishes.'

Sophie felt a pang of affection for the old woman. 'She's truly a marvel.'

'She is,' one of the guards agreed fondly.

Sophie didn't dare straighten even though it was awkward, trotting while crouching low, and her horse's neck almost collided with her face several times. 'Where are you taking me?'

'Don't worry, it's somewhere safe,' said the guard who'd pulled her from the carriage.

A flutter of unease stirred in Sophie's belly. 'Where?'

'We can't tell you.'

Unease became panic, clawing to get out. Had Sophie made a terrible mistake? 'Why not?'

The guard tutted. 'Dio's orders.'

Sophie clutched her horse's mane. 'I don't understand.'

The guard gave her a placating look. 'We're taking you to Dio's own private retreat. Not many know of its existence. It's not far.' Sophie relaxed a little, the guard seeming genuine enough, although Hale's words kept playing over and over in her mind, *Do you trust me?*

They rode past the lake and into the woods, and Sophie was finally able to sit tall in her saddle, protected by the trees. The path narrowed, and their party stretched out into single file. They flew along at a canter, the horses' hooves muted by the soft ground, and it felt to Sophie almost like a dream, or more accurately, a nightmare. She wished it were, that she would wake to find her wedding day not yet begun, but the pinch of her ill-fitting saddle suggested otherwise.

They reined in their horses in a small clearing by a tall tree, and Sophie looked around, expecting to find a house—or at least a shed or shack—but there was nothing.

'You and I will stay here,' said the guard. 'The others will go and fetch the carriage Dio requested. We'll be safe here.'

Sophie looked around, entirely confused. '*This* is Dio's hiding place? A clearing in the woods?'

The guard dismounted, as did Sophie, and the others wheeled around and rode swiftly back the way they'd come, taking Sophie's riderless horse with them.

'What is this?' Sophie demanded, her voice shrill as panic coursed through her again. 'What's going on?'

The guard visibly softened, maybe remembering that for Sophie this was a life-or-death situation. 'You have nothing to worry about. There's a place a little farther along the path.'

'There is indeed,' said a male voice, and Sophie whirled to see a familiar face stepping out from behind a tree, 'but you're not going to get to it.'

Sophie gasped in shock as she came face to face with the man she'd been supposed to marry. 'John?' He was hardly recognizable, relaxed and commanding, a short beard on his face, making him seem older and more grounded.

John moved closer, and Sophie's guard drew her sword, but many more figures appeared through the trees, making fighting futile.

'Did you think you were free of me?' John asked, tilting his head to one side, the movement threatening.

I'd hoped. 'What do you want, John?' Her heart was hammering at a thousand beats a minute and she already regretted her rash decision to flee.

He exhaled a low laugh. 'It's what the Goddess wants that concerns us.'

Us?

A woman with long dark hair pulled back in a ponytail stepped up beside him. 'And the Goddess wants you.'

Sophie's mouth went dry, and she willed her brain to come up with some argument to justify her actions. 'The Goddess doesn't care who takes the wands through the gates. It could be any woman. I read a book in my father's library that said—'

'I don't care what some old book says!' John snapped. 'Celestl can't afford to take chances, especially in its current state. When the Goddess abandoned us three hundred years ago, the ingenuity of the Claws saved us, and Blades and Claws worked together to survive, but our world is fractured now, tearing itself apart, and the Goddess is angry.'

The dark-haired woman cocked her hip, her arms folded across her chest. 'And sacrifice is the purpose of your life, after all—the justification for the opulence of the Blades. But instead of fulfilling your birthright, you ran like a coward.'

Shame flooded Sophie's veins because this woman was right. Sophie had run when she should have stayed, despite Dio's wishes. What would Hale think of her now? She'd run from him, too, when he'd told her he would protect her, had asked her to trust him ... Maybe her actions meant she'd never see him again.

'How did you find us?' asked Sophie's guard, her sword still drawn, even if there was nothing she could do, hopelessly outnumbered as they were.

'Gabriele and I had eyes on your wedding,' said John, looking down at the woman beside him, his demeanor turning tender.

Gabriele smiled wolfishly back at him. 'The Claws have eyes everywhere.' She flicked her gaze to Sophie. 'And when we saw you run, we followed.'

'Although, given you were with Grandmother's guards,' added John, 'it was obvious where you were headed.'

'She thinks her tree is secret,' said a clipped, commanding voice from behind them. Sophie turned with a start, barely daring to believe her eyes. 'It is anything but, at least not since you followed her and blabbed about it to anyone who would listen, brother, which was even more of an outrage given you're not even brave enough to climb to the top.'

'Hale?' Sophie breathed, but he didn't look at her, and Sophie's heart splintered.

'Brother,' said John, seemingly unphased, 'what a lovely surprise.'

Sophie took a tentative step towards Hale but stopped because his expression was cold as a frozen sea, and guards from both Alter and Laurow flanked him.

'You thought to take my bride?' growled Hale, stepping menacingly towards his younger sibling.

The others from John's party melted back into the trees, knowing their plan was in tatters, only John and Gabriele remaining. There would be no fight, and Sophie's knees almost gave out in relief, her head swimming, making her faint.

John gave an amused shrug. 'Seems only fair, seeing as you did the same to me.'

Gabriele's features blackened. 'We are doing the Goddess's work, seeing as the first families have forgotten their responsibilities.'

'Who is the Alter sacrifice?' John demanded, not seeming to notice that his brother's gaze threatened violence, or perhaps not caring.

'Grandmother,' Hale bit out. 'It's the topic she used to detain me so she could help my *wife* escape.' Hale cast a chastising look at Sophie, and she bowed her head, wishing she could melt into the ground.

John chuckled. 'Grandmother always was a devious old handbag. And congratulations, by the way, even if your marriage is not destined to last.' A smirk danced at the corner of John's mouth, and Sophie wanted to punch him, or cry ... Maybe both.

Hale exploded across the clearing, tripping Gabriele, who tried to intercept him, and punched John with a left hook so hard he fell to his knees.

'You find this funny?' Hale hissed, grabbing the front of his brother's shirt and hauling him up until their faces were only an inch apart. 'You see this as a victory? Our grandmother, my wife, and, if Mother is correct, our sister, will all be sacrificed to the Goddess, and you laugh at that fate?'

'Maria?' breathed John, shaking his head in confusion. 'But Oshe has a daughter ...'

Hale released his brother so he fell into the dirt. 'Pixy.' Hale crossed to Sophie in three quick strides, then slid his hand into hers, and as soon as their skin made contact, calm washed over her, bolstered her, at least until he yanked her forcefully behind him as he headed back along the path.

'I'm sorry,' she breathed, half-running to keep up.

He marched her out of the woods, guards surrounding them on every side. 'I told you I would never let the Goddess take you, and I meant it,' he hissed. He handed her up into the back of a waiting carriage, then climbed up behind her and slammed the door. 'What the fuck were you thinking?'

She looked down at her skirts. 'I didn't think ... I shouldn't have ... It was a decision made in a flash, and Dio seemed to have a plan ...'

'*I* have a plan,' he said in an urgent whisper.

She looked up, a bead of hope making her lean forward, desperate for details. 'You do?'

He clamped his lips shut and shook his head. Of course he wouldn't trust her now. Perhaps he would never trust her again.

'I'm sorry, Hale. I didn't mean to hurt you. I ran because I want a life with you. I thought—'

His lips crashed into hers, the contact overriding her ability to think, emotion welling inside her, rising until it caught in her throat. And then she was sobbing into his kisses, clutching at his hair, terrified this would be all the time they would ever get.

'They'll be listening,' he whispered, kissing her ear.

She nodded, knowing he was right, especially seeing as this carriage was one of her father's. Hale tucked her under his arm so her head pressed against his chest, and she breathed him in, letting his stroking fingers and the rocking carriage and the rise and fall of his chest calm her frantic heart.

'Trust me, my love, you're not going through that gate.'

CHAPTER FIFTY-FOUR
AVA

SEEING AS BILLY NO longer had his drinking habit for company, he was all over Ava all the time. They worked spells, made potions, practiced illusions, spent time in the echo chamber—probably because Billy wanted her to hear all the bad things going on across the Federation—and read endless books.

It meant the time she spent with Kush decreased, and he went back to swimming, gardening, reading, and making trips for food. He seemed content, so Ava told herself not to worry, but a nagging voice at the back of her mind said he wasn't happy, that the arrangement couldn't last. Kush wasn't made to sit around the house.

'He-llo!' sang Billy, snapping his fingers in front of her face. 'Billy to Ava! Are you there?'

She sucked in a breath, snapping herself out of her thoughts. 'Yes, sorry ... Just tired I guess.'

'Well, we know that's not because of the magic ...' He waggled his eyebrows suggestively.

She scowled, turning away to drop a handful of bay leaves into the potion bubbling above the fire. Billy made a delighted sound designed to rile her, but she'd learned to ignore his frequent provocations.

She gently stirred the mixture, watching the steam disappear up the chimney, and thought back to her mother's notebook, to the question that had been on her mind for weeks. 'Billy,' she asked, still with her back to him, 'do you ever wonder what it's all for?'

'Ha!' he barked, then he held his hands open theatrically. 'Whatever in the name of Atlas do you mean?'

'Well, magic.' She turned her head to look at him. 'The Atlas Web. Portals ... All of it! Why does it exist? What's it for?'

Billy scowled as though she might have fallen off her rocker. 'Magic is for lots of things, as you well know! To make life easier. To heal. For fun. For throwing the web out of balance and finding other worlds to exploit.'

Ava huffed in frustration. 'But ... why?'

Billy crossed his arms and legs, balancing on one foot and pouting, deep in thought. He narrowed his eyes as though he'd genuinely never considered it, then shrugged. 'Why anything?'

'Urgh.' Ava dusted off her hands and returned to the desk, looking down at the vicious scalpel and twisted length of wood lying there. 'Why were these in the package Novak left for me?' The house shook, as it always did when she mentioned the package. 'Did you give it to Novak?' she asked, looking up at the sloped attic ceiling, speaking to the house. It shook a little, as though purring.

Billy leaned his elbows on the desk and rested his chin on his hands, eyeing the mysterious magical objects. 'You'll have to ask Novak if you want answers.'

Ava's heart lurched. She had mixed feelings about meeting the man who'd abandoned her into B's care. 'When?'

Billy tapped his fingers on his cheeks. 'Oh, I don't know.' He let silence settle, Ava not filling it, hoping for more, but then he yawned and shook his shoulders. 'Nap time.'

Ava pulled out a book on root systems, trying not to be disappointed, while Billy rushed from the room. She settled down in an armchair and lost herself in the book for who knew how long, not moving until it was dark outside and Kush appeared in the doorway. Whereas Billy's attention span was short, Ava's was the opposite. She would regularly pour over problems and pages for hours, lost in the search for any tiny nugget of useful information until Kush found a way to entice her away. But today, when he interrupted, his features were serious, and her stomach sank.

'Hey,' she said, catching his fingers between hers as he reached her side. 'Everything okay?' She stood and tipped her head from side to side, stretching out her neck, their fingers still entwined.

He hesitated, fighting some internal battle, then said quietly, 'Have you given any thought to what happens next?'

She stilled. 'Next?' A million images raced through her mind. The two of them married with little children running around, the two of them living together in the Clouds, the two of them hiding somewhere in the Atlas Tree and Ava sneaking off to learn from the physics there.

Kush puffed out a heavy breath that did nothing to ease the tension in his shoulders. 'I'm, well, I guess I'm bored, Ava. Of course I want to be here with you, but there are only so many irrigation systems I can build and so many laps of the pool I can swim. I'm not someone who likes to sit still, and it's not healthy for the three of us to live here together like we are, sniping at one another, not trusting each other, helping no one.'

Not trusting each other. Those four words repeated over and over as she looked up at him. She still hadn't told him about her trip with Billy to the Atlas Tree or about the three physics she'd met there. She'd come close a few times, but every time Billy's warning had rung loud in her ears. Ava trusted Kush with her own life, but she didn't know if she could trust him with theirs, and she couldn't risk it, especially as they were the only other physics she'd met. If Billy decided to abandon her or drank himself into an early grave, they were the only contacts she had. Anyway, even if she wanted to tell Kush, too much time had passed. He'd be hurt she'd kept the secret for so long.

'I love you, Ava, but—'

'We could move to the Atlas Tree,' she blurted. 'It's big enough for us to find somewhere to hide.' He froze, looking momentarily suspicious, and her heart tugged in alarm. 'Isn't it? Billy successfully hid himself for years ... Over a decade.'

Kush's shoulders relaxed a fraction. 'Billy wasn't really hiding. The other Gods left him alone because he wasn't important enough to find.'

'Oh. So it's not possible?' She asked, even though she knew it was.

Kush considered it, staring into her eyes as the cogs in his brain turned. 'It ... might be. I could ...' He paused. 'Let me think about it.'

'Really?'

He nodded, and her lips split into a broad smile. 'I want to explore the Atlas Tree with you,' she breathed, wrapping her arms around him and squeezing elatedly.

'Ava,' he cautioned. 'Don't get excited ... Not yet. I might not be able to find a way. I won't risk you. If it's not safe ...'

'I know,' she said, tipping her head back and inviting him to kiss her. He did, and she sighed, everything about him so very very perfect. 'I love you.'

'I love you, too.'

'Just imagine,' she said, as he led her downstairs to the food Kush had prepared, 'getting out of here, discovering all the secrets we're not supposed to know, finding others to learn from ...'

He shook his head, but he was smiling when he turned back to face her. 'I told you, don't get excited.'

She threw her arms around his neck, and he lifted her down the last two steps. 'Too late,' she whispered. 'So now you have to make it happen.'

Billy was already helping himself to the soup simmering on the stove when they entered the kitchen. 'Help yourself,' Kush muttered bad temperedly, pulling two bowls from the cupboard, then filling one and handing it to Ava.

Ava sat opposite Billy at the table, a smile tugging at her lips. 'Billy,' she said, her tone playful, drawing out his name as though she needed a favor. He looked guardedly up at her. 'How do you feel about moving to the Atlas Tree?' If he came with them, it would be the best of all worlds. Billy could still teach Ava, and Kush could do ... whatever he wanted.

'Ava!' barked Kush, the ladle in his hand dripping tomato and bacon soup back into the pot.

Billy's spoon clattered to his bowl. 'What do you mean?' He looked at Ava with such fear in his eyes that a pang of guilt stole Ava's good humor. Was he worried she'd told Kush about his friends?

'We can't stay here forever,' Ava said brightly, hoping her tone didn't sound too forced. 'Kush is bored out of his mind.'

'I'm not ...' Kush put down the ladle and leaned back against the counter, crossing his arms. 'That's not what I said.'

'Okay, but either way, a change of scenery could do us all good.' She looked at Billy. 'Don't you think?'

Billy shook his head, his gaze carefully blank. 'I'm quite happy here, thank you.'

Ava's features turned skeptical. 'Teaching me and searching every nook and cranny for hidden alcohol?'

He narrowed his eyes. 'Don't judge me you little limpet.'

'Hey!' Kush snapped. 'Don't call *her* a limpet.'

Billy batted Kush's comment away with his hand. 'Oh, give it a rest. You act like you're some knight in shining armor, but really you're just Daddy's pet. What's the plan? Lure her back to the tree and deliver her to Var?'

Ava sucked in a sharp breath. 'Billy! It's me who wants to go to the tree. Kush isn't even sure it's a good idea.'

'Oh, really. Well, I can tell you for nothing it's not a good idea, and he knows that as well as I do.' Billy pointed an accusing finger at Kush. 'Or maybe his plan is to hand *me* over to Var now I've served my purpose.'

Ava covered her face with her hands. How had this conversation taken such a terrible turn? 'No one's handing anyone over to Var, Billy, and it's just an idea. Even if it happens, you don't have to come.'

Billy threw up his hands. 'And what exactly do you suggest I do instead? Rot here in this house, slowly starving?'

'You could—' Ava stopped herself as her brain caught up with her mouth.

'What?' he demanded, with a triumphant look that was also a sneer. 'Use the Atlas Stone to get food? You're going to leave that with me, are you?'

Ava lowered her head.

'No, didn't think so.'

'There's a solution to this,' said Ava, as much to herself as to Billy. 'We just need to find it.'

Billy leaned so far across the table towards her, his chest nearly knocked over his soup. 'Var wants me dead. That's the only way this ends. And he wants you dead, too.'

Kush let out a frustrated growl. 'It doesn't have to be like that.'

Billy jumped to his feet and faced Kush, his chair scraping loudly across the stone floor. 'If you're stupid enough to believe that, your father has you exactly where he wants you. But then, you think the Federation is all kittens and rose petals, so that's exactly how stupid you are.'

Ava winced. She shouldn't have asked Billy like this, and now she had to find a way to undo the damage she'd done. 'Billy, there's no need for—'

'They're going to kill me!' Billy wrapped his arms as far around himself as he could and rocked from side to side. 'But first, they'll experiment on me. They'll pump me for information, desperately searching for ways to find their souls. That's what they'll be doing to poor old B right this very second—if she's even still alive.' His eyes bulged.

'Billy!' cried Ava, trying to sound supportive but not quite managing it. 'No one's going to make you do anything you don't want to do. All I'm saying is that we need a plan. We can't stay here forever.'

Billy went unnaturally still, his hands pressed against his shoulder blades. 'Why not?'

Ava gave a disbelieving huff. 'Because Kush has run out of things to do, you're running out of things to teach me, and I have no desire to spend my whole life rotting between these four walls.'

'So now you've sucked me dry, you'll cast me aside and find a better teacher, is that right?'

'If I have anything to do with it,' said Kush.

Ava rounded on him with imploring eyes. 'Kush!'

Kush gave an exasperated head shake, then said through gritted teeth, 'But nobody's going to hand you to my father or tell the Gods where you are.'

Ava nodded encouragingly at Billy. 'And no one's casting you aside. We're a family, the three of us, and you don't throw your family to the wolves.' Ava was surprised to find she meant it. She'd grown attached to Billy, although Atlas only knew why.

But Billy cocked his head conceitedly, like a poker player about to reveal a winning hand. 'And who is Kush's family, Ava?'

Oh, shit. She hadn't thought that through. 'No, I—'

'*Ava* is my family,' said Kush. Ava's chest constricted.

Billy pouted. 'Only Ava?'

Ava knew she should step in, that she should tell Billy to stop, but she didn't because she wanted to hear Kush's answer more. She was being ridiculous. Of course she wasn't his only family—she wasn't even his true family. He had a mother and a father, a godfather, and probably a small army of other relations. And yet ...

Kush's eyes met hers. 'Ava matters most.'

Her heart swelled.

'But we don't throw any of our family to the wolves,' said Billy, bludgeoning them over the head with his point, 'even if they're not our favorites. Wasn't that what you meant, Ava dear?'

'That's not what I said!'

Billy lifted his hands to his hips. 'No? Care to clarify?'

But Ava didn't know what to say. Whatever she came up with he would find a way to twist. She'd grown up in a tavern, neglected and alone, she had no experience with conversations like this one.

Billy raised an eyebrow in mocking challenge. 'Didn't think so.' He headed for the door.

'Right on cue,' said Kush, pushing himself upright. 'As soon as things get difficult, what do you do? You run, hide, bury your head in a bottle, or stand aside and watch while others commit atrocious acts.'

Billy froze, then turned his head to face Kush. 'Fuck off, *demi*-God. We both know you'll run to Daddy and leave Ava behind the first chance you get. You crave his validation, his approval. You even killed a man for it, did you not?'

Ava's stomach sank, knowing how deeply the terrible task had affected Kush, how much he hated himself for it.

Kush folded his arms defensively. 'I did what I had to do, but I will never choose him over Ava. You, though ... What would you do if the price was right? Oh, right, you never *do* anything. You're a lazy, good for nothing—'

'Kush!' cried Ava. 'Can't we just—'

'Better to do nothing than trash the Atlas Web for greed,' spat Billy.

Kush took a threatening step towards him. 'You can't even see what's right in front of you! Without the Federation, the Web would be a worse place. Poverty, instability—'

'For fuck's sake, Kush! Think for yourself! It's you who can't see what's right in front of you. You've been brainwashed, and not only by Var. They have you exactly where they want you, putting your life at risk for their gain.'

'To help the Federation!'

'To help *Daddy*.'

Kush sneered. 'What would you know? You're just a leech. You do nothing but suck everyone else dry.'

Billy pressed his pointer finger repeatedly into his own chest. 'I've done plenty, which is why I know when it's best to do nothing. You're just a kid. One day you'll realize you've been played for a fool, but by then it will be too late. I own the choices I've made, and one day you'll have to do the same.'

Billy stormed from the kitchen, leaving behind a pile of emotional rubble so high, Ava wondered how they could possibly scale it. 'I'm sorry,' she whispered. 'I shouldn't have said anything, it was impulsive.'

Kush's shoulders dropped and he padded to her side, wrapping her tightly in his arms. 'Fuck him. This is your house and you can do and say what you please.' He pulled back, cupping her face. 'And I meant what I said. You are the most important person in my life.'

Ava's mouth went dry as she looked up into his blue, blue eyes, relieved he wasn't angry with her. 'Same.'

He slid the pad of his thumb across her bottom lip, and her lips parted, her eyes fluttering closed. 'But Ava ...' Her eyes flew open, her heart rate rocketing because his tone was a serious concern. He dropped his hand, and she almost grabbed it, desperate not to lose his touch, although something in his features warned her not to. 'Billy is no family of mine.'

CHAPTER FIFTY-FIVE
DIO

'IT HAS TO BE *me*,' insisted Bianca, following Dio like a stray dog.

Dio widened her eyes in irritation. She'd never liked her daughter-in-law, and now the blasted woman was ruining even this. 'No,' said Dio, for what felt like the hundredth time. Dio had tried to get rid of Bianca by fetching a carriage to take her to Spruce, but Bianca had refused to take the bait, deciding that going through the gate was preferable, convinced Pixy would be waiting on the other side.

The area before Alter Bridge was a crush of humanity, but a quiet hush settled as they passed through the channel the guards had cleared through the middle of the crowd. An occasional, 'Thank you,' or, 'May the Goddess save you,' floated quietly on the air, but unfortunately, as soon as they stepped onto the bridge itself, Bianca's incessant whining resumed.

Dio squared her shoulders and blocked out Bianca's voice. This was Dio's moment, clad in the purple of her people, anxious excitement gripping her chest. The sun was setting and the bridge had never looked so splendid; it was perfect.

Bianca grabbed her arm. 'Let me go, Dio. Do you have no compassion?'

Dio stopped dead, then spun with lightning speed, moving away so she had space to whack her cane across Bianca's chest.

Bianca doubled over, wheezing and spluttering as she tried to catch her breath.

'The rules are the rules,' Dio said in a deathly whisper. 'You are not born of the Alter line. And if you are so concerned about the welfare of your daughter, perhaps you should have ridden at speed to Spruce instead of buzzing in my ear like an irksome fly.

'I will let you walk the bridge with me out of respect for my dead son, who, for some unfathomable reason, loved you. But when the gate opens, you will stand behind my guards, and if you utter one peep between here and there, they will escort you off the bridge. Are we clear?'

Bianca's face pinched, reminding Dio of a furious toddler, but she bowed her head and muttered, 'Yes.'

'Good.'

The walk to the Toll Gate went quickly, Dio's excitement growing with every passing pace. This was the kind of adventure she'd always longed for, bigger and more glorious than anything Celestl had to offer. And if stepping through the gate spelled death, well, so be it. She was old, and she was tired of her monotonous life and the war-mongering men who dominated it. It was a risk she was happy to take just to see the other side. Perhaps she'd even meet the Goddess herself.

Dio stopped a few paces from the gate, looking back over her shoulder to ensure Bianca was behind her guards. The gate called to Dio, so much so she barely registered the administrator from the temple who was already waiting under the Alterwood wand. Dio's eyes snagged on the magical object and then on the carpet of little white flowers adorning the roots around the gate.

'We thank you for your sacrifice,' the administrator said piously, then bowed her head low.

'Oh, come now,' snapped Dio, 'it's what my family's here for.' Her fingers itched to snatch the wand, to get this over with before anything could stand in her way, but the gate was not yet open.

The administrator half rose, seeming unsure of what to say next, but if she said anything, Dio didn't hear because the gate was starting to glow around the edges.

Behind her, Bianca gasped, and Dio whirled around to ensure the woman was contained—Bianca was nothing if not resourceful. Satisfied, Dio returned her attention to the root gate, her heart thrumming in a frantic rhythm, anxious for the gate to let her pass, some part of her worried this was all a ruse, that the greatest adventure of her life was nothing but a cruel hoax by an uncaring deity, that it would be snatched away.

But then the sound of bells tolled once more, lighter this time, and although Dio couldn't see from where the sound came, it resonated through the wood beneath her feet and up into her soul.

It was happening. This was it. She was about to leave Celestl forever. She would never see her family again. The thought sent a pang of melancholy through Dio's chest because Hale, Maria, John, and Pixy had been the only true light in her recent years, even if they were a troublesome lot.

The administrator said some words Dio couldn't decipher, then stepped back and left her alone. The light around the gate burned bright and vivid, and all thoughts flew from Dio's mind, no room for anything but awe.

Dio reached up and snatched the wand with greedy fingers, and it released without protest, a shiver of something powerful coursing through her as her skin made contact with the wood.

And then the gate swung open, and she could see something green beyond—perhaps a garden—bathed in light as though it were midday on the other side.

A commotion started behind her, and Bianca's screams pierced the otherwise reverent moment, but Dio refused to take her eyes off her future for even a heartbeat, worried if she did, the gate would snap shut and steal it away. She gripped the precious wand even harder and stepped quickly across the threshold, practically floating on the swell of elation bubbling up inside because finally, finally, the greatest adventure of her life had begun.

CHAPTER FIFTY-SIX
SOPHIE

PANIC AND FEAR GRIPPED Sophie as Hale swept her along the bridge towards Laurow's Toll Gate. It was an emotion more potent than any she'd felt before, all consuming, robbing her of thoughts and making her breaths staccato things that didn't have a hope of sustaining her. So she was dizzy, too, the world floating in and out of focus, and she heard only a handful of the words spoken by her father and mother and Hale, understanding none of them.

She registered another figure by the gate—an old man wearing robes of the temple—an administrator, she realized. She hadn't expected to see one here, but it made sense, she supposed, that something so important as a sacrifice to the Goddess should be independently verified and officially committed to the annals.

The administrator bowed his head. 'We thank you for your sacrifice,' he said gravely.

Sophie looked at the bald spot on the top of his head and her legs suddenly gave way so she slumped to the wooden slats beneath her feet. 'I can't ...' Her breaths were frantic. 'I can't ... breathe ... Hale ... I ...'

Hale crouched in front of her, pulling the thin burgundy fabric of the skimpy dress her mother had insisted she wear over her bare legs. It felt alien now, the Laurow style. Somehow she'd grown accustomed to Alter's fashion in the short time she'd been there ... Such a short time ... A time that was over.

Her chest heaved in and out, her lips tingling, as were her hands and feet, and she wondered if she would pass out, her mind dizzy, nothing making any sense. Hale had said he had a plan, but they were by the gate, and ... Goddess ... it had started to glow. She clamped her eyes shut and clenched her hands together.

But Hale held her hands, easing them apart, then forced her to look into his eyes, encouraging her to take longer breaths, to slow down, to forget everything but him for a moment. But how could she? This was their *last* moment together. Probably the last moments of her life!

'Sophie,' said Hale, stroking her hair. 'Sophie, it's okay. It's going to be okay.'

It wasn't going to be okay. Nothing was okay!

Hale moved to sit behind Sophie, his legs on either side of hers, cocooning her in his arms. His chest came flush against her back, and something in her eased, slowed, felt right. So when his lips moved against her ear, she thought she heard the words he spoke ... but, 'What?' she breathed, finally able to suck in a full, nourishing breath, a terrible, numbing kind of hope taking hold of her insides.

'It is time,' said her father's disdainful voice. 'She's fine. Get her up. And no one is to hear about this embarrassment, am I clear?'

Of course, his reputation was his primary concern. The thought steeled Sophie, especially now she knew Hale's plan.

The journey across the bridge had taken a lot out of her father, and he leaned heavily on the barrier at the edge, unused to walking anywhere, let alone the distance of two trips to a Toll Gate in one day.

'Up!' shrieked Linella, her voice merging with the ringing of the Toll Bells. She rushed forward and grabbed Sophie's arm. 'It's opening! Now! You must go now!'

Hale helped Sophie to her feet, and then he strode to the gate and seized the wand, seeming a little surprised when it came away in his hand.

'No!' Linella screeched, throwing herself towards him and snatching it from his grip. 'You may not touch the wand of Laurow.' Sophie moved closer, her eyes wide, her blood standing still in her veins.

'Neither of you may touch the wand!' cried the administrator.

Linella tried to press the wand into Sophie's grasp, but in a move so quick Sophie hardly saw it, Hale grabbed Linella, spun her, and shoved her with brutal force through the now fully open gate.

The gate's bright light extinguished as it snapped shut, and they waited with bated breath to see if Linella would be rejected by the Goddess. She was a member of Laurow's first family by marriage only, not by blood.

Still nothing happened, but only then did it occur to Sophie that perhaps the Goddess would make all of Celestl suffer because of this. Perhaps the ground would shake or the waterfalls would stop or the bridge would break and they would plummet to their deaths.

But nothing happened. At least, not yet ...

Sophie turned to face her father, to see what he would do, if he would punish Hale for tampering with the Laurow sacrifice, but it was the open-mouthed administrator who spoke first. 'This is not right,' he sputtered, seemingly in shock. 'Unprecedented. An insult to the Goddess. We will suffer because of this, mark my words.'

Sophie's father shrugged as though he didn't give a damn, then pushed himself off the rail. 'Well, this one,' he said, pointing to Sophie, 'is more useful to me than that one anyway. We must have a Laurow-Alter heir to fulfil the pact, after all. What is done is done, and now I have much to do. The balance of my home will be skewed without Linella, and I must select a new wife without delay.'

He turned and started slowly back across the bridge, and it seemed to Sophie that he had a new spring in his step. The administrator followed, jabbering on about reports and inquiries and records, leaving Sophie and Hale alone.

'This was your plan all along?' Sophie demanded. Her legs threatened to give out again, her head swimming, and she clutched at Hale to keep herself upright.

Hale pulled her in front of him, wrapping an arm around her waist and cupping her cheek. 'Are you okay?'

'I'm f——' But she wasn't fine, not by a long shot. 'I just ... I ... I think ... I ...' Her body shook as it finally began to sink in. 'I'm still here,' she said, looking up into his amber eyes, tears spilling down her cheeks. 'I'm still here. We're still here, Hale. We're married ...'

Hale smiled tenderly down at her. 'We're still here,' he agreed, and then he kissed her.

CHAPTER FIFTY-SEVEN
PIXY

As Pixy stood before Spruce's Toll Gate, she prayed to the Goddess. They'd decked her out in the dark, drab green of Spruce Blade, her necklace the only thing she had left from her homeland, the disk of Alter purple warm against her chest. But even though she was a child of Alter—meaning her sacrifice most likely wouldn't work—she prayed that it would.

Please, Goddess, allow me to travel through your gate. Save me from the man they call my husband.

The man in question conversed pompously with the young, female administrator from the temple, standing too close—as was his way—lecherous and disgusting. He'd forced himself on Pixy one single time, saying he had no choice, that it was his duty to consummate their marriage. In his arrogance, he'd made the mistake of rolling off her when he'd finished, lying panting on his back by her side. She hadn't hesitated to punch him so hard in the balls he'd been impotent ever since.

She'd left him squealing like a pig, rolling around in agony, and had announced loudly to the servants that he required a large team of healers as she returned to her own rooms and locked the doors. It had been the last time he'd underestimated her, and he'd never tried to touch her again.

Her sacrifice was good for them both. They would escape each other, although she pitied the poor woman he chose next, especially if he ever regained the function she'd taken from him. How he'd managed to keep the story from his father's ears, Pixy would never know.

The sun sat ponderously on the horizon as Spruce's Toll Gate began to glow, a streak of blazing white light shooting around its circular edge. Pixy felt as though the light had circled her heart, warming it, giving her hope. The Goddess would accept her. She would. It was happening!

Tiny white blooms grew overhead, and it was yet another sign. The Goddess surely wouldn't send flowers unless she was happy with the sacrifice. There was no mistaking that Pixy *was* the sacrifice, for everyone else had moved back, not wanting to get too close lest the gate's magic suck them inside. *Cowards.*

Pixy exhaled the breath she'd been holding. It was all going to be okay. It really was. She wondered briefly if she would see the other sacrifices once she stepped through, and who they were, but then the gate began to open, and all thoughts were wiped from her mind as she focused on its progress.

The gate swiveled from a point almost midway through the circular structure, so holes appeared on both sides, and Pixy's eyes flitted back and forth between the two, desperate for her first glimpse of what lay beyond. If death awaited her.

The Goddess wouldn't kill her, would she? Pixy had dutifully worshipped the deity her whole life, even when her family had called her foolish. And why would the Goddess waste the lives of her wand-bearers? It made no sense for her to do so.

The wand. *Shit.* She'd almost forgotten. She reached up and grabbed it, pulling hard, a sharp pulse of fear expanding through her chest as she worried it wouldn't come free. It came away in her hand just as the gate stopped turning, and she clutched it to her chest as her eyes locked onto a lush, green garden beyond. *Not death.* This was not death! And as euphoria filled her up, she ran.

CHAPTER FIFTY-EIGHT
AVA

A NIGHT LATER, AVA sat in the solarium with Kush, lounging on a day bed, Ava holding tight because he'd been avoiding her all day, and in her gut she knew he was going to tell her something she didn't want to hear. She pressed her face into his chest, and he tightened his grip, seeming to be clinging to her for dear life in the same way she was to him. That only made Ava's fear worse. She breathed him in, her heart feeling strangely like it was breaking, although she didn't know why.

He gently tipped her head back and kissed her, the kiss desperate, deep and poignant, the kind of kiss that stole one's mind, and when he finally released her, resting his forehead against hers, they were both panting.

Light from the light stones danced off the crystal-clear water of the swimming pool and the glass of the dark windows, the green plants and tactile furniture softening the harsh lines of the walls. The space was usually a balm to Ava's soul, but not tonight.

'What is it?' Ava whispered. She didn't want to hear whatever he had to say, but her stomach was bunched in knots so tight she thought she might be sick.

He brushed his lips across her forehead. 'I have to go back to the Atlas Tree alone,' he said, his grip tightening on her as though scared she might run away. 'I want you to come with me, and I hate the idea of leaving you here with Billy, but it's not safe. I've wracked my brains, but any way I look at it, I've been away for so long, it's impossible to say what my father and the other Gods will do when I return, what they might have done in the meantime, and some of them ... They're not nice people, Ava, and I don't know what they'd do to you if they found you.'

Ava shivered, and he stroked his hand up and down her bare arm as though she was cold. She wasn't cold, she was terrified.

'I need time to find a place for you,' he continued, 'for us … somewhere safe. Perhaps we could keep you hidden in the tree—only a handful of people know who you are—but me? Everyone knows who I am. Father parades me around, one step behind him, and I'm the God of a world. I sit on the stage every year on Federation Day. My face is well known, and I don't want to be the reason you get caught.'

Caught. Like an animal. Hunted by Kush's father. The man Kush worked for. The man whose domain Kush was returning too.

'If I could, I would take you with me, but I can't, and I can't sit around here any longer like a spare part, doing nothing of use. There's still no sign of your parents' Atlas Stone …'

Ava tensed. Was that the real reason he'd been there all along? She'd never got that impression before, but now he was leaving her, going back to the tree, maybe even to his old life …

'I'll leave my stone with you, of course. You need it. I'll tell father you hid it, that I couldn't find it and that's why I was away so long.'

Ava sat bolt upright, forcing him to release her. 'You're going to see him?'

Kush gave her a perplexed look. 'How could I not? He'll know almost as soon as I'm back in the tree. He has spies everywhere.'

Not everywhere, she thought. Not wherever Billy's friends lived. But now, more than ever, she couldn't tell him that, and she'd been right to keep them a secret. Billy had been right about Kush. He was running back to his father just like Billy had said he would. Ava moved across the daybed, putting clear space between them.

He reached for her hand, but she pulled farther away. 'If I pretend to work with him, I can help you, Ava. I can find Novak and ask him about the past, about what happened to your parents, the package he left for you, if he has your Atlas Stone …'

The Atlas Stone, there it was again.

The house shook, and for some reason, that made tears pool in Ava's eyes.

'Only pretend to work with him?' she choked out. 'You've said it a hundred times, you believe in what he's doing.'

'Ava!' He reached for her again, but she stood and paced to the window, folding her arms across her chest. 'How can you think that? I believe in the Federation. I believe it makes people's lives better because I've seen it, and you have, too. But that's not the same as believing in ...'

She looked over her shoulder at him, but he couldn't even say it. 'Your father and everything he stands for?'

'Please,' he said, his eyes begging her to be reasonable, to agree to his plan, to tell him she understood.

But she didn't understand.

'I'll come back every chance I get. I'll say I'm visiting my mother, and I'll send notes, and you can work with Billy to hone your magic, and when I have everything in place, I'll come and get you. And I'll find out if Billy's stories are true, if we can trust him, if Novak—'

The house shook harder, and the chandelier over the pool swung so wildly, three light stones fell off into the water.

Kush stood, taking a few steps towards Ava. 'I can be so much more useful if I'm out in the open.'

A tutting noise came from behind them, and Ava turned to find Billy sashaying into the solarium in a flowing kaftan that had definitely belonged to Polly. 'What have you two done to upset our dear old abode?' Billy asked, perching on a daybed.

'Kush is going back to the tree. Alone.'

Billy raised an eyebrow in mock surprise. 'Is he now? I'm shocked.'

Ava didn't even have the energy to chastise him, and she didn't want to, anyway.

Kush's forehead scrunched into a forlorn frown. 'It's the only way.'

'Is it?' said Billy, in an animated, over-the-top manner, as though speaking to a small child, a tone designed to rile.

'What would you have me do?' Kush demanded. 'Stay here like this for years on end?'

'We could go together,' said Ava, hating the tremor in her voice, the desperation.

'We can't.' Kush implored her to believe him with his eyes. He moved to her side and tentatively took her hand. She let him have it because soon he would be gone; he'd obviously made up his mind. 'Father has spies everywhere. I can't think of a single place that would be safe either in the tree or in any of the worlds I've visited.'

She lowered her head, searching for another way, but she could think of nothing. Kush couldn't stay in the house much longer—he'd already run out of things to do—and according to him, she couldn't go to the tree. She desperately wanted to tell him there were places in the tree where others successfully hid, but those places were only safe because people like Var didn't know about them ... People like Kush.

Billy threw himself back onto the daybed, arms and legs outstretched like a starfish. 'He has spies everywhere, controls everything, and still you want to return to his side. How can you believe a man like that has good intentions? That he wants to make the Federation fair for everyone?'

Kush closed his eyes for a beat. 'If the Federation is really as bad as you say, and if Father is as selfish—'

'Oh, he is.'

Kush yanked himself free of Ava's grasp and rubbed his hand across his face. 'This is why I have to go!'

Billy barked a laugh. 'Don't blame me, pickle. But I suppose you could be useful and try to free B while you're there. Although for that you'd have to defy Daddy and the other Gods, so ...'

Ava suddenly felt like everything was going too fast, like Kush might storm out and she might never see him again. 'Billy,' she snapped, 'you're not helping.'

Billy rolled over onto his stomach and gave a full body shrug.

Ava glared. 'Or maybe Kush should let B rot.' She turned back to Kush. 'But I do want to speak to Novak.' Again, the house shook.

Billy shot to his knees and threw up his arms. 'Alright, alright! We get it! You don't like the man.' The house shook once more, this one a short, huffy vibration. Billy shimmied as though proud he'd brought the house in line, then sat back onto his heels. 'But B is your family, Ava, she raised you, and I believe it was you who said we don't throw family to the alligators, was it not?' He gave her a look of pure challenge.

'No, Billy, B killed my family, then used me as her slave.' Ava turned her attention back to Kush, who was watching her closely, studying her face. 'So you get to have all the fun while I'm stuck here with Billy?' Her tone was a light, fictional layer atop a raging sea of loss and disappointment. If Billy hadn't been there, she might well have thrown herself at Kush's feet and begged him to take her with him, even though she knew he never would. 'What am I supposed to do without you?' she whispered.

Kush pulled her into his arms, and she offered no resistance. 'I'll find a place for you,' he said, his voice barely more than a murmur, 'for us both. But it has to be safe.'

'Oh, dearie, don't be such a sad turtle. Just think of all the things you can do without him!' Billy's words smashed their moment of intimacy. 'Your options are endless.' He held up his hand, ticking them off on his fingers. 'Physic, web wanderer, lady of leisure—my personal favorite—potionist, socialite, cartographer, web master, portal pirate ...'

Despite Kush's imminent departure, one stood out, calling to her. Ava wanted to be a sorcerer, a magicist, a physic. That's what her body itched to do. Her blood sang when she used magic, just like it had for her mother, and she wanted to learn, to help people, to solve the problems of the web. 'I want to develop my magic.' And maybe with Kush gone, Billy would introduce her to other physics ...

'Fucking Atlas,' cried Billy, throwing himself back onto the daybed once more. 'Of course you do. The world at your feet, and that's what you choose.'

Kush stroked Ava's back. 'I'll find someone to teach you.'

'Ha! Good luck with that,' Billy said dryly.

'I promise,' said Kush, breathing the words into her ear. 'And I love you. Always. No matter what.'

Ava squeezed her eyes shut, wanting time to stop, wanting to hold him there with her. 'You're going now?'

She felt him nod. 'I'll go to my mother's, then use the portal.'

'Not taking the stone?' asked Billy.

'It's Ava's for as long as she needs it.'

'Well, I suppose that's decent of you,' Billy said begrudgingly.

Kush led Ava to the hall and she waited while he retrieved his long leather coat from the closet, watching as he slid it on in a smooth, practiced movement, and then he kissed her like they might never kiss again. She committed every press of his lips to memory, knowing she wouldn't see him for weeks, months, maybe ever ... When he broke the kiss, it seemed to take physical effort, and he crushed her to his chest.

'I love you,' he said, squeezing her hand.

Tears blurred her vision. 'I love you, too.'

He slid his hand through hers, her fingertips kissing his perfect skin one moment, then nothing but open air the next, and a tear slid down her cheek as he opened the front door. He looked back for a brief moment, his features those of a tortured man, and then the door clicked closed and he was gone, the house seeming to amplify the noise of his feet walking away, adding to Ava's torment.

Silence descended, punctuated only by the deafening tick of the clock in the drawing room, and Ava's whole body felt wrung out, shaky, in shock. She stared at the door for many long moments—she had no idea how many—and then Billy stepped up beside her and huffed.

Ava turned her face slowly to look at him and found his head tipped to one side, a grim smile on his lips. 'I told you so.'

She balled her hands into tight, painful fists, her arms rigid at her side. In that moment, she saw Billy in a new light, perhaps the light Kush had seen him in all along. He was nothing, and she didn't need him. She didn't need anyone.

Ava sneered, pain and anger mixing like a toxic fuel in her chest, or perhaps a poison spelling her demise. 'Get the fuck out of my house you lowlife.' And then she turned and headed for the stairs, for her bed, where she fully intended to wrap herself in the smell of Kush and wallow in her pain.

Chapter Fifty-Nine
Maria

Maria stiffened her spine, holding her head high as she approached the bridge, Elex by her side. The search for Rosalind had been fruitless, just as Maria had known deep down it would be. Rosalind had lived in Oshala her whole life, so of course she had places to hide.

The others had repeated over and over that maybe Rosalind would turn up at the bridge, but Maria had seen that for the false hope it was, too. Only one solution remained: Maria would be Oshe's sacrifice.

But she would not go meekly. She would show the people of Oshe the kind of first lady they were losing, and that this was a sacrifice for Elex, also. It would serve as a reminder to those who doubted him that he was a man who deserved their trust. A man who did the right thing even when it came at great personal cost.

The thought almost made Maria stumble—hurting Elex—and then her mind took a downward spiral because it occurred to her that he wouldn't mourn her forever. He would take lovers, remarry, have children, as was his duty as the leader of a Blade. She bit her lip, the sharp sting forcing her mind to stop. Much as she would like to rage and cry and scream at the injustice of it all, she would do none of those things. She would be strong, and make him and her people proud.

Elex's brooding presence was a comfort, as was Nicoli, a pace behind. She was glad he was there, that she would be lucky enough to say goodbye to her best friend as well as her husband.

Maria recalled some of the adventures they'd had together, climbing trees, spying on Danit, triffling, and then her mind turned to what she would face on the other side of the gate. The land of the Gods? Would she become a servant to the Goddess? A slave? Or perhaps it was far simpler than that. Perhaps she was walking to her death.

'I'm sorry,' said Elex, taking Maria's hand now they'd left the crowd behind. He'd already apologized a thousand times since sunrise, but apologies wouldn't save her, and this wasn't his fault.

'Morbid realities aside,' said Nicoli, 'I must admit I'm interested to see the mechanism inside the gate.'

It took a moment for his words to register, but when they did, Maria couldn't help but huff a laugh. 'I'm so glad my demise provides an educational opportunity for you.'

'Oh, good. I knew you would be.'

Maria turned her head and gave her oldest friend a broad smile because this was the Nicoli she knew and loved, the light-hearted, often flippant, opportunistic inventor version of himself. He'd disappeared since the pact had come about, yet here he was again, finally. Maria returned her eyes to the path ahead and blinked back tears. She would not cry.

'Perhaps you can figure out a way to pry it open so you can rescue me from the evil Goddess.'

'Careful,' said Nicoli, 'she's probably listening.'

Maria's mouth split into a wide smile. 'I'm sure she has better things to do than listen to your nonsensical whittering.'

'Yeah, you're probably right. It's not like I keep this place running or anything.'

Maria squeezed Elex's fingers. 'Your head has grown larger than is healthy, my friend.'

They went on like that for the remainder of the walk, Maria clutching Elex with everything she had, Nicoli distracting her from her fate. But too soon they were at the gate, where an administrator was already waiting.

The administrator gave a pompous nod. 'We thank you for your sacrifice.'

'Thank you,' said Maria, and then Nicoli surprised her by pulling her into a deep, solid hug.

'I love you, Maria,' he whispered in her ear. 'I always have, even when you were being a total ass. Even now.'

Tears sprang free as Maria hugged him tighter. 'Nicoli—'

Nicoli kissed her cheek, then stepped back, making space for Elex while he moved towards the gate, which had started to emit a white light from the edges. 'Fascinating,' said Nicoli, leaning close to the gate, studying it closely.

Maria and Elex crashed together, pressing themselves to one another as though trying to fuse their bodies, as though if the Goddess saw the strength of their love, she might spare Maria this terrible fate. But of course, it was hopeless. 'Elex—'

He kissed her like a man starved, and even though the gate was already opening, she reasoned she could steal a few more moments, so she sank into the kiss, letting herself forget for just a second, inhaling him, his big, strong arms cradling her as though they would never let her go.

They might never have stopped kissing had the administrator not let out a garbled sound of alarm. Their heads snapped apart, and Maria's teary eyes found the source of the administrator's distress: Nicoli.

'What are you doing?' said Maria, trying to move towards him, but Elex's hands were clamped around her waist, refusing to let her go.

'Elex! He's got the wand!'

'What are you doing, Nicoli?' asked Elex, his tone uncertain, but perhaps a little encouraging, too.

Nicoli gave an exaggerated shrug. 'I've had enough of this world. None of you can lead us to peace. The first families are obsessed with war and power and dominion. I can see you're happy with Elex, Maria, and if even you are now one of them, what hope is there for Celestl?'

'You can't do this,' Maria sobbed, trying to get to him, but Elex held fast.

Nicoli grinned. 'Says who?'

'Elex,' she breathed, the word choked, 'we can't do this.' But Elex said nothing, his arms still locked around her.

'She's right,' stuttered the administrator. 'Hand over the wand or there will be consequences.'

Maria looked imploringly at him. 'Nicoli, it has to be a woman!'

He barked a laugh as he backed towards the fully open gate, Toll Bells chiming all around. 'Well, Maria, I don't really give a fuck. And I want a word with the Goddess.'

Chapter Sixty
Ava

Billy disregarded Ava's order to leave, which she only knew because she could hear him clattering around downstairs. But seeing as she refused to leave her room for anything but essential reasons, and he didn't darken her door, they coexisted happily by ignoring each other. At least until, after three days in bed, and having exhausted her stack of reading material, Ava became bored.

She swung her legs out of bed and wrapped a robe around her, no doubt looking a state. She hadn't washed since before Kush left, and she didn't even bother to finger comb her hair before padding down the stairs and into the kitchen, where Billy was cooking eggs. The smell made her empty stomach growl.

'Breakfast?' asked Billy, ignoring her disheveled state.

Ava climbed onto a stool and accepted the plate he slid across to her, eating ravenously. She requested seconds, then thirds, then finally pushed her plate away, stuffed to the rafters. She washed it all down with a large mug of tea, and then looked up at Billy, who was surveying her from behind his coffee cup.

'Are you ... feeling okay?' he ventured, seeming to cringe as he said the words, compassion apparently making him uncomfortable.

'We don't have to talk about it,' said Ava, wiping her mouth. 'But now Kush has gone, you can tell me more about those people who saved you in the tree.'

Billy tapped his fingers on the counter. 'Ava ... I'm not ... How to put it ... I'm not in good standing with that lot.'

'And yet they saved you, which indicates you once were, or at least that you have some kind of joint history. And one of them has my eyes ...' She leaned forward, resting her chin on her fists. 'I'd like to know more about that.' Ava had shoved the niggling feeling that there was more to those eyes aside for weeks, telling herself she'd imagined the close similarity, and not wanting to risk Kush overhearing her and Billy discussing it. But now there was nothing to hold her back.

Billy's tapping stopped. 'What do you mean?'

'The one with purple hair, the young one, she had my eyes.'

He looked away. 'No.'

'I need to go back there.'

'No, you don't.'

'I want to go back.'

Billy folded his arms across his chest, his shoulders hunching inwards, making himself small. 'That wouldn't be wise.'

Ava scowled. 'Why don't they like you?'

He sighed. 'Because they blame me for ... Oh, well ... everything, really. Enabling your parents by being their guinea pig, keeping secrets from the Cloud families, allowing B to kill your parents, then lying low, then not telling them where you were—even though I didn't know to start—then drinking all their best booze. Not to mention, they're annoyed I won't get back to brewing. Beverage quality has diminished since I scuttled away—scuttled was their word, not mine. And now they're probably angry because I'm helping you.'

'Then why did they save you?'

Billy reeled back as though shocked. 'They're not barbarians!'

'But they banished you?'

He made a weary noise, like it was too much trouble to explain.

'Who are they?'

His eyes avoided hers, like he wished he was anywhere else. 'Billy, tell me, or I'll go back there right now and ask.'

'Urgh, well, you know how I told you that only some of the Cloud-dwellers were made into Gods?'

'Yes,' said Ava. 'Mainly the ones the same age as my parents.'

'Yes, well, that meant the other Cloud families could still have children. But, scared they'd be held captive and forced to breed—which would never have happened ... Well, probably not, but, anyway—they were scared and angry and some of them fled the Clouds and started their own community away from the limelight.

'They still attend Federation Day, and the Synod—those eligible—and unlike Var and his besties, they still take their duties seriously. They just have to do it from the shadows and be careful not to get caught. The place we went is a kind of research laboratory.'

Ava's chest tugged tight with hope. 'So they are physics?'

Billy gave a little nod. 'Probably the best we have left.'

Excitement filled her up. 'Then I have to go back.'

'No.'

'But you said it yourself, we're reaching the end of your knowledge.'

He shook his head in short staccato movements. 'They despise you almost as much as they despise me.'

Ava waved her hand. 'I'm sure they're reasonable. They don't even know me. They despise the idea of me, but once I show them what I can do and what I've learned in the short time since we last met.'

He narrowed his eyes. 'And what about Kush?'

She stilled. *Kush*. It was still so raw, so painful. 'We can come back here every night to sleep, and we'll leave him notes when we're gone, but we can't sit here and do nothing in the meantime.'

'I can, quite happily, I assure you.'

'Billy! You can't criticize Var and the Federation and whatever else the Gods get up to if you're not willing to do something about it!'

He leaned casually back against the counter. 'I think you'll find I can. Have been for years.'

'So you'll just let the web crumble?'

His eyes widened. 'All I want is my soul back and a peaceful life, preferably surrounded by good liquor. Is that really so much to ask?'

'Perhaps not for another person, but that's not the life you have, and wishing it to be different won't make it so.' Ava knew all about wishing. It had never given her anything but a headache and a sour mood. 'You have to get off your backside and work for what you want, I'm afraid.'

'Darling, acting like a grown-up doesn't suit you. Please stop.'

'Someone has to.'

He leaned forward and gave her a salacious look. 'Lies.'

Ava took a long, deep breath, then hummed an exhale. 'I'm going to the echo chamber.' Billy raised a judgmental eyebrow, but she ignored him. She missed Kush, and if she was about to beg the echo chamber to show her some glimpse of him, what was so wrong with that? 'And unless you give me a good reason not to,' she said as she headed for the door, 'tomorrow morning I'm going to find your friends in the tree, whether you come or not.'

Billy tisked at Ava's retreating back, but the door slammed closed before she heard his answer. She put him from her mind as she lay on the flower bed in the echo chamber and focused on thoughts of Kush, but the damned chamber didn't show her a single glimpse of him. It showed her nothing for a long while, and then it dropped a notebook in her lap. She thought at first the potion she'd taken to aid with opening her mind had made her hallucinate it, but when she closed her fingers, she found it quite real. She pulled out a light stone and flipped the notebook open, the handwriting unmistakably her mother's.

It was less clear than the other works in her mother's hand, this one filled with emotion, crossings out, and doodles that seemingly bore little resemblance to anything magical. The writing was dotted about in small fragments, an idea here and there, a shopping list, an innermost thought. It was so much at odds with the calm, rigorous, brilliant physic Ava had been introduced to in the other books, the work of a dreamer and artist, someone human, fragile, vulnerable.

Grandmama brought me here to the Clouds—to the top of the world—but I don't belong. They look at me with contempt in their eyes, seeing a social climber, a gold-digger, but I'm not here for gold. I'm here because Grandmama gave me no choice.

Ava flipped the page, gobbling up the words.

Grandmama may be brilliant, but she hates me because she's not as brilliant as me. She tries to control me, to wield me like her weapon ... I wish I could say I resist, but ... how?

The word Rupert caught Ava's eye at the bottom of the page, and she scanned the words, which had been written at an angle and circled several times.

Rupert likes me. I like Novak. Novak's scared of Rupert.

Then opposite: *Everyone here has a motive. What's Rupert's? His eyes light up every time he sees me.*

Then: *Found it: Rupert loves power and he's scared of losing it. And he wants to fuck me. I'm not sure he's ever done it before. Should I tell him I have? Would that get us thrown out of the Clouds? Maybe I should ...*

Ava flipped through the pages, seeing snippets about her mother's first kiss with Rupert—after her first kiss with Novak—about how she felt like a fish out of water, an intruder, important only for her magic. And then how she felt trapped in her marriage.

Rupert's not so bad, I suppose. I think he might even love me or perhaps he's merely infatuated. He gets a hard on any time he sees me use my power. Unfortunately, I mean that literally. I've had to ban him from the attic. But being married to him does have its benefits. They don't treat me like a gold-digger any longer, that's for sure, or maybe it's my power that did that. They call me a perpetumot, but I like the term magic-maker more.

Rupert certainly loves his family's return to dominance, the expansion of the Federation, the new portals. I suppose my power did that, too. But what's it all for? They call the Federation one thing in public, but behind closed doors ... it's unnatural. All of it. Perhaps evil, even. We have wealth and power, more than we could ever need! For Atlas' sake, why?

Ava breathed a sigh of relief as she read those words. She'd been hesitant to believe her mother was evil, even when Billy, and her mother's other journals, had hinted otherwise. It had been easy to believe that Rupert was, because of the family he'd been born into, and Novak because he'd abandoned Ava in a hovel of a tavern with his bitter cousin, but not Polly.

Not the owner of vibrant yellow dresses. She'd never understood how her mother could be the woman Billy described, and here was proof that she wasn't, something concrete. Ava was so happy she wanted to cry.

But then: *It's all going to shit, and I have to stop it. B and Billy want their souls back. Don't they realize we have more important things to do? We need every physic we can get, every good, honest person from the Clouds. We have to stop this.*

Ava closed the book. What did that mean? She lay back on the bed of flowers and hugged the journal to her chest, staring up at the roots on the ceiling. What had her mother been trying to do, and why did she need other physics?

A small white flower sprouted from one of the roots, and hope bloomed in Ava's chest. Perhaps now the chamber would link her to Kush. But the voice when it came didn't belong to him, it belonged to a child begging for mercy. Ava shook her head, trying to make the sound leave, but then another flower bloomed, and a woman's voice accompanied it, a woman desperately seeking a trade for food.

'We have enough corn,' said another woman.

'But we need to trade! We need—'

'Next!'

Another flower, then a man's voice. 'We'll slit their throats while they sleep. They treat us like criminals, so criminals we will be.'

'We'd never get close,' said a second man.

'Then we'll die trying. They call themselves Gods, but really they're parasites.'

The voices went on and on, and Ava was frozen in place, too full of shock and sick fascination to make it stop, to leave the echo chamber. Each one was worse than the last, children dying, uprisings violently quashed, attacks on the portals, gangs forcing their way into the temples to use the healing waters reserved for the Gods.

On and on until there was no denying Billy's criticisms of the Federation, until Ava's brain could absorb no more. It was only then that the chamber finally brought her something good, children playing a harmless trick on their parents, then falling about in fits of giggles, reunited friends after months apart, singing around a crackling fire, the sound of a stream trickling over stones that lulled Ava to sleep.

When she emerged the following morning, bleary eyed, head pounding, she found Billy leaning against the apple tree, one leg crossed over the other, a coffee in his hand.

'Well?' he demanded.

Ava scowled. 'Well what?'

'What did it show you?' Billy seemed eager, energized and expectant.

She rubbed her tired eyes. 'Death, destruction, suffering ... Is that what you want to hear?'

Billy reeled as though she'd slapped him. 'Don't blame me! I don't *want* the Federation to be like this. I'm not sure we should have a federation at all!'

Ava shook her head sadly. 'But what can we do about it?'

Billy shrugged. 'Not much.'

'Then what difference does it make if I know?'

He launched to his feet. 'Knowledge is a tool, Ava.'

'Knowledge in this case is worry and guilt and ...' A division straight down the middle of her relationship with Kush. Although, Kush knew the Federation wasn't perfect. 'The chamber showed us some of it when Kush and I were in there before, but nothing like last night.'

Billy put one hand against the tree trunk and leaned against it. 'Kush doesn't want to see the bad stuff, and the chamber knew that. Still, that it showed the bad things anyway is testament to how bad it really is. Your mind is more receptive, so the chamber had free rein to show you whatever it pleased, and that will be useful when Var eventually catches up with you. Your eyes will be open, unlike poor Kushy-Kush.'

'*When* he catches up with me?' Ava's heart fluttered in panic as she fought the temptation to scan the garden for Var.

'Oh, my dear, you don't think you can outmaneuver him forever, do you? He's the most powerful man in the federated world. There's nowhere you can go that his fingers do not touch, Kush was right about that, at least.' He sighed dramatically. 'No, all we can do is fly under his bat-like spidey-senses for as long as we possibly can and deal with the consequences when he finds us.'

'No,' said Ava, refusing to believe that was her only option.

'Yes!' he said in a high-pitched tone accompanied by a patronizing nod of his head. 'Var controls the Gods, the tree, the Federation, and even the House of Portals itself ... in theory. Just be thankful you have an Atlas Stone so you can hop about as you please. Most of us aren't so lucky.'

'Then that's the place to hit him,' said Ava, her mind racing a mile a minute. 'The portals. If we can take those, we can ...' She trailed off, finding she wasn't sure how to finish her sentence.

Billy waved his hand in a circular motion, gesturing for her to continue. 'We can ...?' His tone was somewhere between condescension and mockery.

She huffed. 'Well we have to do something! It's not fair for one man to have such vast, unchecked power, especially when it's causing the kind of suffering the chamber showed me last night.'

'Ilyavra,' he said, his use of her full name making her skin prickle, 'I don't think you quite understand what you're up against. Maybe that's on me—I often forget how little you know.'

'What do you mean, *What* you're *up against*? This affects you too!'

Billy inhaled noisily, held it, then exhaled in a rush. 'Give me the stone,' he said, setting down his mug and stepping forward with his hand out.

She took a half step back, wings of panic fluttering in her chest. 'Why?'

'You should see what the portals are like. The unnatural ones, anyway. Good time of year for it, actually, when Var keeps the true state of things under wraps. Maybe seeing them will get the message through to you. I think you're a visual learner.'

Despite the sinister edge to Billy's words, Ava's heart leapt at the idea of getting out of the house, of seeing more of the Atlas Tree, and she handed over the stone. Maybe she'd even convince Billy to come with her to see his friends after they'd been to see whatever he wanted to show her. Despite her earlier threat, Ava didn't want to go alone, even though she'd memorized the coordinates.

Billy grabbed her arm. 'Stay quiet,' he said, spinning the stone, and before Ava had even had time to take a stabilizing breath, they were there, in a huge cavern of some sort, but a cavern made from roots. All around them, on the floor and domed ceiling, flowers bloomed then wilted, bloomed then wilted, in all manner of colors and shapes and sizes. It made the place feel as though it were alive, a living, breathing thing.

She looked at Billy, not sure what to do, but he put a finger to his lips and fiddled with the Atlas Stone, then handed it back to her. 'If this goes to shit, run,' he whispered, no hint of levity in him at all. In fact, she'd never seen him so serious.

'Over there is below the Atlas Tree's Bridge,' he mouthed, pointing to an opening through which Ava could see more flower-covered roots. 'It houses the portals of the federated worlds. Looks like the coast is clear. We'll go through, then turn to the right. Stick to the shadows at the edge. You'll find it shocking, but do not scream.'

Shocking? 'Billy!' she hissed, suddenly filled with fear and trepidation, desperate to know what he meant. But Billy was already moving, sauntering across the space as though meant to be there, giving Ava little choice but to follow.

They passed through the circular opening into the second cavern, and Ava's eyes flicked up to what looked like the sky above a cutout in the ceiling. Billy pulled her back into the shadow of an overhang that ringed the whole room. 'It's an illusion,' he murmured. 'We're inside the tree. When people look down, they see a lake. Works in our favor right now, but the balcony above us, and the bridge across the middle, they're real.'

Ava's eyes traced the straight lines of the wooden bridge that crossed that hole in the ceiling, then she took in the clumps of roots that rose up from the ground, twisting together into ropes that ended beside the bridge. At the top, each clump formed a large, hollow oval, the space in the middle shimmering with blue light. Portals, Ava realized.

'Natural portals,' said Billy, with a hint of wonder. 'A thing of beauty, formed by the roots over hundreds of years, bit by bit, only taking what they gave, using magic they'd inhaled from across the web. A true marvel. Most are extensions from the main portals in the House below, but still, they radiate balance, unlike those around the edge, filthy, unnatural things.'

Billy pulled Ava farther into the circular space, careful to keep them hidden under the overhang, and as her eyes slowly adjusted to the gloom, a stone dropped through her stomach, and Billy's warning not to scream hurtled to the forefront of her mind.

Shapes appeared. Human shapes with open eyes, entwined and held up by the mess of roots they were pressed against. Ava sucked in a sharp breath and clamped her hands over her mouth.

'Disgusting,' Billy hissed, Ava drawn along in his wake like a puppet on a string. 'Unnatural. Barbaric. Wrong.'

It certainly seemed that way to Ava. But ... did Kush know about this? Had he kept this from her, too?

'We should go,' said Billy, at this time of year, the succaplents are frequently checked.

'Succaplents?'

'That's what these people are called, but they run out and need replacing. Sometimes they need—Oh creeping cracklejacks.' Billy pulled Ava back against the roots, wedging them between two bodies, and she squeezed her eyes shut and clamped her lips together, telling herself to breathe. She wrapped her fingers around the Atlas Stone, ready to use it, the voices Billy had heard coming closer, and they sounded familiar.

'Please,' said a woman's voice. 'Please, don't hurt him. He didn't mean—'

'Stop, woman,' said a man, and when they appeared through the opening, Ava's suspicions were confirmed. It was Yella and Var, Kush's parents. 'I'm not going to sacrifice my own son! I need *you* to heal a succaplent.'

Yella drew back. 'Me? But what about the women of the Bridge Temple? What about—'

'The situation is delicate. I need discretion.'

'But—'

He rounded on her. 'You will heal the succaplent or I will replace them with you. Which would you prefer?' Var was entirely confident in his power, his tone more businesslike than threatening, although the threat was plain.

'Of course, my divine lord,' Yella stuttered. 'Only, it will deplete me a great deal. I—'

'Yes, yes, you may use the temple pool when you return.'

'Thank you. Thank you, my—'

'Ahhh,' said Var, turning to face another set of approaching footsteps. 'My wandering son.'

Ava moved forward, drawn to Kush like a moth to a flame. He looked tired, tense, pale, but also divine, and her chest squeezed tight at the sight of him. 'Father,' said Kush, bowing his head in deference.

Billy grabbed Ava and forced her back, violently shaking his head. She would have shrugged him off, but Var's voice snapped her out of her stupidity.

'Your mother will heal the succaplent, then you will escort her to Santala and heal her in the pool. Do not let her die, I have need of her yet.'

'Yes, Father,' said Kush, his hollow tone making Ava want to cry. He was so close, right there, the missing piece of her heart, and he needed her, but she couldn't go to him.

Ava was so preoccupied by Kush, she almost didn't notice the deep rumbling noise coming from the roots three or four bodies to their right, at least until Billy squeezed her arm so tightly she almost yelped.

'What?' she mouthed.

Billy's face was a picture of horror. 'We have to leave. Now, Ava. I mean it.'

'Why?'

'Fuck!' shouted Var. 'Fuck!'

'What is it?' asked Kush, stepping to his mother's side as though ready to shield her.

'The portal,' snapped Var.

Kush seemed at a loss. 'What do you—'

Var grabbed Yella's arm and dragged her forward. 'Heal the succaplent, now!' He forced Yella into the shadows so close to where Billy and Ava stood that Ava stilled, not daring to breathe, even though the rumbling all around them had become so loud she couldn't hear herself think.

Billy took Ava's hand, tugging her away and mouthing for her to use the Atlas Stone.

Yella cried out, and Var screamed, 'More! Faster! Fuck!'

'Father! It's too much, she'll die!' Kush's voice was so desperate, Ava planted her feet and looked back at him.

'If she doesn't do this, we'll all die,' Var screamed.

'Balance is binary,' Billy shouted at Ava, having to raise his voice so she could hear him above the near-deafening noise. 'And this means things are out of balance. We have to go!'

'I can't leave him!'

Billy tugged on Ava's hand, but she yanked it free and ran into the light.

'Kush!' she screamed, no time to think. 'You have to leave!'

'Ava?' Kush paused for a moment as though he didn't believe his eyes, then he ran for her, but so did Var, impossibly fast. And then Billy was there, too, protecting Ava, using magic.

Kush crashed into Ava, wrapping her in his arms and lifting her off her feet, crushing her to his chest. She was so lost in him, the feel and smell and warmth, that she didn't realize he'd moved them as they embraced, until he put her down and pulled away, and she found they were back by the hole in the wall.

'Kill the succaplent! Close the portal!' Billy shrieked the words right in Var's face, their bodies chest to chest. 'Var! Kill the succaplent! Close the portal! It's the only way!'

'No!' Var bit out, trying and failing to get around whatever magic Billy wielded. 'It needs more power, that's all.' His eyes flicked to Ava.

'You're not having her,' Kush shouted, pushing Ava behind him.

'It's too late, Var,' said Billy. 'And if you don't do it now, Yella will die, too. We all will … Perhaps the whole damn tree!'

The floor started shaking, and Yella fell to the ground on the edge of the shadows, lying on a carpet of flowers. Her appearance galvanized Var, and, nostrils flaring, he spun, drawing a knife from his sleeve as he disappeared into the shadows.

Var appeared again moments later, his hands covered in blood, and hauled Yella up, the rumbling, crashing noise deafening.

Billy sped to where Ava and Kush stood, neither of them moving a muscle, stuck in a dreadful trance. 'We have to go. Now! The magic, the energy, the … whatever the hell that is, it's still coming. We have to go! Ava! Now!'

Ava gave a shaky nod and pulled the stone from her pocket, grasping it between her thumb and forefinger. Billy held tight to her arm, but Kush stepped back, watching as Var rapidly closed the distance to their side, dragging Yella with him.

'Now, Ava!' screamed Billy.

'Come with us!' she begged Kush. 'You can't stay here.'

Kush shook his head and took another step away. 'My mother needs me. The Federation—'

'Kush! Please!'

The noise was like a living, roaring thing, the pitch increasing like water filling a glass, and then, with a great slamming noise, it stopped.

'Fuck!' said Billy, and just as a cracking, splintering, ripping filled the air, Billy flicked the stone, and they were gone.

'Noooooo!' Ava screamed as she and Billy landed in the library. She tried to reset the coordinates, but Billy had done them on the way there, and she hadn't paid enough attention. 'We have to go back!'

Billy bent over, panting hard, his hands on his knees. 'There's nothing we can do.'

'You knew!'

He collapsed onto the floor, his arms and legs flying wide. 'That the portal was going to implode?' He gave a weak laugh. 'How could I have?'

'You took me there to show me that. So I'd see. So I'd know how bad things are.' It felt like her heart was fracturing all over again. 'To see Kush …'

Billy shook his head, clutching his hands to his chest.

'I don't believe you.' Ava paced back and forth, trying to think of something she could do, some magic that might help.

'I didn't know, Ava.' He tipped his head back and closed his eyes. 'I took you there to show you the unnatural portals, so you'd understand the cost, the lengths Var is willing to go to in order to keep his precious Federation going.'

'You knew the web was out of balance! You've been saying it for weeks, months!'

'If I'd thought that was going to happen today, do you really think I would have put myself in the middle of it? I'm no hero, Ava.'

'And yet you held off Var. You didn't even break a sweat!'

'Well, yes. His magic is portal magic, whereas mine's more ... belligerent. Comes in handy for moments like that, you know? And thanks to you, I've been practicing.'

'Fuck!' Ava screamed, grabbing her head and crouching to the floor. 'What even was that?'

Billy shrugged. 'Damned if I know. But balance is binary.'

'I know the second fucking principle.'

'Mmm hmm,' he said, then opened his eyes and looked at her expectantly.

Ava rocked her weight back and sat on the floor, shaking her head. 'I get it, it's out of balance, but how do we fix it?'

'Ha! *We?* My dear Ava, *we* have no business fixing anything. Someone else will do that. We will do nothing and evade capture, although first we'll decompress after that traumatic experience.' A tumbler full of chestnut colored liquid appeared on the floor beside him, and Billy let out a moan of utter joy. 'Oh my good gracious Atlas. Thank you! You wonderful, delightful, clever house, you.' Billy snatched up the glass and took a delicate sip, closing his eyes and sighing with pleasure as he rolled the liquid around his mouth.

'But what would it take?' Ava pressed, refusing to be deterred. 'To fix it?'

Billy reluctantly opened his eyes and pinned her with a pitying look. 'Oh, I don't know, I suppose it would mean learning to give what we take—collectively—and for us to give more than that to start to balance things out.'

That didn't sound so hard, and surely now Var would act ... If he was still alive. If Kush—*No*, she wouldn't think like that. He was still alive, he had to be. She shook away the thought and forced herself to focus. 'So we need to stop people from taking so much? To ration the use of magic and create ways to generate more?'

Billy's mouth dropped open and he gave an incredulous laugh as he saluted her with his drink. 'Good fucking luck with that, my dear.'

Ava flung herself back onto the rug and stared up at the map of the Atlas Web. It was wonderful, precious, depicted a connected universe that deserved their respect. The whims of her mother and father and Var might have caused this mess, but it wasn't a game. There were tavern girls and stable boys and temple women across the web who had done nothing wrong, whose lives were at risk because the Gods refused to play their parts. Well, she would find a way to fix it. For them. She would force the Gods to do their duty, to restore balance, to curb their greed, no matter what it might take.

Thank you for reading *Daughter of Secrets and Sorcery*. The story continues in book 3, which is coming soon. For release date updates, sign up to my newsletter (where you'll also get a free story!): https://hrmoore.com/blog/cruelgoddess/

If you enjoyed *Daughter of Secrets and Sorcery*, I would really appreciate a review on social media or wherever you buy books. This helps others find my stories in this algorithm driven world. Thank you for your support.

READ NEXT: *Kingdoms of Shadow and Ash*, book one in the *Shadow and Ash* Duology.

CONNECT WITH HR MOORE

Find HR Moore on TikTok and Instagram: @HR_Moore

See what the world of *Cruel Goddess* looks like on Pinterest:
  https://www.pinterest.com/authorhrmoore/

Follow HR Moore on BookBub:
  https://www.bookbub.com/profile/hr-moore

Like the HR Moore page on Facebook:
  https://www.facebook.com/authorhrmoore

Check out HR Moore's website:
  http://www.hrmoore.com/

Follow HR Moore on Goodreads:
  https://www.goodreads.com/author/show/7228761.H_R_Moore

ACKNOWLEDGEMENTS

Those who follow me on social media or are subscribed to my newsletter will know that this series has recently been rebranded (because turns out the word *Celestl* is an auto-correct fail ... ah, the life of an author). As ever, I'm eternally grateful to my wonderful author friends for all their help and advice, but they really went above and beyond this time (especially Vela Roth and Jeffe Kennedy), so THANK YOU.

Thank you to Alice for your honest feedback (keeping track of all the moving pieces in this series is hard!), to Patcas for another stunning piece of cover art, to my wonderful ARC and street teams for your ongoing reviews and championing, and to all my readers, I appreciate you more than you know.

TITLES BY HR MOORE

The Relic Trilogy (complete):
Queen of Empire
Temple of Sand
Court of Crystal

In the Gleaming Light

The Ancient Souls Series (complete):
Nation of the Sun
Nation of the Sword
Nation of the Stars

The Shadow and Ash Duology (complete):
Kingdoms of Shadow and Ash
Dragons of Asred

Stories set in the Shadow and Ash world:
House of Storms and Secrets
Of Medris and Mutiny

The Cruel Goddess Series:
Bride of Stars and Sacrifice
Daughter of Secrets and Sorcery
Book 3 – coming soon

http://www.hrmoore.com

Printed in Great Britain
by Amazon

59956536R00236